A Thirst for Water

The Last God War part 2

Stephen B5 Jones

Christian Speculative Fiction

Printed by CreateSpace

The cover is
"Underwater Light"
by Petr Kraochvil
found on
PublicDomainPictures.net

*There is a list of characters
in the last pages of this book.

The orbit of the world of Perma
crosses in the shadow of its gas giant
every four revolutions,
or, about 0.26 Earth years.
The sky is dimmed.
The temperature drops.
The wind blows.
It is the beginning and ending of the year.
The inhabitants call this eclipse
winter.

1

Sharo made warm the Commons. Strong double doors, just up the steps, rattled in the face of the winded days of winter. In the last days until the distant sun returned, the wind was released with fury over those not yet touched to chill. Snow was lifted from the ground and swallowed any who ventured out under the dimmed sky with a blinding blizzard.

Around Sharo the business of the Shanties was being done, what little there was for these days. Deals were made and promises kept; goods were offered in trade and alliances mended. If there was not a pura, a warmer, like Sharo in the midst, the Commons would be put to closed for the length of fallen winter, and the Shanties would suffer for it.

Once, long ago, the Shanties had been a city, one of the two cities established on Perma at the first, when the colonists arrived. They had never agreed. There had been wars, named 'The God wars' for the initial point of contention. In the second city there were those who were genetically adapted to life on the world of Perma. In Cityscape such adaptations were not wanted nor welcome. The wars had put the second city to ruin, lost and gone. Those who survived rebuilt in secret under the ruins to keep Cityscape from knowing there was a remnant. This was how the Shanties came to be.

Sharo had been born in Cityscape. She was once a keeper. In the twenty-two winters she had been in the

Shanties, she had been a pura. In Cityscape keepers were of no use except to do the labor, but Cityscape had no concept of anything beyond its streets and towers. They believed their ancient opponents lost and gone.

The doors of the Commons rattled for the air pushing on it, Sharo glanced up to assure herself the doors were still emplaced. Traversing beyond doors was dire, most knew not to leave their threshold for the handful of days as winded snow filled the deep cyan sky of the world of Perma. The movement in the Commons slowed to a crawl with only a handful of people about, some present only for the cause of warm shelter.

"Athan," Sharo called to the young man who entered, pushed through the doors by the wind, then shaking his cloak dry as he jaunted the steps. "Are you warming at the work site on this day?"

Athan was a young man of the Shanties. He had taken his growth five winters before, and with it uncovered his gift of warming. Sharo taught him to be a pura in the same way she had been taught. The young man did not hold the same strength she held, but was befitted to any task he was called to.

Lately he had often been seen in the company of a befitted young woman named Paige. Chatter spoke of the possibility of a union, but chatter often traversed beyond the bounds of truth. Thus far he had made no move other than being seen in her company.

"Presently, Pura Sharo," Athan said. "I listened to the keepers chatter as they worked before the turn of the day. They talk of building the same kind of work shelters in Cityscape to labor in the chill of winter, and warming them with only a fire at either end. It's a wonder any of the keepers stay alive."

"Some do not," Sharo said. Athan had heard how keepers were worth less to house lords than dust in a cup, but he had not perceived it. It was not a bitter thing if his heart was too soft to fathom the hardness of Cityscape. "It is well you are handy to keep for them."

"We require that new lane," Athan said. "We have need of the dwellings on it. With the turn of every season a handful of keepers arrive, leaving Cityscape. We must meet the demands of proper harborage."

"Much is given," Sharo said. "Much is appreciated."

"For the Shanties as well," Athan said. "I would be happy if more of the keepers lived in the Shanties than live in Cityscape."

It was a sentiment Sharo had heard often in the turn of the last few winters. It was well the Shanties thought so much of the keepers, but only a very few would ever traverse across the sandscape.

"I would too," Sharo said.

#

It was in the mid of the day when Chimo stumbled through a single open door of the Commons. He had run a straight line to the door, his movments spoke of purpose and urgency.

Chimo was a young initiate of the Shanties. He was often called upon as messenger for his love of running. He could traverse quite swiftly, even over long distances when there was need.

"Pura Sharo," he said as he stopped at her side. "You are needed."

"For what cause?" Sharo asked as she moved

toward the door. Being a pura she hardly needed the cloak she put on, even in the fullest of dread winter, but she chose to wear it nonetheless. She was often called for emergencies of various kinds, especially in winter when losing warmth could quickly put one to lost for the chill. Sharo knew there were limits to her gift. If ever she had need to call upon the fullness of her warmth she would not have it already squandered on herself.

"The work crew on the new lane," Chimo gasped. "You are needed quickly."

Every home and workplace was emplaced within broken ruins and surrounded by broken streets, all in the hope that they would never be seen by the ones who had once broken the buildings. Even on a summer day one would have to stand close nearby to see the Shanties. In the winter when the distant sun hid behind the gas giant Hera all was dim. The Shanties could be lost to even the eldest initiate.

Yet the keepers, the lowest class in all of Cityscape, had found the Shanties, or more to the point, the Shanties had found them. The fear of being known in Cityscape was forced to stand aside for the cause of proper harborage. As the number of keepers from Cityscape traversing to the Shanties had increased, proper harborage had demanded more dwellings be made available. The space was near at hand, one need only jaunt to the next lane and repair dwellings from within. The once second city covered more than a large area.

The keepers were not in the habit of waiting for anything to be placed in their hands. They were handy to the work and would see it done, even in the full of winter.

Footing in the Shanty lanes was a matter of care, especially if one sought to traverse in haste. Sharo had to force herself to walk slowly and deliberately as she chided herself for expecting the worst. Perhaps they had found something extraordinary. The workers on this crew were mostly keepers, transplanted from Cityscape. Whether or not she accepted the title, she was seen as leader and elder by many of them. In their excitement she would be the one they might choose to make their report.

Even if there was an injury Kassi was ever near at hand to the workers. Kassi, the woman walking with Sharo's younger brother, was a sozo, a healer. There was little her touch could not fix. However, if the situation was sufficiently untoward she would send for Sharo straightaway to warm the place where she worked as an aid to the healing or recovery of whichever of the crew was hurt.

Sharo pushed into the work tent, and found the workers, from the eldest to the youngest attentive to the small temporary shelter in the center. Sharo no longer had need to guess at the truth. It was obvious in the concern of the workers, someone had indeed been hurt.

When they ushered Sharo into the room Kassi was kneeling over a small form on a folding cot, someone very young. Children had been present at the worksite from the beginning--they were curious. It tugged at her heart to know one of them had been hurt. It was most untoward.

Sharo instantly set the room to warm with her gift. As the chill was chased through the door Kassi's back straightened and she glanced behind her.

"Kassi?" Sharo asked. Kassi stood up from the table. Her hands awash with blood and her breaths short, indicators that she had been using her gift to the limit in order to mend the small body. Sharo could also see on her the bulge heralding yet another child for her brother.

"He wanted to see you first," Kassi said, indicating the child on the table. Then Kassi looked up at the worker who had fetched Sharo. "Has elder Jenne been found, or Ryalt?"

The worker ducked his head and backed out of the shelter.

"Keeper Sharo?" a tiny voice whispered from the table. Sharo let close her eyes for a moment. It was Joska, child of her dearest friend Jenne and her partner Ryalt. Of all the children in the Shanties, he was the most favored in her eyes. She was as much family to him as anyone in the Shanties.

"Yes Joska," Sharo said moving around to see. The child was not mortally injured; Sharo could tell he still held to his warmth. Knowing all this, Sharo was still surprised when she saw his face. One of his eyes was permanently closed and covered with the smallest of scars. Only Kassi could have done work so fine.

"Everything I can do is not sufficient," Kassi said on the aside. "There are injuries I cannot cause a body to mend."

Sharo only nodded, Kassi was distressed enough by her inability. She did not need someone to add to her regret.

"Keeper Sharo," Joska said as he touched her

arm. "Have I become unbefitted?"

Kassi backed away. Sharo glanced after her. How quickly she forgot the ways of keepers. She no longer knew how to swallow her tears for better days. At least she knew enough not to weep in front of the child.

Sharo looked down and saw Joska looking up at her with his remaining eye.

"Not in the least," Sharo said. "You have become distinct. Yet you will be obligated to learn how to reimburse for what you have lost. Not everyone you encounter will be able to see you past your injury, especially at first look. You will sometimes have cause to regret."

"I regret not turning the other direction," he said.

"You are not the only one who would say as much," Sharo said. "But your situation could have turned much worse. Your mother will arrive soon."

"My mother will tell me of her love for me," Joska said, "and not put an answer to my question."

"Her love for you will never end," Sharo said. "Even if you had no face at all. She will tell you much the same as I have, though likely in softer words. She will be at your side for the worst of it, and the best. You may be glad to have a mother who loves you so well."

Joska smiled and settled down in the cloak he was covered with. Kassi had learned how a body made its own barrier to pain, which often brought sleep. She sometimes used her gift to hasten that sleep. Sharo saw that at work now. The child had suffered harm, and his body had been caused to make him well. It would be enough to put anyone to weariness.

"Kassi does not want to look at me," Joska

observed.

"In you Kassi sees her limits," Sharo said. "She would rather put herself to lost and gone than to fail to restore you in full. Her love for you makes her inability hard and bitter. Don't fear to talk to her. Let her see that you are well. She will recover."

"Keeper Sharo," Joska said sleepily. "…So wise." Then he fell into slumber.

Sharo put her hand over Joska's as he slept. Despite the violence done to his face he slept as peaceful as a newborn. Behind her she heard Jenne arrive, filled with concern and fright. Kassi spoke to her with weariness behind her voice and told the whole of the circumstance.

"He is well, and he sleeps," Sharo said, stepping up from the cot. "At the moment."

"Sharo," Jenne said, approaching for a warm embrace. "He called for you first."

"He feared he had become untoward," Sharo said, putting her hand to Kassi's shoulder in silent support. "And he knew you would love him despite all. He requested a clear opinion."

"Then I am pleased you stood ready to keep for him," Jenne said. "Ryalt will arrive presently, and we will keep for my son along with you."

"I leave him with you," Sharo said. "I suspect I should return to the Commons."

"Go," Jenne said. "And have no worry for Joska. Chatter would have it I love him despite all."

"He is in the best of hands," Sharo said.

"If you have no plans for the first bright day of summer," Jenne called after her. "Plan to celebrate with us."

#

Sharo left Joska safely emplaced in his mother's arms and walked, not to the Commons, but to her house. The way was treacherous even if it were not a winded day of winter. It made the jaunt by necessity a slow one. On most days she had sufficient patience for the time it took, but on this day she found herself in want of a faster pace. Her heart beat in double time with her steps and refused to be slowed.

When she had first been an initiate of the Shanties had wanted to provide her with the largest and finest of all houses, yet Sharo would not have it. She was more grateful to the Shanties than they could ever be to her, and had accepted a smaller house with some anticipation. It was not far from the Commons. Pytre, her brother, was placed in another house with his new bride Kassi, and Sharo was set to be alone.

At times living in a house could be a bitter task for one who had slept in her cloak during the summer and in the midst of huge sheltering along with handfuls of other keepers in the winter, still in her cloak. A cloak is easy to clean and does not require any great amount of attentiveness. A larger house would only have been more empty and would have brought with it more labor.

On this day, however, her house was well suited to her need. The wind pushed her as she entered the house. She turned and assured herself that the door and windows were closed. Then Sharo sat on the floor to cry until she could cry no more.

2

The towers of Cityscape fell under a chilled hush, one which extended to the outermost reaches of the world of Perma. The distant sun was hid behind the blue giant Hera's back for the circle of fifteen days. With dimmed light and gathering of snow the season had tested the strong and culled the weak.

The winter chill had taken for lost those who were touched by it and could not retrieve their warmth. Now the harsh winded days portended the soon coming end of winter, fighting its worst at the last of it, throwing clouds of snow even over the Cityscape weatherscreen. Deep blue skies had ruled the early of the day, but the later of the day would see the distant sun escape the bounds of Hera and shine its warmth and renew the world. With its rising Hera revealed the bright leading edge where the distant sun would soon emerge.

Opposite the sky from Hera, a tiny speck of bright dust had appeared; it slid below the horizon as Hera emerged. The astronomers named it a comet, and marveled that none had been seen since the early days of the colony, when the population still lived on the great colony ship and invented new kinds of trees and plants to cover the land of a barren world. The comet, it was thought, may draw close to Perma, as close as such things would likely come.

"Will you attend the celebration tonight councilman?" the aid asked.

Iance, a councilman of Cityscape, had spent the

day enmeshed in his work. There was information to find and deals to be made. He, of course, was equal to the task, even on the last day of coldest winter. The work of the day would not be put aside, otherwise it would add bitterly to the work of the morrow.

"I suspect I will Backe," he said. Iance smiled and nodded. Backe had been sent to gain employ in his office covertly. The councilman had yet to distinguish which of his opponents had sent this spy, but with the information the aid was being allowed to discover, it would only be a matter of time.

"Early on the morrow then," Backe said.

"I will see you then," Iance walked out of the office, not once reacting to the search his new aid would probably make of his papers and effects once he was out of seeing distance. Backe was one of the better spies who had been sent to his office; therefore he would allow this one time to do his work.

Though, not every thing he found would be as useful as it appeared, nor as honest.

Iance was the young dark haired and steely eyed initiate of the council; the penultimate son of a proud and potent family. He was a prince of Cityscape, one of three chosen to replace the Regent when his term circled to an end. If softly spoken rumors were to be held as true, the Regent would be replaced before the next winterfall.

In the back of a cart Iance rode the short distance to the roof of a nearby tower. Unlike many of the council, he did not own his own tower complete. Iance could have, but rather chose a befitted floor in a convenient tower and kept his compensation for more important matters.

He walked the stairs alone, the building was as secure as it could be and he gathered no comfort from having needless guardianship hovering over his every step. His rooms were secure, well lit and warm for the number of clear panes surrounding it. He barely glanced to the winter sky outside as he organized his real files and put them to hidden storage.

He had put much work into the day, but whether he had accomplished anything was yet to be seen. He sighed and put it all aside. Today was finished for him, there would be no change to what had been, he could only plan for what he would do next.

After a befitted length of time he prepared for the celebration. It was to be yet another opportunity for him, perhaps. He dressed his part and steeled himself for the onslaught he would face once he arrived.

As for any frivolous occasion, the higher society of Cityscape had organized a celebration for the first bright day of summer. His driver conveyed him to the highest open balcony in Cityscape, nestled against the top edge of the security tower. There were gathered the city lords in their finest and most unreserved. To enjoy, to laugh, to see and be seen, and perhaps to witness the distant sun emerge before the late of the day.

The event itself was of second import, celebration among the proper company was first.

"Iance," dour Forst, the council organizer said as Iance entered. "Eat and drink, the summer will return and all will be well and warm. Have you considered our newest proposal?"

By plan, Iance had entered a befitted time after the celebration start. He was not the eager follower of influence, he was the wielder. His moments were to be doled out with care; generous as it suited him, but never in abundance. Even those who could not put words to it knew this was true of him.

"Considered?" Iance said in passing. "Hardly at all." Then he let the crowd carry him onward. Forst should know not to introduce debate in the site of a debacle. Little of the council work was done in the council hall, yet there was no cause to introduce every meeting and greeting with terms of commerce.

Iance retrieved a beverage and stood at the edge of the gathered mass, and at the edge of the overlook. He could see the sky entire as well as the lane far beneath his feet. One misstep, he judged, could send him to lost and gone.

"A sight truly to inspire the eyes," A soft voice said at his shoulder. It was Raisia, a befitted child of the Cityscape elite. She had not kept secret her designs to be at the side of the next regent. To that end, she hovered in the circles meant to sustain discourse with the most likely candidates. Iance did not avert her attentions, as guarded as they oftimes were. She had been a comrade to him from their earliest days, and he intended to see that comradeship continue.

The street below and lights of the city glowed in the cyan glow of winter last. They stood above it like giants who owned the world.

"Mintel considers the regency his to own," Raisia said.

"As do we all," Iance said accepting her hold to his arm. Those who put eyes to them so entwined would chatter of it for the turn of a few days. Iance had made it clear he intended to win the regency, and Raisia

"Rugre does not aspire as highly," Raisia said. "He plans ways to divert water to the river and reopen the Drydocks for shipping and perhaps for fishing."

"A worthy goal," Iance said. "Only spectacular for the first day. The results would be temporary."

The three intenders knew the rules of the game. Whichever of them had the most noteworthy accomplishments when the Regent's replacement was at hand would be given the place and position. To have captured the support of Raisia would be a fortune, but at the finish it was not a consideration.

"Mintel is closed and mysterious," Raisia said. "He has made himself impossible to keep track of, and he hints of some ingenious scheme, but has not whispered the first word of it."

"And I?" Iance asked.

"You connect well in the council, and the city," Raisia said. "You aspire to the topmost of Cityscape, but you have yet to grab hold of a cause or a course. It will be your undoing."

Raisia glanced about, to assure none were within range to hear her soft words.

"You know of the Forst scheme to speak into truth less work for Keepers," Raisia said. "To lead to lower recompence for them, and in the end to diminish their excess population."

"I know of this," Iance said. "And the results which were as expected."

"As you have been told," Raisia said. "The need for hard sheltering this winter was lowered, yet the expected revenue from the ovens of the lost is less than even a normal winter. The numbers of keepers at the corners to be hired is diminished a small amount."

"Have they chosen a new method for their lost and cold?" Iance asked.

"None than I can uncover," Raisia said. "And if their laboring population continues to decrease, the Forst scheme could be reversed."

"So what has become of the surplus keepers?" Iance said.

"That is the question," Raisia said. "Perhaps in the answer you will find something worthy to display and win the regency."

"Or construct it into one," Iance said. "Moments are many but days are few. I will see if there is something to this."

"Haste would be befitted," Raisia said. "There is but one regent and he will be replaced but once in the circle of our lives."

"The distant sun emerges," Iance said. From the trailing side of the gas giant Hera, the distant sun showed an edge at first, a diamond of bright light to herald the ending of the winter eclipse. In the first few moments the light was too bright to look at directly, then it would settle out over the whole of the distant sun to warm the world of Perma.

As the remainder of the city lords watched the sun begin to shine around them, Iance leaned in to speak to Raisia in a quiet voice. "...and I will emerge as well."

3

Daine awoke, as she had on every day of her life thus far, in the shadow of the Holding. It was a building like many others, yet its walls were not adorned with sun panes nor even a place for them, and the top of it reached half to the sky. The building was different in that for as massive as it was, it was not claimed or owned by any City lord. It was set aside for a different purpose.

The young girl looked out from her cloak as the distant sun touched the sky and sublimated the frost of the night direct to the air. Often Daine wondered at the poor souls who were consigned to the Holding—criminals of various kinds, the misfortunate and even the teras-- if such monsters truly existed. For the longest time she had believed that the doors of the Holding were for entrance only, lately she had learned something closer to the truth. There were those who were put in the Holding for a short time, some for longer, and some few who were put within its walls never to emerge.

The last set was still a matter of conjecture. Everyone claimed it was true though no one in her reach could put a name to a prisoner consigned to the Holding so permanently.

It was the first full day of summer. The distant sun had escaped its exile behind the gas giant Hera on the mid of late yesterday and now again warmed the world of Perma. The keepers were once again free to live and sleep on the street, no longer closed up in hard sheltering required by the chill of full on winter. Keepers were not at their best when they were enclosed by walls, especially, one might add, the walls of the Holding.

The lane was named Trawler. Back in the circle of years a well meaning house lord had built rows of cubbies into the walls for the keepers to sleep in, giving them the hope of partial shelter. Half of them were placed wrong for the wind or the sunlight, and were used for little beyond storage, the rest were set aside for elders or families with small children. Daine's father had been placed in a cubbie for the time after she had been born and her mother had been lost and gone.

Her father, Nyel by name, began to stir. Daine glanced around to see other keepers along the lane also stirring beneath their cloaks. It was close to first early and the keeping of the day would not do itself—keepers would need to be awake and on hand and at their best.

"Papa," Daine said as she climbed out of their cloak. "See how I've grown. Soon I will start to keep."

His eyes always held a pained expression when she reminded him. He had kept for her and protected her from the beginning. He would continue to do so for longer if he could. She reminded him often so when the time came he would be ready to allow her to keep.

She was already among the eldest of the crèche. Daine taught the children more than she learned. Of late the keepers used a book recently found for their scholarship. It was the holy writ, put in the language of keepers. It spoke of God and truth. There were stories there she could not fully fathom, but on the whole what she found in those pages was good for learning and telling.

"Mind the book child," her father said as he

folded his cloak back together, and she wrapped herself in her own, smaller cloak. She picked up the white book from where she had put it down to sit on through the night. The holy writ was scarce in the Drydocks. They would only have the book for two more days before it would be passed to the next family.

Nyel quietly walked her to the crèche as most of the keepers of Drydock traversed in the other direction. Their goal was an old warehouse over the edge of the shallow depression. Chatter was it once held the fish caught when the drydock flats were filled with water. Daine could almost see how it once appeared, but the buildings and streets in the depression had been there for a long time. She had to wonder what had become of the water.

"What have you read of late?" he asked.

Her father had looked at the words of the book, and had touched them with his fingers, but he had never learned to read them. He relied on her to read for him and to speak of what she had learned.

"The world is given to God, and everything in it," Daine said, remembering what she had seen in the mid of late of yesterday. "I suppose God is a planet-lord."

"If that is true," her father said. "Is there a benefit for us?"

Her father always asked her questions about what she read. He had heard that the words held no meaning unless it was put to work in some way.

Daine considered as they walked to the end of the lane where Nyel stopped by a morning vendor and bought two coppers worth of fruitage for her. It was a meager meal, but far better than none at all.

"It means we have little to fear," Daine said taking her food to eat. "The house lords only own buildings, but not a whole world. If he is by our side he outdistances them. He even has the hold of the place where they stand."

"As long as we stay at his side, where we belong," her father said. "And here you are where you belong-- in the crèche."

"Oh Papa," she chided. "You know it won't always be so."

He put his head down, then looked back up at her.

"Of that I am aware," he said. "But allow me this day to see you as my child."

"This day," Daine said. "And perhaps a handful more. I keep enough here, but work without recompense is not befitted work, not in the least."

Daine entered the crèche. She put to open the door and entered the second floor of an unused warehouse which the keepers were allowed to use as long as it was kept to clean, something the keepers could accomplish without difficulty. She received a nod from a parent who made her way to the exit and the hiring corner to obtain keeping for the day. In her heart Daine longed to accompany her, but it was not yet to be, not on this day.

In the turn of a few moments there were almost two handfuls of children in the creche, every last one younger than her.

"Children," Daine announced. "Play if you like, or finish your sleep. We will have scholarship starting at the last of early."

The children nodded and continued whatever they had been doing before she arrived. Daine walked about, preparing for what she would teach on this day. Reading and writing would be a benefit to them when they became keepers, sometimes numbers could be a help as well.

In the circle of winters back, when Daine had been one of the younger of the crèche, there had been a keeper who chose not to keep, but to stay with the crèche teaching and caring for the children. Her name had been Kassi. Daine remembered her well. Kassi was quite recently joined to the man at her side, something an unrelenting mother would not allow for the cause of her young age. Therefore, according to chatter, she and her man had joined and then jaunted to the drydocks. The other keepers had taken to passing her a coin or two at the end of the day in recompense. Then Kassi had gone somewhere else and the crèche was again cared for by whatever keeper did not manage to find keeping for the day.

Daine sometimes considered what Kassi had done as she cared for the crèche, even if an older keeper returned. She had a pattern which counterweighed play with scholarship, and few other keepers had cared to interfere with her.

"Gather children," Daine said, standing at the place where Kassi once stood when she played at scholarship. "First I will read to you from the holy writ, then we will learn to spell words found in the story."

"There is chatter that some of the scholars from the cathedral would take away our copies of the holy writ," Sele said. She was young and had a head full of bright yellow curls.

"Truly?" Daine asked.

"I heard it in the Cathedral," Sele said. "We went for summer's first day to walk by and see the holy writ."

"What did you see?" Reny asked. He was not as boisterious as Sele, but he was always curious.

"I saw a part of a story Daine told us about a hero named Dan-iel," Sele said. "But when I went to speak of where I'd heard it, my mother would not let me talk."

"And she was right to do so," Daine said. "A mouth kept to silence cannot speak untoward words."

"That's what another keeper said," Sele said. "The one in the line beside us. She said there are those who would take away our copies of the holy writ if the knew we had them."

"Then they won't know," Daine said. "And now, may I continue with this story."

"Yes ma'am," Sele said.

Daine gave them a moment to hold to their silence before she started the scholarship again.

#

Nyel arrived after the last of the children had been retrieved by the keepers, and Daine had finished putting the room to right and clean.

"That is a fine cleaning," he noted as he walked through the open door.

"True," Daine said. "Note how befitted I am for keeping."

Her father ignored her comment, instead he looked about to assure there were no prying ears to hear what he said.

"This even there is a meeting," he said.

"Authority Taylo will bring more copies of the holy writ and chatter is she has some manner of opportunity for us. It is not for the whole of the Drydocks, just for a few."

Daine had heard of Authority Taylo but had never seen her before. She was the authority that believed just was for keepers as well as house lords. She had begun her work in the Cathedral district, but had found plenty to be done in the Drydocks as well.

"That may be well befitted," Daine said. "Did you fare well at the hiring corner this day?"

"Well enough," he said, and produced from his cloak a bag which looked to be half filled with bread. "And you?"

Daine held out three coins. It was little. She would make much more in the work of keeping, if her father would only relent.

They traversed down the steps and jaunted down the lane toward the Drydocks. The distant sun was low in the sky and would soon fall below the horizon. At the top of a hill they could see the whole of Drydocks, the many small buildings in the center and the factories at the edges. Many of those small shacks were eateries and clothiers, owned by house lords and toiled at by keepers.

"Shall we eat on the hill?" her father offered.

They found a befitted place off the lane and sat in the corner to take their share of food as the sun slowly sank in the sky. Blue Giant Hera had set ahead of the sun, and would precede it to rise in the morning. As a child Daine had often wondered at how close Hera was, and wondered what it would be like to stand on that world and look out over little Perma. She wondered what the towers of Cityscape would appear as seen from above the sky.

She had been told it was not possible, but Daine liked to dream of impossible things.

"Were the children well-behaved?" Nyel asked.

"As well as always," she said. "They are still excited over the first day of summer. I also heard chatter that house lords are taking away copies of the holy writ."

"Then we should keep it hidden," he said.

"I had thought of that," Daine said. "In it I read we are to hide its words in our hearts."

"That is best," Nyel said.

#

"How fare you Kene?" the other keeper asked.

It was the end of the work day. Kene stepped from the cart, collected his recompense and walked into the Drydocks where he sheltered at night. He could scant remember a time before his days were filled with keeping.

"Older by the day," Kene said.

"And wiser by far," his friend added.

"And yet… older," Kene said, rubbing the soreness of his back.

He walked slowly, there was no cause to hurry. Lately he had been reading the holy writ, the book once found only in the Deep Cyan Cathedral. Some found in it reason for hope. For Kene it was too late for hope, the circle of his years would turn to a close soon enough. His children had gone their own directions and he was alone. A life filled with anything more than simple keeping was late and gone for him.

He could only wish the young ones well.

"Authority Taylo," Kene said, recognizing the woman in front of him. She was shorter than he, with dark hair and eyes, yet she stood with a confidence which belied her size and her years.

Even with their weapons and their training, and the cause of just behind them, few of the authority could stand with confidence in the places where keepers lived.

"Elder Kene," Taylo greeted in turn. She had been naming him an elder of late. She joined him, walking at his elbow. "I have called for a meeting at mid late on the square. Will you be in attendance?"

"If my old legs are sufficient to carry me there, ma'am," Kene said. "What have you to say?"

He had forgotten once again how little authority Taylo enjoyed being called ma'am. Proper address was the way of keepers and the way of all of Cityscape, but Taylo would not have it. She did not see the need to be set above others in action or in word. She glanced at him as he recognized his indiscretion, and he turned his eyes downward as apology.

"I have more copies of the holy writ," Taylo said, allowing the matter to pass unspoken. "And there is an opportunity for some of your younger ones."

"I trust it is not a dire opportunity," he said. "Join me for a meal?"

"Not today I think," Taylo said. "There is much to be done."

"...And only one of you to accomplish it," Kene said. "Keepers have added strength when we work together authority Taylo. You work too often alone. If you were to be gone what would become of those who depend on you?"

"I dare say I may never be alone," Taylo said. "I won't be as long as there are keepers in Cityscape. But in this one thing I persevere, whether alone or alongside cohorts. Good day, friend Kene."

"Good day Taylo," he said in response.

He walked into the Drydocks with more purpose than before. Moments were many, but his legs were slow. He stopped at a vendor and bought a handful of bread, eating it along the way. Keepers had already begun to gather as he arrived.

"Kene," Asheya said as she fell into step to the side of him. "Fare you well?"

He wondered for the moment why each conversation seemed to begin with his well being. He would have rebuffed her, but Asheya was one of the most respected of the keepers. She had stood for the keepers for longer than Kene had, and she had proven her wit more than once.

"Well enough," he said. "Authority Taylo is bringing more books and some sort of news this time."

"Authority Taylo is a gift to us," Asheya said. "I understand you don't always think so. But on this point I would disagree with you."

"She is a gift," Kene said. "But should the world turn she could become a dire gift. Is it best I do not speak?"

"Never," she said immediately. "I value your words, even when they do not agree with mine."

Taylo met the two of them as they approached the center, which was raised half a knee level from the rest of the street. Taylo always seemed to be in the forefront, even when she deferred to the leadership of others.

"I am glad you are here," Taylo said. "We have much to consider."

"About the matter we talked of earlier," Asheya said. "Keepers are present, and more keepers arrive as we speak. It is best we proceed now, for there will be sufficient work for us to accomplish after."

"Fair enough," Taylo said. Then she looked around the square, taking in the numbers and the faces of the keepers surrounding her. Then she stood to the forefront and waited a befitted amount of time for the keepers to become quiet.

"The children of Cathedral district have been leaving Cityscape for the circle of a season to attend a new kind of scholarship," Authority Taylo said. "I can bring two from Drydocks for this session. They will be safe and warm, sheltered and fed and they will be returned after the turn of the next winter with a most befitted scholarship."

"Is it not dire to send our children to a place without the shelter of family and other keepers?" one keeper asked. Kene had been thinking the same question. Keepers are stronger as they stay among each other.

"The students are safe and sheltered," Taylo said. "There are other keepers at hand, and they are beyond the reach of Cityscape. I dare not tell you more."

"We have talked of this, and my support is unwavering, but my question also remains," Asheya said. "How do we choose two from so many?" Many of our children are worthy of scholarship."

"Choose for need," Authority Taylo said. "And choose those who learn best. It may be best to choose from the older. The younger will have opportunities after the turn of winters."

Asheya turned to the other keepers she had gathered, Kene being one of them. She had often said the best decisions were made with the voice of several, and though many looked to her for the last word, she often decided what to speak after talking with others.

"Speak what is on your mind," Asheya said.

"What do we know of this scholarship?" Kene asked.

"Little enough," Asheya said. "The children are taken out of Cityscape to a place Taylo will not name, and they become students at a rare scholarship. They are sheltered and kept for, and Taylo insists they are safe. Authority Taylo would rather not say more."

"Just as well," Another keeper said. She often kept quiet in meetings, hoping that her silence would lend strength to her words when she did speak them. "It is best for us not to know."

"We cannot carry the worry over something we know little about," Kene added. "Any step can be dire, whether here or in some unknown place. We should trust Taylo."

"Do you know which two we should send?" Asheya asked.

There was some discussion, several names were mentioned. Taylo had been giving out more copies of the holy writ as the elders had conversed. Asheya nodded her readiness and moved to the forefront to voice their decision. She stood before the keepers and spoke with a clear voice.

"We will send Aery," Asheya said. "He is smart,

and a leader among his peers. And… Daine. She will teach the young ones as she learns."

Kene heard the girl exclaim, "What?" as she realized her name had been spoken. He had suggested her first. He knew her well enough, she was as bright as any keeper and was also quick to teach the children when she had opportunity. He also knew this was not something she had considered in her plans.

"It is well then," Nyel, her father, said before the full import of what had been said could impress itself on his daughter. Kene had heard his concern over her desire to begin to keep. Now his voice was touched with relief. The young would choose to be too quickly grown.

"Learn well young ones," Asheya said as the two were brought to the center of the square.

"I will converse with the students," Authority Taylo said. "We will see to the arrangements for their travel."

Kene left as the meeting broke asunder. It was time for the keepers to rest, to be ready for whatever keeping the next day brought. He looked back over the two young ones who would be given a chance at scholarship, and felt a twinge of envy. Whatever adventures they might have, he would yet labor.

Such was the life of a keeper.

4

Taylo chose not to appear weary as she entered the authority building at the first of early in the second day of warming summer. There were only so many moments in a day, and she often chose more of those than one person could grasp. There was no use to complain of her many extra hours, she alone was the cause of it.

There had been business in need of attention out in the Drydocks the night before, and now she had to finish some neglected work even over the caustic glances of the other authorities, those who stood adverse to her connection with the keepers. Only a few said words to her, but their animosity ebbed and flowed. It was at full force now, few of the authority would be found in her presence if they could choose.

There were those who supported the cause of authority Taylo, those who still believed that just was for all, but they did so quietly. They were all convinced the elders still held the last word.

Taylo pulled her dark hair back and put a full satchel aside the seat. She had been given a full day of work, and there was a matter of covert transportation for a number of keepers which had to be overseen. She had often done such transporting on her own, but this time she had cause to put that job into another's hands. Taylo reminded herself yet again she was not the only one with a well befitted set of hands.

Perhaps the keepers were correct; she did take too

much upon herself when there were those who stood ready to help. All she need do was ask.

As Authority Taylo sat at her desk the communication box buzzed its warning. She looked at it, wondering if the cause of its buzzing had somehow known the exact moment of her arrival. There was only one way to know.

"Authority Taylo?" the box asked as she put it to her ear.

"Yes, it is I," she said. Usually a caller would launch directly to the purpose of the call, but this one waited for a time, and when he spoke, he did so slowly.

"There is a matter with which I need to consult you," the voice said. "Is there a place where we could meet far from the eyes and ears of other authority.. or anyone subject to chatter?"

Taylo considered for the turn of a moment. There were those who had in every word and action threatened her. She had cause to be wary, but there were places in Cityscape where none would dare harm her. It would not be difficult to arrange a meeting in one of those places.

"Diametric to the Cathedral," Taylo said, taking note that none were sufficiently close to hear her words. "There is a street named Hopeful. Near the first interchange from the Cathedral there is a red building with the number 301 fixed to the steps. See me there at the mid of the day. Bring no more than one other with you."

"I will be alone" the voice asked. "Dare I step inside the building?"

"None will interfere with you there unless you

interfere with them," Taylo said.

"We will meet then," The voice said. The connection was closed.

Taylo looked at the reports having need to be completed, and breathed a sigh. There would always be work for an authority, it was the way the world was, but none would choose to see it done if they had been warned of the need to write numerous reports.

The day had only so many hours to it, and already she was not sufficient to what was required of her. She now only had until the mid of the day, or somewhat less, and she also had need to contact certain people before attending a secretive meeting.

#

"Authority Taylo," Angla said as she opened the entry door. "Fare you well?"

"As well as ever," Taylo said stepping into the room. "You know you are not to reply at your door. It is untoward for someone of your situation."

"And yet it is toward," Angla said. "This is my entry door. I knew it was you, otherwise I would have sent Chanta and played my part as a weak and spoiled house lord child."

Angla was once an abandoned child of Cityscape. Her parents had taken her one day on a jaunt to the large trees, but had died in an accident with their cart. Taylo had been among those who found her and brought her back to Cityscape. Angla had been in the presence of a keeper, Sharo, who had been abandoned on the far side of sandscape and left to die, and Ryalt from the Shanties, which most of Cityscape could not speak the first word about. They had taken shelter in the winded days of winter in the old colony ship, which again, most of Cityscape did not know of.

Despite a number of misgivings, some of which were directed at her, they had all been friends from that time.

"The latest set of children is prepared to go to the lake," Taylo said. Gabri, an interface robot who was on the ship, taught classes for the children of Cityscape keepers by the day and the year. By agreement they talked of it only circumspectly when others might hear.

"The cause of their scholarship benefits from it," Angla said, as they traversed further into the building, and further from possible listeners. "And their parents benefit from not having to gather recompense for their sheltering until the full of winter next."

"Authority Taylo," Chanta greeted as she turned the corner.

"Chanta," Taylo said in turn. "Is our charge on her best?"

"Of course she is, ma'am" Chanta said. "Her scholarship turns to an end this season, but I dare say the scholarship of life may never end."

"I doubt it will," Taylo said. "For as long as it lasts."

"For as long as it lasts," Angla said, speaking in lower tones. "When the ship is discovered, and us with it, we shall sing to each other in the dark of night at the holding, just like the men in the holy writ. The guards will learn of the truth from our own voices."

One of the discoveries in the colony ship was the great library, and in it the holy writ. In the days of the colony it had been named "Holy Bible". Only three copies had existed in all of Cityscape, and they were held in the Deep Cyan Cathedral and viewed by the passing multitudes only at the fall of winter and on summer's first day. Gabri had translated the holy writ into the language as spoken on Perma and printed numerous copies. Now they could all read it and know about the first world of men and the God who also was present on the world of Perma.

"You always look to the better turn," Taylo said.

"Authority Taylo," Chanta said. "Have you heard there will be less work for the keepers by the turn of the season?"

"I've heard," Taylo said. "Yet not a factory closes, not a farm has lost crops and not a house lord desires for less. I do not see how it could be."

"Proper recompense has been lowered for keepers at every corner of Cityscape," Chanta said. "It may be prudent to lower my pay as well, ma'am."

"Never," Angla said. "You are worth more to me than any recompense. You are a gift Chanta. I will not give you less for the cause of a few house lords and their fears."

"I fathom your concerns Chanta," Taylo said. "But I do not share them. Keep the extra tight to yourself, and be generous with your cohorts when there is need. Perhaps you are emplaced for such a time to be generous with your family. I have hope it will be a short downward turn."

"I as well, ma'am" Chanta said.

"Why have you put your shadow to my door on this day?" Angla asked. "I had not expected to walk with you for the turn of a handful of days."

Taylo looked at Angla, waiting her realization of the second meaning inherent in the words she had used.

"... not that you are unwelcome in my house on any day," Angla hastily added. She had the inheritance of a tower to live in and a number of business concerns. They were being caretaked for the time, but would soon turn to Angla for decisions and directions. She might cause more of a change than the managers expect, her concerns were not a mirror to her father's.

"I have a meeting near the Cathedral with someone as yet unknown," Taylo said. "The last of those kinds of meetings kept me for a full hand of days for the cause of proper just."

"And you wanted someone to fret should you be over delayed," Angla said.

"I want someone to worry from the start," Taylo said. "I have already left the transport of the new students in hands other than my own."

"It is a task you should share," Angla said. "I should soon be able to put a hand to that task as well. Will you be safe?"

"I dare not think it," Taylo said. "It is the place of authority to walk on the edge of dire, sometimes past it. However, our meeting will be in the red building. I am well watched in that sector."

Angla had arranged to purchase the red building after Taylo uncovered a criminal cadre who had utilized it to warehouse stolen articles and hide fugitives. Now it housed keepers in the winter, the occasional medic who would dare care for keepers, and whatever else the keepers might need.

There was nothing unjust in any of their activities

in the red building, yet they were obligated to keep any word of it unspoken. There were those who would take offense at keepers being tended so well.

"That is well then," Angla said. "We will send word ahead of you for keepers to put eyes to the red building. Should you encounter trouble; help will be but a breath away."

"We have sent word already, ma'am and miss," Chanta said, entering the room with refreshment for all three of them. In the whole of Cityscape keepers were not allowed to eat or drink with house lords or authorities, save for the living area of Angla. She would not allow it to be any other way.

"You two have had such adventures," Chanta continued. "And yet you give no pause before going forward again."

"I do give pause," Taylo answered. "I have cause to look twice."

"Is medic Parke well?" Angla asked as the three sat down. The medic had given aid to the keepers more than once, and in an off-hand statement Taylo had admitted to a slight attraction. The admission had yet to be forgotten, in fact, chatter had been spread to the furthest reaches of Cityscape, and grew with every telling.

"I would not know," Taylo said.

"He is well and warm, ma'am" Chanta said. "And as yet he remains without a woman to walk by his side. There is no end to the meals which must be prepared for him by keepers."

"Which provides work for the keepers," Taylo said. "In these times of trouble I dare not think or speak anything to interfere with that."

On that point neither of her cohorts believed her.

#

Taylo turned the corner from the Deep Cyan Cathedral and walked the street to the red house. She kept a watchful eye so she would know if any followed her. And yet she was unaware when a young keeper fell in step beside her. The keepers had a gift for walking silently and beneath notice, even for someone who had learned to notice.

"Aysa," Taylo said, hiding her surprise. "Are you prepared to return to the lake?"

The girl smiled, looking around to assure no untoward person could hear.

"I count the days, ma'am," Aysa said, then leaned in to speak more softly. "I propose to direct my scholarship to the cause of being a medic. Gabri is supportive, but requires also the consent of my family. Keepers are left to keep for themselves, I could learn well enough to assist with any need, and would allow medic Parke to stay warm and safe and attend to matters of more import."

"Matters such as...?" Taylo had to ask. Had she been so transparent?

"Authority Taylo," Aysa said. "You are a gift. I have been sent to tell you about a city lord dressed in the manner of a keeper who entered the red house well before you arrived. He is alone and no one has taken note of him."

"Is the house empty?" Taylo asked.

"The base floor is, ma'am" Aysa said. "At the top of the first landing a work crew plays at repairing the floor. They stand ready to assist as needed."

"Thank you Aysa," Taylo said. "You might also know we have two new students from the Drydocks. They will jaunt with you."

"It is well then," Aysa said.

Authority Taylo approached the steps well aware of the keepers about her who looked as if they were not watching. They in fact were. She need only utter a word to request help, and help would find her quickly. On the other hand, if someone dire stood in close to her, could any help reach her in time?

The air stood still and dim within the walls of the red house. They had done well in their pursuit of the appearance not unlike any other building on the row where keepers had their winter shelter. The first floor was a great open room interspersed with square columns. The floor was polished wood, and not entirely even. The second floor appeared as abandoned offices, some used for storage. Taylo knew those rooms were not as abandoned as they seemed, and what storage was contained within was for the benefit of the keepers.

In the midst of the floor a man stood with his back to her. He wore the drab colors of a keeper, but his cloak was ungainly new and too thin even for the sleep of a summer night. His bearing was incorrect as well. Keepers were not given to standing straight and proud. He could pass as a keeper for one who gave keepers no attention, but none of those were present.

"Authority Taylo," he said with a booming voice. He had not turned toward her. He must have heard the door close or her foot fall. "Your reputation as most beloved of all authority among the keepers has been confirmed. They have put their eyes to me from the moment I left the Cathedral Square, and even now choose to stay nearby."

"I beg pardon sir," Taylo said. "There are those who have spoken against me, and I have learned to have a care."

The man turned toward her, his face partly hidden in the dim inside light. Still, she could quickly put a name to the face. He was well known in Cityscape.

"I did not speak in reprimand," the man said. "But rather in surprise. It is well befitted for an authority to have the respect of the keepers. It is why I have sought you."

"I stand ready to assist," Taylo said. "Councilman Iance."

Iance walked nearer to where she stood. She had never seen him in person before. He was well befitted and still on the edge of young. His figure was imposing, though not overly tall. His dark eyes darted to and fro, taking in the measure of the room and all its contents. He considered her carefully, detailing every last curve of her face before he spoke again.

"I have discovered a problem," he said. "And require you to assist in finding the answer. It seems the number of keepers has been reduced over the last handful of winters—reduced in the order of a hundred or more. No one can account for these. I require to discover what has become of them."

Taylo hesitated. She had not realized how many keepers had gone to the Shanties but the number was not untoward. Sixteen students were at the ship at any given time, and she had lost track of how many had gone to the

Shanties. They jaunted a few at a time, as the need arose.

Taylo had hoped it would have kept them beneath notice.

"I know of no one who would harm the keepers,"Taylo said truthfully, though not completely. "And have not heard any talk of it. I can check the current chatter. It will take the turn of a few days."

"Unfortunate," Councilman Iance said. He stopped to consider the moment. Taylo decided he had expected her to know right off of anything which touched the keepers. In this case he had been correct, she knew straightaway where the keepers had gone, but she dared not mention the first word of it to him or to anyone in all of Cityscape. More than the keepers were at stake; the whole of the Shanties could also be at risk.

It was not for outsiders to know of the Shanties, she had heard it more than once. Taylo had already resolved not to be the proof of their fear.

"Walk with me on the way to the Cathedral Authority Taylo," Iance said. "We have a need to map out the course of our investigation to the cause of these disappearances."

"As you wish Councilman," Taylo said. By reputation Iance was a careful man, one who noticed everything under his eyes. Taylo knew what he would look for, and kept herself from any reaction to his request which would chatter to him about her part in the keeper disappearances.

She followed, her mind filled with the consideration of the moment. On the one hand she knew things she could not tell anyone, especially a councilman. Even one who worked for the cause of right could benefit the cause of wrong. She would investigate, as she must, but Taylo had already resolved to be incompetent in this matter. She would find nothing to clue her to the cause of such disappearances.

"Authority Taylo," a young man approached her on the street. He was one of the students, home for a season. Then as he noticed the man walking next to her he held back the words he would have said at first. "May I speak with you, ma'am?"

"It is well Adison," Taylo said. "What has occurred?"

Adison had attended scholarship at the old ship. She had heard chatter that he had chosen not to return, but none mentioned his reasons. As much as Taylo would like to converse with him, they were not in well befitted company.

Adison looked at Iance once more before he spoke.

"Elder Hector has sent chatter," Adison said. "He has need of a keeper or two for some work, and it will require silence from beginning to end and an instant agreement to every request. Could this be something untoward?"

"I do not know," Taylo said. "The Elder has the best intentions to keepers, but not always the best sense. It would not be too bitter to investigate. Adison, I will need you to accompany me and we will find out whether this unusual request from Elder Hector is at issue with the cause of just."

"Authority Taylo," Iance said. "Perhaps I could accompany you as you investigate this matter."

"This is not the matter of your concern," Taylo

said. She had thought herself about to be beyond the company of the councilman, and able to talk to Adison. Yet he interposed to turn her plan to its opposite. She could not be certain whether he was playing at some game or whether he just held to curiosity.

"I am a councilman of Cityscape," he explained. "I'm obligated to be aware of the lives of those who live here, even keepers. It could be a scholarship for me."

Taylo considered for the turn of a moment. There was no cause to turn him down, and in the matter of the fact, it could turn to an advantage. It would not be untoward for a councilman of Cityscape, one who might turn to be Regent, to know the substance of the lives of keepers.

"It is well then," Taylo said. "Adison, lend this man your cloak. He must appear in the manner of a keeper."

Adison quickly removed his cloak, and traded with the councilman for the thinner one. In the exchange, Iance held out three heavy coins, each the recompense of more than a day's work.

"I would not take your cloak without proper recompense," the councilman said. "Is this sufficient?"

"It is more than enough sir," Adison said, offering back two of the coins which Iance refused with the wave of his hand.

"Shall we jaunt forth then?" Iance said taking a light hold on Taylo's arm. "It seems my scholarship is incomplete. You can verse me on the proper conduct of keepers as we go."

Taylo could not help but feel hopeful. Perhaps if councilman Iance could live the life of a keeper, even if for the circle of a few hours, he could learn to see them differently. This meeting was not like what she expected and thankfully nothing like what she feared, but it could yet turn to adventure.

5

Elder Jenne noted Pura Sharo in the Commons as she arrived at first early. It had been the turn of two days since Joska had been injured. After a full day of rest the boy had resolved to proceed as he had before and learn to counter his injury. The keeper's condition, though she held every glance and look in check, was there for anyone who knew her well enough to look.

Since the day of Joska's injury Sharo stood apart, moving through the day like one who only had thought for the moment, and who only had care for the most basic of need. If the distance in her heart were not reason enough for concern, she had also taken to sleeping in the Commons.

Sharo was in her cloak gathered in a well befitted corner, wrapped in her old cloak from Cityscape, sleeping in the first of early.

"Oh my dearest friend," Jenne spoke to herself in a soft voice. "What is to be done for you?"

As the distant sun climbed into the sky the Commons slowly became awake, as did Sharo. Jenne stood in her place greeting and talking as the day brought alive the heart of the Shanties. In the midst of it all Sharo awoke and stood to lend her warmth to counter the chill, yet she kept any other's shadow from crossing her feet.

Ryalt and Athan entered at near the same time, from differing directions. They took in the whole of the Commons, and traversed specifically to Jenne. Athan was a young pura who had been trained by Sharo. Ryalt was the man at her side and the father to their child.

"I do not fathom how Sharo is here and does not leave to her house," Ryalt said.

"It is unbefitted," Athan added.

"She is grieving," Jenne said. "Every word and movement shows her heart as one broken."

"You know her better than us," Athan said. He moved to say more, to contradict Jenne in support of his view, but she had already abandoned them to approach Sharo. The remedy for the situation could not be found in trying to fathom another's heart, but rather by speaking to it.

"Sharo," Jenne said, catching Sharo in a warm embrace which she held, allowing them to talk closely. "My child Joska is as well as ever and I am still emplaced at your side. Yet you somehow seem to worry."

"Much is appreciated," Sharo replied.

"Why are you in the Commons today?" Jenne asked. "Chatter has it you would not see any other place."

"I have no cause to stay at my house," Sharo said. "And the work of the day will not do itself."

Sharo expected her words to be the end of the conversation. Jenne wondered that her friend had forgotten so quickly the celebrated persistence of her closest friend.

"You know if you but say a word the whole of the Shanties would stand with you for all," Jenne said. "You are well beloved."

"And yet," Sharo said. "I am alone."

"No Sharo," Jenne said. "While I am warm and

well you are not allowed to be truly alone. You have done more for me than any recompense could pay, and I will not abandon you, not for any cause."

"I understand what you say," Sharo said. "And ever before my fondest wish was to live in a real house and sleep in a bed. But now my heart does not find cause to hold those things. I find myself here and find no cause to venture away."

"Perhaps you find yourself here to face the depth of love your friends have for you," Jenne said. "None of us will stand aside no matter how terse your words are. But for now, the Commons are open, and the work of the day will not do itself."

"Then we shall be handy to the task," Sharo agreed.

#

Miko traversed the Shanties, stepping through fallen rock on every lane, looking to whatever he might find and taking care not to be caught in the midst of conversation with himself.

It was difficult to avoid; he had a full share of frustration to speak and none other would listen. He was young, a mere forty-two winters, but old enough to be entrenched in scholarship, and old enough to hear the chatter of the Shanties. He had learned to lend himself to the occasional labor in the circle of winters after his father died.

His father had been far afield in late of summer, hunting to the south for whatever food there might be, and had died at the hand of an accident. It had been sad, but it was the way the world was.

It was the second summerset day. Sky which had

been filled with chill was now touched by the warmth of the distant sun. Within the turn of a handful of days the warmth would entrench itself in the land and the sky, and then summer would be in full turn.

The broken buildings of the Shanties gave way to a flat valley with a stream following the edge of a hill. There and in places like it foodstuffs were grown, not in even rows but gathered and clumped, and under the cover of large trees and ruins which had yet to fall. It was life in the Shanties, it was made to be hid from Cityscape. No one knew when the Cityscape lords might be watching, therefore every growth and every step had need to be hidden by the hour and the day.

Miko chose to join the labor of the day, as the ground was released from chill it was prepared for what would be planted for the season. It was at the fields he found another result of the madness which had overcome the whole of the Shanties.

On a day in which the fields should be filled with labor only a scant few had arrived to do their work. The rest must have gone to the Commons, for this was their one day in seven. A growing number of the initiates took a pause from work and to discuss an ancient book, one which had been given to them by an old robot in the colony ship. The book said that God truly was, and the Shanties had believed it all without question or thought.

Miko traversed the hill and set his shirt to a tree so he could work. He was young for such labor, but since those older than him would not, he would. His size had grown to a befitted level, and working together was the strength of the Shanties.

"The free sun will warm the air," Miko said to a

man who worked nearby. It was the traditional greeting of the first summerset day.

"May the warmth take growth in your heart," the man returned.

Miko set to work then, breaking weeds out of the frozen soil. It was not difficult work, but it had need to be done.

"This work will never be accomplished," Miko commented as he moved from one set to another.

"It will be finished on the morrow," a worker said. "The rest of us only visit the Commons for the turn of a day."

"Combined with the keepers," another added. "The work will be done by the mid of the day."

"Why should the work of today wait until the morrow?" Miko asked. He knew the answer of course, but wanted to see if they would say as much.

"A day for rest has not done any harm little one," the first worker said. "You find offense where there is none."

Miko decided to leave at the mid of the day. The workers in this field had obviously been misled. It was disgrace how many neglected work for their one day in seven—simply for the cause of a book which told them to do so.

#

Miko arrived home after the late of mid but well before eventime. His mother, Sundi, returned his nodded greeting, but held back the words he knew she wanted to say. He was old enough to choose whether to gather at the Commons or to work, and he had chosen the better portion. He cleaned himself at the basin. His mother was already in the midst of conversation with Trina, his sister, who was in the next room.

"If I have calculated befittedly," Trina was saying from the sleeping room. "The comet is moving toward Hera and the world of Perma. In the last third of the summer we should see it cover a major part of the sky."

"A small speck of dust in the sky will grow so large?" their mother asked.

"My scholarship tells me comets are large," Trina said, "as large as the whole of ruinscape, and their tail can stretch as long as the space between Perma and Hera or more. They are only small because they are so very distant."

Trina played at being the instructor. She had gone to the old colony ship three times, and was learning after a category with the cause of being able to teach alongside the old robot. Chatter had it there were a handful of students following this scholarship, ones who would soon be given to teaching old information in new settings.

"I cannot fathom," their mother said. "But if your numbers are correct we will see."

"Yes we will see," Trina agreed. "I understand it will be a well befitted sight. In the first world of men the sight of a comet often portended bitter tidings, or at least some large change to the world."

Miko turned the corner, intent on lounging in his sling with as much silence as his family would tolerate. Trina worked at painting the wall diametric to his bed and opposite hers, near the divider between their spaces. As he looked closer, he could see she was not painting the wall completely. She painted careful words upon it.

"What is this you are doing?" Miko asked. There was always some strange thing for her to be doing of late. He wondered why he bothered to ask at all.

"As it is spelled out in the holy writ," Trina said standing back to admire her work. "I am to etch these words on my walls and in my heart. This one is my most favored."

"Because a book told you to?" he asked. It was beyond annoying. "How can you say it was written concerning you."

"It is the book God instigated people to write on the first world of men," Trina said. "It's what God wanted to tell us, and these words speak an echo in my heart."

"It is a book written by a robot who was bored," Miko countered. "God is not, he cannot write a book."

They had traversed this argument more than once. With his mother he stubbornly held this ground but relented to allow her to have her say, but with his sister he could speak his mind. Thus far she was not smart enough to be convinced.

"God is," Trina said. "He emplaced us in this world so we would find these words and turn to him."

"God is not," he said. "We are emplaced here for the cause of our distant ancestors who chose this world."

"God truly is," she said back, not having the sense to understand what was obvious to him. "You have but to listen and see. He has brought about wonders at every turn."

"God is truly NOT!" Miko yelled. He stood up, wanting to put a point to his words and his opinion. He felt his heart rush as he stood up, and felt the slightest twinge of dizziness.

Then, unexpectedly, every surface in the room including himself and Trina, was layered over in water. It dripped from the counters and settled to the doorway. Trina moved away, as if he had splashed her, but the water had come from all directions. It came direct from the air.

For some reason Miko knew where the water had been moved from.

Their mother walked in, stopped in her footing, and looked about. They were, both of them and their space, well soaked in water. Trina was a sight with dripping hair. Miko looked as if he had been dipped in a pond.

"What has occurred?" she asked.

Trina simply shook her head. She pointed at Miko.

Miko put low his head, knowing he had once again infracted upon the heart of his mother.

#

Chatter of the event preceded them as they walked to the Commons. Miko would have rather put the memory to rest, as well as himself. His mother could be stubborn at times. Miko was the only one who proceeded quietly, his mother and sister spoke to everyone they encountered, near or far.

By the time they reached the commons a curious crowd was waiting.

"It appears we have a new pino in our midst," elder Jenne said.

If it weren't bad enough to suddenly have something make the world turn strange around him,

Miko was obligated to present himself in the Commons, more than half filled with keepers who played at being initiates of the Shanties. His mother stood by, proudly, not noting his obvious disdain.

Once the commons had held great mystery for Miko; the polished white walls, the faint pictures in the tiles, but no longer. On this particular day the Commons was a trap for him. Too much was done contrary to the true Shanties in these walls, and the walls would someday fall on those who had brought them to true ruin.

Miko could not fade into the background, no matter how much he would want to. He had shown signs that he had one of the gifts, a result of the genetic additions the original colony had fabricated so life on the world of Perma would be less harsh. The gifts had been the cause of the god wars. The god wars had been the cause of the destruction of the city where the Shanties had been built. The keepers worked for those who had brought down the city.

"So it seems," Miko said, knowing he had no cause not to answer what was spoken to him.

Jenne was the worst of them all. Her words hung upon by half the Shanties, as if wisdom were found in the mouth of a lost cityscape keeper. If she had been so wise, how had she managed to be abandoned in ruinscape, and near death when she had been found?

There were also other elders around, real elders from the Shanties. Also a number of the initiates had gathered around, mostly it seemed to put their eyes to him, as if somehow he was a different person to whom they were indifferent to not more than a day before. His arrival had almost begun a celebration for the Shanties. Even elder Paol had left his house and hearth to witness the activity of the day.

"There has not been a pino for the turn of many winters," elder Paol said. "Far past the life of any living initiate. It is cause for the whole of the Shanties to be happy."

"It is also a cause to wonder," Jenne said. "Perhaps you are given for a time coming soon, a time when your gift will be required."

Miko realized he was being spoken to again and straightened his back. As he supposed was usual, Jenne was saying words which seemed to be filled with meaning, but in the end had none.

"A time such as when?" Miko asked.

"We may not know until it is upon us, or gone," Jenne said. "There is no one who knows the ways of a water caller to instruct this young initiate. Should we set him to echo a sozo or a pura, or leave him to his own direction?"

"I traversed, I arrived and I talked," Miko said. "Can I now return to my own setting?"

"Presently," Jenne said. "Allow our conversation to be completed before you traverse."

"There is one who knows more of the pino than all of us," Pura Sharo said.

Pura Sharo was a sight to see, she still wore the drab colors of a keeper, which belied the red of her hair. The hair was a trait common in her family. The Shanties had been chattering about how she had taken to sleeping in the open at the Commons, reverting to a keeper in earnest.

Miko was not surprised. Sharo, and those who had traversed the sandscape with her were ever keepers. They could not be anything else.

"You are right Sharo," elder Paol said.

"One of us will be required to remain and so open a place for his scholarship," Trina said from her place beside their mother. "I will gladly relent, knowing the import of the need."

"Then we will arrange it," Jenne said. "Trina, much is given, much is appreciated. You have the admiration of the Shanties."

"Arrange what?" Miko asked. He had been dropped from the exchange, and now decisions were made without his voice. He had seen but not noted the awe on the faces of many of the initiates, and the commencement of tears in her mother and his sister.

"We will send you to continue your scholarship at the old colony ship," Jenne said. "There you will meet the robot interface Gabri, who had a hand in the design of your gift. You will have a befitted scholarship there."

There was no question to whether he would go. Scholarship at the old ship was a privilege reserved for a very few. Miko hung his head. He did not chase the privilege, and had not once considered it. He was more than content to keep his place in the Shanties.

Of all his days, he thought, this could be his worst.

6

It was by tradition that the doors of the Deep Cyan Cathedral were never locked, none of the doors were made with a bolt or a slide, but to jaunt too distant within would be dire without the benefit of a guide. Stories, however exaggerated they were, told of people wandering the hallowed halls for the turn of years without once finding a window or a doorway out. Fortunately Taylo was a sufficient guide and could get from one side of the Cathedral to the other without commotion or fuss.

After she sent keepers to warn others away from inquiring after the work proposed by the Elder, for at least long enough for her to assure that it was all befitted, Taylo approached the building from the front.

"Did not the Elder suggest the Southern face of the building?" Iance asked.

"He did," Taylo said. "There would be a guardian at that door, one who likely knows me. I can traverse through the Cathedral and get us to our destination in good time."

"Then I will follow as you lead," Iance said.

She led the way, hallway by hallway and room by room, wary of encroachment on the Elders who lived in the building. Taylo would not be seen as out of place, either in her uniform as an authority or in the dress of a keeper, but if her investigation turned to serious she would rather not be delayed, nor would she want the Elder warned of her approach.

The last time she had stopped by in the guise of a keeper one of the Elders had commented that she seemed to be more keeper than house lord. He had meant to insult, but Taylo kept it as tribute. Keepers had been teaching her how to dress and act and she had used the talent to the solution of more than one case.

"I dare say I've never jaunted so deep into the Cathedral," Iance mentioned as they walked past a darkened cellar. Elder Harve had once embarked on an investigation as to the purpose of all the rooms in the midst of the Chathedral. It had been when she had first arrived, so far as she understood he had not yet finished.

"Few have," Taylo said. "At the beginning I lived in Agriscape, but was sent to late scholarship within these walls. Some of what I learned was not planned to be taught. I often spent time within those offices for my transgressions."

"On this day it is a befitted scholarship."

"That it is," Taylo said. "Our destination is near and you must take the lead. The women keepers are told not to speak or to lead the way within the walls of the Cathedral."

"A strange tradition," Iance said. "You suspect this rumor of a job is untoward?"

"It is unusual at best," Taylo said. "Since we are here and in the guise of keepers, it may be a benefit to uncover the truth. I suspect nothing criminal but have cause to investigate to determine if there is. Here we are."

They entered the cellar room circumspectly, as if they had just arrived from the street. Taylo was not being unusually wary, but simply did as she had done from her first days as an authority. There was a truth to be found here, a truth behind an unusual request for keepers. Sometimes the unusual was a mask for the untoward. She lagged behind as Councilman Iance approached Elder Hector.

The Elder was well known to her. He had presided over many of her classes, and had taken interest in her as she continued to be the cause of untold commotion in the Deep Cyan Cathedral. She knew him as a friend, but his attitude toward keepers was uninformed.

"Elder," Iance spoke contritely as Taylo had instructed. "Is there keeping in need to be done?"

"There is," Elder Hector spoke. Taylo noted how his voice inflected differed from the times she had spoken to him in the form of an authority. There was harshness in his voice, excluded of respect. She had been working to change that frame of mind, not hard enough it seemed. "The books on this table have need to be burned."

With a single gaze at the table Taylo immediately knew which books they were. They were the version of the holy writ produced by Gabri on the ancient colony ship. Many had been brought to Cityscape, including the one on her own table.

Not many of the keepers would have parted with their own version of the holy writ willingly, but surely she would have heard of it had the Elder taken them by force. She had need to find where those books had been taken, and how the Elder had learned of them.

"Burned?" Iance asked.

"Ask no questions," Elder Hector said. "And do

not open to any page in these books. I do not know what brought these about, but they are in every corner of Cityscape, and they must be destroyed…keeper! What are you doing?"

Iance had picked up one of the copies and had opened it. Elder Hector lunged at him without a thought, and Iance sidestepped him. Elder Hector turned again, brandishing an old walking staff like a weapon.

"Councilman," Taylo said, standing tall and throwing the edge of her cloak from her head. "Do you require assistance?"

Elder Hector stood in his tracks.

"Authority Taylo?" he asked, looking, but only just seeing her through her cloak. "You mimic a keeper well."

"It is no bitter task," Taylo said.

"And…" Hector turned to his recent opponent. "Councilman Iance I believe. Forgive me. I did not know it was you."

"You would have beaten any other man for opening a book?" Iance asked.

Elder Hector let hang his head, but did not give an answer. When the question was framed so, it did not befit the Elder.

"What are these books?" the councilman asked. "Why are they so troublesome?"

"They are appearing everywhere," Hector answered, his eyes aglow. "I find them in the hands of keepers. They are a distortion, a broken image of the holy writ formed in common words. They are an abomination and they must be destroyed."

Iance had found a page, as if he had been searching something out.

"It says here under the label of Deuteronomy, here it is named the Second Book of Just," Iance said. "Should one become king, he is to scribe for himself a copy of this scholarship. Is that not comparable to the words in the holy writ I read on summer's first day?"

"Comparable, but no true echo," Elder Hector said. "The meaning differs when the words differ."

"I am unconvinced," Iance said, putting the book under his arm despite the elders' unspoken and hastily subdued protest. "Elder Hector, the influence politic is not your office, nor is it the cause of those who hold your office. Hold influence, if you must, within these walls, but with one footstep outside you have no cause to consider yourself above the dust in the streets. These books do not belong to you. Return them. Any remainder when I visit you in the third part of summer will be burned at the base of your bookshelves."

Elder Hector's eyes grew open wide.

"But take one to yourself," Iance continued. "Keep it long enough to scribe a copy of it, from the first word to the last. Then you will be better equipped to report on why this holy writ in slightly different words should be destroyed. At that time I will decide if there is a worthy threat to Cityscape, and I will take whatever action I choose."

"Yes councilman," Elder Hector said.

"You are, however, empowered to insist that these books not be carried within these walls."

"Yes councilman," Elder Hector said again.

Iance led the way in the more direct route to the

street, which was not obvious. As they made their exit Taylo glanced back at the Elder. He was holding one of the books in his hand and shaking.

Authority Taylo could not fathom where he saw such threat in something she knew to be so well befitted.

As their feet touched the lane outside, Taylo looked about. They were alone, at least in the moment.

"You know your own way in the Cathedral," She asked. "Do you not?"

"I would not dare match my knowledge against yours," Iance said. "But I have studied the original plans for the building in my offices. I have noted a number of changes this evening."

They continued to walk about the turn of the lane until, diametric to the Cathedral, they were in sight of Taylo's cart.

"I believe that is your cart," Iance said. "And for my cause you have already worked beyond your shift. I will traverse from here and let you on your way."

"Much is appreciated councilman."

"Continue to pursue this matter," Iance said. "We will converse again."

"That we will," Taylo said.

#

"Iance kept a copy of the holy writ?" Angla asked once again, as if it were important information.

"I told you he did," Taylo said. "It was still in his hand when I entered my cart and left. He instructed me to meet him in the same red building in three days. I fear in choosing our meeting place I may have given him evidence to find the relationship between us."

"The relationship between us is chattered on

every street," Angla said. "You have nothing to explain. You required a safe place for a meeting and you found it in a building you knew belongs to me. There is nothing more."

"I must remind you," Taylo said. "This conversation is not to be repeated anywhere else, not a word of it. That goes double for you Chanta."

There was a muffled "Yes ma'am." from behind the near wall.

"I do not share your fear," Angla said. "He was fair with the keepers he met and he told the Elder to return the copies of the holy writ he had taken. His heart may yet be turned to good."

"He is a councilman for Cityscape," Taylo said. "They work to appear well befitted whenever they are about. It is a benefit to them if they are perceived in the best light by the most number of people. He also intends to reach for the regency. Despite all, his heart is given first to the cause of ambition, and only to us if it is suitable to his first cause."

"And he kept a copy of the holy writ for himself," Angla added, ignoring what Taylo had said. "There may be hope if he reads those words. Allow councilman Iance to grow, to learn and see. Perhaps God intends take him by hand. Perhaps you were emplaced to be the one to speak to him."

"You do not know these people like I do," Taylo said. "There is no room for trust when one is near them. They keep their purposes silent, but will avenge any distraction to it. For them to turn to the truth is not possible."

"I am alive now when I could have been given to

lost," Angla said. "If God has chosen this distrusted councilman, he will be caused to change and he can put up little resistance."

"Well," Taylo said, standing to leave. "When I am consigned to the darkest level of the Holding, at least I will have you to visit me."

"It will be a befitted place to sing," Angla said.

7

Miko stood with his mother and sister Trina at the embarkation. He did everything not to be found looking at them, both bleary eyed for how soon they would miss him fondly, even before his jaunt began. Trina had given him a note with a careful explanation of which book she wanted him to return with. It was something on the next level of astronomy, which was what she had been given to study. He would rather she go and get the book herself, and leave him in the Shanties where he was most befitted.

The embarkation was an outside wall of an old building laid on its side; a flat place to stand at the edge of sand and ruined city. Before journeys were undertaken into the emptyscape of sand, children had played there and imagined all manner of monsters over the edge of the horizon. Since the old ship had been found and parents sent children to scholarship with the old robot, the Shanties had reused the embarkation as a beginning for their jaunt to the ship for scholarship. Trina had gone thrice, returning more expert and self-important each time.

Miko was obligated to travel with a guide and three students he had known before they had gone to the scholarship of the colony ship. Jenk he knew well, they had often scouted the hills around ruinscape as they grew. He knew the two girls, but not as well. They had started to gain womanly curves since the last time he had seen them. Kimi and Rayma chattered among themselves and sometimes looked at the boys they would be traveling with in much the same way a bird of prey would look upon its next meal.

Presently their guide arrived. Miko heard his mother gasp, and looked to see.

A tall man with deep red hair walked out from the Shanties in the company of the former keeper Kassi. Miko had met Kassi more than once; she was a sozo, a healer. Unlike the healers from the beginnings of the Shantyway, Kassi kept no office nor area. She chose instead to do her work in the home of those injured and sick, or in their workplace if the need was great. The keeper did whatever her mind thought to do and had no regard to keep to old tradition.

"Pytre," Miko heard his mother say. "It is well-befitted that you will guide my son to his new scholarship."

"Sundi," Pytre said holding her hand for a moment. "It is well for me to be able to jaunt forth this time. Your Miko is a pino. Wonders abound."

Kassi had disconnected from Pytre in the moment, and took time to touch the other students. As a sozo she would assure they were well with a single touch, it was her gift to see the wrongs in a body and set them to right. She nodded, affirming them ready for a long jaunt, and the time in their new scholarship.

"Pino Miko," Kassi said rejoining her hand to Pytre. "You have my admiration…"

Kassi leaned up to him, touching him as she had the others to assure his well-being, and to send him off. As she was so close, she whispered an end to her sentence which none other but Miko could have heard.

"...and my sympathy."

Miko felt the need to nod, if only to avoid the discussion which might ensue should he mention to her how addled she was. The gifts were gifts, there was no bitterness to be had in them. They could be used for good or ill, but those uses fell at the feet of the one with the gift. Kassi stood entrenched in the Shanties, but she spoke with the cynical words of Cityscape.

Pytre had gathered his other charges and stood to speak to them all.

"It will be a three day trip through sandscape," Pytre said. "It will be warm in the day and well chilled in the night, and also very dry. Keep your water with you, and drink it well. Once we reach the sea of grass there is a water pool we have dug for the benefit of those who travel that way. When we have traversed that far we will wait for a cart to convey us the remainder of the jaunt."

Pytre received a finishing embrace from Kassi before they were underway.

Miko gave a last wave to his mother. She was still proud, and did not seem to notice his disdain for what the world was doing to him. It was possibly better, if nothing else, for the cause of not seeing disappointment touch her eyes.

#

"I have never traversed out so far," Miko said as they topped yet another hill of sand.

"The world is bigger than it seems," Pytre said. "When I first jaunted to the Shanties I thought we had walked the world around back to Cityscape."

Miko had tried not to converse with Pytre on

principal, but the man was difficult to avoid. He had an easy way about him, and was quick with a comment or a question. Miko would not choose to be the untoward one, so he answered when he felt no cause to.

"I first traversed the sandscape on the early days of summer," Pytre continued. The man seemed to consider any length of quiet as an invitation to speak. "We walked complete from the ship to the Shanties the whole time hearing of how Sharo had traversed in the full of winter."

Miko had heard this before, the epic jaunt of Sharo and Ryalt. They were joined on their return journey by Kassi and Pytre. Much had been said about that traverse, much of which could not possibly be true. They had brought the holy writ with them, and many other things which threatened to ruin the Shanties.

"Really?" Jenk said. "Tell me more about it."

Miko let close his eyes. Miko could not fathom that Jenk would ask to hear what he already knew—what the Shanties had been chattering of since the actual event. It was not to be avoided. Miko was obliged to hear the breadth and depth of it all, with more of the detail as Pytre remembered it, and with little regard for proper order.

The sand was soft and warm, walking was bitter work by itself, listening to people who were happy to be walking upon the sand was even more bitter. By the end of the day they were well out of sight of the Shanties. As their camp was being set up, Miko stood upon a dune and looked back.

"You can't even see the fires from here," Jenk asked. "Can you?"

"It's nice to know the Shanties are not so easy to find," Miko said. "However the keepers keep finding us I cannot imagine."

"They look during the day," Jenk said. "Once they know where we are emplaced the ruined city is quite distinctive."

Pytre had brought two small tents for them to sleep in. The girls took one tent for themselves. Miko was obligated to fit into a small tent with Jenk and their guide.

The night was not overly chilled, and the sand beneath them was soft, still Miko awoke with a sore neck. Pytre passed out a small breakfast and reminded them to continue to drink as they willed, then they packed up and continued their jaunt.

#

"You are a pino," Pytre said as they walked in line. There had been other footprints made in this sand, and hastily erased by the winds of Perma. According to Miko, too many footprints had been made. "I've never met one before."

"Few have," Miko said. For as involved as Kassi was with the Shanties, Pytre seemed vastly uninformed about everything of any import. Even the youngest initiate of the Shanties knew there had not been a pino for generations.

"How long ago did you find out?"

"The turn of four days," Miko said. "My sister was putting an argument to me and I mistakenly made the house wet, and us with it."

"Really," Kimi said. "What else have you done?"

"I can pull water out of the air," Miko said.

"Look."

Miko cupped his hands together and looked at it for a moment. He pictured his hands pulling to the water in the air around them. He imagined what it would feel like when his hands contained a full amount of water. As he continued to think water began to collect and form there. The air was quite dry, but what little water there was came to him. Soon he had a half handful of water, clear and pure.

"Such things are not in the habit of being," Jenk said. "How does your gift find water in such a dry land?"

"There's bits of water afloat in the air, and plenty to be had a befitted length beneath our feet," Miko said. "A man with a shovel could reach it easily."

"Really?" Rayma asked.

"Miko," Pytre said. "How did you become aware of the placement of water below our feet?"

Miko hadn't thought about it. The water was there because he knew it was. Then the thought occurred to him that the rest did not know anything about it. He had taken it for granted because it had been there from the first steps of their jaunt.

"Your gift touches the way you see," Pytre said. "Sharo can see the warmth in anything, or the lack of it. Kassi can tell when something is untoward inside a person. You can search out where there is water. It is a most befitted gift, especially in sandscape."

"You give so much trust for what I might see?" Miko asked. "What if I play the young initiate and tell you whatever jumps into my head?"

"When we settle in the mid of late," Jenk said. "I

will take a shovel and prove your sight. It may give us water in a dry land…for those of us who cannot call it out of the air."

"Perhaps by the time we traverse back to the Shanties," Pytre added. "We could use a boat and our friend pino Miko."

"Bah," Miko said. He wasn't sure which was more an annoyance, the assumption of friendship, or the unthinking confidence in the boundlessness of his ability.

"There is not so much water here," Miko said. "And I have not the first hint on how to construct a boat."

"I've read about them," Kimi said. "I would truly enjoy constructing a boat. First one fabricates the framework…"

"Kimi," Jenk childed. "You would love to construct, not matter what the project would be."

"True enough," Kimi said. "I have learned the earliest principles, I am eager to put them into practice."

#

The separation to grasscape could not be found quickly enough. Rayma saw it first, she stopped and pointed. Pytre only smiled, he had been expecting it. Once they were closer he recoursed them to traverse to a particular place. It had been dug out and camped in a number of times. A pile of wood was stacked against a tree and ready for use.

"Is there water here as well?" Kimi asked. They had all found what he saw so interesting, and Miko knew they would now as well. He had hoped to distance himself from these students, yet they could not help but try to bring him to inclusion.

"Over that ridge is where it flows best," Miko

said pointing. It was a fair walk from where the camp was emplaced, whoever put it here did not have his advantage.

As Pytre and Jenk set up the tents, Kimi and Rayma chattered. Miko looked about at the grass and the small trees beyond the edge. He could see the water as it was pulled from the ground, and how it traveled up the plants. In the tree in front of him the water reached up to the most elevated leaves, then jumped out into the air. He had never seen the like, it had never occurred to him that it would be so. He also noted a number of small animals, all hiding. Miko knew their location from the water they held. It would be an advantage in hunting.

"This is only the demarcation of it," Jenk said, appearing at Miko's side. "I cannot wait to watch you when you espy the great trees."

"I've heard of them," Miko said. He had been enjoying himself, would it be so untoward to allow him leave to enjoy alone? It was not the way of people, he supposed, to allow others requisite time to consider and think.

"So had I," Jenk said as he settled onto a fallen tree. "But the hearing is not the same as the seeing. Now join me in gathering dry sticks and branches for the fire. The keeping of the day will not do itself."

"The what?" Miko asked, while picking up a handful of smaller sticks.

"It is something you will hear quite often," Jenk said. "Where we have the Shantyway, the keepers from Cityscape have a wisdom all their own, and are quick to speak it. Your scholarship may benefit more than you think."

"If my scholarship benefits at all," Miko said.

#

It came out of the sky, a rounded box tinted white. Pytre had told them to watch for it, but Miko still found seeing such a sight unsettling. It made little sound, only something like the rushing of wind, and Miko could see the one inside through a clear panel.

"We're going to traverse in that?" Miko asked, pointing at the cart which had circled first at a distance before lowering itself onto the grasscape. He was sitting on the collected tents they had spent the morning gathering and folding. The tents would be staying where they were, Pytre would take them back when he returned to the Shanties.

"It is only a cart," Pytre said. "It will not harm you."

"It will not usually harm you," Jenk said. He did not sound worried in the least.

The cart settled to the grass. Jenk did not think to approach until after the sound of the wind had settled down. A man in dim clothes stepped out and smiled at Pytre.

"Medic Parke," Pytre said. "Is all well?"

"As well as can be," the man said. "Authority Taylo was called away for the cause of her work so I have come to gather the new students from the Shanties. "I must ask about the pool I saw from the air, it looks to be full of water."

"It is," Pytre said. "I dug it out last night under the direction of Miko, who is what they call a pino. He can find water without a second thought."

"I have heard of that adaption in my

scholarship," Parke said as he considered the boy. "It is very rare. You are fortunate."

"If you say so," Miko said. With the passing of every day he thought himself less fortunate by jumps and steps. Perhaps he was weary from traversing sandscape, or as he neared Cityscape he grew the same dour attitude for all things.

Rayma and Kimi were already seated in the cart. They had gathered their packs as the craft landed. Jenk had noted how they had all traversed in a cart before, save only Miko. He had also mentioned how the carts were very safe, they only fell from the sky on rare occasions. Only a mere handful had died in that terrible and painful manner.

Miko took his pack and stepped up into the cart like he had seen the others do. Once inside he found a small space and not near enough room to stand fully upright. There was a seat aside to the doorway which he put himself into, setting his pack under the chair as the others had.

"Fear not friend Miko," The driver said as he emplaced himself at the front. "I hear chatter the first time Jenk jaunted in a cart he cried for fear from start to finish."

"Not true, Medic Parke" Jenk said. "I cried before the start as well."

"And well after the finish," Kimi added.

Pytre waved as the cart took off, then turned to the work of gathering his packs for the traverse back to the Shanties. Miko could not help but touch the envy he felt, and consider how he dreaded the journey before him. Perhaps it would have been better if he had never had the gift, or if he had found it later in the summer. He would be safe at home, and not so far from the Shanties.

After traversing a slow circle once, the cart took off at a run, staying low over the grass. Quickly a mass of trees rose up before them. They were growing in a long curved line, marking the transition between grass and forest.

"So huge!" Kimi exclaimed.

"You have seen the big trees before," Jenk said.

"I know," Kimi said. "Yet they are still huge. The things we could build..."

The trees were every bit as large as Miko had been told, maybe even larger. They passed by too quickly as Miko looked at them with new eyes, seeing dampness traversing in every branch and leaf.

"You intend to take the long way around the lake?" Kimi asked, looking out over the forest with steady eyes.

"We do not want to be seen," Parke said. "This early in the summer the lake is surrounded by city lords and their keepers. They gather to watch the ice break free."

"We are near to city lords?" Miko asked. He had not considered, though he had known the old ship was near the lake, and the city lords often went to the lake. He could not think of anything less safe.

"Fear not," Parke said. "The old ship has been in place for the turn of many years and only one house lord has ever found it."

"One is sufficient," Miko said.

#

The cart was brought to ground in a small

clearing surrounded by tall trees. Medic Parke left the cart to look about before giving the go ahead for the students to come out. They were obviously careful, fearing even the sight of the smallest city lord. Miko could not help but join in their anxiety. It would be well if he never saw a city lord, and all the better if one never saw him.

They walked through the forest, Miko having to redirect himself several times. It was not that he neglected to be careful, but he found wonder in every tree branch and blade of grass.

The old ship was hidden among trees and under the dirt of a hill. It was strange, but Miko knew it was there before they arrived. He could sense it somehow, though it was not made of water. Perhaps, he thought, it was the lack of water to be found which caught his attention.

Parke took Miko directly to Gabri once they reached the old ship. She was the oddest thing he had ever seen. There were whispy wings made of vapor surrounding her, and a shining circle above her head, but there was hardly any water within her at all. She was most decidedly mechanical.

"A pino pneuma?" the robot said. "You are correct, I have much information on that augmentation. Miko, what have you accomplished so far?"

"I've gathered water out of the air," Miko said. "And I can see where water is to be found, Pytre helped with that."

"That is a good start," the robot said.

Miko sat where he was, looking at the machine. For its part, the machine looked at him. Parke took his leave with a simple nod, leaving the boy in the presence of the robot.

"You are not at ease around me," Gabri said once they were alone. "Do you fear me Miko?"

Miko wanted to sink down in his chair, to disappear, but it just wasn't possible. This robot could see through him like he could see the water under the sand.

"I have no cause to be offended," Gabri said. "Nor have I the ability. Say what you will. The truth is of most value."

"I did not want to come here from the first," Miko said. "I was content in my place in the Shanties. I fear because this is so far from home, and so near to Cityscape. I also hesitate because you are the one who pushed the God upon the Shanties."

The robot stopped for a moment, considering his words. Miko had heard that robots use little time to think. For one to consider before giving an answer would be unusual.

"In the matter of the fact," Gabri finally said. "God is the one who forced himself upon the Shanties, though I am sure he used scant little force, not as you would understand it."

"If you suggest," Miko said. He had learned his scholarship, and knew he had no caused to put questions to the teacher. It would do little good to argue.

"It would be most befitted if you were to gain scholarship while you are here," Gabri said. "You will attend class with the other students every morning. In the later of the day I will demonstrate and instruct you as a pino. We will reconsider your position after a few weeks."

"It is well then," Miko said. If the robot put her word to it, he could look forward to the turn of a few weeks when he could be traversing back home.

8

Iance traversed toward his house after nightfall. Above, in the sky he could see the edge of blue giant Hera and its faint ice rings.

In the journal of the first regent of Cityscape, he had called himself a "governor", Iance had read how the engineers had lamented over how little water there was to be found on Perma, and how much was visible in the sky above. They did not have the capacity to go retrieve it from the rings. The first governor had used it as a reminder to him of how helpless he was, how the whole planet was powerless. He used their powerlessness as proof that it was the way it should be. Iance had often wondered whether that was a failing in the man, but he had done many well-befitted things.

As a councilman of high standing, and a city lord with numerous assets and interests, Iance could have easily lived in a single building in the midst of the towers, if not a set. Yet he could not see the advantage of having so much room when the single floor of one of the mid-sized buildings was more than enough. It gave him freedom away from endless planners and keepers to care for a larger space.

He entered the main door and closed himself in. The door led up three steps to the large center room, large enough for a hundred city lords to mingle and chatter without the feeling of crowdedness. Chairs were arranged in a befitted order about the room, even the colors put to the walls had been a matter of careful planning. Nothing had been left to chance, nor to second level workers. There were secrets within those walls, hidden panels to hide objects of interest and hidden causeways to be used in more dire situations.

The cloak he had obtained from the keepers was taken off and thrown against a near wall. Iance considered disposing of it, but it would be handy to his purpose if he ever chose to walk through keeper areas. The keepers had noticed the cloak given to him by a tradesman who said it would mask him from notice. That man had been wrong. The cloak would stay. It could be useful again.

It was late, and Iance had a plan to put himself through a shower then to wander off to sleep. There were many things to accomplish; tomorrow would be a full day. He would need to plan, and plan well, considering which actions to take, and which to avoid. There were too many who watched for his next misstep, and he knew he dared not allow them success.

"Have you made progress?" a sleepy voice asked from the lounge near the wall of windows.

He should have known Raisia would be here. She had, however covertly, chosen in her bid to become the wife of a regent. The choice meant she would channel her increasingly large resources behind him to assure his victory. She would, as a matter of course, check on occasion to see whether she had chosen wisely.

"Progress is slow," Iance said. "But information is handy, should one choose to look for it."

"What have you found?" Raisia asked. Iance had noted how his lifelong friend was quick in some things, but dull in others. He put up with her shortcomings, she was loyal and well connected.

Iance held up the book for her, and let her take it and hold it in her lap, opening it carefully.

"It's the holy writ," Iance said. "Framed in the words of Cityscape."

She turned several of the pages, finally finding what she sought. It was what he had done, and possibly what anyone in Cityscape would do. They would seek whatever segment they had read on passing on the one day a year when the holy writ was open at the first of summer.

"…Perhaps it has been given for you to be the one walking with the regent for a time such as this-- to avoid a crisis," Raisia read. "It's the words I read in the holy writ one summer's first day. It's framed differently, of course. It took the turn of a few years before I found the meaning for the word 'queen'. It is an old word from the first home of men... It is a strange thing to say though, isn't it?"

Raisia soon abandoned the words within and looked at the cover, light colored, and bound neatly to the pages.

"Where did you obtain this?" she finally asked.

"Elder Hector at the Deep Cyan Cathedral," Iance said. "He had as many as fifty of these he'd taken from the hands of keepers. He considered them a threat and intended to have them burned."

"Burned?" Raisia asked. "That would be a bitter offense. This book is immaculate. The cover is perfect, if not understated, and the printing indicates it is from one of the better publishers."

"It was not produced in Cityscape," Iance waited

to let the full measure of his words work into her. It would not take long. Raisia knew to think before she spoke.

"Then where?"

That was the question, and they both knew it. Conventional wisdom knew that Cityscape was the only city on Perma. A few villages dotted the agriscape to the north, but there was nothing else to be found. There had once been another city, but it was a landscape of rubble on the other side of the desert courtesy of the last and final god war.

Could there be a city unknown somewhere on the world of Perma?

"I cannot say I know," Iance said. "It is someplace with access to a copy of the holy writ, but certainly not the Cathedral where all known copies are hid and watched by the day and the moment. It is someplace with capabilities to publish with quality at a high level and in goodly amounts."

"An unknown place on Perma..." Raisia said. "An outpost of some sort, perhaps with a factory. The thought is compelling and frightening. Could it also be a place where keepers disappear to?"

"My investigation of one led to the other," Iance said. "The new books are recent. I may take opportunity to question Elder Hector about the time when the copies first appeared. I already know the numbers for the keepers have been diminishing slightly over the circle of the last twenty winters. We only noted the disparity because the number has grown large over the circle of time."

"Did anything unusual happen within the circle

of those times?" Raisia asked. This was one of the things she excelled at, connecting one event to another. He had anticipated the question and had taken a few moments to search the archives as he traversed back to his house.

"The winter was a day longer than usual, but somewhat milder, a house lord was murdered by a keeper, the keeper was captured and put to lost before winter's end," Iance said. "A young child of house lords was lost in forestscape. Her parents were found dead in their cart. She was not found until after the start of summer."

"Her name was Angla," Raisia said. "I recall that event… interesting how a child alone without sheltering stayed warm and well in the winded days of winter. By all sense and speculation she should have been lost and gone."

Iance smiled. He had taken time to investigate what chatter there was on the event, and what had been recorded. He wondered how well her memory served.

"And," Raisia began. "… and, she was found by an authority named Taylo. Someone you have recently been acquainted with I believe."

"That she is," Iance said. "And she is protective of the keepers. She may know something of these disappearances, but she is hard to see into. I noted how glad Taylo was when I left her."

"Which indicates you should spend more time with her," Raisia said.

"And I should look at her more closely," Iance said. "She may have little to fear, but with the turn of a few days she will be able to hide nothing."

"If she is protective," Raisia said. "Then those

who disappear are being hidden away somewhere, not harmed."

"That is the assumption," Iance said. "Taylo was named as the guardian for Angla when she arrived back in Cityscape. The building in cathedral district Taylo named as our meeting place is among her holdings."

Raisia put the book down on the table as she sat up.

"Perhaps Angla may be easier to see into," she said. "Given the right situation and a certain amount of encouragement."

Iance smiled. It was obvious, yet as much as it had been before him, he had left the strategy she stated without consideration. Raisia had once again proven her worth.

He would consider how best to arrange a meeting with Angla and how to get the words he needed from her.

9

It had been arranged beginning to end, though no one observing would perceive it. In the yard of the old warehouse at Drydocks all was kenetic as ever; carts whispering in and out, keepers being hired and jaunted away as other keepers moved forward; all for the cause of finding keeping in need to be done and trading work for recompense.

Daine stood at the edge of the lane, her delight to have finally reached the hiring corner was tempered by knowing that she was not present to be hired nor to keep, and worst of all, not to expect fair recompense. She had been obligated to listen, several times over, as elder keepers prattled over the import of her opportunity and how it was better than any pay.

She would have gladly let any of them jaunt to this opportunity for scholarship if they would but let her work for coinage and carry her part of the expenses of the day.

Daine still could not fathom why she had been chosen to attend scholarship. There were others much more deserving than she. Perhaps it had become known how she taught the younger children in the crèche as she awaited her day to begin to keep. Daine stood up straighter and nodded to herself. She could not change where she had been placed, she could only accept it and work for the better. Perhaps in the end some good might come of it.

"To avoid the leading edge of the hiring corner is

to avoid being hired," an older keeper mentioned to her as she walked by. Daine stared back at her stupidly. Mere handfuls of the Drydocks knew of authority Taylo and her actions. Those who knew thought it best to exclude those not involved, to be less dire. She had not considered what to say should anyone questioned her presence at the hiring corner, or her actions.

"One has already arranged our availability," Aery said, linking his arm into hers. The keeper walked away, shaking her head for the shame of it. Daine turned her eyes away. Their hiring would not be near what the elder keeper was thinking, but the rumor would serve to quiet curious keepers.

"We are to look for the medic Parke," Aery said to her in aside. "Do you have note on how we would know him?"

"I hear he is well befitted," Daine said. "Chatter is that he is a good match for authority Taylo."

"That is scant helpful," Aery said. "Perhaps he is tall, has dark eyes, or perhaps he wears a hat? More information would have been befitted."

As Aery complained, Daine noted a cart come to a stop at the corner of the street. A man stepped out, well-built and bold. Daine had never heard of a house lord who actually stepped out of his cart to do his hiring. He talked to one of the elder keepers, holding her hand as he did so, also something unheard of. Daine began to recognize the defining attributes they were to look for in meeting the medic were not in dress or appearance, but in action.

The elder keeper turned to look through the crowd, and then pointed direct at her and Aery.

"Our house lord has arrived," Daine said. "Follow me."

Aery was confused, he had not seen what Daine had seen, yet he followed as he was led by the hand of Daine.

"Daine and Aery," the man said as they approached. "I am Parke."

"Of whom we have heard much sir," Daine said.

"We stand ready to serve," Aery added.

"Then you know what will be required," Parke asked. "And what the recompense will be?"

"Well then, sir," Daine said using the proper form. She covertly looked about, feeling the actor as she played the keeper who had just been hired. Her father had said it would be most befitted if Daine would not be hired as a keeper until the turn of another winter or more. Daine had wondered whether somehow he had arranged for her to be chosen to attend this unknown scholarship to separate her from the start of keeping. She could not truly fathom his reluctance. Keepers were born for keeping and work was made to be done. There would never be a shortage of keeping, nor of keepers, in Cityscape.

As they approached, Daine could see two keepers already in the cart, a girl and a boy who were a similar age to Daine and Aery. She had heard they would be students from Cathedral district. Authority Taylo had been working among them for some time. Aery gave a curt nod to the two as he sat down. In such a setting keepers would not converse, save for what had to do with the keeping they were hired to do. Their task at the moment was to appear in every way like they were keepers being hired, and to give no observer reason to chatter.

Daine settled to her place in the cart. Medic Parke walked into the first seat and did not wait for the circle of a moment before his cart whispered them up and away from the Drydocks.

Once above the ground, away from curious eyes, the other keepers lit right into conversation, with hardly any note or consent from the city lord driver.

"I am Aysa," the girl said. "And this is my friend Masey. We are from the Cathedral district."

"I am Aery," Aery said. "And this is Daine."

"How much has been spoken to you of the scholarship?" Masey asked.

"Almost none at all," Aery said. "Except that it is beyond the bounds of Cityscape, and that it is a well befitted opportunity."

It seemed Aery had been hearing the same words which had been spoken to Daine.

"None of what you know or discover is to be repeated in Cityscape," Aysa said. "The scholarship is found near Purgatory Lake. It is within the original colony ship."

"Was that not the ship destroyed in the last God war?" Daine asked. Some of the keepers who would play at scholarship in the crèche had some grasp of history. Daine had always found events from before her life to hold her interest. If something happened once, it could always happen again.

"It was supposed to have been," Aysa said. "But it had been moved and hidden by the scientists from the second city. It was found by a child of Cityscape who was lost in the great trees."

"Would that be Angla?" Aery asked.

"It would," Aysa said. "It was there she obtained the holy writ which has introduced us to God."

"There is no end to wonders," Aery said. "I wondered how the books had appeared so suddenly."

"That is just the beginning," Masey said. "The scholarship is taught by an interface robot which was on the ship when it arrived on Perma."

"And yet she does not appear old at all," Aysa added. "You will quickly be fond of Gabri."

"Also," Masey said. "You will be studying along with students from another city on Perma."

"There is no other city on Perma," Aery said.

"It was supposed to have been destroyed in the God war as well," Aysa said. "But there were those who lived after their city was put to ruin. I would say that they rebuilt their city, but it is not entirely true. They built it to be hidden."

Daine looked at Aery and saw the wideness of his eyes which probably echoed her own.

"There is so much I do not know," Daine said. "And I have yet to be introduced to any formal scholarship."

Aysa turned her attention to the driver of the cart. Medic Parke had visited the Drydocks on occasion to check on the keepers and offer his support. Not many medics would serve for the keepers.

"I fathom we are to be especially careful on our way to the ship," Aysa said.

"You are," medic Parke said. "Authority Taylo has advised caution for a time. The disappearance of so many keepers has caught the consideration of the power politic."

"We have never had their consideration before," Aysa commented.

"As a whole no," Parke said, "but keepers have had the consideration of diverse and scattered persons all the while."

"Like you and authority Taylo?" Masey asked.

"Yes, like us Masey," Parke said as he turned a course toward the lake. "Aysa, I have heard chatter that Gabri has allowed for you to turn your scholarship toward being a medic."

"It would not have the official seal of the Cityscape medic scholarship, sir," Aysa said. "But it would be a help to the keepers in my area."

"And to me as well," Parke said. "It is a befitted course of study, and it will be a long one. For the times you return home I will arrange a clinic for the keepers, and you will be an aid to me."

"That would be most appropriate, sir," Aysa said. "I can see from you the practice of what my scholarship will tell me."

Daine was thinking how befitted it would be to have a keeper trained as a medic. Keepers were given to care for keepers, and none other desired to intervene. Cityscape would not allow a keeper/medic if they were given leave. There would be no end to the trouble, or the chatter, if one were discovered. Daine was given to be in the midst of those who considered ideas not thought of in the whole of history of Perma, and not just considered, but spoken aloud.

Cityscape gave way to landscape, Daine looked

out over an endless sea of short grass which would be tall by summer's end. The towers huddled ever closer behind them as tall trees rose up ahead.

"The lake is ahead," Parke said. "It's not too well filled with people."

Daine had heard of the lake, mostly when someone kept for a family on an outing. It was as round as she'd been told, with hills on the upper side. There was sand on two thirds of the edges, and a straight cliff ahead of them which some said was perfect for diving into the water. Tall trees stood around the lake in vast array, one could not see the sky through them.

"On the trailing edge there is no one emplaced at all," Aysa said. "I know the way from there the best."

"Then that is where we will settle," Parke said. "You two and I will go out and set up a small meal near the water for the sake of form, and watch for our time to see you off."

"You take so much care, sir," Daine said.

"If authority Taylo feels ill at ease," Parke said, "wisdom would have the rest of us knowing true terror."

"On that I would agree sir," Aysa said.

Daine let her head look down for a moment. It was difficult for her to see a keeper talking so openly with a house lord, one who was a medic as well. Much of her life had taught her such conversations were not welcome, and should not be attempted. It was strange and unsettling on the one hand, but on the other it was exciting and full of wonder.

"It is not untoward," Masey said, putting a hand to her shoulder. "You need only know Medic Parke is a friend, and he considers us family. It is what he has learned from the holy writ."

"I would dare not contradict the holy writ," Daine said.

Medic Parke smiled when she said that.

"Daine of the Drydocks," he said. "You are as wise as the chatter suggests."

"Chatter?" Daine asked.

#

"Slowness is not befitted young keeper," Parke said loudly to Aysa as she finally delivered his platter. "If you cannot be quick your recompense will suffer."

Parke had made a show of impatience from the moment they had stepped from the cart, standing by as the girls set out a table with a chair, and then made to deliver his lunch. Aysa, for her part, had to stifle her giggles as he ordered them this way and that.

Daine was not so amused.

"We beg your pardon, sir," she said, taking the platter from Aysa's hands and setting it in front of Parke.

"Daine," Aysa whispered to her. "It is well. Medic Parke is a friend. He reprimands us in jest."

"It is difficult," Daine said. "My eyes are not so new."

"All things change with time," Medic Parke said, looking about to make sure no one was watching or listening. "Know in your heart that I am not upset with Aysa or you, and would not have you anxious for the smallest moment."

"He criticizes us to make us safe," Aysa added.

"No one is about," Parke said. "When I raise my hand sprint back to the cart and retrieve your friends, and then go out the other side to be on your way."

"Much is appreciated," Aysa said.

"And much is given," Parke said as he raised his hand. The two lit out back to the cart. Aery and Masey stood ready, and followed them through the cart's other door and into the depths of forestscape.

"Stay warm and well young ones," he said out loud as they left.

"Medic Parke is truly a befitted man." Masey commented. "Authority Taylo could not do better, if she would only make the choice everyone else knows is the obvious one."

"It is her choice to make," Aysa said. "It is not ours. Allow them time, I believe they both see what we do. Perhaps they feel the recompense of a short delay."

"You believe their delay will be short?" Masey asked. "Neither will yet admit to seeing the shadow of the other."

The keepers proceeded with requisite caution, Aysa leading the way and Daine a few steps behind. They had explanations on the ready, should they be discovered. The worst possible outcome was their return to Medic Parke at the lake, where he would reprimand them yet again, then see them off after a befitted amount of time.

"Wait here," Aysa said, putting her hand to a tree. "I will look ahead."

The rest of the keepers turned aside to allow her to scout. Aysa made a point of having a care in every moment. No one was to know about the old ship, and she was clear that she would not be the one followed to it. Daine could appreciate the cause of quiet.

"There is no one about," Aysa said as she

returned. "Let's follow the trees around this clearing and we will have a clear path through on the other side. I know this place well. We will arrive in good time."

Daine wondered if Aysa knew how much she mirrored a city lord when she took the place of the responsible one. For herself, Daina realized, she was more at ease being alone with only keepers, despite being a fair jaunt from her home in the Drydocks.

"There is no need for haste," Daine said.

"And every need for care," Aysa agreed.

"It has occurred to me," Daine said, after a time. "I have no concept of what the old ship might look like."

"And you had not even put a thought to it until now," Aysa said. "I was the same way the first time I jaunted to the old ship in the company of Angla. I was thinking so much about the ship still being whole that I had not thought for any other detail."

"You accompanied Angla to this ship?" Aery asked. "Is this where she was when she was lost in forestscape?"

"Not at first," Aysa said. "She was found by Sharo, a keeper from Cityscape who was abandoned on the far side of the sandscape, and Ryalt, who is from the Shanties. Angla completed much of her scholarship here at the hand of Gabri."

"There is much I did not know," Aery said.

"Daine," Aysa said. "The ship is like a tower, though more wide than tall, and hidden buried in the ground."

"But it's also not like anything you know," Masey said. "It is a wonder, your eyes will not want to close for the turn of a few days for the cause of so much to see."

"Sometimes we are given to sleep past the dawn of the day," Aysa said. "Once even to the mid of early."

"Such a thing cannot be," Daine said. "You play at me with stories which cannot be true."

"There are more wonders to be found in the old ship," Aysa said. "And there are events even more difficult to believe. I think that is why those of us who have been to the old ship have so much to speak to each other."

#

It was near the late of mid before they arrived at the old ship. They had stopped to rest twice, creched in the underside of handy shrubs and looking for signs of pursuit. They were keepers, wandering about in the forest would not be tolerated when they should be keeping. They struggled under the surrounding undergrowth and approached the door. After awaiting a befitted amount of time the ship recognized them and let them in.

Daine had never seen anything like it. The huge metal door slid to the side as quiet as the night, inside was a hallway stretching into the distance in either direction. The walls were hard and textured, given a light color. From above a double line of light followed the top of the hallway lending every surface a befitted amount of light. Her first thought was to compliment the house lord who had built such a place, but then she remembered this was made before the time of house lords in a place far away.

Aysa took hold of Daine's arm to walk her into the structure. She had been so captivated by the sight her feet had forgotten how to walk.

"It's Aysa of Cathedral district," a young man said as the door slid shut behind them.

Daine looked at the young man who had greeted them, and found him the oddest person she had yet seen. He was young, as they were, but dressed in the most colorful clothes. And his voice was inflected differently than any she had ever heard. He, as she understood, had to be from the other city.

"Jenk of the Shanties," Aysa greeted in return. "You've grown since the last I've seen of you."

"Not overmuch I hope," Jenk said as he overlooked himself, then used his hand to push his tummy inward. "I arrived only yesterday, and now you arrive with your cohorts."

"Were the Shanties as you left it?" Aysa asked.

"A few more new keepers are emplaced," he said. "We work to open a new lane with its houses. We consider it befitted to be allowed to offer them hospitality. Is there news from Cityscape?"

"Authority Taylo still hesitates with the medic," Aysa said. "And if the elders portend clearly, we would have a new regent by the fall of winter."

"Are these the new students I have heard chatter of?" Jenk asked.

"Jenk," Aysa said. "I present Aery and Daine, of the Drydocks. They are the first students from that section of Cityscape to ever step into the old ship."

"You are most welcome Aery and Daine of the Drydocks," Jenk said.

"You are from the other city?" Aery asked.

"The Shanties," Daine amended. "Before today I had never heard anything about another city on Perma, and now I meet one of its citizens."

"In the case of the Shanties," Jenk said. "I would be named an initiate, and I am most pleased to make your acquaintance."

"We will walk you to the upper levels," Aysa said. "It is where the students live and eat. The levels just below those contain rooms set aside for classes. You two will need to converse with Gabri."

"Then lead," Aery said. "And we will follow."

"Adison will not return this term," Masey said as they walked through dark colored hallways. "His mother needs him to keep, to add to their total recompense."

"She asked him to stay?" Jenk asked.

"She never would," Aysa said. "And he would never ask for help even though we would give it freely."

"He will be missed," Jenk said.

"He said he'd already learned a sufficient amount to be a benefit," Aysa said. "How is Kassi?"

"Kassi is well," Jenk said. "She will deliver yet another child by mid-summer."

The sound of a familiar name gave Daine a turn. It took her the turn of a moment to remember whose name it was.

"Kassi?" Daine asked. "The keeper who once lived in Drydocks?"

Daine remembered how Kassi had been keeping the crèche one day, and then gone on the first warm day of summer. No one had spoken of it near the children. It was the way of keepers. To keep too keen an eye to what is past is to allow what is before you to pass by.

"I believe she did," Aysa said. "She had a need to

leave the shadow of Cathedral when it was found she was a sozo, before Sharo returned to take her brother and her out of Cityscape."

"What is a sozo?" Daine asked.

"You would name it as a soul thief," Jenk said. "In your stories you take the gifts designed by the colony scientists and change them into monsters."

"Are you saying Kassi, the one who once kept our crèche, is a stealer of souls?" Aery asked.

"Far from it," Aysa said. "Kassi is a healer. She can heal physical harm and put it to right."

"In the Shanties we do not know these people as monsters," Jenk said. "They are needed for those of us who don't have the technology of Cityscape."

Daine started to speak, but then was reminded of a time when she had hit her elbow on a doorway, and how the bruise faded away under the care of Kassi who kept the crèche that day. At the time she hadn't had a second thought about it, she simply returned to her play.

"What I haven't spoken yet," Jenk continued, "the Shanties are alive with the most amazing of all news."

"What would that be?" Aysa asked.

"We have uncovered a new pino," Jenk said.

"Beg pardon," Daine asked as politely as she could, "What is a pino?"

"A pino pneuma," Jenk said. "A water caller. There hasn't been one of those in generations. The elders are considering instituting some kind of celebration."

"A Thunder Eater," Daine said. Aysa looked at her for a moment, the childhood stories jumping to her mind. Of all the teras the thunder eater held the most terror for Daine. When she was young she would cover her ears when those stories were told, and cry at night when she had dreams of it. She would not want to die at the hands of a thunder eater.

"You will meet him on the morrow," Jenk said.

#

Aery walked through the door and left it to open. He did hold the same look of nervousness on his face that he had when he had entered.

"Gabri will converse with you," he said simply. "You have no cause to worry."

Daine had only just heard of the interface robot which lived on the old ship. She had only just heard of the old ship and the scholarship there. The other students spoke well of Gabri, calling it a her, and chattering about it as if it were a dear friend.

Daine had espied robots at various times, when accompanying her father into a shop. They followed after their house lords and did not notice keepers in the least. They were cumbersome things, more boxlike than curved, with faces sealed in wax which only vaguely appeared like a person.

The room was large with huge clear windows on the obverse side. There were seats and desks, and small lights on a few of them. Those lights would do little for illumination, perhaps they were some sort of decoration.

"Welcome Daine of the Drydocks," a young voice said from aside.

This was the first time Daine had seen Gabri, immediately she knew why the other students called her a she. The robot looked everything like a child. Daine noted her eyes first. They were a solid color with hardly any texture to speak of, but they noted her at once.

As it approached her Daine noted what had the appearance of avia wings linked to her shoulders. They were wispy things, moved by every gust of air. She also wore a ring of faint light above her head. What the significance of those embellishments was, Daine did not know, but they did make the robot distinct.

"You have been highly recommended by your elders," the robot continued. "Would you like to sit?"

Gabri pointed her to a chair in the center of the room, it was elevated and had narrow desks to both sides, and looked as if it would turn to face any part of the room.

"What is that chair, ma'am," Daine asked. No one in all of Cityscape would ask a keeper to sit, it was an honor given only for guests who were house lords.

"It was once the Captain's chair," Gabri said. "Geo often said it was once vital to the ship, but once the ship was put to ground, only made poorly placed furniture."

"What is a Captain, Ma'am?" Daine asked. She yet hesitated to sit. On the one hand Gabri was a robot and not a house lord, on the other, she was the one in charge of the scholarship. In the end she only stood in her place for being unsure of where to proceed.

"It would be the regent of the ship," the robot answered. "Your elders thought it best you direct your scholarship to teaching."

"Yes ma'am," Daine said. It was what she had heard when she had been chosen for scholarship.

"Is teaching what you think your scholarship should attend to?" Gabri asked.

"Beg pardon ma'am?"

"In this scholarship it is given for the student to decide what they are to study," Gabri said. "You may take the advice of others, and I will test you to reveal where your abilities sit, but the final choice is always your own."

"Then I do not know what I would study," Daine admitted. "I have not given it the first thought."

"You should give it a thought then," Gabri said. "Attend to your basic studies and see what captures your attention. I will report to you what I learn of you from your studies, and put the question to you again in a befitted turn of days."

"That would be well, ma'am," Daine said.

"Daine," Gabri continued. "You are not required to name me as ma'am, I am neither house lord nor a person. Now, on the matter of your sleeping. You could sleep in a bed, though I understand some keepers would rather sleep in their cloaks in a befitted room with a view of the sky."

It was another item Daine had not given the first thought to. She knew she was jaunting to a new place, but expected she would be given to her own means for finding a place to rest. Never had she imagined she would be allowed a choice.

"If I could, ma'am… I mean Gabri," Daine said. "I have always wanted to sleep on a house lord bed."

"Then you will have that opportunity," Gabri said. "You can tell me whether it is as befitted as you had hoped."

"Much is given," Daine said. "Much is appreciated."

10

"Miko," A voice said. "Arise sleepy one."

The voice that woke him was not befitted at all. It did not sound the first part like his mother. Miko went to turn to the wall, to face it as he added a handful more of sleep, but found it missing. His hand found only air and he was not asleep in a sling.

Miko opened one of his eyes to strange white walls and one of his past cohorts in the Shanties standing over him

"Jenk," Miko said. In the moment he remembered his traverse to the old ship for his new scholarship. He was no longer to be found in the Shanties. Through no fault of his own, Miko was the world traversed away in the old colony ship, a ship owned by a robot.

Being awake was not befitted at all. Only in his dreams had he forgotten the bitterness of his waking life.

"First a meal," Jenk said. "And then class. You no longer have cause to rest."

"I rest for the cause of my weariness," Miko said. "I have traversed too well and too much lately."

Miko thought to get perhaps the turn of a moment's more of sleep, but Jenk pulled the blanket from his bed.

"Now arise for the cause of your comfort," Jenk said. "And join your friend in a meal. There are those who would like to meet you."

"Me?" Miko asked. "Why..?"

Then he knew. The chatter of him, and specifically what he was, had preceded him to the old ship. Then for the overnight after his arrival the whispered had turned to talk. He was given one of the gifts and was to be on display for all to see. There would be questions yet again, and some would want to see him act out his gift. It was a most wearying consequence.

"Can I traverse back to the Shanties now?" Miko asked as he put his feet to the floor. Jenk chose not to hear, he had moved back to his own area and was putting the finishing touches on his clothes and attempting to arrange his hair.

Dressed and somewhat arranged, Miko followed Jenk to a place he called the lounge, two sets of steps above their room. The room was filled with young people and the far wall was clear sun screens showing the tops of the trees around them.

"This is my friend Miko," Jenk said as they approached the long table where two convenient places to sit waited. The table was overfilled with keepers.

"You are from the Shanties?" a young keeper asked. She was perhaps his age or a little younger and dressed in the drab clothing of keepers.

He had known how word of the Shanties had touched the keepers, but had not considered it traversed much beyond those few who had relocated to the ruinscape. Miko cringed at the thought of it. It was not for anyone who actually stayed in Cityscape to know about the Shanties, any mouth with knowledge could be found open at the wrong moment. Perhaps it was time for the Shanties to vacate ruinscape in favor of a location more secure.

"Yes," he managed. There was not a call for unbefitted manners. She was only a girl, and a keeper from Cityscape.

Miko would have much to say in the Commons when he returned. The danger was never more clear than from hearing the words flow freely from the mouth of a young keeper from Cityscape. Armed with this information the elders would have no cause but to listen to his complaints, and to make changes accordingly, even those keepers who played at being elders.

"I am Aysa," she said, motioning for him to settle down beside her. "From Cathedral district. Rayma has told me much of the comings and goings of the Shanties. I love your clothes, you wear such color."

It seemed even Rayma, the quiet one, was treasonous to the Shanties. Miko could only begin to see how relenting to the needs of proper harborage would bring about the end of the Shanties. One untoward word and the whole of Cityscape would know there had been survivors of the last God war. If history had its say, survivors would not be tolerated.

The Shanties would have been better had the keepers never been found.

As Miko sat down and picked at a dish of food, they stared at each other. He knew they wanted to talk at length, but he was not as sure it was conversation he wanted.

"What has become of my manners?" Jenk asked himself.

"I've often wondered," Miko answered, which Jenk again ignored.

"Everyone is here," Jenk said. "At the far end of

the table there is Dathe and Yendi, who you know from the Shanties. They stayed at the ship for extra scholarship over the break. Aside from Kimi and Rayma, who you also know, are Masey and Emne from Cathedral district in Cityscape."

Miko nodded to them, ignoring their curious stares as Jenk continued. As annoying as their words were, their silences were worse. He could only imagine what traversed through their minds as they turned their gazes upon him.

"Here we have Aysa and Jerin, from Cathedral district and our new students, Daine and Aery from the Drydocks. Miko is quite pleased to meet all of you."

"Thanks," Miko said, and put his head down, pretending he had any appetite remaining. His plan to stay silent and persevere through his time of scholarship was not working as he had hoped. He had not considered how much he had become a point of interest.

"Miko," Aysa said, breaking the silence. "There is chatter you are a Thunder Eater."

"I am a pino pneuma," he said, "in the old language. I do not know what a thunder eater would be."

"What is it like?" the one called Daine asked. "What do you accomplish?"

"I am able to see water without putting my eyes to it, and I am able to draw water out from the air and collect it when I need to."

"It's like our stories," Jerin said from across the table.

"He's from the Shanties," Aysa said. "They don't tell the stories of the Teras. He wouldn't know what is like or unlike and we have no cause to speak around his ears."

"I understand you turn our gifts into monsters with your childminder's stories," Miko said. "I am no monster."

"Of course not," Aysa said. "They tell us those stories to make us afraid of people like you. Do you want to hear it?"

"Don't tell him," Jerin said. "He'll hit you."

"He wouldn't do that," Aysa said, then stood up and bent slightly forward to tell the tale in all of its suspense. "The Thunder Eater is the most mysterious of all creatures. Thunder heralds its arrival, and its feeding, for it pulls the water direct with the soul."

"The soul does not contain water," Miko said putting his eyes up into his head. "Only the body."

"He's always wet, the Thunder Eater," She continued, becoming more dramatic as she continued. "He stays to the shadows near the pools and rivers and waits for his victim to swim alone, then in an instant, swish, the body is left as a dry husk and is dissolved into the water, but the soul of the poor swimmer is caught up in the Thunder Eater, screaming in pain and fear through every pore of the Tera…"

"Wouldn't that be annoying?" Miko said. "I could not draw the water from a living person."

"You don't know what you could do," Jenk said. "There hasn't been a pino in the Shanties for the turn of twenty generations, since the time of pino Heniry."

"That's what they said then they made me come here," Miko said.

"They made you come?" Aysa asked. "For your

sake Trina remained at the Shanties. You would forsake her gift so easily?"

Her eyes widened with the thought. Miko knew the value the other students placed on attending scholarship in the old ship. More than once during the journey they had spoken of the many who wanted to attend but were prevented.

"Gabri holds knowledge of my gift," Miko said. "More than anyone else on Perma. The elders thought it best…"

Miko let his words trail off when he saw the looks of the other students. They had stopped with the admission that he did not want to attend, and would not move any further. He would now be known as the student who was made to traverse to the old ship, the one who had taken the place of one more befitted.

Miko had been correct, their silence was worse than their words.

#

"Will you be in attendance?" Jenk asked as he walked into the room aclutter with books and pages which he put down, unarranged, on the desk to the side of his bed. It was a wonder Jenk ever learned anything, and when he did, it was a wonder he could figure out where he had learnt it.

The first few days of scholarship had been hectic in attendance, organizing and taking part it what work had need to be done. Miko had requested a chore from some of the harder tasks, ones which would allow him leave to be alone while he worked, but found each and every one reserved by the keepers. He could impune their intelligence or their social skills, but he could not say the first word against their will to work.

"Must I?" Miko asked, knowing what the answer would be. He had already asked once and Gabri would not hear the first word about how he had heard all about the comet from his sister Trina.

"Of course you must," Jenk said. "We are given to scholarship, and this is a chance to do so."

"A moment then," Miko said.

"Moments are many," Jenk said, taking his arm. "And you use too many of them for nothing. You are the object at rest, and you will stay at rest until changed by contact with another object."

"Are you that object?" Miko said, reluctantly walking out into the hallway with his once friend.

"For today I am," Jenk said. "Am I not a gift?"

Miko left the question unanswered, knowing Jenk would not have an ear to hear him anyway.

They walked up the steps into the lounge where most of the students were already gathered and the lighting put to dim. Jenk disappeared once they were in the room, and Miko found an open place to sit on the floor as they had been instructed.

In the course of time Gabri entered the door, looked about, then put the door to closed. She walked quietly to the center of the group before she spoke.

"Stay closed your eyes," Gabri instructed. "I will count to the full circle of time for your eyes to adjust to the dark."

If there was any benefit to the activity, it was the the first activity beyond the morningtime classes which had nothing to do with him.

"Miko?" a voice in the dark asked. "Is that you?"

"Who else would I be?" Miko answered. It was the keeper Daine, she had no scholarship to leaving him be, no matter how well he had offended the rest.

"It is well then," Daine said, settling down. "I will observe from beside you."

"Eyes closed," Gabri reminded.

"Our eyes are closed," one of the students repeated.

"Then you are not the one to whom I speak," Gabri said.

The room fell to silence for the turn of a moment. Miko could almost see the other students, using the eyes of his gift. The outlines of the water contained in them made an impression in his mind, down to the mists of every breath they took. He had asked, more than once, if such sight was a quality of the gift he had, or if he could see more than most. Gabri was irritatingly non-definitive in her answers.

At the full of the moment, Gabri spoke again, "Open your eyes and observe."

From their vantage on the floor the students saw the night sky filled with stars and the edges of wispy rings which surrounded Hera. They had been born among those stars and under the blue planet. They had seen those moons for the whole of their lives. And yet the moons were spectacular.

The students made note of one thing more. It was a small thing, like a moon or a distant star, but fuzzy at the edges. It appeared to be traversing on a ghost of a trail.

"What is that?" A student asked.

"It is named a comet," Miko said. He had

suffered much under the scholarship of his sister, but knowing about this particular thing was well befitted at this moment. It lent him the appearance of being well taught.

"Correct Miko," Gabri said. "From the outer edges of the star system it has turned to dive in toward the distant sun. It is a ball of ice and rock, as big as the distance between Cityscape and the Shanties. As it travels some of the ice is melted by the face of the sun. It will turn very near our world before winterset next, after which it will curve around the distant sun and return by a path distant from Perma."

"Isn't it beautiful?" Daine asked.

"I am not programmed for aesthetics," Gabri said.

"Beg pardon?" Daine asked.

"I am a robot interface," Gabri explained. "I make no assessment of beauty. I am not able. However, I fathom this is something you might find pleasing to look upon."

"How can you know then what I might find pleasing?" Aysa asked.

"I have observed people for the turn of many years," Gabri said. "Even I can learn."

"But you never see beauty?" Daine asked again. She was usually one of the smarter students, but on this point she seemed unusually dense. Gabri had explained this once already.

"A robot does not have the ability," Gabri said.

Daine stood in her place for a moment, thinking.

"I'm sorry," she said softly.

"Does clay say to a ceramicist, 'what are you doing?'," Gabri asked. "Aesthetics is not my function. It is no bitter circumstance

"Students, who can tell me when a comet was last seen by the inhabitants of Perma?"

11

"Chanta?" Angla said one early as she sat to eat her first meal of the day.

"Child?" Chanta answered in kind.

Angla often thought of things in the night as she slept, thoughts which could not intrude on her mind in the busyness of the day. Sometimes her thoughts were fanciful, sometimes serious and clever. Chanta had grown comfortable with her mid-early questions, no matter what they were. It made the first of the day more interesting.

"Is it insult that I give you recompense?" the girl asked.

It was time for Chanta to think. Never had she considered recompense to be insult. Though she would readily admit that in this case she would do the same work for no recompense at all. Angla was dear to her.

"I am not insulted," Chanta said.

"You are the closest I have to family," Angla said. "You and authority Taylo, and I would never think to offer recompense to Taylo."

"You do recompense Taylo," Chanta said. "But not with coinage. You join in her work and her life... Do you no longer wish to pay me?"

"No, never Chanta," Angla said. "You are worth more to me than any coinage could be. I should not give to you, you should have a share and a voice as any family member should."

Chanta felt her heart warm, knowing Angla

thought of her as family was a gift without measure. However, it was not something accepted in all of Cityscape. Keepers were to be keepers and house lords were to be house lords, and the two would never be more than worker and supervisor.

"It is not the way of things," Chanta said.

"We both know the way of things is not always the right way," Angla said.

"I would not have you reviled for the cause of me," Chanta said.

"Nor I for you," Angla said, then fell to silent eating.

After a few bites had gone their way, Angla looked up.

"If we could change anything about what is," she said. "What would be changed first?"

There was a knock at the door. Chanta stood and walked to the viewer. It appeared to be a messenger and he was holding something small and light colored.

"Chanta," Angla said from behind her. "Would it be a bitter task for you to retrieve whatever package the messenger has brought?"

"Absolutely not ma'am," Chanta said.

The messenger handed her an old style note, printed upon gilded paper and folded into a packet. Chanta had never seen something so fancy in all of her days.

"What shall I do?" Angla said as Chanta gave her the note.

"Open it child," Chanta said. "It holds a message meant for you."

Angla unfolded the letter and held it flat in front

of her.

"You are invited," Angla read, then fell silent. Her eyes widened and her breaths became more swift. Chanta wondered if the girl would fail in the use of her legs and be forced to sit.

"To what?" Chanta asked.

"It's a state event," she finally said, "a dinner. Councilman Iance has invited me."

"That is wonderful," Chanta said. She stood up, thinking through what Angla would require for such an event.

Angla had stood, she was transfixed on the letter.

"This is terrible," she whispered.

"This is a befitted event for a young lady of Cityscape," Chanta said. "Be calm."

"Taylo warned me," Angla said, putting the letter down on a flat table. "Leave me alone Chanta."

Chanta knew her charge, Angla, was not in good spirits.

If Chanta could do as she willed, she would pull Angla into her arms and hold her until the problem was diminished.

Chanta could read the alarm in her eyes. There was little she could do, she did not fathom the problem in the situation. Not too many days before Angla had happily talked about the ways councilman Iance might be walked to a place where he could know the truth. Now, when invited to spend an evening with him, Angla's first thought was to panic. Chanta did not know the first thing to do.

However, she did know someone who might.

In most of Cityscape keepers were not given leave

to call and converse with someone on their voice box, but again, this was Chanta and she was talking to Taylo. For a moment Chanta wondered what life would become if she were no longer needed in her present situation, and she was put back to the street as a normal keeper.

She shuddered, such a thing would be too terrible for words, not that Chanta in any way feared keeping. The thought of never seeing Angla was a terrible one. Chanta put those thoughts aside, there was no good to be found in fearing the worst.

"Chanta," Taylo's voice answered in the box at her hand. "What has occurred?"

#

"It is simply an invitation," Angla told herself once again.

She looked at the folded page, set on the flat table against the entry wall, as if it would make some move against her in some untoward moment. She could remind herself there was no cause to be alarmed, but the fact did not change. It was simply an invitation, and Angla was quite alarmed.

Chanta had read the page, had cooed and told her it was wonderful. She was a keeper, she did not know the labyrinth it represented. Angla could hardly explain. Finally Chanta began to realize the alarm Angla felt was real, and knew just as quickly it was something she could not begin to touch.

Not too long after there was a commotion at the door.

"Angla," Taylo said as she entered. She had been called from her station, and set to find the cause of her distress. For a moment Angla felt relief, but just for a moment. Not even authority Taylo could lend her help.

"What has occurred?"

In wordless answer Angla handed Taylo the offending document. Taylo read it, looked up at Angla, and read it again.

She set it down as she looked up at Angla, and laughed.

"It's not humorous Taylo," Angla said.

"It is somewhat," Taylo said. "You keep telling me to allow councilman Iance to grow, to learn and see, and perhaps God will take him by hand. Then when you have a chance to participate…"

"This is not participation in anything for the cause of God," Angla said. "This is an invitation to a state event, one I dare not refuse. If there was ever a den of vipers, that is where it would be. I am being compelled to step into the midst of it."

Angla could see it in Taylo's eyes when she began to fathom. But Taylo was not one given to fear, and quickly the fathoming turned to something more of sly wit.

"Perhaps you were given for a time such as this," Taylo said. "You were given to lend a hand to save your people."

"Perhaps I could be found out as the cause of their problems," Angla said. "And set in holding, or sent to lost."

"Angla, the true God has prepared a table for you," Taylo said. "You are alive now when you should have been lost as a child. Is this any more dire a circumstance than being in a downed cart, lost in Treescape in the full of winter?"

Angla had been neglecting that memory of late. It seemed so long ago when she had lived with a family and had held herself in highest esteem and all others as nothing if they were not useful to her. She had been well on her way to being someone who would crave such invitations.

That had all been turned, for the better she thought.

"When you turn my words back on me," Angla said. "You make arguing difficult. I have received this invitation, I know it could all work to good. Yet I am still alarmed."

"Being lost and cold does not hold the terror for us it once did," Taylo said. "This is not so dire as seeing the face of your own end. And in any circumstance, you know you will never be alone."

"You could be my guard," Angla said. "For my many years in confinement."

"If need be," Taylo said. "I doubt my involvement along with you would be neglected. Perhaps we could have adjoining accommodation in the Holding."

"The event is in the circle of two days," Angla said. "What must I do?"

"Reply as civilization requires," Taylo said. "As I have heard from chatter, these events turn to a certain amount of fussing over your appearance and wardrobe."

Angla gazed on her shoes for the moment. The fearlessness of Taylo was beginning to touch her, to give her the hope that all could maybe turn to the best. She had read as much in the holy writ, but translation from reading to living was not always an easy one.

"Chanta will be a help to me in that," Angla said. "Would you attend with me?"

"I have received no invitation," Taylo said. "But I will gladly convey you to, and from… unless you have fallen into the arms of a bright young city lord who will convey you on his own."

"You are not humorous," Angla said. "Not in the least."

"You will need something befitted to wear," Taylo added. "Something new is required I believe."

"I find myself happy that this is not my normal manner of operating," Angla said. "Chambers filled with clothes and pockets filled with invitations-- the thought makes me weary."

"It easily could have been who you became," Taylo reminded her. "And for this occasion it is who you should appear to be. Councilman Iance does little without good reason. At this point I do not know that reason."

"Then I should keep my eyes open," Angla said. "For I doubt there is much protection for me in a fluffy dress."

#

"Dare I ask what you wear?" Sharo said. It was the last of late and the Commons were all but empty, all empty but for Sharo and Jenne.

Sharo had been walking the four corners of the room, assuring herself it had been vacated for the day, and seeing all was in order. When she returned to the place which suited her best for sleeping, Jenne was awaiting her, wearing a cloak which was bedecked with bright colors.

"Some of the young students thought to go camping after last winter," Jenne said. "They constructed cloaks like we have in Cityscape thinking they would outdistance the tents they have used before."

"They constructed to ill," Sharo said. "There is nothing of such color to be found in all of Cityscape."

"Yes," Jenne said. "Their cloaks with keeper form and Shanty color. I could not help but obtain one for my own use. This one is as good as the best cloak I ever owned when I jaunted about in the shadow of the Towers, and the addition of colors makes me happy."

"You intend to sleep in the Commons?" Sharo asked. The answer was obvious, but it had need to be spoken.

"As much as you" Jenne said. She settled down in place next to Sharo. "No keeper should stand alone in the night, or sleep without company nearby. You know this as well as I."

"There is little need," Sharo said, but knew her word would not be heeded. Jenne had arrived with her plan in hand, there would be discussion but no variation. Sharo knew not to argue too much, there was no point. As soft and quiet as Jenne appeared, when pushed on some matter she had already chosen she was formed of metal inside.

The Commons were quiet at the end of the day. The last of the initiates left for their homes as the distant sun slid below the horizon.

"Due to your befitted wisdom Joska can fathom every reaction to the loss of his eye," Jenne said. "Excluding only yours."

"I might join him in that," Sharo said. "I know he

is still the Joska I know, nothing of the most value in him has changed, but to turn away from his pain…"

"Joska has no pain," Jenne said turning to her friend. "Kassi has done her work well, and he is already learning how to see without the benefit of his other eye. He is well and happy. He does not have the first bitter tear to swallow."

The silence settled between them grew for the turn of a few moments as Jenne settled herself into her befitted place. It was directly next to the place where Sharo had settled.

"Do you ever wonder what occurs in Cityscape?" Sharo asked as each leaned against the other. "Or where we would have been had none of these events ever happened?"

"I do consider sometimes," Jenne said. "Long enough to know I have little clue to what I would be doing by now. But I also know this is where we should be."

"How do you know?" Sharo asked.

"Because this is where we are," Jenne said. "As much as you might miss what life we had before, and as much as the Shanties can still hold more than a share of confusion to us, dear sister and friend, trust me when I say running from a problem does little to solve it."

Sharo could not help but smile at that last bit. When they had first met Jenne had been the first to run when there was a problem, an act she duplicated once she was in the Shanties when she had been lost to those who had shown her hospitality in the full of winter. It had been before Jenne was given to understand the Shanties.

"That is a wisdom you would know," Sharo said.
"All too well," Jenne said.

12

Miko awoke as the brightness of the morning warmed the small clearframe in the room. This time he knew where he was immediately. As much as he would rather be in his bunk at home, he was at the old ship where all was spent for the cause of scholarship. He was given to spend too much time spent with young keepers who knew too much. As he opened his eyes and began to sit up he realized he was alone, none other occupied the room. Every bed was empty.

"I have been left behind," Miko observed as he put his clothes on. There had to be some purpose to why the room was empty. Such things as the other students gone to nothing was not in the habit of being. He thought to revel in his new found freedom, but without knowing what had happened he thought better of it. The moment he did anything untoward they would all return and question his every movement. It was the way the world was.

No one was in the lounge. A befitted amount of food remained. Miko filled his plate and contemplated as he ate. The view through the window was singular. The trees still held a fascination for him, he watched as moisture in the leaves obverse from the window jumped out as mist in the air.

He would even see the edge of the lake. It was warmed from below, and the warmer water was more likely to flow up into the air. It was likely the cause of the water throughout the forest, and the reason the trees were able to grow so tall.

Miko had learned how the world of Perma was deficient of water. The first colonists lamented the fact in more than one report found in the pages Gabri gave to him. Yet there was water to be found, if one looked. Much of it had been under the ground and brought to the surface, but it was not a sufficient amount, and much had to remain where it was.

It made him wonder what a world would look like with sufficient water. It stretched his imagination to think of such a place.

"And I am yet alone," Miko said aloud as he completed his meal. Usually someone had come into the lounge by this time to remind him of early scholarship, or of some special event Gabri had planned.

Whatever had occurred to the other students had not happened to him.

None of the rooms were occupied. Miko put his shadow to the doorway of each one and no one was in any of them. At every step he expected someone to challenge his presence, or tell him of some work he had neglected. He wondered even more what had become of the other students.

Miko walked down another set of steps to the classrooms. The rooms were put to dark and there was no one within. His sight, by which he could see people around him, was blocked by the walls and the metal of the ship, but with the doors open he would see someone, even in the darkness.

He was beginning to be alarmed. There was no one to be found anywhere he put his eyes to see.

Yet, the ship was large, perhaps Gabri found

something of interest in a lower level, the ones which were never used.

...something of interest to everyone save him.

The control room, where Gabri conducted her business, was empty as well. Miko had need only to open the door. No one living was within, and Gabri would never let a student open her door unquestioned. Neither student nor robot occupied that room.

Miko put his back to the wall and stopped to think. The ship was vast. He had taken an afternoon to explore it once and barely made it back in time to put his head down and sleep. There were many rooms, most of them put to empty or filled with unused machinery.

He had decided the safest course would be to withdraw back to his room and wait until someone returned, when in the distance he heard sounds.

They were faint sounds, like voices from far away, but having no better course to pursue, he tried to follow their direction.

Miko had to retrace his steps twice before he began to move closer. He began to draw near enough to hear more clearly when he recognized what he was hearing.

They were singing.

Finally, Miko decided he had set his course and he would see it through. The corridor he followed enlarged as others joined it to a large meeting room without proper doors to block it in. The students were all there, as was Gabri. They were sitting in seats arranged into a half circle facing a center where there was a slightly raised circle.

"Join us friend Miko," Aysa said. She had noted

his approach and walked back to meet him. He had arrived and observed long enough to know what they were doing.

"This is your one day in seven?" Miko asked. He had already decided it was, but could not think of any other question.

"It is," Aysa said. "We are only the first part through. There is much left to be said. You can sit to the side of me if you choose."

Aysa did not understand any more than his cohorts at the Shanties. It was well enough for them to follow this god created by a robot, but it was not something Miko wanted to touch, even in a superficial way. They would never understand.

"Enjoy your day," Miko said, then turned and traversed away.

#

Jenk joined the tableful with his dinner. He was in a mood to converse, but as any of the students would say, he was always in a mood to converse.

No one had mentioned the first word to Miko about his walking from their one day in seven, for which Miko was appreciative. As much as he disagreed, perhaps it was best to allow them their wrong thoughts. Yet, he was allowed to sit at the edge of the table, and few worked for the cause of talking with him.

"I begin to understand the ways of the world," Jenk said before he had even taken his first bite. "From my course of study on the science of politics."

"What is politics?" Aysa asked. Eating at leisure was a new idea to her. Though she made the attempt, once she put her actions to consume her food she was compelled to bring that action to its prompt conclusion. She had put herself to sit at the table a few moments ago, and already her meal was mostly consumed.

Jenk continually conversed on whatever subject he had studied last. Miko had concluded it was part of the way he put it to scholarship. If he was prohibited from speaking he might not learn at all.

"It is the way groups of people direct themselves," Jenk said. "I think the advantage of the Shanties is that we work together. But our disadvantage is that it takes us overlong to decide, for we must all speak our view."

"That may be true in part," Kimi said. "But have you considered the other advantages we have?"

Jenk only smiled and waited as Kimi realized how she had just given proof to his point. It was a given on any point that the students from the Shanties would want to converse on any counterpoint which might exist.

"The advantage of keepers is also that we work together," Aysa said.

"Not so much in my estimation," Jenk said. "Keepers work from the beginning of the day to the end, and that is your advantage. But your disadvantage is you think of others overmuch, and yourself not at all."

"I can see that is true," Kimi said. "You often fail to see how much of a gift you are. If the Cityscape was deprived of keepers it would quickly fall."

"No," Aysa said. "They would simply find other keepers to accomplish what has need to be done."

"And Citylords," Jenk continued before the rest fell into discussion over what he had said so far. "The Citylords have the advantage of technology. Their disadvantage is they believe they deserve to have hold of everything they see."

"Not all Citylords are given complete to the cause of themselves," Aysa said.

"Of course," Jenk said, taking a sideways glance at Miko, which he quickly tried to hide. "I speak of the group complete, there are differences when you look at single people."

Jenk had taken a sideways glance at Miko, and Miko had seen it. In his eyes he was the one who was different. They were wrong, of course. He only wanted the Shanties to be what it was, and for it to be left alone.

#

"Now Miko," Gabri said patiently. She was ever patient. For some reason her patience was turning to a source of irritation to him. His daily lessons were all too recurrent. "See if you can move the water from the bowl and back into the air."

"I don't see the need…," Miko said as he turned his attention to the bowl. He had been picturing keepers under the water, being lost and gone and therefore unable to speak of the Shanties ever again. It was an unworthy thought, he knew, but none would know of it beyond his own head.

"The purpose need not be obvious," Gabri said. "Water is not lost and gone when it is in the air, it only changes in its form."

For the latter part of the days Miko was given to the individual attention of Gabri. Other students stood by, out of the way, observing. Some stayed and some left, but Miko was not given the choice but to remain.

"Stay to the task, Miko," Gabri said. It seemed

her most favored phrase.

"In vapor form it would take less effort to carry," Miko heard Emne's voice as she spoke. She had a befitted understanding of those things Gabri named science, and had given help to him as he tried to understand his lessons.

"Only if the wind never took to blowing," someone else mentioned. It was what Miko had been thinking, but then he considered a flooded sub-floor or a puddle blocking a path. Then he went further in his imagining to bricks in need to be dried—he thought he could accomplish that in the turn of a day instead of the usual handful.

"It is a benefit for Miko to know what he can do," Gabri said. "And what he cannot. Sometimes God uses the most useless thing for tasks with the most import."

There was murmured agreement. Miko was weary from studying, he was weary from leaving unspoken what worried him most, and he was weary from hearing about this God over and over again with belief presupposed.

"If there was a God," Miko commented.

There was a rustle and commotion from those who observed. It was almost as if he had said something most unexpected. Gabri, however seemed untouched.

"If you do not think God is," Gabri continued, as if she had this discussion on every day. "Keep a thought that you are among those who do, and practice a befitted regard. There may come a time when you are convinced, and it would limit the amount of pardon you may need beg."

Gabri had once told him she had no feelings to

offend, it seemed she was truthful in saying so. It was difficult not to see human feelings in her because she had the appearance of a human.

"I do not expect to be convinced," Miko said. "Would you seek to show me that God truly is?"

"I would fail," Gabri said. "And it is not my concern. If you would choose to know whether God truly is, it is to him you must put the question."

"Ask?" he stood up straighter than he had been. The conversation had taken an untoward turn, one he had not anticipated. "But what if God is not?"

"There will be no answer," Gabri said without the hint of hesitation.

That should have been the end of the matter. It had already gone beyond his well practiced arguments. But Miko had seen something in the interface robot, something he had to pursue.

"You think there will be," he said. "You have the belief just like my family."

There was a moment of quick chatter among the students in the room. It was quickly cut short for the cause of whatever the robot might say next.

"I do not believe," Gabri said. "I do not suppose, or think, or cause myself to have faith. I am a robot interface, not a living person. I am constructed and programmed. For any matter of fact I either know or I don't know. In this case I know."

"How can you know?" Miko asked. It stretched all credibility that a robot would be conversing about knowing there was a God.

"God does impossible things. He accomplishes them in ways they could not have been done," Gabri said. "Not the least of which is we are conversing when we should never have met at all."

"Mere happenstance," Miko said.

"From your point of view that would be one possibility, Miko," Gabri said. "Now if you would stay to the task, and finish putting the bowl to empty..."

13

The event was to be held at a posh and shiny building near the center of Cityscape, in a tower given the diminutive name 'Fief'. Angla knew the building, as she knew many of the towers from the investigations of her youth. Once they had been a fascination to her. They were the currency of power in Cityscape and she once wished to have supremacy over them all.

Taylo would be the one to deliver Angla to the event. At least for a time she could feel safe, as safe as anyone could feel. She could not walk away from the anxiety which walked with her every step. It was not to be ignored.

Chanta escorted Angla to the top entry of her tower, cooing the whole way over how she looked in her new dress and holding her hand. Angla appreciated the company, for even though Chanta did not understand the situation, she was aware Angla worried, and that was enough. After Chanta put shut the door behind them Angla turned and held her close for a long moment. The events of the night would turn out as they chose, and would not be turned aside for the cause of one young woman.

"Chanta did well," Taylo said.

Taylo stood ready to the side of her cart with the door open. Angla feared for a moment Taylo would make some unkind remark, but she only nodded and allowed Angla to sit before returning to the controls.

The jaunt to the other tower was shorter than

Angla would have wanted it to be.

The entry was a wide row of steps so far above the road below that those who walked there could hardly be seen. Taylo had expertly hovered her cart over the second step, allowing Angla to navigate her dress around to let her put her foot down on a step without fear of tripping to a fall out of the cart. They had spoken little as they traversed past the towers and into the district politic, never out of sight of the Holding. Crowds of people gathered about the steps, looking to see what was produced from the latest cart. Not a few chattered about her. Though Angla did not fathom it, many still recalled her early story.

"My heart walks with you," Taylo said as Angla let the door close behind her. The other carts whispering fancily dressed house lords and ladies were all much fancier than the one Taylo drove, but hers was the only one with the seal of the authority. That in itself distinguished it.

With the whisper of the cart engine, Angla was alone.

She looked about at the crowd she had joined. Some of the faces seemed distantly familiar, like those she had meet once in passing. As much as this had once been her destined world, it was no longer. The course of her life had been stopped, and then changed to the better. She could not fathom why she had been called back to this world, but after many conversations with Chanta and Taylo, she had promised to be the best of her new self in an old situation.

"Welcome Lady Angla," Iance said, approaching her from the top of the steps. She recognized him at once, as would most of Cityscape. There had been much chatter lately as to the condition of the regent, and the possibility of a new one. His name came up often in those conversations. "I have anticipated making your acquaintance."

"Mine?" Angla answered. She had been practicing coyness in her effort to assimilate into the crowd she once knew, one of the many things she had neglected in her latter upbringing. She had hoped it had been a lost art to her.

"You are one of the most famous women in all of Cityscape," Iance said as he ushered her into the entry lobby. The walls and windows were high and bright, the floors polished to a shine. Their words added to the faint echo of so many people, not a few of whom turned to see the councilman and the young woman was on his arm.

"Angla," a young woman greeted as they passed. It took Angla a moment to remember her in her place, they had attended scholarship together. Now her classmate was dressed in fine silvery cloth and on the arm of a man who had traversed many more winters.

"Lizbet," Angla greeted in turn. Then her classmate was gone, turned back into the churning crowd. Angla wondered wether she had just seen an echo of who she could have been. The thought filled her heart with a heaviness for the cause of a life lived for the cause of unreachable ambitions.

"The complete number of these people will be attending the dinner?" Angla asked, wondering at what manner of table would seat so many.

"No," Iance said as he finished exchanging a greeting with a set of befitted young men. "The meal is only for a few. These are the ones who desire to be seen, with hopes to be integrated with others in the memories of those here."

Despite what Iance had told her, the table in the main hall was huge. Angla estimated seating for a hundred or more. The table was clothed in bright blue, set out with dainty china and slivery utensils. More food was emplaced on the table than Angla had seen in all of her years.

As she was seated she was surprised to observe several familiar faces in such an unfamiliar setting. They were among the keepers who were arranging the tables and serving the meal. She captured the eye of one nearby and gave a covert nod. She did not know if conversing with them would cause undue trouble, and decided to await their actions before deciding on her own.

The covert nod was returned, then she noted as one keeper talked into the ear of another. She would ask Chanta when she returned home, to see what the proper response should have been. She had walked the ways of keepers, but hardly ever in the sight of house lords, and did not have the experience to know what she should have done.

It was more comfort than anything in this lavish, overdressed event, for Angla to know keepers were nearby.

"You are near the end of your scholarship," Iance asked as he barely touched the ample food set before him. "Are you not?"

"It will end before winter next," Angla said. Her plate, by comparison, held only what she thought she could actually consume, and even that was an excess. "Though it is my consideration that the scholarship of life should never end."

"Well said,"Iance said.

The meal was serviced in the most befitted of ways. A crowd of keepers moved as one to deliver filled plates to all who sat in the hall.

"Thank you," Angla said as a keeper put a plate before her.

"It is well, ma'am," the keeper said and immediately retreated. Only then did Angla look up to see a number of the house lords considering her curiously.

"Your association with Authority Taylo gives advantages," Iance said to her. "I dare say the keepers in this room would jump to any request you have."

"As they would for any of us," Angla said, wondering why she would be made to feel so awkward for an action so ingrained in her. To fail to be grateful is insult to those who fill a need.

"I would not be surprised to find that any of them would die for you," Iance said.

"It is rare to find one who would die for someone," Angla said, "even for someone who is good."

Angla realized she had just given an answer from the holy writ, and wondered how many question she could answer so. It could make befitted conversation, and allow her to imagine she was working for good, even in this overornamented setting.

Angla had a number of conversations, her name and face were known in these halls, mostly from the time she was lost in forestscape. Eventually the meal came to an end, and Angla wandered out into the entry hall, where a number of people still mulled about. She may have been one of the few who made note of the keepers within, waiting with patience to do their part in clearing up after the meal.

Keepers were present throughout the whole of Cityscape, though not everyone considered them.

Angla was prepared to call for Taylo, to take her away from this gilded hall, but she held back her hand as she noticed Iance approaching her.

"Angla," Iance said from her side. "Step into this room. I have something to show you."

The room was befitted more for business, with a large square table and chairs along the perimeter. A woman sat in one of those chairs.

"This is Raisia," Iance said. "My associate."

"It is well then," Angla said in greeting. The woman stood, a striking figure. Angla would have considered her further if she was not distracted by the map on the table.

It was an impression of Purgatory Lake and the treescape around it, the demarcation to grass-scape was along the edges. She knew that area well, better than anyone in Cityscape would guess.

"I have a question," Iance said without need for preamble. He pointed at a spot on the map. "Your cart went down here."

"What a calm set of words for a truly traumatic event," Angla said. "I was in the safe chair, therefore I survived. My parents did not. It appears to be near the right location."

"Yes. Quite," Iance said, then pointed at a place

obverse of the lake, to the inlet side. "You were found in a cave, according to the report of authority Taylo, here."

"I believe here," Angla said, amending his indication by a fingernail's width. It was a cave she had played in before, it was why she had suggested it to Taylo. "It was twenty winters ago. The remembrance is not new."

"Am I meant to believe a young girl walked for two days and two nights in the winded days of winter before she found shelter?" Iance asked.

"It was not the winded days of winter until I was emplaced in the cave," Angla said. "I would have gone forward from there but there was a blizzard. Authority Taylo found me as the distant sun emerged and the winds died away. As for the rest, believe what you want."

"I do not want a belief," Iance said. His voice rife with suspicion, as if her being alive was the result of some sort of wrongness. "I want truth. Why do you lie?"

"I did not cry until I was emplaced in the cave," Angla said. "I've not mentioned that to anyone, though not saying is not the same as a lie."

"Who stood with you?" the woman, Raisia asked. "You could not have traversed so far alone."

Angla held her words back. They had invited her to the dinner for the cause of making her the accused, when they had no clue what to accuse her of. They would draw words from her in the hopes she would allow some untoward information to pass her lips. She had conversed with Taylo enough to know the rules to this confrontation. They would examine every word for the clues to what she would hide.

"This area," Iance said, brushing his hand over a section of the map. "Here. We've traced some of the missing keepers to this place. What will I find if I look there?"

"Trees," Angla said, holding her face to hide any feeling. "I believe… There are keepers missing?"

"Yes there are keepers missing," Iance said. "And I will seek them out."

"Perhaps authority Taylo has her own cadre of slaves," the woman offered.

Angla looked at the map. Iance pointed at the place where the old ship was hidden. She wondered whether it would be hidden well enough when someone was looking. Even if they found the old ship, they would not find a cadre of slaves, or even the majority of the keepers who had left Cityscape. Yet what they would find would be the beginning of a disaster.

"Perhaps the keepers chose not to starve in Cityscape when councilmen like you withhold their just recompense," Angla said.

The back of Iance's hand met her face, tumbling Angla over a nearby chair. She pulled herself back up, resolute. She had done nothing wrong, and now she was being corrected and coerced by people who did not know the first of her.

"Even what you think you embrace will be put to lost," Angla said, and then backed through the door and into the great hall.

#

Angla swept into the cart, almost not waiting for Taylo to bring it to a stop. When she was emplaced with the entry closed she kept looking at her feet, willing herself to be still until the cart was well clear of the building. She would not feel safe, she knew, even in the confines of her own tower. They knew where she had not told the truth, and they would follow it until everything close to her heart was lost and gone.

"Angla?" Taylo asked.

It happened then at once. Tears flowed from her eyes and down her chin. Her whole person shook with the pent up feelings she had swallowed for the last few moments. Angla knew then she was not as strong as Taylo, nor as brave, but if her life was to progress in any way past the turn of this day, she would have need to be. The confrontation of Iance had been a challenge, it would not discontinue because she had sense enough to retreat.

"There is a problem," Angla managed to say.

14

Daine awated for the last moment to go to the lounge for her mid of the day meal. Her cohorts thought her daft, but she would hear none of their ravings on the subject. Miko had been eating later and she proposed to talk to him.

"He increases the distance between him and his friends by the day," Kimi said. She was one of her new friends from the Shanties. "There is hardly a thing he does not see the need to contend with."

"Whether we name it correct or not, he runs," Daine said, "If he runs it must be that he runs from something."

"Yes," Kimi had said. "But perhaps he runs because he does not have any real fondness for us. He would avoid us in total if he could. He does not think any keeper should know the first word about the Shanties."

"No," Daine replied. "Miko may think he runs from us, but in truth he runs from God. This is something which has been under my eyes before."

Kimi had shrugged and left Daine to her own direction. It seemed one of the things the Shanties practiced was letting another do as they wanted, though they did not practice such self direction without discussion. The Shanty students would argue in the worst ways, even saying cruel things to one another, but then once a decision was made, they were yet fast friends and the topic was never brought up again.

Not a handful of days before Daine had not known of such a place as the Shanties, and now she knew people who lived within it. It was odd how the whole world turned on such a small hinge.

Daine entered the dining room late, as she designed. Miko occupied the far table, alone, as he designed. He had a large book open in front of him but he was looking at his own finger.

Jenk had said Miko would talk the night away about the way his gift allowed him to see. Daine imagined the seeing of water in one's finger might be a sight to keep one's attention. Such things were not in the habit of being seen.

Jenk had also mentioned how Miko had tried once to pull the water from his hand, just to see whether he could. He had failed utterly. Jenk supposed it was like trying to bite one's tongue enough to cause hurt. One could not do it willingly.

Daine had grown up hearing stories of the soul thief, how he would drain the water from a person whole and leave them as dust. Somehow the being she had pictured looked very little like Miko. Conversely, Miko did carry more than his share of anger, against almost everyone under his eyes. In her heart she did not want to believe Miko would hurt any of them, but what her eyes espied told her another story.

For the cause of his own heart Miko needed to relent and let those who would be his friends gather around him. Others willingly turned from him, it was what he thought he wanted. For her part, Daine could not leave his secluded condition so unaddressed, even if she did not know the first word to say to him.

"Was your early of the day well-befitted?" Daine asked. He looked up at her and smiled a light smile. He must have noted how she was increasingly in the same place as he, but he had yet to comment upon it. The colony ship was large, but the spaces used by the students was small and left little room to avoid any of the other students for any length of time.

"I begin to fathom my sister's interest in astronomy," Miko said. "Rayma is teaching me so I reach the place were the rest of the students are. We touched on the purposes and uses of the numbers for it today."

He put the book he had been reading aside. Daine noted it as she approached, that it was bound in the manner of the holy writ she now had at the side of her bed. It was a larger book, and the printing on the front and side spoke of reports on something it named an augmentation.

"This is the book on your gift?" she asked. "I had learned such scholarship was destroyed at the start of one of the God wars. They had cause to keep such information out of untoward hands."

"It was," Miko said. "The robot Gabri produced a copy from her memory. She considered it appropriate that I have the schooling of my gift in its first form. I have much to read, and the time I have to read it is short."

Daine picked up the book and was turning the pages carefully, reading some of what she found there. Miko had put it to the side carelessly, but she could see he wasn't willing to let her read, yet he did not say the first word to stop her.

"Many of these pages are written by one named

Geo," Daine said. "Gabri speaks of him often."

"He was the scientist she worked for when he was constructing the gifts," Miko said.

"Have you learned anything of import?" she asked.

"Some," he said. Daine thought he might want to take the book. She kept a wary eye out, waiting for his indication. "The pino pneuma augmentation is the least likely to manifest. The designers justified it because there would be little need for more than one for each city."

"A single pino could keep the water of a city-full of people?" Daine asked.

"It seems," Miko said. "The world of Perma does not have enough water, not by half. The technicians of that time could not introduce more water to the world, but with this augmentation water can be found and controlled."

Daine flipped a few more pages.

"Imagine our world if there was water in plenty to be found," she said.

"Perhaps it would be more green," Miko said.

Daine continued turning the pages until she came to the part in the end with the many formulae and numbers.

"All these numbers," she exclaimed. "I have found working with numbers difficult beyond measure. I have been given to remedial scholarship, but only now have I begun to grasp the basis the first part of it."

"Some are better at it than others," Miko admitted.

In the brief lull of their conversation Miko took

the opportunity for a bite of food.

"How many dwell in the Shanties?" Daine asked, handing the book back to him.

Miko looked up from his meal.

"It is not for outsiders to know of the Shanties," Miko said. "It is a basic of the Shantyway.

"I'm not an outsider Miko," she answered without a thought. "I'm Daine, a keeper, a student and your friend. Not many turns of the world ago I had no idea someone like you was even alive on this world."

"Any ill spoken word," Miko said. "Or loud thought could bring destruction to the Shanties. The Cityscape tore us down before, just short of completely. One keeper speaking one word of our existence would bring destruction on us again."

"You would not surely think any of us would give you up," Daine continued. "It is not the way of keepers."

"But you are the city lord's slaves," Miko said. "You live and work by their lead. You rise for them and fall down for them. If they tell you to speak, they would hear of the Shanties, every last word."

Daine stood up, horrified. He casually accused her of the worst of offenses, of being disloyal and turning against those who had show her proper hospitality. For just a moment he began to see herself as he must see her.

"You must think me as such a monster," she whispered, her eyes dampened with the realization. He tolerated her, but every part of him must have wanted to withdraw. She was untoward in his sight, untoward in every way.

"I'm the monster," Miko said, "the Tera who draws the life and water out of my victims-- remember?"

She turned on his heel and walked from him and into the outer hallway. There was not a thing left for her to say. Miko would think what he thought and consider her foolish for not thinking the same. His mind had taken a course, and that course could not be changed, not by a young keeper from Cityscape, possibly not by anyone.

#

As Miko arrived he noted the number of students present to observe had grown steadily lower as the time passed. Daine was not present at all. Gabri, without preamble, set to work on his practice.

"Attend to the task, Miko," Gabri said more than once. On this day, for some cause, Miko could not keep his mind from thinking of other things.

Gabri did not seemed pleased with his inability to give complete focus to the tasks she gave him until the mid to late. He did make the attempts, but he did not attempt with the whole of his attention. The time of his lesson moved slowly, as slowly as the water he attempted to pull from the plant Gabri had put in the room.

After an impossible amount of time, the time for his tutorage came to an end.

"Miko," Gabri said before he could get complete to the doorway. "The next two books Trina will need for her continued scholarship are on the shelf by the door."

Miko looked and two large books were sitting there. He picked them up. Between the two they were a load to carry.

"The message Trina sent indicated she would like to see the next book," Miko said. "Not the next two."

"She will benefit from having both volumes,"

Gabri said. "Especially if her return to the school is delayed."

Miko stopped for a moment as he put the books into his pack.

"You suspect I will choose to return?" he asked. "To augment my studies?"

The robot took a moment to consider her answer. It was unusual for her to take even a moment to form an answer.

"Miko," Gabri said. "I can only plan for likely events. I do not hold the future in my hands."

"No," Miko said, turning to the door. "You do not."

#

Authority Taylo arrived at the old ship near the last of late. She walked through the doors, walked direct to Gabri, and then called the students into the lounge room.

Miko had heard chatter of Taylo. She was an authority, something unheard of in the Shanties. Jenk had tried to explain the purpose of the office at length. The keepers held most of the authority at a distance, but Taylo was beloved. They considered her a strong collaborator, and a friend emplaced among their opponents.

"The city lords suspect something has occurred in this place," Taylo said. "They will be here the first of early."

"Has someone chattered on the old ship?" Aysa asked.

Authority Taylo shook her head.

"A city lord became concerned about the number

of keepers who could not be traced," Taylo said. "And somehow he followed our steps to this section around the lake."

"That is not possible," Aysa said. "We have been more than careful."

"And yet they are on their way," Authority Taylo said. "They will search, and it is possible they will find. I am not given to the cause of assigning blame. I am here to see you safe."

"How do we return to the Shanties?" Jenk said. "Shall we pack what we can and head out into the desert?"

"You will be found easily," Taylo said. "And taken back to Cityscape for a fate even I cannot discern or dissuade. We must find a place for you to hide, at least for the turn of a few days. It will also be difficult to transfer the keepers back to their places as a group."

Miko had been staying to the back. Everything he had supposed and feared was coming to pass. The keepers could not even hold back the secret of the old ship. Was it that many more steps to the demarcation of the Shanties? He could only guess it would be known in Cityscape sooner more than later.

Someone had to bring word to the Commons.

The problem was they had need to depart from the ship but an exodus of the initiates would attract undue attention to people who were looking for something unusual. If only they could traverse in some hidden space.

And as suddenly as that, Miko knew they could.

"There's another way," Miko said, hardly believing he was the one standing up. It was a short step, though, from protecting the Shanties to protecting those who knew about it. "There is a tunnel under the ground which reaches from a hill near here in treescape into the midst of the Shanties."

"A tunnel?" Taylo asked. "How do you know?"

"I saw it," Miko said. "With my gift. I did not know what it was then, but now I'm sure of it. It can be found on the other side of the north clearing."

"Initiates, grab what you need quickly," Taylo said. "Meet at the entrance to follow Miko to the tunnel. For those who would return to Cityscape, make your way to the north of the lake and find Angla's cave. I will traverse you from there quietly in turn, by night if I must."

As students, keepers and children of the Shanties alike, scattered to gather their most needed possessions, Gabri, who had been standing near the wall aside from Taylo approached her.

"I cannot leave the ship," Gabri said.

Miko had been awaiting his turn to egress through the door, but at her words he stopped. The trouble was impending, Gabri would do well to vacate the ship with the rest. He could not say he was fond of the robot, but he did not hold ill will toward her.

"You cannot?" Taylo asked.

"I obtain my sustenance from the ship," Gabri said. "My batteries will run empty in the turn of three days and there is no one remaining who could properly restart me. I must stay."

"Are there places on the ship for you to hide?" Taylo asked.

"There are," Gabri said.

"Then hide," Taylo said. "Though I fear you will be found once the scientists enter the ship to deconstruct it and learn its secrets."

"I will consider hiding," Gabri said. "But yours is not the only voice in my hearing. You need only assure the children are safe, I will assure no untoward information can be taken from me, and I will keep for myself."

Miko exited at that point. He had been using his pack as storage, and would need little time to repack it. He considered dropping the books for Trina, they were heavy, but chose to keep them close. His pack was not full as it was, and the books would be better used in her hands than in the hands of the City Lords who would soon hold onto the ship.

Students rushed through the halls, obtaining belongings or stopping to say farewell to friends. Miko walked alone as he had planned. He would return home, the Shanties would be warned, and all would be set to right.

As he worked his way toward the entrance of the ship, he saw Daine not far in front of him. She was talking to Jenk.

"You would be welcome in the Shanties," Jenk said. "You all would be. It would be no bitter task to make proper harborage for any of you, and entering Miko's tunnel would be safer by far than hiding in the hope of a quiet return to Cityscape."

"Jenk," Daine said, putting her hand to his arm. "You are a gift, but I must go home."

"Cityscape?" he asked. "Are you sure?"

"I am sure," she said. "I don't know why, but

there is ever, always, only, one right thing to do."

"God told you this?" he asked. Miko had heard of this before. It was the way that group talked. They often justified their actions by blaming the God that the robot invented. It served to keep others from opposing even the worst of ideas.

"Perhaps," she said. "It is where my heart is drawn. It is where my father is. I will go home, but I will not fail to remember my friends from the Shanties."

"Then fare well," Jenk said. He put a hand on her shoulder and nodded his head to say farewell, however, she was not quite finished with her goodbyes.

"Do not give up on Miko," Daine said. "He doesn't yet fathom, but I think his heart wishes to."

"We trust in hope," Jenk said.

Miko fought the urge to throw up his hands and question the skies. They spoke without taking time to hear. Did they never fathom how much he did not want to become like they were?

Authority Taylo was outside the entrance, in a small open area before the wall of trees.

"Miko," she said pulling him aside. "I have instructed the initiates to gather on this edge of a clearing thirty paces from the large tree. It is a small closed area. Do you know the place?"

"I do," Miko said. He felt like he should say more, but wasn't sure exactly what was befitted for the moment, so he simply said. "Thank you for your concern Authority Taylo."

"If you are correct about this tunnel," Taylo answered. "Then you may have kept the lives of your friends. I hope you fathom how much of a gift you are."

"I may never truly fathom that," Miko said. "Stay warm and well."

"Stay warm and well," Taylo answered.

Miko decided he liked Taylo, she held no pretension and kept to the point. If she had not been from Cityscape he might have one day seen her as a friend.

Miko walked out through the entrance he had walked into not too many days before. The air was still and the trees lent themselves to cover the sky and the leading edge of Hera, above, glowing in the light of the distant sun. Once the ship was in the hands of house lords it would be lost and gone to the Shanties, and the keepers.

Part of him had wanted something like this the whole time, Miko thought. The scholarship of the old robot only added to the dire situation of the Shanties, yet in the face of it Miko felt the touch of sadness as he walked out from the ship for the last and final time.

#

"Right here," Miko said, pointing at a square mound surrounded by small trees. "I think the door must be on this side."

The night was not a dark one, Hera was three parts lit by the distant sun, and lent more light than a full winter's day. The six students returning to the Shanties managed to move through the darkened forest with a minimum of commotion. It was not too surprising, they had all been born traversing over uneven rock and narrow paths. It was the world of the Shanties.

With only a little digging they found metal doors which, once they were cleared off, opened easily to their touch.

"We could use this tunnel to return," Jenk said. "Should the city lords not find the old ship?"

"How would we know if they don't?" Kimi asked.

"The first one to speak seems correct," Jenk said, using a phrase Miko knew was not part of the Shantyway. "Until someone puts it to question."

There were steps inside the doorway, leading down to a dark area.

"Torches," Jenk said. "Dathe, search out a handful of befitted branches. Kimi, find a full branch large enough to cover this entrance. We do not want it to be easily found."

As always the Shanties went to working together to accomplish whatever was needed. Jenk and Miko opened their packs and found the pouch containing cloth crowns for their torches. As Dathe returned with branches they were stripped and wrapped. Kimi returned pulling a branch taller and wider than herself.

All the while some fragment of a memory kept bothering Miko. He tried to think around it, but found he could not. He had set out to be the wounded, but in the attempt had wounded someone else. It was not acceptable; he could not leave it as it was.

He handed his torch to Kimi as Jenk set to lighting them.

"I must go back," Miko said as the others entered the tunnel.

"Why?" Jenk asked. "We have all we need."

"I must talk to Daine," Miko said. "She should be at the lake, or in the nearby cave."

"Do you know what you risk?" Jenk said. "You

must not be found by the city lords."

"I will not be caught," Miko said. "I must speak with Daine."

"Why?"

"I used unkind words when I spoke to her last," Miko said. "We will not meet again and I must make sure all is put to right."

The initiates looked at one another before turning to face Miko again.

"Then we dare not stand in your way," Rayma said. "At least not longer than in takes to caution you again, and add my hope that you can make amends. A bitter word spoken may leave the speaker as hurt as the hearer."

"Is that the keeper way?" Jenk asked.

"You know it is," Rayma answered.

"It's a minor thing," Miko said. "But I have no wish to leave it undone."

"I will leave a torch and some spark stones at the entrance," Jenk said. "For your return. Do not wait too long."

"I don't know if I'll need them," Miko said. "I can see the tunnel from here. It's all in my mind. I imagine I could traverse it completely with my eyes closed."

"Perhaps," Jenk said. "Yet I will leave the torch anyway, for the angled rocks you may need to stand upon may not hold water at all and they may be invisible to your gift."

"If you would leave my pack on the steps," Miko said. "I would travel faster without the weight." Miko had kept the book about his gift alongside the ones he had obtained for Trina. Together they pulled his pack close to the ground.

"I will carry it," Jenk said, "until you reach us. Do not delay either in going forward or in your return, but have a care and go quietly."

#

The young keepers had stolen into the extreme reaches of the cave, the one called for the time someone named Angla had stayed there. They were gathered about a warming fire in the back as the light from the soon rising sun played at the entrance. They were well hidden, Miko was not sure it was the correct cave until he had walked into its entrance.

"Authority Taylo should arrive soon," Aysa was saying. "We can only hope she will manage to return all of us to Cityscape without incident. While my heart would have me stay at the old ship for every day I could, I have missed being in the shadow of the Cathedral."

"Beg pardon," Miko said as he approached. "Where would I find Daine?"

They turned to look at him, surprised at first, then with disdain. Not many of the keepers had sympathy for him. He had been the cause of that, and had not taken note of those he had kept away for the sake of his own displeasure.

Miko had never been so harsh before. Had suddenly being given to one of the gifts changed him to the worst?

"Why would you have any concern," Aysa said. "Considering what you have said to her?"

Miko should not have been surprised. The keepers never considered keeping secrets from each other. Every secret conversation was shouted from the tops of houses. He would complain about it, but in many ways it mirrored the way the Shanties worked together, and some of his best friends were quite given to the cause of chatter.

"I said what I should not have to her," Miko said. "And now I have need to beg her pardon."

Aysa sighed.

"It is well then," she said. "She lit out from here toward the ship, to see whether you had made it away safely. She thought there were words left to be said between you."

"Then I will seek her there," Miko said. "And draw her away before she faces the hazard of being found."

"She is light on her feet and is as quiet as a keeper," Aysa said. "She will not be found."

"It is well then," Miko said. "I will seek her out carefully."

"Keep yourself safe," Masey said. "The house lords know little of kindness in regard to those they consider less than they are. And they consider all less than they are."

"When you find her," Aysa said. "Have your say, and then send her back here straightway. Taylo should be back by the mid of the day to take us home and I don't want her to end up walking the long distance back to Cityscape on her own feet."

15

As the sun turned into the sky three carts filled with house lords arrived. Iance had spent the day before arranging and organizing, and assuring that no one would be available to monitor his progress. More than once in history a bid to the regency had been derailed by the opportune application of spies. On this day the spies who had been following him would find themselves jaunting deep into agriscape following nothing more than a well placed rumor.

For the short jaunt to the lake he had ignored the landscape outside his cart, opting instead to read part of the journal of the first governor of the City, as it was spoken back then. He found it reassuring to note how Governor D'Ankin so long ago had problems with the people he governed, problems common to any regent.

Once they arrived and landed the craft in a clearing convenient to his objective, Iance let the people of his employ manage the search as he stood atop his cart, the distant sun rising at his back. There was something here, some secret kept. If he had only impressions before they had been replaced with something more sure after the interview with Angla. She had been frightened as he had planned, but she had not been frightened for herself. There was something to be found, something she would never speak of no matter what the cause.

Angla had been more brave than he had anticipated. It was a miscalculation on his part. She had survived at the end of winter after her parents were lost and gone. One does not accomplish such things without some sort of strength. He had planned for her to whither up once she was confronted, and speak all that was in her head like any woman of her station in Cityscape. His plans had not had the last word, but then, neither would Angla.

Angla had not spoken, but what she kept in herself gave him clues. She feared more for who or what she protected than she did for herself.

"I appreciate the big trees," Raisia said as she joined him on his perch. There was scarcely enough room for them both, a fact Raisia seemed to enjoy. "They were developed by the scientists of first colony to provide a break for the wind, and enrich the air."

"Yes," Iance said. "Quite an achievement."

Just then one of his men appeared, running toward them holding a chart in his hand.

"What do you have to report?" Iance said, giving the man scarce time to regain his breath.

"We thought it was a hill at first," the man said, showing Iance the chart. "But it's too even. It is ground cover for something constructed underneath."

Iance looked at the chart, it showed a hill surrounded by trees. It was obviously not a natural hill. The lines, covered by ground and brush though they were, kept to straight in some parts and made long sweeping curves in others. In fact, the form reminded him of something.

To his aside, Raisia gasped.

"It's the colony ship," she whispered.

"Impossible," the man said, looking at the chart.

His words lacked conviction. They had all been taught in scholarship how the colony ship had perished in the second God war. But they had also learned the shape of it, and what was in front of them mirrored it all too well.

"Perhaps it is not," Iance said. "Surround it, survey it from all directions. If it is not the colony ship we shall discover what it is. Either way, it is something unusual and it may contain the answer to our questions."

Iance could not help but let his mind run ahead of him. Verification was their best course at the moment. If it was that ship…

Iance allowed himself a smug smile. If it was, he might have just won the regencyship. To find the ancient ship intact, to disprove the writ of history and best, to be able to study fully the technology which had brought them to Perma; he could use it to prove himself worthy and to gain for himself advantage.

With the right engineers and a befitted amount of time he might even be the one to re-introduce the world of Perma to the stars…

Iance took a deep breath and put himself to calm. Too often the best situations were derailed by someone too eager to take each step in turn. Iance knew to keep his mind about him, to plan at each juncture.

"Should we celebrate now," Raisia asked. "Or wait until it is in our hands."

"Revel in the moment," Iance said. "But not too fully. We went on the proceed to answer one question and found a different answer. The two may be related, but we do not know until we obtain the complete story from what we have found."

Two of the men in his employ approached with a

large bag. Iance saw at once it was moving, but he was not sure what it contained until they emptied a boy out of the bag. At first he would have thought it was a keeper, he had the look of one who remained outside in the sun and wind form work. But it was a boy with quite colorful clothes, and a look in his eyes like one who would not do as he was told. Nothing about him would be at home in Cityscape.

"We find new discoveries at every turn," Iance said. "Boy where are you from?"

The boy kept his silence. He looked frightened. Iance reciprocated by being frightening.

"It matters not," Iance said. "We already know. The one we found in the ship has already told us."

"Ship sir?" the boy asked, feinting lack of knowledge, and pretending to talk like a keeper. He was not particularly intelligent. Iance would quickly discover everything he needed from this one.

"Maybe we should take you home once we finish here," Raisia added. It was a masterful stroke, the boy was shaking. Then, looking at them, his shoulder slumped.

"I doubt you would be welcome in the Shanties," he said.

Then one of the men walked up to report to Iance.

"We found an opening," he reported. "It is the old ship, and even better, one of the original robot interfaces still functions. It awaited us at the doorway."

Iance fought the temptation to look at the boy as the realization came to him that he had just been lied to, and made to speak more than he was willing. The councilman had seen the look on many occasions.

"Good," Iance said. "Take the interface and this boy to the Holding. It will give me time to consider what to do with them."

Iance pushed the boy into the arms on his man, who caught him deftly and held tight.

"You cannot separate Gabri from the ship," the boy said. "She will cease to function."

"All the better for my engineer," Iance said. "To take it apart and consider how it works."

The boy was not happy to be taken away. Iance did not care. The robot interface had a name, and its power source was in the ship. Iance wondered how many of the old machines still functioned.

"No hearing for him?" Raisia asked.

"Not yet," Iance said. "He will be put to holding until I learn all I can from him. He's from somewhere. Whatever place it is, he fears Citylords in a different way than a keeper would."

"But he has been around keepers," Raisia added. "He knows how they talk."

Iance nodded, agreeing with her assessment.

"First," Iance said. "We should take a look at the colony ship. It will be most enlightening."

"That it will," Raisia said, joining his arm to walk to the ship.

The men had cleared a number of trees, and made open some areas around the ship. In the midst of it all, there was a cleared area where they found a door. It had been opened. Iance stopped to look at the side of the ship, the small section which had been cleared of land and plants to show the smooth metal.

At one time this ship had jaunted through the

emptiness between suns. Iance could not help but be impressed. There was power here, not just the simple power that kept a robot moving, but power to change the world.

"Wouldn't it be strange," Raisia mused. "If the boy turned out to be from the second city."

"The one that was destroyed?" Iance asked.

"Yes," she said. "Destroyed like the colony ship."

She stepped into the corridor with a flourish, making her point. The ship was said to have been destroyed in the same war which ended with the destruction of the second city.

"If everything we thought destroyed still is," Iance had to ask. "Did we ever actually accomplish anything in the god wars?"

"Perhaps the wars have not yet reached their conclusion," Raisia said.

#

Daine ran the last few yards to the cave. There was no one about to see her, and she had spent overmuch time moving slowly and carefully. She had seen enough, but if she were found and prevented from making a report, her sight would be for nothing.

She could have screamed when she noted Miko caught by citylords and put roughly into a bag. Daine had seen the young man's arrival at the ship and was moving with care to approach him and pull him aside, but he had worked himself into a place where there was no escape. He was in their hands now.

She followed them back to where a councilman waited, and Miko was dumped out in front of him and watched carefully. Then as she waited for a chance to covertly intervene, Gabri was brought out of the ship and put next to Miko. The longer she waited the more she knew would be no chance to secret them away. And if she remained too long she could join them all too easily.

As she returned she noted Taylo's cart near the lake. It was parked to the side so to divert suspicion. It was well. Daine knew more than anything her need for assistance, and Taylo was the one who could provide it.

She entered the cave carefully, but was noted right away. Taylo was talking to the group near the fire. As she approached they turned to look at her, the import of what she had need to say must have been imprinted on her face, for they waited silently until she could regain her breath enough to speak.

"Authority Taylo," Daine said. "Miko, from the Shanties was taken by Councilman Iance and the city lords, along with Gabri. They are to be put to the Holding. We must intervene."

Taylo considered for a moment before she spoke. She did that often, weighing the situation and considering which strategy might be best. It was easy to see what lay ahead would be filled with difficulty. Her dark eyes steeled themselves for the worst of times.

"It took me the greater part of a day to return," Taylo said. "I am under the eyes of many and have little room to breathe. If I have a chance at retrieving them, I must act without delay. The rest of you, can you be well until the mid of late? I will send medic Parke to retrieve you."

"Take Daine and Aery now," Aysa said, stepping forward. "They are from the Drydocks, near to the Holding, and they can assist you. Parke will be given the added advantage of fewer students for his concern. We will bide our time here for the day."

"I stand ready to assist Authority Taylo," Daine said. "There are keepers in the Drydocks who hear of every person taken to the Holding, and would be able to find where Gabri and Miko are taken."

As Taylo moved carefully to check the cave entrance, Aysa caught up Daine in a deep embrace.

"You are a gift," Aysa said. "It has been a joy to walk with you this short time. I hope soon to renew our acquaintance."

"I plan to visit the Cathedral on summer's eve next," Daine said. "Perhaps we will renew our conversation then."

"I will be on the northwest corner of the steps," Aysa said. A tear touched the corner of her eye, which was of course quickly held back. Both keepers knew there were many steps to be taken before the next summer's eve, and many things could prevent either or both from attending.

"It is well then," Authority Taylo said. "Daine, Aery, follow me. The rest of you, stay quiet and out of sight, and be ready to traverse when Parke arrives. We face the circle of dire times from this moment on. Keep yourselves ready for the worst of circumstances."

"But always hope for the best," Daine added. "Stay warm and well, friends."

16

Miko was obliged to sit upon the ground next to Gabri as the one they named Councilman Iance continued to come and go, and talk about the great discovery he had made. Two men were given the task of keeping him from running, and he was placed where he could not hope to make his way to any place safe. Miko listened with all intent, knowing his speaking had already started trouble which he could not control. The man had lied, he had said someone had told him about the Shanties, and in the moment Miko had said more than he should have.

"What have I done?" Miko whispered.

"You have been captured," Gabri said just as quietly.

"I was tricked into naming the place I am from," he said.

"Let your words be few," Gabri said. "They intend to learn more from you."

Miko nodded.

As the distant sun fell toward the horizon Miko and Gabri were put into a cart. Miko had ridden in one only once before, and even then it had frightened him. A man stayed at the entry to keep them within.

Miko looked over at Gabri, intending to speak something, but Gabri shook her head quickly to keep him from speaking. Miko could not help but agree. In so small a space every whisper could be heard, and every word carried with it the threat of being misspoken.

He had to consider how ironic it would be if he were the one to inform the city lords about the Shanties. Not too many days before he would have thought he would choose death first. Yet words had flowed from his mouth before he took time to consider.

It was the turn of a few minutes later when Councilman Iance and those with him came to the cart.

They looked at him and Gabri, but did not speak.

One of the other men sat at the controls, and with a whisper the cart lifted to the sky.

Despite himself Miko was drawn to the scene without. They passed huge trees as they traversed all the faster. And then suddenly they were in the open, flying above open areas covered with unkempt grass. In the distance were buildings and square fields, organized in row after row.

Miko had never seen so much food being grown, and all in organized rows and plots. The Shanties could not afford such open farming. It was one of the ways they could be found out.

As if the cart as miracle enough, the city was near impossible. The students at the school had described it more than once, but the actual sight of it forsook even his most wild imagining. They arrived as the distant sun was fallen from the sky. Lights appeared spontaneously in the city, pure light with no flickering at all. Miko knew he was not seeing fire. Cityscape had something more akin to the channeled light in the old ship.

He would have asked about the lights, but already knew he would not be spoken to. When he had tried to sit up straighter the better to see he had been given a cuff in the face. Miko did not appreciate the rough treatment, and did not want to have it repeated.

They landed on the top of an imposing building, as wide as it was tall, marched out and into steps which led into the heart of the building.

"What names should be put for them on the Manifest, councilman?" a guard asked as they were taken inside.

"None," Iance said. "My people will care for them, and no one else need know they are here."

"As you say," the guard said, and turned his back on them.

They were walked down level by level on steps which retreated after they had been walked upon. There were doors upon the walls, too many to count as they walked by. One of the men pushing him along had called it 'the Holding'. Miko wasn't sure what that would be, but it did not sound inviting.

Eventually they entered one of the doors, and found inside a hallway covered with more doors. Every so often there were crossroads in the hallways, with guards at each station. Miko began to realize he was being put aside, locked away like a stray animal. Miko had learned of such things, but it was not the Shantyway.

The two of them were put to a small room with a single bed and little else.

"Gather your rest," Iance said from the closing door. "For when we meet on the morrow you will speak all you know."

"And if I don't?" Miko asked.

"Then you will reside here for a very long time," Iance said. "And I will yet hear what I want to know."

Then they were alone.

"It would be wise not to allow him to cause you to talk at all," Gabri said from behind him. "He can extrapolate information from every word."

"I've noted as much," Miko said. "But he causes me to be so mad."

"Anger is a poor strategy," Gabri noted.

"Do you know where we are?" Miko asked.

"They called it the Holding," Gabri said. "The keepers speak of it. It is the place where criminals and teras are put to be held."

"Teras like…" Miko started but Gabri held up her hand to acquire his silence.

Gabri put her finger to her mouth, something the students had told him was a sign for quiet. She was correct, of course. The worst thing he could put to words in this place would be words about his gift.

He had heard it said that Cityscape would not have the gift, they were rejected along with those who had them. He had never thought to visit Cityscape, and had reinforced that decision when he found he had one of the gifts. Somehow he had still arrived in the midst of it, and every breath was the most dire he had ever breathed.

"You think there are ears put to these walls?" Miko asked.

"It would be very likely," Gabri said. "What they want from you is information. We are more likely to speak to each other than to them."

"Then we should speak of things they already know," Miko said. "Or of things they don't want to hear."

"Why would we do so?" Gabri asked. "It is best

not to speak."

#

Masey had gone out of the cave at the early of late. He intended to keep watch until the medic Parke arrived, and return to the cave so the keepers could meet him part way to the lake and save the turn of a few moments on their return to Cityscape.

From the moment Masey had left, Emne had glanced out the entry every few moments. She did little to hide the concern on her face.

"Could medic Parke have been delayed?" Emne asked, looking once again toward the opening of the cave.

"Nothing is more likely," Jerin said. From the start he had ever been at her shoulder. Aysa had not noted it before, but each was often found in the company of the other. They were like two halves of the total. If they chose to walk together it would not be untoward in the least. They were each befitted for the other.

They all went to quiet as a soft shuffling entered the cave entrance. There was no real place in the back of the cave to remain hidden, not when the fire still burned. Aysa kept herself from breathing hard. If they had been found out they would be taken away and there was nothing to be done.

"Masey?" Jerin said, standing up. Masey had indeed stumbled out of the shadows. His eyes were turned down and his face was pale. "What has occurred?"

"The worst," Masey mumbled.

Jerin moved to one side of Masey as Emne stood at the other. They walked him closer to the fire to warm him, but he seemed untouched by anything. His mouth moved to talk, but it was the turn of a few moments before the words found their way out.

"Medic Parke," he said, then swallowed and took a deep breath. "Medic Parke is lost and gone."

"What occurred?" Emne asked.

Masey looked up at her, then looked down again.

"He was set upon by three men when he walked from his cart," Masey said. "They knew his name. Then they took to beating him. Parke barely fought them, but they did not stop. They didn't stop until…"

Emne let tears touch her face as Jerin's eyes turned to red. They all knew Parke as a kind and gentle man, for him to be so callously attacked was unthinkable.

"We cannot stay here," Aysa said.

"We have to oppose those…" Jerin started, but Aysa put her hand up.

"No," Aysa said. "We can't. Parke would not have us set in the Holding or put to lost for his sake. We are obligated to leave the cause of just in the hands of God and keep for ourselves."

"Should we jaunt our way to the city on foot?" Emne asked. "We would be easily found."

Aysa looked at all of them, their fright was almost tangible, and they all felt there was nothing to be done. If there were men to intercept Parke, they might question why he was at the lake. That question could lead in a straight line to them.

"I suggest we follow the cave Miko spoke about," Aysa said. "We leave the lake and Cityscape behind before we are put to lost in it."

"Aysa, I understood you had no desire to see the

Shanties," Emne said.

"I have a desire to remain warm and well," Aysa said. "Therefore I have sufficient cause to visit any place away from here. To stay emplaced in the cave would be foolish, not when we have another option so readily available."

"I have no hesitation to visit the Shanties," Jerin said stepping forward. "Masey, will you join us?"

"Someone has to keep for you," Masey said. "Aysa, how do we proceed?"

"We must leave here now," Aysa said. "If those men search for us they will soon look in the caves. There is a stand of trees part way around the lake which we could emplace ourselves under. We should wait there till the first of early before we trace the path to the tunnel."

"Either the men at the old ship will be fewer," Jerin said. "Or they will be easier to avoid in the light."

"We should leave now," Masey said. "Quickly and quietly. Aysa can lead the way and I will follow behind. No one need speak until we are hidden below the trees."

"Keepers, prepare yourselves for a long walk through unknown places," Aysa said. "It is not the path I would have traced, but it is the path we must follow for the cause of our lives."

17

The tunnel was long and straight, and as near as Jenk could tell, constructed of a continuous length of porcelain. It was porcelain more fine than anything he had seen before. He glanced at the wall every few steps, looking for a joint. There were none. The darkness inside was total and every footfall echoed all around them.

He had heard of such things, wonders put to construction using methods no longer available, but had never thought to see one in his life. It was an effort to task his feet to walking and avoid stopping every handful of steps to admire the walls again. They had need to be constant in their traversing. Overground the jaunt was a matter of five days, he could only assume the underground route would be comparable. What food and water they carried would only last so long.

Jenk could not accustom himself to the everpresent dark. Outside of the flickering light of their torches, the tunnel fell to utter black. Without stars, moons or distant sun it was impossible to know whether the sky outside turned to night or to day. His eyes would not consent to such darkness, they kept imagining light for him to see.

"I wonder if it is yet to the last of day?" Kimi asked, echoing his thoughts. None of them had felt the need to converse in the dark of the tunnel. At first it had been for the cause of the loss of their scholarship to the Citylords, who truly did not have the need, or it was the quickness of their farewells and knowing there would not be hope for fond reunion with those they had named as friends. Each of them had cause to be taken by consideration. Much had turned to change over the turn of a single day.

"I cannot say," Jenk said. "Do you feel a need to rest?"

"I do not," she answered. "But I rarely do unless I stay awake far beyond a reasonable time."

"Chatter has it you do so often in the pursuit of your studies," Jenk said. "We will rest soon. It is a long jaunt, and we cannot walk it to conclusion on the first day."

Kimi was satisfied with his answer, and returned to her place in the line. They could easily walk two or three beside each other, but it was the scholarship of their earliest days to walk one at a time. In the Shanties there was room for little else.

Jenk considered that they were on their way to the Shanties, much earlier than any of them had planned. When they arrived the students would be obligated to take word to the Commons. Much had occurred and the Shanties would need to hear of it. For a moment he wondered which of them would do the speaking. Yendi was the eldest, though not by even the circle of a winter. Jenk was known for talking, but not always for his organization.

Perhaps as they drew closer to their destination it would be good for them to converse on this subject and choose what words they would say.

#

"It's a cart," Kimi said. She had stopped

suddenly in the tunnel, at the moment she was the one in the front, the rest stopped as well.

They had stopped and rested twice since they had left the old ship, though no one could know for sure whether it had actually been two days. Their sadness merged with the darkness to keep them from talking overmuch, and their sorrow brought with it a longing for home.

Jenk walked around her and looked ahead. In the flickering light of their torches was indeed a cart of some sort. It was larger than the carts from Cityscape. It had windows in the front, and was pointed in the middle like a cart would be.

"It fills the tunnel," Dathe observed.

Jenk walked to both sides. It was as if this cart was made to fill the tunnel from wall to wall, and as much, from floor to ceiling. It was old, he could tell by the dust on the upper surfaces. Where once it had moved, it had been put to a stop and had stayed there for longer than Jenk could fathom.

"There is no way around," Kimi said.

Jenk had noticed as much, but did not want to say it until he had looked closely at each side. However, he could not disagree with Kimi's observation. The cart was made to fit into the tunnel like a hand would fit into a glove.

"Sometimes the best way around is to go through," Jenk said. He had read it in one of the ancient books. At the time he had not thought it was not a well befitted phrase, but now that he was emplaced before this cart, it made as much sense as anything.

"Are you kidding?" Yendi asked.

Jenk had walked under the forefront of the cart, there he had seen a square framed out on the surface. He knew from his reading about such things, every part of them was made with a purpose.

"It looks like this should open," Jenk said. "Help me pull."

Three of them pulled for the turn of several moments. The frame gave only a little, revealing it was indeed some kind of panel which had the ability to open, yet it snapped back into place once they released it.

"Wait," Kimi said. "If it was meant to open there would be a way to make it do so."

"Maybe it wasn't meant to open," Dathe said.

"It was," Kimi said. "But it was also made to stay closed. I think this was a cart made only for the purpose of traversing the tunnel. The panel would have need to be secure when it traversed." Her fingers jaunted over the edges of what might have been an entry until she found a small disk protruding to the inside of the panel.

"Can I borrow your knife Jenk?" Kimi asked.

She put the point of the knife into a slot to the center of the disk.

"It should turn," Kim said. "Help me."

Two of them wrapped their hands around the handle and twisted. They were rewarded by a stiff crunch, and the slot turned without any effort at all.

"We broke it," Jenk said.

"Then it should be easier to open," Kimi said and pulled on the panel. She was correct. It opened easily. Inside the entry was a port which opened at the floor of the cart. Kimi entered first and stopped to put her gaze to every part of the cart. There were seats around the sides and the remains of clear panels on the upper edges of the sides and front.

"The main door was there on the side," Kimi said as she stood up.

"That would be silly," Yendi said. "It opens to a wall."

"Here it does," Kimi said. "Do you remember the shelf at the start of the tunnel? The door would be at just that level if the cart was there."

"There are no controls," Jenk said.

"It must have been controlled from outside," Kimi said. "There would be no need to recourse in any direction, only to start and stop."

"It won't work now?" Rayma asked.

"No," Kimi said. "We are given to walking the full way to the Shanties. Though I suggest we stop here, eat and take our rest. These seats will be more comfortable than the floor below."

They put two of their torches on the floor in the center of the cart, and extinguished the other two so they would stay alight all the longer. They silently ate some of their foodstuffs, knowing what they had would need to last until they reached the Shanties.

As most of them settled to rest, Jenk joined Kimi, who was near the port entry of the cart near an open panel, looking at what was within and occasionally putting her hand in to touch some part of the machine. It looked every bit like a solid mess to him, but he was certain she was seeing more than he could.

"This wire traverses the energy to this machine," Kimi said. "The machine moves to activate one of these depending on which direction it is turned to."

"I understand most of your words," Jenk said.

"But you have no understanding of all of it together," Kimi completed his thought for him. "In my understanding of what I see here, I am beginning to see the result of my scholarship. It is quite befitted."

"You believe you could make this cart work again," Jenk said.

"Perhaps with time," Kimi said. "I know I could try. Even if I do not succeed I would gain knowledge from the attempt."

Kimi noted Jenk glancing at the port entry to the cart. She knew what he was watching to see.

"Miko has not arrived," Kimi said. "We would see his torch by now."

"No he has not," Jenk said. "Either he is traversing more slowly than we, or he has chosen to go to Cityscape."

Jenk was trying to speak in jest, but knew he had fallen short. Miko was quite verbal in his disdain for Cityscape.

"We both know he would never go there," Kimi said. "He sees Cityscape as poison to the Shanties, and he knows how they respond to someone who has a gift."

"And yet he progressed enough to see the need to beg the pardon of Daine," Jenk said. "Perhaps he has turned to growing."

"You have yet to mention the worst which could have occurred," Kimi said.

"And I won't," Jenk said. "I will not put it to words. I will not give the first thought to it. It would be too terrible for anyone to be taken by house lords, even Miko."

"It would be," Kimi said. "Do you think we should await him here?"

Jenk had considered it already, and though he truly wanted to remain he knew they could not. Their course had been set and they would have to follow it until the end.

"We dare not wait long," Jenk said. "A meal and some rest is all we can take. The jaunt will not walk itself and our food and water will only last so long."

"Perhaps he will arrive by the first of early," Kimi said. "And you will have worried for nothing."

"I trust in hope," Jenk said.

18

Sharo was aware of falling asleep yet found herself still sitting in the Commons with Jenne, still emplaced at her side. It did not strike her as unusual in any way. The light was brighter than day and the Commons was deserted save for a single man—an extraordinary man. He approached her and smiled.

He was dressed in some kind of loose fitting robe, and had a small cloak around his shoulders, it would have barely covered his head at all. He would be chilled if he went about in the Shanties, even on the full of a summer's day.

Sharo only noted she was sitting on a half wall when the man knelt down in front of her. There was a large bowl there. He took a towel, put it about his midsection, and began to wash her feet. Even though her mind was numb with sleep, she was not completely without her thoughts. The actions he took were something she had read about not long ago.

"This is in the holy writ," Sharo said. "I held no understanding of it until now. It is a tried and true tradition, and a befitted one. It is an action of love."

The man nodded a confirmation, and continued with his work.

"I must echo the words of your follower, sir," Sharo said. "The one who said he was not worthy of such action, not from your hand."

"Then I would repeat again," the man said. "If you do not accept this from me you have no part of me."

"It is well then, sir," Sharo said. Looking over the man as he finished his work. He kept an eye to his task, smiling as he completed it all to the last toe. She knew he would be someone worthy to follow. In fact, and she had known it from the first she saw of him, and it was well that she already followed him. The face was not familiar, but the man was.

Sharo glanced back at Jenne, sleeping peacefully. She wondered whether it would be untoward to wake her. Surely Jenne would want to see this man as well.

Then he stood up, the Son before her. Sharo stood up as well, her feet still tingling from its cleaning. It was not the place of a keeper to sit while a house lord stood, nor one more important. She was honored and surprised that he noted her in any way, and she waited for what words he might speak. Without it being spoken she knew his next words would be of the most import.

"Name what you want of me," he said.

The query was a surprise to Sharo. Never had anyone asked such a question of her. She was a keeper from the shadow of the Cathedral in Cityscape. She was a pura, a warmer of special talent and was truly needed in the Shanties. Never in her heart had Sharo dreamt of someone with such consideration for her.

Sharo could not hold it back. Tears flowed from her eyes. The man held her as a gentle man would, putting his hand to her head and allowing her tears to run their full course.

#

Sharo awoke in the commons, surrounded by her cloak and by the side of her dearest friend Jenne. It was the first of early, light had only begun to dance upon the clear frames on the far side of the room. Sharo noted as she awoke that Jenne was already stirring.

"What are your tears for?" Jenne asked.

Sharo wiped her face, it seemed the tears of her dream had become the tears of her waking life.

"For joy," she said. "And for sorrow. In my dream I talked to the Son. He washed my feet, then asked what I want of him."

"I read of that yesterday," Jenne said. "One would think it would be clear what a blind man would ask from the one known as a healer. Perhaps it is befitted to put words to that which is obvious."

Kassi had entered the Commons carrying a platter. She knelt at Sharo's feet, three cups of warm tea with her.

The cups were of a particular pattern and color, one which Jenne was particularly proud of. She had been giving them as gifts to her friends for the turn of three winters.

"Awake sleepy ones," Kassi said. "Are you warm and well?"

"As well as one might be," Sharo said stretching the stiffness from her arms. "What brings you to the commons in the early of the day?"

"Surely not only to deliver tea to us," Jenne added, taking one of the cups.

Kassi didn't answer, but rather put herself to sit beside Sharo and handed her one of the warm cups. She had known Kassi from her first day, having been in attendance at her birth so long ago in Cityscape. Sharo had been so young at the time, and full of wonder at the way of children as they arrived in the world. Madri had been proud of her daughter, and had always named her a golden heart.

"Sometimes I miss sleeping in a keeper cloak," Kassi said. "I miss the closeness, but Pytre would never to see a cloak again."

"He walks away from his life before too quickly," Sharo said. "Leaving behind the good with the bad."

Kassi breathed for a moment before she spoke again.

"Joska has made amends with me," Kassi said. "Allowing me forgiveness for not being able to fix his eye."

"Joska is a strong child," Sharo said. "He has a heart as big as the world. He will be fine."

"He misses talking to you," Jenne said. "He is afraid he asks too many questions of you. His heart is broken when he thinks he may have offended you and he cannot fathom how to make amends."

Sharo instantly felt regret. She had been staying away from her house, and most every place save the commons. Traversing had become too difficult. Conversing had become difficult as well. Her mind had been too full of thoughts lately. Part of her had returned to Cityscape, to the shadow of the cathedral, and there was only a little room for the Shanties.

"When Joska was given to injury you saw the echo of Rafe in him," Kassi said.

Sharo closed her eyes. There were tears close at hand from her dream, and she did not want to share them now.

Sharo had not given a thought to Rafe in the turn of a winter or more. They had known each other from the crèche, and the elder keepers portended a union between them, but it was not to be. When her mother was lost and gone Sharo was needed to raise her younger brother Pytre, and Rafe would not help, nor would he consent to wait.

Rafe had been injured in a fight for the cause of a house lord with his twisted need for distraction. It was much the same injury Joska now wore. How had Sharo not made note of the equivalence? Kassi so easily drew the line between the two.

When Sharo had been deserted on the far side of sandscape Rafe had sought out those who had abandoned her. The house lord had been killed, and Rafe had faced the authority for the matter. By the time Sharo had returned to Cityscape to retrieve her brother, Rafe had already been put to lost and gone. Taylo had told her the full of it.

She had always thought he would make amends and retrieve their friendship. She had always seen herself as the eventual woman at his side. It had not occurred. The plans of her future had been lost and gone before she had been given time to consider them.

"It was long ago and far away," Sharo said. "Can something so distant put me to hurt?"

"It can because it has," Kassi said. "You carry a hurt I cannot begin to touch."

"Even if it could be, healing a broken heart would be untoward," Jenne said. "You need to walk with the grief your heart holds holds until it is given to a proper place. Grief is born of love. It allows for remembrance."

"When will you allow yourself to touch your grief Sharo?" Kassi asked. "Both for what has happened in the turn of years past, and what has happened in the turn of a few days back?"

Silence grew between them. Sharo knew she had no need to answer, save with action. Her friends would not expect anything else.

Sharo lifted her cup, now half filled with the warm tea.

"Salute to friends," she said. "Near and far, well and lost."

"It truly is," Jenne said in agreement. "Sharo, if you need to converse..."

"I need only speak your name," Sharo finished. "Be patient for the turn of a few days. My heart feels a need to pull aside, to converse with myself, and perhaps to name that which is most obvious to the one who can touch broken hearts."

"Do not stay aside too long," Kassi said. "The Shanties has need of you and your friends do not want to converse too long without you."

19

"Are you awake?" Kimi asked in the darkness.

"I've been awake for the turn of some moments," Rayma said softly. "How long did we sleep?"

"There's no way to know," Kimi said. "A befitted amount I think."

"I would agree," Jenk said. "Did anyone think to have their spark stones on hand?"

"Mine are in my pack," Kimi said.

"As are mine," Rayma answered in kind.

"Give me a moment," Yendi said. "I will put my hands on mine in a breath or two."

"Have you found them?" Jenk asked after the turn of a moment.

In answer a bright flash filled the cart. The light of the sparks seemed all the brighter for the time they had gone without. The second set of sparks was more centered on the first torch on the floor, and within a moment it was lending its own flickering light to the students.

They gathered their packs and gave themselves to eating a meager meal with meager water to drink. Jenk was worried they would take too much, leaving them with nothing for the later end of the traverse.

"If Miko were with us," Yendi observed. "He could pull water from the air and fill our containers."

"If only Miko was in good spirits," Rayma commented. "Otherwise he would only stomp away and give nothing."

"Be gentle," Kimi corrected. "Miko was only with us for the turn of a few days, and he was given much to consider, much more than many of us."

"Maybe he was always ever grumpy," Rayma said. "I was with him more than any of you, and not once was he of good cheer."

"I was with him as well," Kimi added. "And Jenk has been his friend from their earliest days, and yet none of us can discern what might truly be in his heart."

"Are we ready to traverse?" Dathe asked in an attempt to shut down the conversation and give them all a task. Attention to keeping gives distraction from chatter.

"Where is Jenk?" Yendi asked.

Kimi looked about the cart. Jenk was not to be seen. It made sense. He would have been the one encouraging their preparation had he been in sight.

"I'll find him," Kimi said.

Kimi found Jenk standing in the tunnel obverse from the cart. He was emplaced there, like she knew he would be.

"Is Miko approaching?" She asked, drawing his attention from the tunnel behind him. The way was as straight as could be. There could be no thought to hiding if one used a torch or flame of any kind.

"Someone does," Jenk said. "But unless Miko has taken to carrying two flames I dare say it is not him alone."

"Or it is not him at all," Kimi said. "I hesitate to speak the worst, but could it be city lords?"

"It could," Jenk said. "Which is why you will take the rest onward. I will stay here to meet Miko if it is him, or to be taken by city lords. I will make them busy taking me, it will give you time to reach the Shanties."

"I will also stay here," Kimi said. "The other three can care for each other. And it will take them twice as long to subdue both of us."

Jenk looked down for a moment, seeing her feet in the shadows like he dared not look higher.

"It would break my heart to see you taken by city lords," Jenk said.

"And it would break mine to never see you in the Shanties again," Kimi countered. "I believe we can put to closed this door to the cart, and then lay low in the cart to see who arrives. Perhaps we can even devise a way to keep them from taking us at all."

"Your scholarship is a benefit to us all," Jenk said. "Let's send the rest on their way. They can take word to the Shanties."

She smiled at him, and he returned it. They had been friends since childhood, and as Kimi knew, sometimes childhood friends were the most befitted to have walk by one's side. This would be assuming, of course, they were not taken by the city lords before day's end.

"Rayma has in mind to teach the new scholarship," Kimi said. "Perhaps along the way she can practice on Yendi and Dathe."

"Rayma may not take those words as a kindness," Jenk said.

"Nor may Yendi and Dathe," Kimi added.

#

"How long have they been walking?" Jenk asked in a whisper. Without the light the tunnel was darker than night.

It would have been completely dark, but the fire from torches lit the tunnel far ahead, and more quickly from behind.

"Near half a day I suspect," Kimi said as quietly as she could. The cart where they hid was solid, and most likely their quiet voices would not escape to be heard on the outside, but it was difficult not to fear. "I thought you told them to keep their lights hidden."

"As much as possible," Jenk said, looking down the tunnel. They were far enough ahead to be indistinct, but the fire from their torchlight illuminated the walls about them and gave them away. "They require the torches to walk."

They were not near far enough ahead by Jenk's estimation. If their pursuers be city lords they could too easily see there were others yet to be chased, and the destination was obvious in any sense. The worst of it all would be the city lords walking direct to the Shanties.

"Strange how once you have light," Kimi said. "You cannot be without it, and it will not allow itself to be hidden."

"Yes," Jenk said. Kimi was ever the student, considering things in ways no one else would think.

"They approach," Kimi whispered from beside him on the floor. They had closed up the entry to the cart, and made it secure as could be provided by the materials at hand before they had quenched their lights. In the dark Kimi reached out and held to his hand, Jenk held hers in answer.

"It's some kind of cart," a muffled voice said from outside. The shadows of their torches touched the upper surface inside, and danced about. Jenk could see how wide open Kimi's eyes were. The voice did not belong to Miko.

"There is no entry," a feminine voice said. "Perhaps there is a way to traverse to the side of it."

"Aysa?" Kimi asked, then scrambled to sit up and look through the clear frames at the front of the cart.

"If it is not," Jenk said, mostly to himself. "Then our days will not be long."

Kimi pounded on the window, Jenk decided it would be just as well if he sat up. For good or for ill the game was over. They were found. There was not a way to reverse it.

"Aysa!" Kimi yelled at the window. "Stand aside, we will unloose the entry and let you through."

"Kimi," Jenk heard Aysa say. At least at this point they had been pursued by friends and not city lords. Jenk sat back for the turn of a moment and allowed himself to breathe his release from anxiety.

"Why do you give yourself to worry?" Kimi asked as she put her hand to his shoulder. "Instead help me reopen this frame."

#

"Miko and Gabri taken by city lords," Jenk said, as much to himself as to his companions. "And the medic Parke put to lost. This is not fair news."

"Not in the least," Emne added.

They spoke as they walked along the pathway, their mid-day meal still in the midst of settling within them.

"All of Cityscape knows of the caves to the north face of the lake," Aysa said. "We would have been discovered. We thought it best to get far from the lake and traverse to the Shanties to bide our time there."

"You will be safe and among friends in the Shanties," Kimi said. "For whatever turn of time you are among us we will have much to show you."

"Then I have much to see," Aysa said. "Starting first, I think, with our friend Trina."

"She will smile for the turn of many days when she sees you again," Kimi said.

They walked forward, never out of sight of the small light ahead where their friends continued. Jenk could see some pretense at keeping the light hidden on the obverse side of them. It was not worth the effort, the light would not allow itself hidden, not in the least.

"We should have preset some signal," Jenk said. "They will think themselves followed by city lords. It is among Rayma's deepest fears."

"We best not follow too close then," Kimi said. "We will have our reunion at the Shanties, where there is cause to feel more secure. I wish we could do more for Miko and Gabri."

"There is nothing to be done," Emne said. "Authority Taylo will take the task to the face of it, but I fear even her efforts will be a shouting into the wind. The Holding does not release its victims."

Jenk had met authority Taylo more than once, and he knew she had the reputation of being strong in every way a person could be. Anything she could be ineffectual against seemed impossible, and then frightening.

"Perhaps we should leave our friends in the hands of God," Jenk said.

"Which is where they have been for the whole time," Emne added. "Whether we choose to leave them there or not."

Despite the scattered rubble at the beginning of the tunnel, the rest of the way was smooth. It was a round tunnel with a flat floor. It was also very straight. Anyone who found it would have a way direct to the Shanties.

"Kimi," Emne said. "With your scholarship in engineering... Have you looked closely at these tunnel walls?"

"I have not stopped looking," Kimi said. "There isn't much to pull my eyes away. I do not know how this tunnel was constructed, but I've counted the space between supports, and the lines between them. The walls appear to be molded, as if it is one solid brick. I suspect the walls must have been formed from the inside."

"How would one accomplish such work?" Aysa asked.

"I am unsure," Kimi said. "I suspect there would be the need for some sort of machine, it would need to be as large as the tunnel. It would be required to dig the tunnel first, then set the walls as it went."

"Could such machines be real?" Jarin asked.

"I was at the start of the study of such machines," Kimi said. "I have books in my pack to continue such study. They were once real."

"And if Kimi has her way," Jenk added. "They would be real again, and they would work for us."

"If such a thing can be done," Aysa said. "I would expect Kimi to be the one to accomplish it."

#

When they stopped to rest for what felt like the evening Jenk and Kimi sat back against the nearest wall. The keepers, however, kept to their feet, and after a few moments of walking around quite slowly and considering every last bit of space, they chose the most befitted places in which to sleep. Then they took their cloaks off of their shoulders and began to spread them out to cover themselves.

"I had heard keepers sleep in their cloaks," Jenk said. "But I have yet to see it."

"You will see it now," Aysa said. "And it would be untoward if you did not join us. For decency we will sleep here and the boys will sleep there. Kimi, join us. Jenk, join them."

Kimi stood to her feet, partly feeling anticipation but also a moment to hesitate.

"I don't know how..."Kimi said, but Aysa stopped her.

"Then follow as we lead," she said. "It would be untoward of us to sleep together in the warm of our cloaks and leave you chilled and without. No keeper would ever be so cruel."

"It is much like the way we follow proper harborage," Jenk said.

"The reasons are alike," Masey said. "To leave anyone alone in the chill is to turn your heart from everyone."

"Then for my part I will accept your harborage," Jenk said.

"It would be best if you did, sir," Jerin said.

They stood Jenk in their midst and wrapped

themselves together under their cloaks. Jenk had always thought they wrapped up separately, but it was not the case. They sat down together, all warmed under overlapping layers of cloaks. Jenk tried not to lean against anyone else, but realized he was the only one not using the stability of the others.

It was warmer than it would be if he had slept outside the group. At first he wondered if he could sleep, so encased with cloaks and friends, but in a short time tiredness caught Jenk and he drifted into the sleep of the evening.

20

The day had it's fill of meetings and appointments, conviction and concession, every part of which made Iance weary to his bones. This was the way the colonists once spoke, and at times the meaning of their words worked better than the ones he had available to him.

He was doing more than his usual, trying to keep everything close and silent. More than one opponent had stepped up their observation of him of late. Some kept track of him to prevent a loss of power; some did so in hopes of gaining more.

Iance had played this game often enough, and knew how to keep his opponents at arm's length, but it was not without cost. There were matters he could not attend to, not without risk of allowing some leverages over him.

At times he considered taking the keeper cloak he had stored in his closet and disappearing into Cityscape streets. Spending a few days unnoticed would be helpful. However, he knew he could not. Too many matters at hand required constant attention, and few were trustworthy enough to be trusted with vital matters.

"So," Raisia asked as he entered his rooms. "How are your guests at the Holding?"

"I wouldn't know," Iance said. "They have been more trouble than they are worth, and I have been kept busy."

"You've at least had someone listening?" she asked, walking around his large couch.

"I did for the first day," Iance said. "He was named Backe and he was working for Forste and had a need to be put to quiet. It is clear they are not going to talk, at least not directly. It doesn't matter, I have heard enough."

"Any clue what happened to whoever had been on the ship?"

"To my best estimation authority Taylo's medic friend went out to the lake to retrieve them," Iance said. "The men I sent got too enthusiastic about their job. The medic would not give any information. Whoever he was hiding were not found."

"Were they keepers or were they from the Shanties?" Raisia asked.

"We know someone was in the old ship," Iance said. "It seems there were keepers there as well as those from the second city. I think they were young, and given to scholarship at the hand of the robot interface."

"What were they being taught?"

Iance had not taken time to consider it. Raisia always thought to ask good questions.

"The robot is not forthcoming, nor is the child," Iance said. "They are careful to control their words, as if they know we have listened. I put that at the feet of the robot. The child does not know the first thing of technology."

"Do you intend to question them further?" she asked. They both knew the limit of their opportunity was near.

"There is chatter of an attempt to retrieve my

prisoners. It will be made by the turn of the day," Iance said. "When we recapture them along with their cohorts, I will be in a more suitable position to ask good questions and force befitted answers from them."

#

The City lord Iance had not been true to his word. Miko and Gabri stayed in the small room and no one crossed through the door to ask questions. The only thing which came into the room were meals, meager and bland. The food was sent through a slot along the bottom of the wall. The light stayed on always, not changing for the turn of night or day. There were no windows, and no hope.

"It is mid early," Gabri said. "On the third day since we arrived."

Miko sat up. His sleep, when it occurred at all, was fitful and was not encouraged by the glaring light of the room. He was stiff and weary, and there seemed no end for his situation. Gabri updated the times for him, which helped a little, but in the everlasting nothingness of the Holding it could not be more than a minor help. Between times of anxious boredom, he found little to release him from the panic hid in the back of his heart.

He looked at the food which he had retrieved from the floor and put on the table. There was more than he needed, the guards probably thought there were two people in the room. The extra was not a kindness.

"It would be a benefit for you to continue to eat," Gabri said, yet again. She was singleminded in her concern for him. She should have held some concern for herself. No one on all of Perma could keep for her. She had said so at the old ship.

"I don't know if this food was truly made for eating," Miko said, chewing on a dried slab of bread. There was no taste to it, and it was as dry as death.

"It was not made to be pleasant," Gabri said. "But your body will yet use it to give you energy which you may soon need."

Miko took a bite and tried to think of other things as he chewed.

"It is ill befitted you cannot use food for energy," Miko said.

"For you it is natural," Gabri said. "For me it would be a most inefficient and bulky system. I do not serve my function if I am not mobile."

Miko paced the room again, not bothering to remind Gabri yet again that she had lapsed into the old way of speaking. He would have found it interesting to hear how people once spoke if each word did not portend the dire fate of Gabri. Her energy would run its course within the turn of the day. She had said it once, but had not returned to the subject. Miko did not care to speak about it, and Gabri had already provided all the information he needed.

Miko put his hand to the door and noted the man on the outside—he could feel faint echoes of them using his gift. Most of the time there was one, sometimes there were two. He had tried to speak to them. Either they did not hear or they did not care. It was most likely the latter. Those sent to this place were sent to be forgotten.

On their second day Gabri had given him scholarship on the system of detainment coupled with the system of just. It made little sense to him. How could one be required to pay just recompense for wrongs when held behind thick walls and watched over by guards? Gabri had attempted to explain, but so far as Miko could see, it was a most inefficient system.

When he finished pacing the entirety of the room once again he returned to Gabri. She had lain on the bed; a position Miko had never seen her take. Gabri was ever upright, she rarely even sat. She had said rest was for people, she was a robot.

"What are you doing?" Miko asked.

"My final battery has a three percent charge. Sitting requires as much energy as standing," Gabri said. "Lying requires less, and is safer, should I topple when my energy is at an end."

"Does speaking require energy?" Miko asked.

Gabri turned her head to face him. It was as if that task took much effort. She looked at him and smiled.

"It seems I would choose to stand less in exchange for talking more," Gabri said.

Miko was not sure what to say to her. If it was to be their last conversation he had a need to fill it with the most important information he could consider. Yet at the moment he did not know what that would be. Gabri was not like a person who would find comfort in words of fondness or encouragement.

"Is my scholarship complete about…?" he asked, stopping himself before the mention of his gift. More than the Shanties, the city lords must never know of his gift. It would be dire for him from the first to the last.

"You have a sufficient amount of scholarship for your... life," Gabri said. "Any more will be taught in the practice, and from other friends."

Miko had expected the question to illicit a flood of information. It usually did. He was surprised at her lack of response. The use of his gift had once been in the forefront of her thoughts.

"…I trust you will be a benefit to your peers."

"What are peers?" Miko asked.

"Cohorts," Gabri said, using another word he had no knowledge of. "The people around you."

"Oh," Miko said. "Those who walk with me." For a moment he considered it interesting that the people who colonized Perma would have so many words for the same thing. At one time they must have been a friendly people.

It made him wonder at how the people of Perma must have changed from their beginnings. It would be of interest to hear what Gabri would say, but he did not want Gabri to finish her energy for the cause of his curiosity.

"How long before you are lost?" Miko was not sure he really wanted to know, but could not think of anything else to say. It would be better to leave all to silence, it would help Gabri last a bit longer, but he could not help but talk.

"I do not have anything to be lost," Gabri said. "I am a robot interface. Robots do not die, they simply cease to function."

"Why are you smiling?" Miko asked. Unlike everyone else Miko knew, Gabri never smiled; not unless she had a reason.

"Geo would have thought it ironic," Gabri explained.

The stories of Geo were often mentioned in the

old ship. Miko had wondered if Gabri knew how often she spoke of him. Somewhere back in the turn of time that man had made his impression on the robot. Her students sometimes took to the stories as well, Geo had been well-spoken much of the time. Miko remembered thinking it would not be possible for one person to be so wise on so many subjects.

Gabri's eyes stared forward, turning to a pale color. Then her eyelids shut mostly, as if there was little energy even for that.

"You will feel lost to me," Miko said, "to many of us."

Miko had been in preparation for this for three days, and yet he was increasingly aware he would break the word he had put to himself not to let his tears fall free. He was so quickly acquainted with the robot interface, when Miko arrived at the ship he did not have the first befitted thought about her, but in the midst of it all had formed a connection. In it all she had acted in his behalf.

"Do not grieve," Gabri said. She no longer attempted to look at him. Miko supposed her darkened eyes could no longer could trace where he was. "As if you are people who have no hope..."

"What hope is there for one who is lost and gone?" Miko asked. He turned to look at her, but she was staring straight up with empty eyes. She was moving, but slightly, and her movements appeared random, without purpose or control. It was the end, her power was near gone and she no longer had the ability to control what movements she did make.

Miko caught himself watching her slight and

purposeless movements, wondering if he should be looking at all. He reminded himself that he was looking at a robot,and she had no sense of embarrassment.

"I am named Gabri," she said suddenly, as if to one one at all. She looked up, appearing as one who spoke to someone unseen. "Geo named me as Gabri Noel."

Her voice became lighter by the moment, by the end of her sentence Miko thought her gone, completely lost. Her batteries were emptied, she had grown truly still and her face was locked in position. Miko could not fathom what to do. He had never been present at the point when someone was lost and gone, even a robot.

He knelt next to her and put a hand to her shoulder. They were meaningless gestures to Gabri, and would have been more so had she still functioned. Somehow it meant something to Miko.

Then he heard the robot interface speak, as soft as the most quiet of whispers. It was bereft of human undertones and was simply a mechanical sound. Miko leaned near to Gabri so he could listen to the words the robot spoke at her last.

"...so beautiful..."

#

Miko sat in the corner diametric to what was once Gabri. He truly could not recall how he had arrived there. Yet he had no will to stand or to move. The light hadn't changed, but the whole world seemed darker. The room hadn't changed but it seemed empty.

Gabri was a machine. It was plain to see even if he had not known before. The power had gone and the parts had ceased their movment. She had been a wonderous machine but everyone on Perma knew machines had no heart. Gabri was an object, not a person. She was given to the physical, not the ideal.

Gabri had said as much about herself. She knew beauty only as something people understood, to her it was a simple definition.

Yet, Gabri had said "beautiful," at the moment of being lost and gone.

"Such things cannot be," Miko said out loud. Gabri was not capable of such a thing, even at the end of her power. It would be especially impossible at the end of her power.

Miko stood up on shaking legs and proceeded to pace the room. His hands and toes tingled as his mind fought to understand what he had seen. More than once in his scholarship Gabri had coursed him through the process of considering a difficult problem.

Tears which he had held back poured onto his face. When something which could not be obviously was, then some view had to be reconsidered. Either he lacked understanding on the way a computer interface worked or he held to believe something about it which was not true.

Miko sought to avoid it, but he had no cause to deny his error which Gabri in her death had proven. There was one way it could be. He would have never thought to ask for this proof, but it was the proof he needed. Nothing else could have held what truly was in front of his eyes. He could not help but see.

"It must be," Miko said. "It is... God truly is."

21

Sharo sat in a corner of the Commons, wondering once again when she might return to the home she had occupied from the day of her arrival in the Shanties. In her time at the Shanties she had collected a number of things, things she would have never possessed had she remained at Cityscape, but even the allure of belongings did not tempt her back to the house. It was as if her life had been a dream, and she was ever a keeper—even in the midst of the Commons.

She had faced the sorrow which sent her to sleep away from her house; the past injury to her friend in Cityscape and the present injury to the son of her friend in the Shanties, but her continued desire to sleep in a cloak sitting on the ground was hard to explain, even to herself. She felt as if she were awaiting something. Whatever that something might be, she did not have the first guess.

"Pura Sharo?" a voice called out from the entry. "Are you still in attendance?"

"Of course I am friend Ryalt," Sharo said. "What brings you out to the Commons so distant into the late?"

"Worry for you," Ryalt said as he sat himself on a block near her. If there was ever one who took no time for anything less than honest it was Ryalt. He did not know how to speak an untruth.

She could witness his thoughts on his face. To him it was unbefitted for her to sleep in the open; even the open of the Commons, which was not much more than a large open shelter, certainly not someone so beloved in the Shanties.

"Every keeper in Cityscape would desire to sleep in a place such as this," Sharo said. "Under the sky the air draws away all warmth, and the most befitted places are the most difficult to get."

"Yes," Ryalt said. "But I can offer nothing to every keeper in Cityscape. If you cannot return to your house, my beloved Jenne has allowed you room at our hearth. What is it keepers say? 'To stand alone against your sorrow…'."

"…Is to invite your sorrow to stand closer," Sharo said. "You learn the Keeperway well."

"My teachers are numerous and most befitted," he said. Ryalt had never been to Cityscape, though he had been as close as any other.

When Sharo first arrived at the Shanties, and had gone to retrieve her brother Pytre, Ryalt had been sent by Jenne to watch over Sharo for her jaunt. Fortunately he had stayed in the colony ship to recover from the chill while Sharo had gone into the city. It would be most dire for an initiate to take the first step into Cityscape.

"Much is appreciated Ryalt," Sharo said. "But sometimes sorrow must take its course, and sometimes a misplaced keeper must touch the life she once was required to live in order to know the true recompense of what she has now."

"You cannot say I did not show a care," Ryalt said.

"I never would," Sharo said, knowing his smile was a real one. "My heart has drawn me here, and I cannot say I know the course of it. For the circle of this time, here is where I belong. I find nothing ill-befitted in it."

"I dare not impugn your heart," Ryalt said. "But I will not allow you to traverse without knowing the care of those who walk with you. Jenne is concerned, though not as much as I."

"Jenne's heart is taken by the Shanties," Sharo said. "Yet she has the wisdom to walk with every keeper who has chosen to join us. She is a gift to all of us."

"It may be well that so many keepers have joined us," Ryalt said. "If Jenne is to join you as often as she has, I will need a cloak of my own."

"I am certain Jenne would correct your lack of propriety should you attempt to gather under your own cloak," Sharo said. "It is the way of families to sleep under the same cover, more than one if the night is well chilled."

"Do you hear something?" he said suddenly.

Sharo gave her ear to listen, and was instantly to her feet when she heard a scrape. She held up her palm and made a fire in it, enough to illuminate the whole of the commons. Ryalt had seen her make fire before, on more than one occasion, yet the fire in her upraised hand still held a fascination for him.

"I have seen a wonder today," Ryalt said, neglecting to search out the source of the sound he had heard. Sharo herself found it, walking direct to a wall on the side of where they had been.

"Here," Sharo said putting the palm of her hand flat to the wall. "There are people obverse to this wall."

"Who are they?"

"We will not know until we find a way to open

the wall and retrieve them," Sharo said. "I believe there is a bachelor covey not too distant from the Commons."

"There is," Ryalt said. "Will you fare well until I return?"

Sharo looked at the fire coming from her hand, then back at Ryalt.

"If I keep my wits I suspect there is little I cannot weather," she said. "Go quickly, return with a befitted measure of haste and with some amount of strong help."

Ryalt ran, keeping mind of his feet as he traversed the rubble strewn path. She turned back to the wall.

They carried fire with them, Sharo could feel the points of warmth even through the wall. She considered their torchlight and realized they would not be city lords. If they were from Cityscape they would use another form of light, one which her gift would not see so well.

Holding to the hope they were not enemies, Sharo hit her fist against the wall twice.

There was a pause, as if those within were startled that someone would be near. It was possible they did not know where they were, or what was obverse to the wall which hid them.

Then they answered her knocks with pounding of their own from inside. The third knock dislodged a tile from the wall which Sharo noted, on further inspection, to be a locking mechanism.

"I see," Sharo said to herself. "If I can loosen this, the panel should slide open."

Sharo took hold of the old latch and started to pull. It moved, however stiff it was.

"I ask that these not be enemies," she whispered softly. "For I am allowing them entrance to the heart of the Shanties when I alone am here to stand for it."

#

The edge of the sky still held the brightness from the distant sun which had fallen below the horizon. Ryalt believed Sharo, that she would fare well until his return, but his trust in her was not at hand. Someone unknown was obverse to the wall in the Commons. What could that mean?

On further contemplation Ryalt realized whoever it was would have stayed on the other side of the wall, or would have emerged into an empty room had Sharo not been present in the Commons after the remainder of the Shanties had gone to their homes.

Perhaps at the end of it she had been led to the Commons for this reason.

The bachelor covey was before him, a larger house with many rooms. Ryalt shouted greeting before he reached the door.

"Ryalt?" a face appeared at the opening of the door. "What occurs?"

"Someone is within the wall in the Commons," Ryalt said, knowing he could not tell the story in detail, not until later. "I need help to open the wall, and to discover whether these are friends or not."

"We will follow," the young man said. "Allow us the turn of a moment to grab our coats."

Five young men followed Ryalt down the lane and into the Commons.

"What has occurred?" Ryalt asked. As he entered the commons he noted Sharo standing where she was, but with the inclusion of other people. If this was some sort of Cityscape incursion, it was not a well-equipped one.

A section of the wall where they had heard the sounds was open, it slid on some unknown rail above and hid itself on the inside of the wall. Beyond that was darkness and a hollow sound which bespoke a large size.

"It is not what I feared it would be," Sharo said, turning the face them. She was not in any form of distress.

"Rayma," Ryalt said, recognizing the young woman. They were in fact, from the Shanties. "Dathe and Yendi, How are you back from the old ship?"

His thoughts quickly went to his cousin, Jenk, and he wondered if these students had returned what had become of him.

"The ship is in the hands of the Cityscape lords," Rayma said. "We all traversed away as quickly as we could so as not to be taken as well."

"This tunnel was found by Pino Miko," Sharo said. "He could see it where no one else could. He kept the lives of our young students."

"Where is Jenk?" Ryalt asked, recalling the students at the ship. "Where are Kimi and Miko?"

"Miko went to speak to a keeper before they were returned to Cityscape and did not quickly return," Rayma said. "We traversed without him and hoped he would join us. Jenk and Kimi stayed behind in the tunnel for the cause of our being followed, and they did not know whether it was by Miko or city lords. We have seen their light following us, but without knowing who it was, we pressed all that much more to reach the Shanties."

"That is well," Sharo said. "We will watch for

them in either case. Send these young men with Dathe and Yendi to assure they arrive home and are settled with their family. We will discuss this new occurrence in the Commons on the morrow."

"And I will traverse with Rayma," Ryalt said. "Her family is but a lane down from mine."

As the other students walked out of the Commons, Rayma held up a pack, it seemed heavy.

"This is Miko's pack," she said. "He sent it with us when he left to find the keeper. I believe one of the books he carried was for Trina."

It should not have been surprising that the students would bring books with them. If the old ship was lost, at least a part of the library could be brought to the Shanties.

"We will set this aside for the moment," Sharo said. "When we see Sundi again we will give it to her with hopes that her son will soon follow."

"I am truly sorry," Rayma said. "I have brought such poor tidings to the Shanties."

"You brought the truth, Rayma," Ryalt said. "Because of you the Shanties will be ready for whatever may come to pass next. You should not be sorry for that."

"And yet I feel sorrow," the girl said. "For everything we hold to could be changed with so few words."

Sharo stood by the now open panel—a panel in the commons that opened to a tunnel which led direct to the area of the lake and the old ship.

"What occurs Sharo?" Ryalt asked.

"There are fires distant in the tunnel," Sharo said.

"They do not approach. I suspect they have stopped for the night."

"How does one tell whether it is night or not in that tunnel?"

"We stop when we tire," Rayma said. "It is a long jaunt."

"More than our three then?" Ryalt asked.

"More," Sharo said. "I cannot see them distinctively, but there is more warmth than can be counted for three people."

"How close are they?" Rayma asked.

"Less than a day's walk," Sharo said. "I would not expect them before mid-late on the morrow. And then we will know who they are."

"Did I lead them here?" Rayma asked putting her head down.

"Are there branches or turns in the tunnel?" Sharo asked.

"There are none," Rayma said.

"Then they were given to finding the Shanties from the moment they entered the tunnel," Ryalt said. "You have led no one to the Shanties save for your companions, and for that we are ever grateful."

"And I believe they are glad to be home as well," Sharo added.

"I suppose you will not be sleeping at my hearth tonight?" Ryalt asked.

"I wonder if I will sleep at all," Sharo said. "Accompany Rayma to her family while I put this door to shut. Then I will stay here to watch."

"Until the morrow," Ryalt said.

"Until the morrow," Sharo echoed.

22

Without Gabri to mark off the time, every moment followed every other moment in the Holding stretching to an infinite doldrum. Miko could note the change of the guard by putting his hand to the door, which he had marked at twice a day when Gabri had kept watch of the times, but otherwise nothing differed. The walls were barren, the light was from one source, and though it was a wonder to Miko, it was also harsh. There were two cots, each less a comfort than the other.

Nothing was toward about his place. Gabri was lost and gone, a motionless machine laying on the cot, and he was yet held in a place he knew little about in a city he had never wanted to touch.

He paced the floors and gathered his thoughts. Miko was not sure whether to feel rage or fear at being at the mercy of Cityscape and alone, but ended up with a parcel of both.

He considered what had occurred to accompany him to this place, both good and ill. He remembered what Gabri had taught him about his gift, but found nothing which would end his custody. Perhaps it was one of those events which had to traverse full forward until it reached the other end.

The only best thing was that he knew God walked alongside him, even in this place. He wondered whether it would have driven him mad to be in such a place without knowing. He had come close to missing the truth.

Miko sat on the cot next to Gabri. It was an empty gesture. He thought to talk to her in memory but found he did not have the heart. The machine no longer contained Gabri and it served nothing for him to speak to her shell.

"God," Miko said suddenly. Some of what his family had been saying, and what he had heard on the old ship began to make sense to him. "I have heard chatter that you hear every word spoken and see every move made. You know I am here even if I have been abandoned and forgotten by all else."

Miko was not sure whether it was permitted to ask to be let out. It seemed God would be aware of his situation and would move to change it when he chose. He also wondered whether one could presume upon God to speak a message to Gabri. In the size of the world his concerns seemed little. In the end he simply smiled and looked back down at the remnant of Gabri. For the moment he would be content and allow for events to happen as they would, and know there was one who was in charge of it all. There was little else to do.

"I must beg your pardon for not listening sooner."

Somehow in those words he found a parcel of hope which he hadn't held to before. Surely God would know how many people who had need to give Miko pardon. In order to accomplish such a thing he would need to be away from the Holding.

Miko jumped as the door swung open on the sudden. A blue clad guard, a large man, walked in the room and located him sitting on the cot, then retreated.

When he returned a girl dressed in drab and layer followed, carrying a metal bucket.

"The keeper is here to clean," the guard said. "Best leave her be."

"Okay," Miko said, not sure what was required of him, or whether he was permitted to speak at all.

The guard gave him a menacing glance, then backed through the door and pulled it closed. Only then did Miko think he could have tried to use his gift. He might have been able to pull at the water in the man and touch him to illness. In the commotion he might have made an escape. Miko was not sure he had the heart for the attempt. It would be more dangerous, he thought, to reveal himself.

"Miko?"

Miko had been returning his attention to the still Gabri, but there was something in the voice, something familiar. He looked at her again, and recognized the one in the drab clothes.

"Daine," He said, then softened his voice, remembering they might still be listened to. "How are you here?"

She started to respond, but was caught up in his embrace and lost her words.

"I must beg your pardon," Miko said. "I accused you unfairly. It was for the cause of my own fear and not for any fault of yours."

"Your fears ended up as exact," Daine said. "The whole city is chattering about the ship being found, and the great library for which they have no end of words. There have been celebrations among the gentry."

"Do we know who..?" Miko moved to ask, and then reconsidered. "I do not have need to know."

"More than one person," Daine said. "The

knowledge was coerced by a sinister man. The one you met, who brought you here. Somehow in the midst of the information he pried from a handful of different people he found his way to the ship."

"Then councilman Iance is the cause of all bad things," He said, glad she had not named any name. There was no need to know, anyone could have been worn under by the man who told lies to force out information. Miko had named the Shanties to the man without the cause to do so. He could only hope he grew silent before the damage was fully done.

"Miko," Daine said. "Quickly wear these clothes."

Miko looked at the bundle she had given him, pants and a shirt both drab and dim, and dark shoes with heavy tread.

"Why..?" Miko started.

"Because keepers are ever present and never noted," she said. "You change while I look to Gabri, then we will leave together."

"Daine," Miko said. "Gabri has lost all power. You should go while you remain safe. I will stay at the side of Gabri."

"I understood Gabri would be gone," Daine said. "She would not have you give us more cause to regret. There is nothing to be done for her, but you may yet be retrieved from what fate the house lords would give you. You are important to your friends. We may even be able to jaunt you home in the right turn of time."

Miko walked to the corner and changed his clothes for the drab clothes of a keeper. He had noted how they wore little color in the old ship, but these were even more drab. If these clothes were what they normally wore, they had taken a step away from their lives in the city when they traversed to the ship.

Daine was here to retrieve him. It had to be a risky venture on the best of days, and this was not the best of days. In the end he decided the risk of leaving outweighed the risk of not leaving, in turn, he would have to see to the young keeper. He would not see her caught or harmed, not for the cause of him.

He returned to Daine, who was still sitting over Gabri, tears touched her eyes.

"They will expect you to have cleaned," Miko said. Without awaiting her answer he raised his hand. The water in the bucket was warm and light. He pulled it all out into the air as a fine mist, then pushed it to the floor and the walls, taking care not to dampen himself or Daine.

In an instant he pulled it back and gathered it above the bucket where he let it fall in. The bucket was less full of water and mixed with the dull brown from the floor.

"You clean better than a keeper," Daine observed. She only had eyes for the walls about them.

"Is it overly clean?" Miko asked.

"It will add to my reputation," Daine said. "I can only trust I will be able live up to it later."

"How do we proceed?" he asked.

"I will put a question to the authority in the hallway," Daine said. "As I do you will walk through to the opposite hall, turn to the right and walk alongside the wall without touching it. Walk as if you have a destination. Linger after the first corner, hidden away from watchful eyes, and I will join you presently."

"Okay," Miko said, wondering how such a simple plan would accomplish anything save his reinternment, perhaps with a new cellmate. But even as he considered she knocked for the door to be opened and lit into conversation with the one who opened it.

"Grant pardon sir," Daine said, suddenly looking less than she was. Her manner and her voice were much more timid than he had yet to see her. "I stand ready for any other task. Do you still have need of keeping?"

The guard caught the eye of his cohort, who shrugged.

"No," the authority said. Miko had already passed, unnoticed as Daine had portended. The simple plan had worked thus far, then the building began to shake.

"Quake," one of the authority said, then all three put their hands to the wall. Miko had turned as the building twisted, then, seeing what they had all done, he put his hand to the wall as well.

The shaking quickly stopped, but now Miko was facing opposite his goal. He considered for a moment continuing on in that way, but had no way to know what might lay in that direction, or whether Daine might be able to retrieve him. In the moment as he paused, Daine started walking toward him.

"Boy," Daine said tersely as she walked past him. "With me."

He turned obediently and followed her and the authority did not note him in the least. They walked upward through the maze of hallways and stairs. Daine led them direct to another set of stairs, this time she took them downward.

"That was not a normal quake," Daine observed when she was sure they were out of the hearing of anyone. "It did not feel right."

"I had wondered," Miko said. "But I don't know what it might really have been."

"Perhaps we will learn in time," Daine said. "Stay at my heel and do not look about more than you have need."

#

Miko followed Daine as they joined a horde of keepers as they traversed to the outside. They were noted by an elder keeper. She glanced about, then leaned down to the girl.

"Have a care child," the keeper said in the lowest of tones. "Is this one worth the dire situation you put yourself in?"

Miko tried to look worthy of something, knowing there was no good direction to take should the elder keeper choose to alert the authority.

"That much and more," Daine said confidently.

The elder keeper seemed surprised, stood up tall, and then studied Miko with gleaming eyes.

"Then good fortune young ones," she said. "Do not accompany us complete to the cart. You would surely be noted there as one out of place."

Daine nodded as they walked past a row of fencing, then caught hold of Miko's sleeve and pulled him into the tall grass on the side. The distant sun was on the horizon, and would soon slide out of sight of the world.

"Have a care," she hissed. "It would be untoward

for us to be found unattended in this section. It would bring attention to us, even as keepers."

After staying in the tall grass for a befitted length of time, Daine led them carefully, putting their back to the Holding, which interposed the sun and made itself to a large shadow looming over them. She stopped twice, kneeling to look about and listen. Presently she led them in the direction of a small clearing.

"There she is," Daine said, indicating a dark form leaning against a cart. "Authority Taylo."

Miko was about to stand up and walk across the clearing, such hiding was not his usual operating. But Daine grabbed at his shoulder and pulled him down.

"Something is untoward," she whispered tersely.

The whispers in the grass had turned to rustling. The rustling turned to commotion. Miko chided himself, he should have been using his gift to see what was about them. Perhaps he feared someone would see what was only in his own head.

The clearing was suddenly illuminated.

"Authority Taylo," a loud voice announced. From his place hidden in the grass he could see her, blinking the illumination out of her eyes. Scores of guardians stood up from the grass to detain her. Taylo did not cringe in fear; she simply crossed her arms and looked determined.

Miko knew that voice. It was the worst turn of events yet.

"I see you have Angla with you as well," the voice said. "We need to have a conversation."

"It is most befitted," Authority Taylo said as she stood to her full stature. "For you have many answers to give, Councilman Iance."

"But where are your young friends?" Iance asked. He was not intimidated by the authority, or at least he did not show it. "They should have arrived by now. Nevertheless, we will seek them out. They must join us."

Daine turned to Miko, her eyes wide open, and whispered to him.

"We must go."

She started to lead him away, but Miko stopped her.

"Not this way," he said softly. "There are four of them obverse to those trees. Follow me."

"How do you know?" Daine asked as she followed closely behind him.

"My gift touches them," he said. "They all contain water."

They picked their way through the trees, aided by Miko's ability to know where the pursuers were. In a short amount of time Miko had led them to a lane where a few people walked. Daine kept to his hand and led him across and away from the Holding.

"We need only cross the bridge and all will be well," Daine said. "We can lay low in the streets of Cityscape and never be looked at twice by any House Lord."

"They follow," Miko said as he looked behind them. "I wonder if they have some technology to see us like I see them."

"It is of no import," Daine said as they gained a foothold on the bridge.

"Children," an elder keeper said from a place at the bridge entrance. "You cannot cross the bridge today.

The flooring will not be put back to place until the morrow."

"Could we look?" Miko asked, trying to mimic the contriteness of Daine. He knew he had not succeeded when the keeper looked at him twice.

"It will do no harm," the elder keeper said. He turned and no longer gave them note.

They walked up on the bridge. A light fog hid the lower areas below, and the distant sun was but a light glow on the horizon. Only a quarter of angry Hera and a few stars lent illumination to the world.

"If we cannot jaunt across," Daine said. "Will that not trap us on the bridge?"

"If they know we cannot traverse," Miko said. "Will they bother to seek us out here?"

"I trust in hope," Daine said.

The bridge angled up to a solid plateau, where the center section ended at a crease. There was a sound here, a new one. It was like the rustling of the leaves of a tree held in the wind, but somewhat different. As they watched the form of tree branches slid between the massive edges of the bridge. The tree had to be huge, and yet it was floating almost upright, indicating a fair amount of water below. Daine left her emplacement at Miko's side and rushed up the bridge to where the lane ended abruptly and stood on the edge.

"Someone has put water in the river!" She exclaimed.

Miko glanced at her and wondered. Where else could one find water? But he understood something had changed what she thought was a normal situation. Then a feeling began to encroach on his awareness, the seeing part of his gift gave him a warning he had hoped not to need.

"We have been followed," Miko said.

Daine looked behind not yet seeing what she knew would be there. Their pursuers were relentless and now they were trapped. There was no place to hide, and no other way off of the bridge aside from where they had just been.

"God, I am afraid," She said, closing her eyes against a tear which had formed there. Miko could see her tremoring, and realized how much fear she must have swallowed to make herself walk into the Holding. Now she faced the possibility to being put there complete, and it was a bitter thought to her.

In the moment Miko knew what to do. He grabbed her around the middle and with her in tow, jumped over the side, down a building's depth, and into the crowded, swift flowing water.

In her surprise, Daine had little time to yell out.

#

"We must converse," Iance said as he entered the room and dismissed the guards who kept heed to their every breath.

"Yes, we must," Taylo said standing to face the man. Angla was conspicuously quiet.

"The young boy we found at the colony ship," Iance said, "the one you conspired to release from the Holding. Who was he?"

"Young boy?" Taylo asked, not allowing him any hint that she knew of whom he spoke.

"After Angla told me where to find the colony ship," Iance said. "We found it easily enough. We took the boy along with the robot interface from the ship. A young keeper led him from the Holding and to avoid us they entered the river and were lost. So now only you can tell me, where are the Shanties?"

Taylo covertly put her hand to Angla, probably in the case she would be tempted to speak some untoward word.

"Let me fathom your words councilman," Taylo said. "In addition to striking young women without cause, you have engaged in the theft of a robot, the abduction of a child, and now you are the direct cause of two children being lost and gone. Is this the limit to your crimes, or shall I investigate further?"

Iance glared at the authority. He had hoped the mention of the Shanties by name would loosen their tongues, but Taylo was too well versed in the verbal games of interrogation. It was sloppy of him to make such an attempt. Now she had named his actions as crimes. Given her pattern, Taylo would seek the proof of his actions and never stop until he was disgraced in all of Cityscape and put to the Holding.

However, his play was not yet complete.

One of his men entered the room, just as he had planned, and talked to Iance in low tones.

"His cart is wrecked?" Iance said. "Unfortunate."

The man retreated, leaving him alone with his two detainees.

"I understand you knew a medic named Parke?" he said.

"What have you done?" Angla found her voice.

"I've done nothing," he said, keeping his face serious toward them. "You were the ones at the beginning of this turn of events, and only you can bring it to a close. I urge you to do so before more of your friends are lost and gone."

Angla was holding back her tears. Taylo was much more controlled, but he could see the anger in her eyes. Whether it would give him the results he wanted, it remained to be seen.

"No one is beyond the cause of just councilman," Taylo said. He knew as well as she the accusations alone would topple his plans, and some could be shown to be true.

"I will not be accused by you," Iance said and turned to leave. He traversed complete to the doorway before he received an answer.

"Who then," Taylo's words followed after him, "would you be accused by?"

#

"What do you think happened to Parke?" Angla asked once she was sure Iance was away from hearing.

"I know what we are meant to suppose," Taylo said. "There may be some measure of truth to it, but we cannot know until we know it by hand. He holds control of each word we hear, and we must suspect all of it."

"I did not point the way to the colony ship," Angla said.

"You were not required to," Taylo said. "There are ways to exhort information from what is not put to words. He would have found the information in either case."

"And now he knows about the Shanties," Angla said.

Taylo raised her hand to her mouth and indicated

the walls about them. Iance would have someone listening to their every word.

"He knows but a name," Taylo said in a low voice. "He does not know the first of what the meaning of the name is."

Angla nodded her affirmation. Knowing the name was nothing more than a clue. Hopefully he did not have his hands on other clues. She looked around, they were being listened to, there were subjects they could talk about freely, especially ones which were not the most welcome by their captor.

"Did Iance truly murder those children?" Angla said. "How could he?"

"How dare he?" Taylo added. "It is not beyond him, but we have need to question those words as well. We cannot truly know, but it may be they are not in his hands."

"They should be happy then," Angla said. "To be out of his hands is ever a good thing."

"Perhaps now," Taylo said, emplacing herself to the side of Angla, "is a good time for those songs you wanted to sing."

"Yes," Angla said, "for those who listen to us in order to know our secrets."

#

"Such things are not in the habit of being," Daine said. She had lost her wind as they struck the water. Even Miko was surprised at how hard it was at the speed of falling. The water seemed determined to put up a wall between itself and the air. At first he thought he might use his gift on that wall to keep them on top of the water and flow away with the tide. But he had seen a bubble of air underneath, at the bottom of the river in the wake of a large rock. He had brought them down to it, had used the water to bring other bubbles of air to join them, and had held all of it together in a well befitted living area.

His reaction was not far from hers, he didn't know such things were possible. When it was at hand and he did not have time to think about it, the task was easily done and now they were in a dry place underneath the flow of a river.

The view from under a river was singular, Miko had never seen anything like it.

"Are you well?" Miko asked. She only had eyes for the bubble around them, and the brackish water without.

"Well enough," she said, marveling at the dry ground in the middle of a flowing current.

"Don't move too quickly," Miko said. "They have not seen us yet, but we must carefully hide."

"You think they would yet find us?" Daine asked. She sounded surprised.

"Do you not see them standing on the bridge?" Miko said looking up through the water. "They have yet to notice us down here. Some were sent to look for us downstream. If we keep to cover we can walk upstream and avoid them in total."

"How do you see that at all?" Daine asked, looking up but not seeing.

"You do not see them?" Miko asked.

"The water is the color of dust," Daine said. "I could not see a hand's span beyond the demarcation of the water. There is nothing to be seen."

Miko looked again and realized he was seeing

that which no one else could. The dust had filled the water, but somehow his gift allowed him to overlook it. His first thought was to ask Gabri if anyone had ever done such a thing before, but then he was reminded. Gabri could no longer answer him.

"I wondered why they hadn't seen us," Miko said. "I thought it was for the dimly colored clothes we wore."

"We can stand openly," Daine said, standing to her feet. "Trust me, they will not see us."

"I think I can take this bubble of air with us," Miko said. "And we can walk."

"Then we should do so," Daine said. "The further we go from here the better."

The water had melted away the dust of the dry river, leaving a road of uneven stones for them to walk. They were not like river rock which was rounded and even, these stones were all angles and sharp. Miko had traversed many such paths in the ruinscape around the Shanties, but Daine was unprepared. For her walking such a path was slow tedious work.

"We can't walk the distance to the city's edge," Daine said. "Or even the lake. We are too unprepared."

"Are you sure?" He asked.

"I'm sure," Daine said. She stopped and looked at her feet. "A coin."

She stooped down and retrieved the coin.

"Finding a coin is luck for us," she said, holding it up for him to see.

"And what do we do with his luck?" Miko asked.

"Find place to walk to shore," she said. "If they search us out, they will look for two keepers damp from the river, and we are not. We can go to my family on the Drydocks. There are keepers who stand ready to lend us aid. They should hear what we have to say."

"There is more to say than you know Daine," Miko said.

"It is the way the world is" she said. "What do I not know?"

"Daine," Miko said, letting bow his head. "I was with Gabri at the point of lost and gone."

"Her end is a sadness for us all," She said. "But Gabri was a robot interface. She is gone but she could not be truly been lost for she never truly lived. Her power ebbed and her workings ceased to move. She would not have us grieve for her as if she were a person."

"She said as much," Miko said. But I'm not so sure."

"Grant pardon?" Daine asked.

"I can only speak what has touched my eyes and touched my ears," Miko said. "When her power was almost gone I heard Gabri whisper, 'beautiful'."

Daine considered for a moment. She would know as well as any these were words the robot interface would not have said, not under normal conditions.

"Robots know nothing of beauty," Daine said. "They are not equipped to perceive what is beauty and what is not. To them all simply is. Perhaps she was dysfunctional because of the low amount of power she had remaining."

"Perhaps," Miko said. "Yet I think not. What if something is so beautiful that even a robot interface would see it and know it to be?"

"Like what?" Daine asked.

"Like Paradise," Miko said.

"I do not fathom," she said.

Miko shifted on his feet and put his eyes to look down. He had given more than a day's worth of consideration to this, and the more he considered it the more he knew it to be true.

"I think the true God took hold to Gabri as she was given to lost and set her to a place in paradise. She looked to it as she traversed from this world and spoke her last word at the sight."

Daine looked at him intently for a moment, letting his words make their way through her heart. Her eyes began to glisten at the moment she stood at the point of fathoming. It was an unknown occurrence, yet there was a truth to it which could not be questioned.

"Then God is better by far than anything I could have imagined or thought," Daine said at a whisper.

"Is that not the way God is?" Miko said. The words came so easily to his mouth, he did not even stop to consider how adverse it was to what he had been saying since he had met Daine. She, however, recognized the difference at once.

"You once said God was not," Daine said.

"Once," Miko agreed. "As Gabri portended, I have been given the answer I did not know I required. Now I am truly an initiate into the truth. And there are many from whom I must beg pardon, starting with you I think."

"The wonders on this day are many," Daine said, taking hold of his arm to steady her feet as she walked. "There is no end in sight."

23

"What have you found?" Ryalt asked the moment the duo of young men returned from the tunnel. It was unlike him to be so terse, but he was given to the cause of anxiety. The tunnel was danger to the Shanties, and to the Commons.

"The stage opens for a handful of steps," the first said. "It leads to the round tunnel, as round as anything could be. We followed it to where the light from the Commons was but a small flicker in the distance, and the course stayed true. We could also see the flickering light ahead in the distance."

"Then they could see you," Sharo said. "Did they attempt to hide their light?"

"Not that we could tell," the young man said. "They kept a steady pace which did not waver. They could see us but they were not detered."

"They are not afraid," Ryalt said. His thoughts returned to those who approached often, but though he could say some true things about them, nothing he knew would reveal who it was who approached or if they intended ill or good.

"We could go meet them," the young man said. "They could be kept from the Commons."

Ryalt had thought as much himself. They could send a group of well equipped young men, ready in case of a fight. But he knew if those who approached were from Cityscape they would likely be much better equipped.

"We don't know if they should be stopped," Sharo said. "For now we should put the door to closed, and have three or four of us put to watch in case something ill comes through the door. There may be a handful of them, but not many more."

There were nods from about the room. Ryalt could see they were walking in fear. Sharo knew Cityscape, and she had become an elder in action for how many thought she could match the problem.

"At the same time," Sharo continued. "This is the Commons, there is much to be done, and the business of the day will not do itself."

Ryalt smiled when she said this. She was speaking keeper wisdom, but in the Commons it seemed to fit quite well.

The business of the day was done as usual, but it was done with anxious glances at the wall.

"Perhaps we should seal up that wall and cover it in rock," Kassi said. When Pytre had come to take his turn in the watch at the Commons, she had accompanied.

"A direct route to the old ship, under the shelter of the ground?" Sharo said. "Could anything be more useful?"

"How useful can it be," Ryalt asked, "if the old ship is out of our hands?"

"I would like to know what the city lords intend to do with the ship," Sharo said. "For that matter, I would like to know if they have the slightest glimmer of where we are. We cannot learn such things from here."

The Commons fell to quiet as those who heard those words waited and listened. It was the greatest fear of all who lived in the Shanties, to be discovered. There had only ever been war between the Shanties and Cityscape.

"A keeper should go back," Pytre said. "No one else could uncover the truth while avoiding dire situations."

"A keeper who does not have family," Sharo said, standing up to Pytre. "You are needed here."

"As are you," Pytre said in return. "The Shanties could not continue without you, and more than I would do everything to stop you from traversing forth."

Ryalt agreed right away, but his voice was not the only one. There were several affirmations from about the room.

"Perhaps," Ryalt added, "we should wait until authority Taylo can send word to us. She is already emplaced there and will know the answer to every question we need."

"We don't know what answers we need," Sharo said, looking at the closed entry. "Yet I dare say a number of our answers are drawing near."

#

"They arrive," Sharo said, pulling her hand from the closed door. Her ability to see what was warm was abridged by the wall, and she could only tell a small part of it when she had a hand to it. But no one wanted the doorway to remain open. There was too much risk which could come through. The tunnel was anchored on its other end in a place where citylords were in abundance.

"Open the entry," Ryalt said. "And stand ready."

The doorway was open, flickering light could be seen from within. The best of the Shanties waited in the

Commons, Sharo hoped they all held to the prayer that they would not be needed for any sort of struggle. If Cityscape had indeed found them, it would mean dark days for the Shanties.

Jenk was the first to appear at the entrance. He looked through and smiled, seeing the Commons. The chatter of relief filled the Shanties. Kimi emerged close at his side. Then there were four more, they were strangers to the Commons, and the Shanties. They looked about, eyes wide for the unusual building they emerged in, and for the number of people set to greet them.

"They are keepers," Ryalt exclaimed.

"Of course they are," Sharo said calmly as she approached one of the young women. "Are you not Aysa, of Cathedral district?"

"That I am, ma'am," the girl said. "I remember you from when I was a child."

Sharo smiled. On the one hand, it didn't seem so long ago when she had walked on the streets of Cityscape, but on the other, the children she once knew had grown beyond those early years. The first handful of years seems forever to the young, but a mere breath to their elders.

"Tell us what has occurred and why you are here," Sharo said.

"There was little choice, ma'am" Aysa said. "Miko and Gabri were taken by the house lords and Taylo was needed to confront the situation. The medic Parke was sent to retrieve us, but he was set upon by wicked men and violently put to lost. Rather than remain placed at a cave near the lake where we might be discovered, we chose to traverse to the Shanties where we could stay until such time as we can be returned to Cityscape."

"Send word to Miko's mother," Ryalt said.

"There is no need," Miko's mother Sundi said from nearby in the Commons. She was surrounded by friends who held her against the anxiety she would be feeling. "Do we trust Authority Taylo?"

"With all our hearts, ma'am" Aysa said. "She will do all she can to retrieve your son, up to selling her life for his."

"There is something worse Sharo," Kimi said as she stepped forward. "I heard Gabri say she would be at the end of her power in three days after being removed from the ship, and no one would be able to start her back up."

"Then it is likely Gabri is gone," Sharo said.

The Commons whispered at the thought of a world without Gabri. Only a few of them had conversed with the robot interface, but all of them had heard her stories.

"She will be remembered," Aysa said.

The crises over, many of the initiates started to shuffle out of the Commons, conversing as they walked to their houses in the rubble. Most of the elders stayed about, knowing there would be a need for proper harborage, and some continued discussion over the matter of a tunnel which opened in the midst of the Commons.

"You are welcome in the Shanties for as long as there is need," Sharo said to the keepers. "And the hour is late. Along that wall is well befitted shelter. We will talk about what we do next on the morrow."

"Guests of the Shanties set to sleep in the Commons?" Ryalt said as he stepped forward. "May it never be so."

"Elder Ryalt," Sharo said in her characteristic calmness. He had missed seeing that in her of late. It was good to see its return, even if it was in her disagreeing with him. "They are keepers. It is not untoward, and this corner within a building is a better shelter than they would have in Cityscape. Allow them to be who they are. I am emplaced to assure that every step of proper harboring will be taken."

Ryalt considered it for a moment. Jenne had tried to explain this to her when she had gone to spend the night with Sharo. It made no sense to him, but he was aware of how much more Sharo knew of keepers. Jenne's advice had been to let keepers be who they are, and teach them that in the Shanties people keep for each other. She said it had been the first most important lesson she had learned when she was a new initiate.

"Then allow me to be myself as well," Ryalt said. "If it is not untoward, I would like all of you to gather at my house in the early of the day for breakfast."

"It is well then sir," Aysa said. "We will serve a truly befitted breakfast for you to celebrate our arrival, sir, well worth any recompense you care to pay."

Ryalt was left speechless. The keeper had spoken an answer he did not anticipate, nor one he readily understood. Sharo, who had a hand in either world, recognized the error at once, and Ryalt's surprise. A few more words would be needed to put all to well.

"Aysa," Sharo said, putting her hand to the girl's shoulder. "This is a meal to be served to you."

24

Angla stood at the window and looked. In the narrow space between a pair of towers she could see but a sliver of her building. It was only a place, a setting, yet nothing matched her longing to return to her home, except perhaps for the need Taylo had to discover the true condition of the medic Parke, and if he was found lost and gone, to lay that crime at the feet of councilman Iance.

Taylo would not talk about it except in circumspect. They both knew their every breath was being heard, and she did not want Iance to know how much it weighed on her. Angla knew that was the best course, Iance already knew she was his opponent, but he did not know how much fear he should have.

"You want to return home," Taylo said. It was not so much a question as an observation.

"My home is with my friends," Angla said. "While my tower is not so much more comfortable than this one, it is mine and I would rather be emplaced there."

Every necessary thing was provided by a pair of stoic guardians, and the door was carefully locked each time. Taylo checked the door and the walls on occasion, in case their guards grew lax. Until they did, or some other occurrence conspired to set them to autonomy, there would be no way out.

"I would rather you be home as well," Taylo said. "On the other hand, I desire to speak to the Councilman at length."

The councilman had not visited since the first few moments of being held. He had demanded to know about Miko and about the Shanties. Taylo had told him nothing of what he had wanted to know and only said if she were to have the last word he would be required to pay for his crimes.

In those words she had given him the cause for their continued holding. If Taylo were set free she would take to the pursuit of him for his crimes. Her pursuit would obviously interfere with his ambition to the regency.

If he was given to set them free, or to send them to the Holding, it would be after he had become regent. His position would be more secure at that point. Even then Taylo would not relent. Taylo always had a need to speak for the cause of honesty, even if silence would be the more secure route.

Taylo would wait, and watch, and on occasion sing a song with Angla. Taylo was sure an opportunity would yet reveal itself. Angla kept her words to herself, but could not see forward to any change which did not turn their situation to the worse.

#

There was little time, Iance knew. His schedule kept him moving from the first of the day to the last, he had barely seen the distant sun in a handful of days, and there would be more to it soon enough. He evaded those who watched him and returned to his building circumspectly. With a few moments stolen from meetings and reports, he had a reason to visit his guests one more time.

"Has your comfort been properly seen to?" Iance asked as he stepped into the room. Those who guarded them quickly put the door to closed.

"As well as needed," Authority Taylo said. "Save for our autonomy."

Angla sat still and looked at him. She did not have any words to give to him, and would not probably for some time. It was a pity, if not for Authority Taylo's influence, the young woman could have been a good source of information.

"I am confused," Taylo said. "Why are we here and not in the Authority building or the Holding."

"You have yet to be charged," Iance said. "The events over the circle of the next few days will tell me whether you should be charged officially, or simply put to sentence."

"Then you have been called to account," Taylo said.

"Yes," Iance said. "I have much to say, but perhaps you could tell me more."

"Perhaps not,"Taylo said. "May the decision be a wise one."

In those words Taylo made it clear how she hoped the decision would be. She had no idea of the convolutions of the power politic in Cityscape. Iance paid no mind to her, but instead he turned to Angla, her back already turned to him.

"What befell you at the old ship ten winters ago?" he asked.

Angla suddenly turned to him. In the stead of usual glum fear she smiled.

"Something extraordinary," She said. "I was

convinced that God is."

"God is not," Iance said at once.

Angla only smiled-- a knowing condescending smile. It was as if she knew something which was in front of his eyes, but he could not see it. The genuineness of her smile unsettled him.

"Those were once my very words," Angla said. "But now I know truly."

"You also think God is?" Iance said to Taylo.

"God is," Taylo said. "There is no cause to doubt, and he placed his son to the first world of men where he was put to lost by untoward people. His death paid the recompense for all the wrongs we have done. With the ability of God he returned from lost and gone, and allows for us to traverse alongside God."

"Phaw," Iance said. "Such stories were almost the end of the colony."

"Such stories may turn all of Perma from lost and gone, both inside and out," Angla said. "Even you, if you would but listen."

"I have no need to listen," Iance said. "If God is, it could not do for me what I have done for myself. It is me, and not a silent God who will decide about you once I am regent."

He turned to walk away, keeping the appearance of being in charge. The questions he asked had a low chance of gaining him information, but what he did receive was not expected, not in the least.

#

Iance arrived, as was his plan, at the moment he was required to. He did not want Cityscape to think he was not active and working at his job, and would always be. Every movement as he entered the building had been mapped out and ready. Every word he would soon speak was well coursed. There would be some variation, but he had planned for those, and if he had not, his opponents would be at the mercy of his wit.

The room was filled with mute witnesses, the platform empty save for the three for whom the assembly had been called, the three who dared stand in the place of a regent. The whole of Cityscape had appeared, anxious and excited. Every seat in the hall was filled, and more than a few dawdled outside.

The room fell to silent, even their breaths were hushed as the light over the audience dimmed and those over the stage flared to bright.

"Gentlemen," the moderator said, as was his traditional say. Those who waited had anticipated those words. "Cityscape is in need of a new regent. Those who hope to lead, must have already been a leader. Lay out in front of us all your accomplishments so we may choose from among you which is best."

"I have opened the upper lake at Penitent point," Rugre announced. "The river now has a steady flow and the dry docks are wet again. We can utilize the southern agriscape, there will be food, and work, in abundance."

"All will be well until the Penitent Lake runs dry," Mintel said, calmly. He had obviously known about Rugre's plan and had sought out its drawbacks. "Between the winter next and the one to follow the lake will be empty, and the dry docks will once more be dry beginning on the summer after. I do not see value in a temporary solution to a problem we do not have."

"Nor should you," Iance said. "I salute you

Rugre for at the least the lower lake bed will be filled and can be used to irrigate the southern agriscape. Mintel, I hear your sharp wit, but none of the epic deeds you have accomplished."

"Cityscape has certainly heard of yours," Mintel said. "It is commendable that you have found the ancient colony ship, and have returned the old library to the halls of Cityscape. I'm sure scholars will be reading the knowledge of the first world of men for years to come. But is digging up the past the best course for a regent who will lead us to our future?"

It was a hint, Iance could see, of what Mintel was arranging the conversation to allow him to reveal. But it was also designed to minimize his accomplishments in the minds of those who would soon decide. As much as he did not want to play the defender for himself, Mintel had given him little choice.

"But I have also found the future," Iance said. "Or part of it. In the last God war we reduced the second city on Perma to rubble. Yet I now know there were survivors, there are numerous descendants who still live, hidden. They call it the Shanties, and they live to hide from us."

"Wonders abound," Mintel said. "You have discovered an old library and an old enemy. But I have found an enemy older still.

It was a master stroke. In once sentence Mintel had the attention of everyone in the room. Iance put his eyes to closed, his retort would need to be formed of his finest speechcraft, else he would not keep the day.

"The colony ship," Mintel said. "The one which you found, Iance, held a thousand colonists destined not for this world, but for a world closer yet to the distant sun. Our ancestors lit out to that world but never arrived. They were attacked in route, and ruthlessly abandoned on a world of deadly cold and common quakes. Our colony world, a warmer more hospitable world, was nearer to the distant sun and it was taken from us and sold to others who took our place.

"Those thieves built their colony on our bright warm world. Their decedents yet live on that world, where they have built towers to their skies. I have contacted them. I will establish trade with them. I will be the regent who will stand on the world where we were intended to live."

#

It was over as quickly as it begun. Thunderous applause made it clear how much sway Mintel had, and how fascinating his story of the colony was. Iance's retort was lost in his mouth. The vote was called and the assembly spilled out into the lobby where the winner was surrounded and, by tradition, the losers were hardly spoken to or seen.

Iance saw Raisia, hopefully approaching Mintel. The new regent must have known of her intentions, all of Cityscape did, but Iance was not sure whether he would choose her. Mintel was a master of keeping control of information, even more than Iance had been aware. Elder Hector attended, part of the group at Mintel's side. The elder was searching the crowd, not hiding his haughty delight. Iance thought he was looking for him. He kept the crowd between them, not giving Hector the satisfaction of seeing him defeated.

Iance walked from the hall alone, as alone as he

had ever been, and traversed to his house. He did well to breathe and to put one foot ahead of the other. He was in his rooms before he realized.

Iance locked himself in his furthest room and left the lights to dim. It was unthinkable, a crime against reality.

He should have been chosen regent. In every way he was the better man.

Iance sat in a chair near the center of the room and drank a bitter liquid, considering the sky though the opening of his balcony. Once there had been talk of providing a watcher for those who were not chosen regent. Many of those who aspired to lead took their lives when they failed. There had been talk, but none had ever been watched. New regents secretly appreciated potential opponents eliminating themselves before they could cause some undue commotion.

Iance went to the demarcation to the outside and threw his half-filled cup over the side—a gift for those who waited below for his body. He could see them, the speculators and the curious. They would know he had failed. His aspirations had ended lost and cold. And they waited to perhaps see his fate. One of those, no doubt, would report to Mintel.

Iance sat back down, weary to his bones. He had worked so hard, had made connections throughout Cityscape. He had accomplished tasks no one had thought possible. He had found the old colony ship intact. He had recovered the ancient library. Even more, he had found knowledge of the Shanties, the remainder from the last god war. He suspected they could be found in the ruins of their city, or near it.

He sighed for the weight he carried. If he were remembered at all, he would be known as one who failed.

He was not sure why, but he remembered the words he had recently read in the holy writ, the one he had taken from the hands of Elder Hector. He had thought to only read a few pages, but he continued to read and could not hope to stop. He had read words once spoken to a regent, "Your rulership's days have been counted, and will soon be brought to the last number. You have been measured and have been found insufficient..."

Iance looked through the window and did something he had not done for the turn of many years. He put his face to his hands and cried.

25

Traversing through the water took more effort than Miko thought, it was at the start of early before they arrived on dry ground, and both of them were weary for their effort. Daine found a well befitted nook, away from used streets and in the shadows. They bundled together in her cloak and slept for the turn of a few hours. They slept fitfully, then arose and prepared to jaunt forth at the mid of the day.

Miko tried to keep his eyes forward as he traversed Cityscape with Daine, but it was no easy task. Miko was new to Cityscape and so many wonders pulled at his eyes. Buildings grew taller in Cityscape, tall enough to touch against the edge of the sky.

"Keep the pace friend Miko," Daine said. "If you are to act the part of a keeper you must not play the untraveled child."

"I try," Miko said. "I have not asked after any building for the turn of some time."

"I told you what I would do if you continued to ask," Daine said. "Your actions are not self-directed, therefore you have no cause to be commended."

"Do we yet draw near?" he had to ask.

"We have crossed the threshold of Drydocks district," Daine told him. "But we have more cause than ever to step carefully. There are those who might know where I am from, and they may seek us here."

"We could have just as easily jaunted here under the water," Miko said. "It was foolhardy to jaunt to the place where they would seek us first."

"Not so much," Daine said, keeping her eyes to the streets. "I know this place well. I know who belongs to it, and who doesn't. Like the man at the end of the street."

"The one we walk toward?" Miko asked, looking forward to see the man. He would seem inconspicuous enough, but Daine knew better. It was her place and she knew the man was one who did not belong, like Miko would know someone who was uninitiate to the Shanties.

"If we make any untoward action he will notice," Daine said. "We will simply walk as if there were no cause to fret, and turn our feet to this byway."

Walls stood over the streets, hovering like a new mother over a cranky child with rows of blank windows and designs of solid brick. Miko kept his eyes away from the man who did not belong in places where keepers lived. But his breathing did not become calmer until they turned onto a side street.

"Just down here," Daine said, then stopped short at the top of the rise. Something was strange. She had only glanced over the Drydocks three days before, while not even taking the first step from the cart when authority Taylo stopped to let Aery out. Taylo had formed a plan, and she was the best one to make it happen. Nothing had seemed different at the time, but now, everything she could see was changed.

"The Drydocks are filled with water," she said.

From the crest of the hill they could see the whole of the Drydocks where the tops of buildings barely cleared the water. Daine blinked several times and yet the sight remained in front of her eyes.

"Is Cityscape always so filled with water?" Miko asked.

"Quite the contrary," Daine said, not taking her eyes from the strange sight in front of her. "This is a new thing."

They walked to the edge of the water, Miko's eyes grew large as he looked about with increasing anxiety. His face turned to pale and his breathing became rapid.

"Miko?" Daine asked.

At once Miko turned to run toward the top of the hill they had just traversed. He did not stop until he reached a wall, then he knelt down and emptied the contents of his stomach onto the ground, and continued to do so until well after nothing remained.

After a time Miko began to catch his breath, and he sat down to the side. Daine knelt in front of him. His eyes leaked tears like a rooftop melting frost. She came to realize he had used the sight of his gift to look through the water that covered the Drydocks. It had revealed to him what lay beneath the water.

"Miko," she asked. "What do you see?"

"It's terrible," he said, shaking his head.

Daine let him sit long enough to end his tears and begin to regain most of his usual countenance. She had some idea of what he might have seen, and decided it would be better not to cause him to speak of it.

"We must move along," she said, lifting him to his feet. He followed her sluggishly, but his actions were not too untoward. Many of the keepers she could see were wandering aimlessly.

Daine looked about as she approached a group of

keepers nearby. Among them the keeper named Kene. She had known him for all of her life, and knew to trust him.

"Daine," Kene said as she approached. "I am surprised to see you here."

"I had need to return," she said, keeping herself from saying specific names or events. There were many keepers around, and some of those may have been prone to chatter. "I only just arrived."

"I am so glad you were not here when the water came," Kene said.

"What has occurred?" Daine asked.

"Just as the keepers were returning from fair day's work there was a rumbling," the keeper said. "We thought it a quake at first, but it was wrong. Then water started flowing down mid street, and it grew and without introduction swept half the Drydocks away."

"Have you seen my father?" Daine asked.

"I saw him pulling children from the water," another keeper said. "And turning to retrieve more. I have not seen him since."

Others agreed that he was involved in the rescue efforts, and none had seen him since the waters leveled out.

"You suspect he…?" Daine said.

Kene reached out and put a hand to Daine's shoulder.

"I do," he said. "You have walked with your father and know him as well as any of us. He would not abandon the effort to retrieve us until all were safe or he was lost. He may yet appear, but in the case he does not, my sorrow walks with you."

"Daine," Miko said, moving up to her side. "Is your father lost and gone?"

"It appears so," she said, then turned back to the keepers. "How many of us?"

"More than fifty," Kene said. "We will know better in the turn of a day or so."

Daine nodded and wandered away, looking over the water and thinking of where her father would go when the world was in such a state.

"My sorrow walks with you Daine," Miko said, markedly not looking over the water.

Daine looked at her feet for the moment, then took a deep breath and swallowed. She had begun to understand what Miko had seen when he looked through the water, and how terrible it truly was.

"Keepers are lost by the day and the hour," Daine finally said. "My Mother was lost soon after my arrival. My father was keeping for the rest of us, something his heart was given to. And I must continue to keep for you."

Miko watched behind Daine as she walked about the edges of the new lake. The river spilled into it, and on the far end spilled out into a deeper channel. She kept her words to herself, Miko knew enough not to cause her to speak until she was ready.

"We must try to find Aery," Daine announced.

The two spent the remainder of the day walking carefully about the water, asking about Aery and Daine's father. No one could tell them the first thing about either. As they sun dropped low in the sky and keepers returned from work, Daine asked for recompense from some friends, and purchased a bit of food for them both.

"We have found no one," Miko said.

"We will continue our search for Aery in the first of early in tomorrow," she said. "As for now, our only recompense will be a full night of rest."

"I cannot but agree," Miko said. "My eyes have a cause only to close. I do not fathom why I would be so weary."

"You have done many things," Daine said. "I heard chatter that gifts like you have need to be well fed. We need only find a befitted place and we can rest."

Miko followed her as she walked up a street, looking around at all angles.

"Here is the place," Daine stopped mid street and announced. She looked relieved, as if she had just arrived somewhere.

"Where?" Miko asked.

Daine smiled, he had no cause to fathom the life of a keeper. At the old ship he had never thought to question anything about Cityscape, he had ever been busy holding information back about the Shanties. He did not realize he had said something truly funny.

"This is the place where we will sleep," Daine said, sitting down and leaning up between a building and a set of stone steps. "The wind will not bother us even a little, and in our cloaks we will be warm and safe."

Miko looked up the steps at the building. He still had no comprehension though she had said it all to him.

"We will sleep inside here?" Miko asked.

"No," Daine said. "That is a factory where keepers sometimes are employed. We only live in hard sheltering during the dark of winter. I meant to say, here, where I stand, is where we will sleep."

Slowly it became clear to Miko that Daine meant for them to sleep on the street, outside under the stars and the dark of the sky.

"Such things cannot be," Miko said. "You mean for us to sleep on the ground, in the street?"

"Such things are Miko," Daine said. "Do you find it so hard to fathom?"

"I cannot see the cause," he said. "You are left to the streets when buildings like this are left empty in the night, and could be used for the benefit of those who are employed here in the light of the day. There would be little trouble to it."

Daine looked up at the building.

"Perhaps it could be," she said. "But such things are not done. Sit here Miko, we will unravel our cloaks and gather them together to give us a double layer against the chill of the night."

Miko hesitated, but his weariness was by far stronger than he was. He would not be accustomed to sleeping close together with family and siblings like the keepers did in the circle of every day. Daine settled him to a place in the corner, aside where she sat with her back on him. Even separated by layers of two cloaks, she could sense Miko felt like the awkward boy.

"What will be do if we cannot find Aery on the morrow?" Miko asked.

"Do not weary your mind with the worries of the morrow," Daine said. "The day has all the worry it needs."

"That sounds like something from the Shantyway," Miko said as he sat next to her, careful not to actually touch her.

"Do not speak of that here," Daine said. "Too many ears hear what they are prone to chatter. You are to be only a friend from the Cathedral district and nothing else."

"Then that is what I will be," Miko said.

"We will keep for you as there is need," Daine said. "I have no thought of what we might do if we cannot find Aery. Perhaps we could traverse to the Cathedral district. It is not an easy jaunt, and we have precious little coinage."

"Perhaps I can work," Miko said. "I have put my hand to labor in the… at my home."

"There are differences you have yet to be aware of," Daine said. "There is peril in that plan."

"But that is a trouble for the morrow," Miko said.

"That it is," she agreed.

Miko was asleep in the turn of a few moments. Daine looked out from her cloak as other keepers wandered in and found befitted places about them, filling the street from start to end. It was the way it had been from her earliest memory. Families gathered together and spoke in hushed voices as they opened their cloaks to each other, gathering the youngest to the center. Old friends gathered each into the other's cloak and mulled over the actions of the day. She allowed herself, at the end of it, to miss her father. He should have been with them, she needed him more now than ever. As tears touched her face she recognized how befitted it was for her to be in this place. There was nowhere else on all of Perma where she could touch her father's memory so well.

Miko snorted and shifted in the cloaks. He was from the Shanties, and he could not see the simple beauty of sleeping under the open sky, he espied only lack of shelter and dire situation.

That view could change quickly under the turn of a few days more, as he played at being a keeper.

26

It was late in the mid of the day. Taylo had been standing at the window of their holding room while Angla paced for impatience. They were given to the growing realization that while events continued in the world around them, little of it would touch them.

Taylo looked out over Cityscape. They were a distance above the level of the world, but even from half into the sky some few things could be noticed by one who had given to such pursuit. The movements of those walking below had changed from telling of anxious anticipation to resolute purpose.

"They've chosen," Taylo said.

"So soon?" Angla asked. "The last choosing took the turn of ten days."

"In those days the choice was complicated," Taylo said. "Each of the candidates had broadcast lies about the others."

"Have they chosen Iance?" Angla asked.

It was the question Taylo had been asking herself. She knew of the candidates, and had in mind which she would choose, especially after she had walked with Iance for any measure. But she did not walk in the circles of those who held sway. From the last she had heard, the choosing could have gone in any direction.

"I cannot tell from here," Taylo said. "I trust we will know soon enough."

"Soon enough," Angla said. They both heard a shuffle in the outer room which told of one entering the floor. Their room was not made to be a part of the Holding, and did not block every sound, and Taylo could turn many sounds into information.

Two of Iance's men entered the room, another watched them from the door.

"Wear this," one said simply, giving Taylo a mask which covered her eyes. He did not wait to see whether she put it on, he was already giving the same article to Angla.

"Do we?" Angla asked. The man had backed away, waiting to see whether they complied. It seemed the mask was required for whatever the next step might be.

"I don't see why not," Taylo said.

Taylo had considered running at that moment, but knew it was pointless. The man at the door was set to stop them, and even if he failed, they would not step foot beyond the limits of the floor before they were caught by the others. She could possibly fight her way out, but Angla could not. Taylo would not leave without her.

After the mask was in place they took her arms and bound them and checked to see if the mask was secure. Taylo had known they would, and thus had not bothered the attempt to put it on lightly.

She was pulled from the room by tugging on her wrist straps. Whatever was to be done with them, it would not be done in the rooms of Iance.

"Are we to be put to our leisure?" Angla asked. The question was unanswered.

"Taylo?" Angla asked as they were guided up steps.

"I'm ahead of you," Taylo said.

"What is to be done with us?" Angla asked.

"I do not know," Taylo said. She had her guesses, but chose not to speak them. They could be brought to the Holding, or there could be a more dire consequence in store for them. She suspected the latter, but chose not to let the men see her fear. Speaking her suspicions would only cause Angla unneeded anxiety.

Presently they were put into the back seat of a cart, which launched straightway. Taylo could not discern its direction, but kept track of the time. They had traveled far enough to be deep into Cityscape on one side, or out into agriscape on the other.

The cart landed and they were taken out and put to the ground, sitting back to back. They were in a place where grass grew long and stiff, the ground held to some of the chill from the night before.

Taylo had heard of such things being done in Cityscape, but not for generations. Inconvenient people were ofttimes put to lost, and any attempt to investigate soundly blocked. It was not her desire to be famous for the revival of such practice.

"Angla," Taylo said. "I think this is a befitted time to sing."

Angla started singing, one of her favorite songs which had to do with God and how he gave a care. Taylo sang along, awaiting the sound of gunshot to herald their end. At one time the prospect would have left her with nothing but fear, it would have controlled her, but now not as much. She had heard of paradise which God invented for his own and at the moment could only manage curiosity about what it would be like.

She did have a few questions she would ask God when they met face to face, and she wondered whether the medic Parke would be at hand, assuming Iance had not lied about his outcome.

The song was finished, and yet nothing occurred.

"Taylo?" Angla asked.

"Patience," Taylo said. She took a deep breath and struggled to her feet, expecting to be thrown back to the ground.

Nothing happened.

"Angla," Taylo said. "Can you stand?"

Taylo heard struggling for a moment.

"I hardly think so," Angla said.

"Be still," Taylo said, walking until her feet touched Angla. "Let me help."

Taylo sat down with her back to Angla and found where her hands were bound. Then she followed the bindings with her fingers until she could feel the knots. It took the turn of many moments, but finally she pulled the first cord free. After that it was little time before Angla had her arms free.

"Taylo!" Angla sounded as if she were surprised.

"Are we alone?" Taylo asked.

"Yes," Angla said. "And look!"

Taylo took the mask from her face. At first the world was blurred, but then as Taylo blinked her eyes clear she looked around.

"The grassy area," Taylo whispered. They were in the shadow of the Holding in the very place where Iance had surprised them. It was mid of late, the distant sun had begun its pilgrimage down the sky.

"My cart is not here," Taylo said, looking at the

place where she had placed her cart not too many days past. "The authority would have taken it back. I wonder if my disappearance has been investigated or ignored."

"I'm sure Iance made the investigation fade away," Angla said. "Why have we been let go?"

It was the question. Taylo started wondering of it the moment she realized they had been abandoned. She could not make sense of it, except to conjecture they were no longer a threat.

"I think Iance failed in his bid for the regency," Taylo said as she put to the dirt the last of her bonds.

"What do we do?" Angla said.

"My rooms are not far," Taylo said. "Shall we walk?"

"It is a fair day for it," Angla said and took Taylo by the arm. They quickly entered the lane which traversed the side of the river on the way down to Dryscape.

"There's water in the river," Angla noted.

"I suspect one of the candidates opened the river," Taylo said. "It would be something impressive for the house lords."

They walked to the bridge and started to cross. The water filled the banks of the once dried river, and flowed slowly on its path.

"If this flows this way," Angla said. "Would it not flow to the Drydocks?"

Taylo stopped in her tracks. She had not considered it, a testament to the addled condition of her mind. Taylo let go of Angla and ran to the other side of the bridge, barely slowing to turn.

The river once flowed, as they had all learned in

their scholarship, into the Drydocks where boats were kept and commerce was done. But now keepers lived at the Drydocks.

Taylo stopped at the crest of the rise, Angla caught up to her moments later.

The street which once led the way to the center of the Drydocks led only to a mid-sized lake, covering where people once slept.

"Do not look at me," a voice said from the periphery of the lane. It was a man who spoke, someone familiar to Taylo

"I am not looking," Taylo said, consciously turning toward Angla.

"You are being closely watched," the voice said. "Did you not see the tell-tale flash of ruby light on you as you walked?"

Taylo sighed. She had seen it, but had failed to gather its significance. It was high level surveillance, something she should have anticipated.

"We are watched even now?" Angla asked. "But to what purpose?"

"To note who you contact," the voice said. "I for one would rather avoid being sent to Holding for a conversation."

"And you are right to say so," Taylo said. "How many keepers were lost in the water?"

"Too many," the man said. "I suspect the device is very small, but would be befuddled by being doused in water."

"There is water here aplenty at the foot of this lane," Taylo said. "Much is given, elder Kene."

"And much is appreciated," the keeper answered.

"Leave swiftly once you have drowned the devices. Those who watch your every move will not be happy when they are perplexed."

"Understood," Taylo said. She was already walking with Angla to the water's edge. They both ran in straightway, feeling the bracing of the cool water. Taylo made sure they both properly wet their hair, one of the more likely places for the device to be installed. Then they walked up out of the water and changed their direction.

"Not the most comfortable of escapes," Angla noted as they crossed yet another lane. Angla was probably more uncomfortable than Taylo, and she wanted to complain, but she would not say more than she already had. They would soon reach Taylo's rooms. The clothes she had would not fit Angla well, but they would be dry.

"Stop," Taylo said, putting her arm out to keep Angla from walking out into the lane. "My building is being watched."

Angla glanced around the edge of the wall, seeing the building where Taylo lived. She would not see the three men Taylo had seen. There would be more, she looked around trying to see signs of them, and holding to hope they had not been found so easily.

Angla put her back to the wall and adjusted her shoes again. The water had caused them to stretch at one point, then as they dried, to stiffen.

"There are ways into my tower," Angla said. "No one knows of them but me, even Chanta only knows of one. Do you think they would have secreted someone to the inside?"

"With your security net in place they would dare not," Taylo said. "I will lead us away from those who would watch for us and then you can lead us into your tower."

"Fair enough," Angla said. "They would still be watching from the outside."

"Yes they would," Taylo said. "We must have a care not to be seen."

Taylo walked them back the way they had approached, then around to the towers where Angla once lived. Once they reached the edge of the district, Angla led Taylo unerringly to an alley where in a small alcove she pushed a pattern into the stones of the wall and a panel opened.

"No one has been here," Angla said as she closed the door behind them.

"Not even you," Taylo said, taking note of the dust on the floor. "Not for some time."

"Secrets are best left sleeping until they are needed," Angla said. "The way to the right is the one we need, but I feel the need to walk further in and circle back."

"It is best to be safe," Taylo said, following Angla, but taking curves and walking in random directions on her own.

The way to the right was a small narrow way which hardly seemed large enough for a child to pass. Yet both Angla and Taylo fit in handily, and found the spiral stairs which led them upward, well past the level of the ground.

"I did not know the first thing about this," Taylo noted as they continued to climb.

"No one does," Angla said. "Chanta didn't know there was more than the one I taught her."

"How many are there?" Taylo asked.

Angla looked back at her and in the dimness of the stairwell gave a small smile, obvious in her intent not to answer. She turned to a section of the wall that looked like any other, and opened a doorway. Many of the towers, so the rumor went, were filled with secrets.

"Where are we?" Taylo asked.

"The scholarship room," Angla said. "If I'd only known of this when I was young..."

"If I remember what you were once like," Taylo said. "Your scholarship would have suffered."

"This way," Angla said.

She led them to a hallway, then down two sets of steps to another level. Then she walked to the left and into a room which was dimly lit. It was set up as a sleeping room with storage along one wall.

"We'd best not increase the lighting," Angla said. "It could be seen."

"Which room is this one?" Taylo asked. She had been in Angla's rooms, more than once, and this was not one of them.

"Chanta's," Angla said.

"She's not here," Taylo said.

Angla went to the clothing storage and pulled out a couple of cloaks and some other clothing.

"We will leave as keepers," Taylo said.

"It seems most right," Angla said. "Though I want to check every room."

"I do as well," Taylo said. "However, if Chanta was aware of our situation she would have disappeared back to the keepers where she would be safe."

Angla finished dressing and stepped toward the doorway.

"Do you think she abandoned the tower in time?"

"I have hope she did," Taylo said. She would have liked to offer more comfort, but could not speak with confidence without speaking in falsehood. "She knew to steal herself away should anything happen to us."

"She is clever and has her ears to every bit of chatter in Cityscape," Angla said. "I trust in hope that she is well."

Taylo followed Angla as she walked through her tower, looking into every empty room and every lonely hallway.

"We cannot contact our friends," Taylo said. "They will look for us among them."

"I know," Angla said. "Where shall we go?"

"We must leave Cityscape," Taylo said.

Their eyes met. There was an understanding between them. They both knew there was only one place where they could go, but they would not put the first word to it, not yet.

"You are correct," Angla said, putting a hand to the wall for just a moment. "And we may never have leave to return."

"I suspect this is what Iance had in mind when he let us go," Taylo said. "We would discover we were watched and choose to leave Cityscape. That is why we were marked. He wants to follow us to where we would go."

"Are we sure we are no longer marked?" Angla

asked.

"I can be sure," Taylo said. "Our next stop is the kitchen for a quick meal, and there I will use your communication equipment to assure we are not being traced. I must beg your pardon, I will leave a mess."

"There is no reason to beg my pardon," Angla said. "I doubt I will ever see this tower again."

"My sympathies walk with you," Taylo said.

"You will walk with me," Angla said. "I have no need to grieve for a building-- I walk among friends."

27

Sharo walked the Shanties under the mid summer sky.

It had been more than a handful of days in which she was entombed in the Commons. She was thankful for the time to step aside and rethink parts of her life. She was thankful to be present when the group of student emerged from the wall.

However, there were other considerations on this day. The time for sitting aside had gone. On this day she had need to converse with a friend.

Sharo stopped at the door. Too long she had been entrenched with the need to knock at a door, even the door of a dearest friend. The motions were so unthinking when she chose not to do them she stood in front of the door, unable to proceed. If she knocked once more Sharo would hear no end to the chiding of Jenne.

"Will you stand at the door for the day," Sharo head Jenne say from behind her. "Or will you enter to a place where you are more than family?"

Sharo turned, knowing she had been caught. There was no need to explain, Jenne was well aquainted with Sharo's problem with the door.

"I have need to speak to Joska," Sharo said.

"Yes you do," Jenne agreed, then walked around Sharo to enter through the front door of her house. Sharo followed.

Joska was much as Sharo expected to find him. Playing at the hearth near the warmth of the fire well. It was his most favored place. Jenne nodded, and walked from the room. She would be nearby, but would not interfere.

"Are you warm and well Joska?" Sharo asked.

"As warm as can be, Keeper Sharo," Joska said. His response was not as open as it once was. Sharo could not complain. She had abandoned him. She sat down just to the side of him. He was aware of her, but appeared to give her little notice.

"I must beg your pardon friend Joska," She said.

The young one stopped for a moment, then moved steadily to put his toys aside. Sharo knew Jenne, and she would not tolerate his leaving her hearth cluttered. Sharo waited patiently, knowing his acceptance, or refusal would follow in the turn of a few moments. If his acceptance was not heart felt their friendship would suffer.

He sat down next to her on the hearth.

"My pardon you have, keeper Sharo," Joska said. "But I do not yet understand what occurred."

Sharo suspected he would ask such a question. It was not untoward, but yet it did not have an easy answer. Her understanding of the situation was limited as well.

"I did not act to cause hurt in you," Sharo said. "I would not willingly put you to harm or even cause you anxiety. Your injury was an echo of one who had much the same injury, one I once knew. Many memories I had neglected returned, and many of those were not happy."

Joska nodded. He was a thoughtful child, one who sometimes could see beyond the words he was told. Jenne had tried to allow him less than the whole of the truth on more than one occasion, but he readily walked beyond it.

"Did he intend to hurt you?" Joska asked.

It was not a question Sharo had thought to answer, but the answer was not complicated.

"No," she said. "He did not."

"And yet he did," Joska said. "How does that happen, when no one has intentions to hurt anyone, and yet they do?"

"It is the way the world is when it is not under the hand of God,"Sharo said.

Joska put his hand to her shoulder.

"It is a wonder God can take so many bad things and turn them to good," he said. "He arranged all so you would be placed in the Commons to greet our students as they returned, and to see the others as they approached."

"I suppose that could be true," Sharo said.

"You know it is," Jenne said, entering the room with three cups of tea on a tray. "Your time in the Commons began with sorrow, but it was filled with the love of friends and family. God saw fit to allow you time for your sorrow, and put you in place for the benefit of our students, and to benefit us all."

"Will wonders ever stop?" Sharo asked.

"Do you truly need to ask?" Jenne said.

#

In the short time the keeper students had been in the Shanties, they had taken to sleeping in the Commons with Sharo. Some of the other keepers who had come to the Shanties in the turn of years before had joined them to make a well numbered group. They happily chattered away so no keeper was unaware of any event worth a mention in their new city, and none was unaware of any keeping in need to be done.

The Shanties had taken pause at the sight of it, but then moved as one to make the Commons as well befitted a place to rest as any keeper could ever dream of. In the day the keepers worked as hard and as well as anyone, and most all of them marveled at the amount of recompense given to them.

Ryalt entered the Commons in the late of early. Pytre stood before the steps, instructing the keeper students sitting about him on how to converse with the Shanties, and where their eager hands could find befitted work.

"Elder Ryalt," Pytre said as he approached. "Fare you well?"

"Quite well," he answered. "When you have a moment..?"

"Moments are many," he said. "Allow me to finish what I am saying, then I will have both ears to hear you."

Pytre turned back to the young keepers and answered a couple of incidental questions. They were filled with energy, these keepers, and did not know anything outside of constant work. When they were finished he turned to converse with Elder Ryalt.

"Have you heard about the meal I served these students?" Ryalt asked.

"I've heard much of the breakfast you served to these young people by all in attendance save you," he said. "I suspect your view will be unique."

Ryalt had mentioned something of that day to a

number of his friends, most of whom were as puzzled as he. The best advice echoed with every telling, it was clear to all if he wanted to fathom keepers he would need to converse with a keeper. He partly expected to find Sharo in attendance, but she was not to be seen. Pytre, however, was once a keeper as well.

"Jenne tried to tell me what might occur, but I could not listen enough to what she said," Ryalt said. "I've never seen the like, nor could I have imagined. We prepared a befitted table, worthy of proper harboring in the Shanties. Yet as Jenne and I served the meal both Aysa and Emne were crying. We did everything to fulfill their needs, yet it only made them more distressed. Finally they said they were crying for the cause of our kindness to them. Have they never been treated well?"

"Not so well," Pytre said. "It is unheard of for a keeper to be put to sit at a table, and then served a meal by the hands of a home owner. They have never seen such kindness, not for them. Keepers are given to understand from their very first days how they are to expect no consideration. Nothing is given to them unless it is earned."

"I don't know if I can do something like this again," Ryalt said. "It was unsettling."

"I hope you can sir," he answered. "I hope we all do as you have done. The kindness you do for them now will live in their hearts even if they do not fathom it for the circle of many years. They must learn it is proper for them to be given kindness and respect in the same manner they give it."

Ryalt took his words into himself, giving his heart time to consider. He glanced at the edge of the

Commons as they walked toward it. A metal bar now held closed the door and a watchful young man stood nearby.

"It is still hard to fathom there was a door in the Commons unknown," he mentioned.

"I'm sure many things are unknown," Pytre said, "for the time until they are known. We should learn that no place is ever secure and complete and be watchful about what is around every corner."

It was when they were traversing by the door that a set of sharp taps sounded from within. For a moment they both looked at the door, wondering whether they had really heard a knock, but then it was repeated.

"Cityscape lords have found us!" Ryalt said as he took a step backward. "I will call out the initiates."

"Wait," Pytre said approaching the door and nodding at the young men to remain at the ready.

"You don't mean to open it?" Ryalt said.

"I do," he said.

"You'll let them in!" Ryalt said.

"If they are opponents," Pytre said. "They surely would not knock."

Ryalt stood back for the moment, but considered Pytre's words for a moment and knew they were true. There would be no good way to transport an army though the tunnel, the way was narrow and the first to step through could be stopped cold and would be a hindrance for the ones who followed.

There was commotion in the tunnel, Pytre stood at the entry looking intently in, only now letting himself appear anxious. There was fire inside, a torch quickly extinguished upon meeting the illumination from the

Commons.

"Authority Taylo," Pytre said as two people walked through the opening, blinking for the increased lighting of the Commons. With the second blink Taylo put her arms around Pytre for a hearty embrace. The two had been friends from the time before Ryalt had met them on the colony ship. If the chatter was true, each had kept the life of the other in the most dire of circumstances.

"Angla," Ryalt said. When he first met Angla she was little more than a child and could barely see beyond her own face. He had heard news of her, but had not seen her since those early days. The version of her before him had left the child behind and was more woman. "I see you finally traversed to the Shanties."

Angla had wanted to see the Shanties from the moment she had found where Ryalt was from. She had filled his day with questions as they waited on the old ship for Sharo to return from Cityscape.

"What has occurred?" Pytre asked. "Why are you here?"

"We have need to stay away from the Cityscape for some time," Taylo said. "We have both been marked as enemies by a power filled city lord, and would be sent to the Holding or worse if we were found."

"We heard chatter that you had gone to retrieve Miko and Gabri from the Holding," Pytre said.

"We did," Taylo said. "Keeper Daine was sent into the edifice to retrieve him. By all accounts they were clear of the Holding but we were taken by councilman Iance and held until the day he failed in his bid to be regent. We do not know what has become of them, there was no chatter of it anywhere."

Angla, standing by, touched Pytre on the shoulder.

"Pytre, who did you hear this chatter from?" Angla asked. "The students from the Shanties who traversed into the tunnel were not aware Miko had been taken by the house lords."

"There are four students from Cityscape who did know," Ryalt said. "They had seen the medic Parke set upon my evil men who put him to lost, so they chose to traverse to the Shanties rather than fall into those same hands. For the past few nights they have lived here in the Commons."

"They are safe," Angla said. "I trusted they were well, but I had no way to know. It is most befitted that they are here."

"...And the medic Parke has fallen," Taylo said. "Councilman Iance hinted of it, but would say no more. I should not be surprised."

Pytre reached out to put a hand to Taylo's shoulder. He had heard of a connection between Taylo and Parke, and had held to hope it would turn to the best for them. In the moment Pytre looked to be the most touched by the loss, but Ryalt knew Taylo, she was as strong as anyone. Her grieving would be done in a more private setting.

"I should take word to Sundi about what we know of her son," Ryalt said. "She has been waiting for some chatter of Miko."

"I will accompany," Taylo said. "I can tell what I have seen with my own eyes and may be able to lend some comfort."

The two were ready to go out into the Shanties when a voice behind them put them to stillness.

"Authority Taylo, it may be that you are one in need of comfort, even if you choose to hide it."

"Kassi," Taylo said, and returned the warm embrace Kassi initiated. "I have looked forward to seeing you again."

"And now you have," Kassi said, turning to put her arm around Angla. "I am glad you both, at least, are safe and well."

"And you truly are growing another child," Angla said, putting a hand to Kassi destended tummy. "I had thought the chatter could not be true."

"True enough," Kassi said. "Taylo, go on your errand with elder Ryalt. I will converse with Angla until you return. We will arrange for your harborage. As much as I would want to have you as guests in our house, my children have yet to learn how to sleep all at the same time, and two of them are prone to rise before the sun touches the sky. You would find the rest you truly require if you stay in Sharo's house."

"Sharo has a house?" Angla asked. She appeared surprised.

Kassi smiled. Ryalt realized it must seem strange to her, for a keeper to have a place to live, a true house. It was a thought she would need to change if she were to spend any time at all in the Shanties. Setting keepers on a lower level would not be welcome.

"She does not use it of late," Kassi said. "She stays here, among the keepers in the Commons."

28

The distant sun put its edge to the sky, announcing the first of early. Miko looked out from his cloak to note how the keepers stirred around them. He was emplaced in his own cloak, but set to the side of Daine. He thought it untoward to share a cloak, them being young and not walking together. Daine had relented, though she would have them together for the sake of shared warmth. She did insist on being at his side.

Daine had already stood up out of her cloak and had started to fold it about her shoulders. It seemed no matter how early he awoke, she was already awake and chiding him for his laziness.

"Awake sleepy head," Daine said as he started out of his cloak. He had not practiced it all his life, so oftimes he took extra time to fold his cloak around him. "The keeping of the day will not do itself."

Miko could not help but stretch as he stood up, evidently it was something keepers were not given to do. Miko did not fret over it. Most of the keepers around them knew he was not, but were befitted enough to keep their chatter among themselves.

"I will be at the crèche again today," Daine announced. "For the cause of my age and the loss of my father the keepers reserve some coinage for me."

"Not overmuch," Miko said. "If we do not find Aery we will need more."

"When you are employed in labor for

recompense," Daine said. "You may then complain."

"I did not speak a complaint," Miko said. "I spoke a strategy."

Miko would spend the morning helping an elder keeper by traversing water from the once dry docks to an old set of troughs he used to grow foodplants. What he did there was not labor for recompense, save for the promise of a share of the plants after they were grown. Miko knew he would be gone by then. But he had seen the need, and had the will to step in and help.

"And I do not complain about your wasted labor," Daine said. "Let us walk into the day, and speak later of what may be done on the morrow."

#

"Not too much water, boy," the keeper said. Miko had been about plants for much of his life, anticipating the time when he could work more constantly with them. It would be his occupation for the day if only he were home, in that place he would not even name in his thoughts. Here he was the untrained initiate, and was told how to do what he had done for most of his life, and watched to assure he did it well.

"No," Miko said as he poured. "Only the perfect amount."

He watched the water as it settled into the dirt, and then as the roots of the plants began to draw it up. It was a patient task, the plants did not have any cause for hurry and too much water at a time was not good for them.

Miko had never really considered plants from the inside. He had never considered their cause for he thought he knew they had none. God had made the plants, and everything they did was invented by him. As he watched minute vapor struggle into the air from a close crop of leaves, he wondered how he had never seen how vastly complicated plants truly were.

"All is well here," Miko said. "I will return in the last of the day to add water to the plants for the night."

"Much is appreciated," the elder keeper said as Miko made his way down the lane.

As Miko entered the crèche the children had settled down for a mid of the day snack, which would be followed by a time for rest.

"Friend Miko," Daine said. She had named him such to belie the chatter that they were growing closer by the day, and each would soon choose the other. "Fare you well?"

"Well enough," Miko said. Then he moved closer in to her in order to keep their words between them. "I have the remainder of the day. I can search the remnant of the Drydocks for Aery.

"If he has taken to keeping," Daine said, "he will not be where we look until the mid of late in the day."

"Then what shall I do?" Miko asked.

"Read something from the holy writ to the children," Daine said, pointing at a book set on a table.

Miko looked at the book, a mirror of the one on his mother's table. Miko had begun to realize how many copies of this book Gabri must have made, and yet they were still scarce. It reminded him that Gabri would no longer be making copies of the holy writ, and he wondered how the need would be filled.

"I thought this book was not allowed in Cityscape," he finally said.

Daine smiled and turned to clean a table nearby.

"Then do not read too loudly," she said. "No one has said it is forbidden, yet it is not always tolerated."

Miko picked up the book, the children had already gathered into a circle.

"Then I will read something befitted," Miko said. "In the case I have no consent to read tomorrow."

#

"Miko," Daine said after the rest time had ended. "It would be a good time for you to go to the hiring corner."

Miko had done this the day before. The early keepers would be returning, and there was a chance he might find Aery returning from his labor.

"If I find him I will bring him here," Miko said, taking his leave.

The children waved him to the door before turning back to their activity.

At first Daine had hesitated to give him leave to wander the Drydocks alone, but the keepers tolerated him and the house lords, what few he had seen, ignored him like the rest of the keepers.

Miko stood to the side of a building, trying to look at the whole area while being beneath notice.

"Are you looking for a keeper in specific," and elder keeper said. Miko had seen the man walk about him, but had thought him on his way.

"I seek a friend," Miko said. "His name is Aery."

"Friend of Aery," the man said. "He has not been seen here since the first of summer."

Miko looked at the man, wondering how much he knew, or did not know. It would untoward of him to mention things he should not. He had to consider his answer with care.

"I heard chatter he was in the company of authority Taylo," Miko said. "She intended to leave him in this place."

"Then much has happened," the man said.

"Very much," Miko said.

"I will spread this chatter through the remnant of the drydocks," the man said. "Perhaps someone has seen Aery."

"If you hear of anything you can let me know..." Miko started. He considered how he might be difficult to find. The two of spent their evening walking through different streets.

"You will be found in the company of Daine," the man said. "She is keeping for the children today."

It seemed the man knew more than he was saying. He nodded, deciding he had a trust for the man, even though he had already decided what would remain unspoken. If one does not want something to be heard, it is best not to put it to words, even in the company of those who are trusted.

"Much is given," Miko said. "Much is appreciated."

Miko stayed his place until the return of keepers turned to a trickle. There had been no sighting of Aery, and Miko wondered again if their fellow student had been caught in the water when the Drydocks flooded. It would be a circumstance most untoward. He took a last look about and returned to the place where Daine was.

It should not have surprised him to find the elder keeper he had conversed with earlier talking to Daine.

He gave a nod to Miko as he walked away.

"Any word?" Miko asked.

"Kene has told me Aery was seen being dropped off by Taylo at the edge of the Drydocks on the same day we... renewed our acquaintance," Daine said. "But no one knew where he jaunted from there. The best of it is he was not seen in or near the water when it came."

"So," Miko said. "We don't know where he is."

"That is correct friend Miko," Daine repeated. "We do not know where he is. We simply have hope that he remains well."

"Then our next step is to keep," Miko said. "And gain the recompense we need in order to traverse to Cathedral district where we have friends."

"Perhaps," Daine said. She had worried about his keeping from the first, but it was the only plan which made any sense. Miko did not share her dread. He knew how to keep his head down and his hands on his work.

He would soon prove to her how much his plan was not untoward.

#

"This is a most untoward occupation," Daine said as she accompanied Miko to the hiring corner. Though they had conversed about the plan late into the night, Miko had chosen a direction and he would not be dissuaded.

"It is what makes the most sense," Miko said, allowing his cloak to cover only part of his back. It was something any keeper would know not to do. As eager as Miko was to play the part of a keeper, he did not study it well. "We might traverse to Cathedral district, but not without eating. If we are to eat we must work and there is little pay to be had in you keeping for the little ones."

"I portend some ill-fated recompense," Daine said. "There may be those who still seek us, you in particular."

"The turn of a day," Miko said. "Perhaps two and we will have earned all we need."

They stepped further toward the new area where house lords did their hiring. The old hiring place remained under the water. This area was the staging platform of a factory which no longer was used. Miko had spoken of the recompense given for labor in the Shanties. He did not understand he would not find such amounts given to keepers in all of Cityscape.

"You have yet to be a keeper," She said. "The recompense you earn will not be so large."

"Stay close," a man said to them as they stepped onto the platform. "Something is ill-befitted."

Daine should have noted it earlier. Keepers milled about on the platform, ready to find keeping in need to to done, yet no house lord carts hovered about in search of labor. The air was clear as if there weren't a house lord to be found anywhere.

"This is most unusual," Daine said.

"We are here," Miko said. "Other keepers are here."

"Yet there are no house lords ready to hire us for work," Daine said. She looked deep into his eyes and spoke in a quiet voice. "Could they have found us?"

"If they find us," Miko said. "I will walk from you and then let them retrieve me. You will hide among the other keepers and never be seen."

"Miko," she said. "I cannot let you..."

Then carts whispered into view. They were not the usual house lord carts, these were labelled for specific use. The keepers mumbled to one another, wondering how they would gain their recompense this day if there was no one to hire them.

"The authority," Daine whispered, holding to Miko's arm all the tighter.

Handfuls of authority approached on foot from all directions. Daine had never seen so many gathered in one place before. She had grown accustomed to the appearance of Taylo, but not so many of the authority together, and showing little regard to the keepers. Daine went weak with fear.

"Keepers," a voice from an authority cart announced. "We have need of labor. All of you follow."

The keepers followed, not knowing anything better to do, Daine and Miko in the midst of them.

"They may not have found us," Miko said in aside.

"But for the authority to hire so many keepers at once, and to fail to negotiate at all," Daine said. "What is the sense of that?"

As they walked along the authority kept pace from the sides. They spoke little, but watched carefully, not allowing any of the keepers to go.

"Continue to walk," a young authority said. "We have much distance to cover."

"Where do we jaunt to?" a keeper asked.

The authority looked at her, perhaps considering whether she had asked a question he could answer.

"We will go past the edge of Cityscape," the

authority said. "Into the grassland beyond."

It was a fair long jaunt. The authority did not approve of the keepers talking, so they kept their chatter to a minimum. In due time they progressed past the end of Cityscape. The occasional house lord would stand out in the street and watch after them, more than a few seemed concerned yet none spoke the first word.

"What is out here?" Miko asked as they continued to walk.

"Nothing," Daine said back. "The lake is to the northern area and if we were to continue this way we would miss the southernmost edge of the tall trees."

"Perhaps they intend to establish another section for Cityscape," a keeper guessed.

"Using the authority to supervise?" Daine asked. "There is no sense to it. Something occurs and we have not heard the first chatter of it."

Near the mid of the day the keepers crested a low hill, and in the valley below was a mass of keepers, more than anyone had ever seen. They were surrounded on all sides by the authority, and in the midst of them other authority were supervising in all manner of tasks.

"Keep moving," one of the authority said. "For the turn of a few days you will be doing what is named training."

"Training for what?" one of the keepers managed to ask.

They were given no answer.

29

Sharo had gone from the Commons in a jaunt to the demarcation. She had not been there in some time. From her vantage she would see the desert, and a hint of the shallow where the ceramicists Amei and Purne worked. On occasion Jenne would join them there, she had been once an echo to Amei as she learned the craft. This had been set into place before Sharo had arrived in the Shanties. Amei often talked about how Jenne had kept her life in the midst of coldest winter. Jenne dismissed such talk and would only say that Amei had restored hers.

Sharo glanced over the sand again. With the concern authority Taylo had brought, perhaps it would be well to have someone to watch most of the time. Cityscape could have found the Shanties were still inhabited, and if history had its say, it would not be tolerated.

So long the Shanties had stood safe and warm, without a bit of change, but with the introduction of a pair of lost keepers a slow curve had started. Now many changes occurred. Sharo wondered if there would be more, and whether they would turn to the worst.

"God, keep for us, for the turn of the days are uncertain," she said out loud.

Sharo sighed, then went her way into the Shanties. The workers had requested her help in the mid of the day on the street of homes they were clearing and preparing.

The work progressed quickly, oftimes aided by former keepers and now the students from Cityscape. They had taken to work as if it were their birthright, and when other befitted keeping could not be found they all joined the labor on the new street.

Some of the houses they were digging into were hid from the distant sun by hills and other buildings and so were filled with ice laced ground. Sharo was helpful in thawing such ground so it could be moved away.

Where a lane once stood fallow, Sharo found the activity of labor, and handfuls of people on hand to see it done. Sharo was not surprised to see Joska, hanging on the rope the workers had put around their area at her request. She had decided the work place would be reserved only for those working, and absolutely not for children.

"Pura Sharo," Joska complained yet again. "This is not befitted in the least."

Sharo hid her smile. It would not be well to aggravate her young friend further. The new rule did that in sufficient measure.

"If you are not a worker on this street," Sharo worded the rule again. "You are not to be on this street. The rule is a good one, and will not be amended, not in the least."

"I am useful for the workers," Joska said. "I deliver their messages and run for their supplies."

"All of which you can accomplish without entering the places where they labor," Sharo said. "If you encroach on the limit I have set once more, I will move you back another five paces."

"It is well then," Joska said, his tone and stance

indicated he did not think it well at all. She put a hand to his shoulder, which was also not completely welcome. Joska was a child of deepest feeling. His anger would burn at her for this perceived slight, but in the turn of a day or two would adapt the situation to suit his needs without infringing the rule.

#

Sharo stopped for a breath before walking into her home in the Shanties. She had been away long enough to know a house was not a needful thing. To be able to share it with those who had the need was most befitted. A house is little good until it is used to practice hospitality among friends. In the Shanties they named it proper harboring.

"Taylo," Sharo said in greeting as she passed through the door. "Angla… and Aysa. How fare you in my house?"

"You have not cleaned for too long," Aysa said. "It took the three of us almost the whole of early to put it to clean."

"I have not been staying here," Sharo said. "As you know Aysa."

"Aside from that," Angla said. "She did more of the cleaning than either of us."

"I would not put to question something so obvious," Sharo said. "What work each of you did is most appreciated."

"You have this house," Taylo said. "Yet you sleep in the Commons. Is there a reason for this?"

"More than one I think," Sharo said. "It was for the cause of pulling aside, and walking alongside who I once was. An event caused me to remember my life in

Cityscape. It is well, for it gives more space for you two. I will stay here at times."

"Since you know more of the Shanties than any of us," Taylo said. "I would appreciate having one to converse about it. There is much to learn."

"There is still much I have to learn," Sharo said. "Some things we may learn together. But whether taken by small steps or large, know you have arrived in a most befitted place authority Taylo. You will always be welcome here."

"Authority no more, I think,"Taylo said. "I have walked away from that world, and I do not think I will be welcomed back."

Sharo nodded. It was true. While they had yet to consider what part Taylo would have in the Shanties, it was given there would be some manner of occupation for her. In the Shanties they all did their share.

"Given your status Sharo," Angla said. "I expected a larger house to be set aside for you."

"A keeper is born to not need a house at all," Sharo said. "When I arrived in the Shanties the elders had set aside a grand house, filled with room and windows, but with Pytre on his own with Kassi I could not fathom any more than this. I told them to set aside the larger house for those who truly need it."

"Sensible," Angla said.

"You miss your tower, ma'am," Aysa said. She had not yet taught her tongue not to use the words she would use in Cityscape. It was not untoward, yet the Shanties did not have anyone given a title unless it spoke of their occupation. Sharo had already spoken to her on the matter, but knew it would take more than a winter or more for her tongue to comply.

"I miss being in my home with my friends," Angla said. "I do not have more than a thought for the tower. And Aysa, you are not required to name me as ma'am."

"You have friends," Aysa said, Sharo noted how she swallowed the ma'am which had threatened to come out of her mouth. "In the course of time you will have more."

"Yes," Angla said. "But I cannot help but consider how not all my friends are safe in the Shanties."

"To have all our friends here would be most befitted," Sharo said. "But such things are not in the habit of being."

#

In the late of the day Sharo returned to the Commons in the company of Aysa, a young keeper from Cityscape. They paced though the corners, then set their cloaks on befitted places to sleep.

Ryalt had been waiting, sitting on the steps at the entry of the Commons. Sharo had gone out today, and chatter had it she had returned to her home. But Ryalt suspected he would find her here. New keepers who had fallen into the proper harborage of the Shanties, were near to her heart and in their first few days she would be on hand to keep for them.

"Is all well in the Shanties?" Ryalt asked.

"As well as can be," Sharo said.

"And yet you still sleep in the Commons," Ryalt said.

"It is a habit at this time," Sharo said. "Taylo and Angla inhabit my house, and I would let them have an eventime to talk between themselves. They understand I will not always be in residence there."

She looked over the students who were settling into their cloaks.

"Also, I stay here for the cause of these young ones. The Shanties are not like Cityscape. They have much to learn."

Ryalt stood across to her, not knowing whether it was proper for him to be near where she slept in her cloak.

"Perhaps we should have someone in residence here at all times," Ryalt said. "I do not mean to say it should be you. Surprises have been coming through that unknown tunnel too regularly."

"I had the same thought as I looked over the demarcation today," Sharo said. "Cityscape is beginning to take note of us, and that cannot be a good thing. Shall we check the tunnel before I sleep so you will be free to return to your beloved Jenne."

"It would be most befitted," he said. "So far the tunnel has only brought friends, but it may not always be."

Sharo smiled, she knew Ryalt only worked for the good of the Shanties and his friends.

He opened the door and they both walked face into the cool wind. All was dark save for the light which came through the doorway behind them.

Sharo walked to the edge of the platform and looked down the long tunnel. There was a wall on one side. Kimi had supposed this tunnel had been constructed to traverse people from the city to the old ship and nowhere else. The young student had requested to be allowed in the tunnel, she believed there was much to be learned from it.

"Will these occurrences never cease?" Sharo asked, looking far down the tunnel.

"What do you see?"

Sharo smiled slightly, then sighed.

"Another set of people is traversing in the tunnel," She said. "We did well to have a final look."

"Do we have a guess at who might be traversing this time?" Ryalt asked.

"There is no way to know until it is at hand," Sharo said. "Friend or foe it is thankfully a small group and we have the course of a day for the preparation. I suspect they will not arrive until the morrow, possible past the mid of the day."

"I will arrive at the Commons at the mid of early, if not before," Ryalt said. "We will make what preparations we see fit at that time."

"Us and the whole of the Shanties," Sharo said, "once word of our newest arrivals becomes known."

"The Shanties function on its chatter," Ryalt said. "It would be untoward if none of the initiates were curious."

#

Angla awoke in the morning, on a bed obverse to the fire well of Sharo's house. She was more rested than she had felt for some time. A small fire overnight had kept the chill of the summer's night outside. She and Taylo had spent the last of the day talking. Sharo had been at the Commons with the keepers who sheltered there.

Outside the distant sun warmed the world.

Angla looked though a clear frame out over the Shanties. She had known of it before most in Cityscape, yet she had never before seen it with her own eyes or walked it with her own feet. As far as the eye could see broken towers and homes lay ruined. There was no clue that anyone yet lived within.

It was every bit as different and wonderful as Ryalt had described it.

Angla had risen quietly and proposed to move about with care, so Taylo would not be disturbed. After a few moments she jaunted through the whole house and realized she was the only one in attendance.

"Where have you gone?" Angla asked. Of course there was no one to answer.

After a small meal she walked out into the lane, which was more a footpath amid broken stones. It was not long before she crossed the path of a woman from the Shanties. The colors she wore were almost vibrant. She was perhaps as old as Taylo, and wore her light colored hair pulled back.

"Are you not Angla?" the woman said as she approached.

"I am," Angla said, remembering the Shanties had a tendency to chatter. "You are?"

"Sundi," the woman said. "I am the mother of Miko."

"There is yet no word about Miko?" Angla asked.

"No," Sundi said. "But most of the Shanties will be gathered at the Commons today. Last night Sharo saw yet more people traversing the tunnel."

"Perhaps it is your son," Angla said.

"Even if it is not," Sundi said. "There may be

some chatter of my son, good or bad. Any mention would be befitted."

"Not to know is the worst of it," Angla agreed. "I have friends remaining in the city, one cannot help but wonder."

"Accompany me to the Commons, Angla," Sundi said. "Perhaps there will be some mention befitted for both of us."

"Chatter about my friends is less likely," Angla said. "But I trust in hope. I know they are warm and well and in the hands of God. Is there any place more befitted?"

"None," Sundi said, taking Angla's arm in hers. "And I should say it is most befitted to meet you today."

#

When Angla and Sundi arrived, the Commons were quite full. Taylo had taken control of the entry from the tunnel along with a handful of young men who would usually be laboring in the warmth of the day. If trouble arrived from that point, it would be obligated to traverse through her and her new cohorts.

Sundi took her leave and Angla searched the crowd. As kind as the people were, they were as unknown to her as the ruins and the hills outside. She had jaunted some of the length of the Shanties, discovering it was once been a vast place, and also discovering how much of the broken city had been taken by the Shanties. The lanes were difficult to find, and the houses were hid. Such was the way of the Shanties. They had been fortunate to survive the last god war and they would rather avoid being found by the next.

"Sharo," Angla said as she approached the once

keeper. "I suspect I would be more at ease in your shadow than anywhere in all the Shanties at the moment."

"Is it for the cause of my ability to make fire?" Sharo asked. "I do not think my gift was given for dealing in harm."

"Not at all," Angla said at once. "I choose to stand here because you are my friend, and you would stand with confidence in any city."

The two were drawn from their conversation by a commotion near the tunnel entrance. Taylo had gone within, leaving the young men to block up the entrance if need be. It should not have surprised Angla how they followed her without question. Taylo knew how to take control of a situation.

The Commons became silent as they waited for Taylo to return.

Presently she emerged with three men blinking at the brightness outside the tunnel. There was a bit of a wry smile on her face.

"Friends," Taylo announced. She had been taught of proper forms of announcement, and she used them to a fault. "Elders, the whole of the Commons, I present to you, Councilman Iance of Cityscape."

Angla had stepped forward despite herself the moment her eyes recognized the man. It had taken the turn of several moments, he was not near as polished as he usually was. The glint which once held sway in his eyes was gone, replaced by a light less bright. He was, as always, a man with a purpose, but now he was a man who had lost in his greatest bid, and here he would not be given the first grain of respect. Angla wondered if that did not make him more dire.

"Councilman Iance," Angla said. "Would you follow us to the ends of the world?"

Iance bowed his head for a moment before he replied.

"Friends of Authority Taylo," He said, stiffly formal. "Elders, the whole of the Commons, and Angla. I follow you because I must. There is much I need to say. There is much you need to know."

"Then say what you must," Sharo said, stepping up beside Angla. "For in this hall we are not in the habit of enduring long and meaningless chatter."

There was a bit of muffled laughter at those words. They were not connected completely to the truth. Angla had been told on more than one occasion how the Commons often contained more than its share of endless and meaningless chatter.

"I jaunt so far to face a keeper?" Iance asked.

"A former keeper," Sharo said. "One for whom you care less than for the dust in a cup. I have more worth in this setting and will not be dismissed."

"Then I note you are one of the many from which I must beg pardon," Iance said. "In the holy writ I have read in a book called Daniel of a King who in the midst of his revel saw the hand of God etch words on the wall."

"What is that to you?" Angla asked.

"If the only God etched words on my wall," Iance said. "He would give the same message. I have been measured and found less than sufficient. Not only in my circle of authority, but within myself."

"You spoke of information," Taylo said. She was skeptical of him. Angla knew it was with good cause.

He had played the well-befitted man before. Iance was involved in the power politic. He did not even know his own real face for it was so seldom used.

"Mintel, the new regent of Cityscape, knows of the old ship and of the Shanties," Iance said. "Both exposed by me in my quest for the seat of power. He is busy rallying the cause of restoring all of Dante to Cityscape. The old ship is now in his hands and he has turned his attention to the Shanties."

"It would be an error," Angla said. "In the whole of history the Shanties never belonged to Cityscape."

"He speaks of the cause of restoration but he prepares for the cause of war," Iance said. "You will face an army and all you have would be destroyed for what I intended and what I said. When they are done, whatever remainder of you there might be would be returned to Cityscape to take the place of keepers. I stand here before you for this cause, your fate should not be written by the new regent. I would stand before the militia and fight alone if I must."

"Then you must," Angla said. He was using fine sounding words, which was his course in Cityscape, but Angla could see beyond his face, and would dare not let him have the last say.

"How soon will this militia reach the Shanties?" Sharo asked.

"When I departed plans were being made," Iance said. "They will prepare quickly, taking five days at most. They could reach this place in four days more, five at the most."

Iance stopped talking, looking over the Commons to see what manner of reply he would receive.

"Your message is delivered," Taylo said. "Do you require supplies before your return?"

Iance considered for a moment before he spoke his next words.

"I fathom," he said. "I am not given to stay."

"You cannot," Taylo said before any other could answer. The Shanties followed closely the cause of proper harborage, but she could not let that principle apply. Iance would be too much a liability. "There are many from which you must beg pardon, and few are here. They are in Cityscape. Accomplish that before you consider where you might take your rest."

"There are still two here whom I have touched to damage," Iance said, looking especially at Angla. "I have a need to make amends."

"Can the end of Medic Parke be put at your feet?" Taylo asked.

Iance looked at his feet for the touch of a moment. Then he set his face and looked back at Taylo.

"It can," Iance admitted. "It was not the action I requested, but it was an action done in my name. I regret it happened."

There were those in the Commons who knew who Medic Parke was. Few were those who had heard anyone admit to bringing another to an untimely end. In the Shanties there was no Holding, but none would offer harborage for those who did such actions. They were consigned to be alone.

"We will still be here once you have made amends in your city," Angla said. "You have begged your pardon from us, and are free to go your way."

The Commons watched quietly as Iance received

a full share of supplies for his traverse back to the lake, and then to Cityscape. He looked about with hope and anxiety, seeing only a sea of faces, many of which would never trust him.

"I wish you well, people of the Shanties" Iance said as he departed. "Prepare your defense without delay."

It was not a happy moment. Though he was unworthy, it was not easy to dismiss the cause of proper harborage. Yet Taylo was correct. Iance could not stay.

"I wish you well Councilman Iance," Angla said. "I trust you will be ever in the hands of God."

#

"It has been the circle of many years since the Shanties have fought a war," pura Athan said. He stood near the center of the Commons. Each word was passed through the room and out into the street. "We live in the ruin of that last action day by day."

"There are but a handful of usable guns here," Taylo said. "A few more bows, and we can construct more. But what we can have will not be sufficient to counter what the Cityscape militia will carry."

"This is not the first threat the Shanties have faced," Elder Ryalt said. "We must entangle ourselves together if we wish to stay warm and well."

There was muttered ascent to his words. It was ever the way of the Shanties, to stand together against any adversity.

"Hiding has served our purpose to this day,"Athan said. "Might it not serve our purpose today?"

"It may yet," Ryalt said. "We need block the lanes

and cover the open areas. Perhaps we should move ourselves deeper into the ruinscape and stay below ground until they pass."

"Would we also cover over our crops?" Pytre stood up, beside him Kassi held to his arm. "Would we pour out our water and fill in our doorways? We cannot traverse the winter next with what we have on hand. If we successfully hide from Cityscape we still do their work to put most of us to lost and gone."

"We cannot stand face to face with a Cityscape militia," Ryalt said. "We would not stand. Perhaps God would show mercy over the next winter. Perhaps Cityscape will think us a myth and leave."

Sharo stood up and approached the center. Over the winters she had warmed the Commons she had only spoken among the elders a handful of times. It was not an office she had desired, but it was one she could fill if the need arose.

"The house lords are certain we are among the ruins," Sharo said. "When they arrive they will search until they find. But perhaps you are correct. They need not find all of us when they search. They do not know how many of us there are."

"But Sharo," Ryalt said without hesitation. "They are many and we are few, they have higher scholarship and we do not. Without the full number of the Shanties how can we hold to hope at all."

"We have hope because we walk in the shadow of God," Sharo said. "He chose to give us the holy writ, and I dare say he did not open that book to let it close again. I am a keeper. I was born to work. I will work to keep the Shanties safe. I will stand against those with evil plans.

"This is the best course. Send as many away as we can, and allow a few to stay to engage the Cityscape army and divert their attention."

Ryalt considered her words for the turn of a moment, and then looked around at the crowd in the Commons.

"Send runners to every corner of the Shanties and bring any who would stand with us to the demarcation at the edge of sandscape," Ryalt said. "We need no more than a third of the Shanties. Tell those who are young, or who have children, to gather their belongings and prepare to traverse from the Shanties."

"And you will walk before them," Sharo said. Ryalt stared at her for a long moment. She was not often vocal in the Commons, when she did her words had all the weight of any elder. For her to send him out was unthinkable.

"I am needed," Ryalt said.

"You are needed with your family," Sharo said, "and for the Shanties. You can hold the remainder of us together in the worst of times. You must be elder for them."

Ryalt stepped down and walked up to face Sharo.

"Lead them a befitted length away," she said. "Keep them hidden and safe. Even if you do not fathom it, the City lords will not show more mercy to those who cower in their homes than they will to those who stand up and face them. They tore down this city before, they will do so again. If they find us all, we will all be lost and gone."

Ryalt was shaking as he stood. The words of

Sharo were not untoward, but neither were they welcome.

"If the Shanties have decided to stand, I would choose to stand with my friends," Ryalt said.

"I know you do," Sharo said. "No one in all the Shanties is as brave as you. But this is what you will do on our behalf. I mean for you to live, to hold life in the initiates, and put to remembrance what will happen to us as you remake the Shanties in a place more hidden still."

Sharo looked across the room for a moment, to the place where Jenne sat, listening to every word. When she looked back at Ryalt she whispered. "You must keep her safe, she is my dearest friend."

Ryalt looked at her for a long moment. Sharo did not impugn his bravery or his resolve. She knew he was the key to keeping the Shanties, if only a part, and she could not see the Shanties kept without the presence of Jenne.

"You will not be forgotten," Ryalt said, then looked around to the whole of the Commons. "None of you will be forgotten. Those who will traverse with me find your way to the area in front of the open bowl."

As commotion ruled the Commons, Taylo found her way to the side of Sharo.

"It is a dire path you have cobbled for us," she said.

"You are not required to stay," Sharo said, putting a hand to her shoulder.

"How could I not?" Taylo said. "I can make the best guesses at how they would move against us. Even if we are all put to lost and gone, I am here for the cause of assuring none will say it was easily accomplished."

"While it lasts," Sharo said.
"While it lasts," Taylo said.

30

"Aery," a keeper said. "You have chosen to put your hand to labor on this day?"

Authority Taylo had dropped him at the Drydocks the day before the river filled. He knew he should have gone direct to rejoin his family, but he hesitated. Until he returned in full he was no longer a keeper-- he was yet a student. Aery chose to take the circle of a day or two to walk through streets and observe with new eyes the city about him. Even in the short time of his scholarship he had learned much of what he had never known before.

"There is no room for any other course," Aery said. "My family is gone, as are many of the Drydocks. No opportunity I've had changes the course of my life. I am ever a keeper."

He had looked at the whole of the city with new eyes. It had been built by the colonists, the ones who desired a place to worship God, and yet in the circle of time God had been set aside into a singular blue cathedral in a corner of the city, not allowed to inhabit the lanes and the houses.

And yet God is not one to remain where he had been set by mere men. Through Gabri and the old ship the knowing of God was remade on Perma. Aery wondered at how many places this knowledge had gone to in so short a time.

One of the keepers drew close to him, putting a hand to his shoulder.

"I had hoped your new scholarship could have changed that," the man said quietly. None other needed to hear what had happened. The way to keep something from being known was to never speak it.

His wanderings had taken him far afield, to the southern edge of Cityscape where Aery looked out at what was once a place on the river where water was taken for irrigation and goods were floated into Cityscape. He had found house lords there, house lords who labored. Aery had approached as close as he dared; pondering what manner of labor it was which was not first and last given to keepers.

The sun had slid beneath the sky and Aery found a secure and befitted place to rest. At the first of early he dared to traverse closer to the old stations, but learned little he had not already known. There was something occurring, something not even keepers were to know, but he could not decipher it with his eyes alone and he could not safely traverse close enough to hear what might be said.

Aery had done what he could, he need only return home now, and perhaps question among the keepers what occurred to the south of the city. Perhaps there was some chatter of it to be heard.

"What was given was not sufficient for the cause of change," Aery said.

"Let not hope walk far from you," the man said. "Hold what is of value close to your heart. There may yet be better days."

As he jaunted back to the Drydocks there was a quake. Aery had stopped and waited, being in the middle of an open lane he had little to fear unless he stumbled. He found the quake to be an odd thing, it did not start and end like a usual quake, but other than the feeling of it he had no clue to what had make the difference.

He had arrived at the edge of the Drydocks and found it filling with water. The rising water was laid at the cause of a quake which Aery had felt during his return. But there was little room to speculate about the quake or the flood. The water was swift and many keepers were in its way.

The eventime turned to endless labor, helping keepers caught in the water to pull themselves out, and salvaging whatever belongings they could. As the night continued Aery helped as he could and moved from place to place looking for chatter of his family. There was nothing to be heard of them. After his second day of searching more than a few cautioned him, someone had been in the Drydocks seeking him. Aery was not sure who it would be, but he hoped they had not found him and had moved along.

He had not found his mother and father, or anyone who could say where they had gone. After a befitted time searching, Aery knew it was time for him to begin keeping.

"There may be better days," Aery agreed. He did not believe his words as he said them. Nothing had gone well of late. He had gone to a scholarship and learned more about his world than most ever knew, but the source of that scholarship was lost and gone, and on his return he found his family was taken by the water. It had been a pleasant side trip in the course of his life but the direction had not been changed, not in the least.

"What occurs?" a keeper near him said. Aery looked up. At a time when the air would be filled with carts seeking to hire keeping for the day, there were none.

Then, just as quickly, a mass of authority appeared about the keepers, on every edge of the hiring corner. There were some in carts, but many authority traversed on their feet.

"Keepers," one of the authority announced. "We have need of labor. All of you follow."

It was all they had said. They led the way and there had been authority following, should any think to avoid this labor assigned without negotiation.

They had been taken to a scantily prepared camp past the edge of Cityscape. There they had divided the keepers into smaller groups of a handful with one keeper responsible, and had trained them how to shoot a long rifle by an authority named Moska. They were only to fire at the robot targets when they were close, so as not to waste a single shot by attempting to hit it from far away. In the eventime they were sent to a cleared area and left to sleep.

The second day was much as the first, and the next as well. One of the authority called it "training" but they spoke little to the keepers beyond the need of the moment, and that was taken up for the cause of their efforts.

On the fourth day each keeper was given a rifle, a pack with food, a container of water. Before the late of mid they were instructed with a direction and told to walk. When one asked the destination the authority would say only a city across the sandscape, and there would be fighting for the cause of Cityscape. There would be additional training each morning, and much walking through the day.

When the distant sun touched the edge of the sky they stopped for rest. Fires were hastily built and meager meals prepared. Though surrounded by keepers he had known his whole life, Aery found he had little to say. He took his food and stepped to the side to eat without company.

He ate slowly, looking ahead but seeing nothing until two younger keepers traversed in front of him, on their way to obtain a share of the meal. Within a moment he recognized how he knew them, and how out of place they were.

"Miko," Aery said, standing up. "How is it that you are here? And Daine with you."

The two noticed him and moved right to his side.

"Friend Aery," Miko said. "I am not here of my own choice. I was taken and put to the Holding. My friends retrieved me and hid me as a keeper until I could traverse to home, but I was taken to be a part of this."

"Do you know what this is?" Aery asked. "The authority will say nothing save to keep training, and to hit the target in the center."

"The house lords know about the Shanties," Daine said.

"We jaunt to your home Miko," Aery asked, "to fight war with them?"

"It makes sense that the house lords would have such a plan," Daine said. "We cannot take part of this. We must not."

"How can we not?" Aery said. "Any who turn back will be put to lost on the moment. I witnessed it the turn of a day ago. One of the keepers decided the labor of training was not worthy of an unknown recompense. The moment after he turned his feet to Cityscape he was shot."

"I don't know how to avoid it," Miko said. "I will die if I must, but I will not raise a hand against the Shanties. I will not shoot anyone there."

"There may be a better way," another voice said from behind them.

A young keeper stood behind them, regarding them with some care.

"Also," he continued. "One should have a care when one uses the names of places which should not be spoken. Can I assume you are... students?"

"Assume that we were," Daine said. "And I suspect you once were."

"I am named Adison," he said. "I was a student for two winters. What has occurred?"

"The place of our scholarship is in the hands of the house lords," Aery said in a low voice. "We were found, and most of us were away before we were found out."

"Who was taken?" Adison asked.

"I was," Miko said. "I am named Miko, I'm from that city we spoke about earlier. Gabri was taken as well, and she is lost and gone."

"This is most untoward. I am glad you are no longer in their hands…" Adison said, then looked about. "Well, not in the same way you once were. But the world without Gabri is hard to fathom."

"For all of us," Daine said. "I also do not have the heart for who they want us to fight."

"None of the keepers would," Adison said, "if they knew the truth."

"We are but four young keepers," Miko said. "What do we do?

"I also have a thought on that," Adison said. He smiled and then abandoned the rest of them and walked up to the fire where a crowd of keepers sat and ate silently.

Aery stood and took a few steps in the same direction. He thought he knew what Adison had in mind, and for any such foolhardy gesture, it would be best not to be alone. He noted Daine and Miko as they shuffled up behind him.

"The city lords have been deceitful to us," Adison said, as he settled in among the keepers. "They have lied in what they have said before, and now even more. We have been brought here to enact murder for them, murder they don't want to soil their hands with."

"We are but keepers," someone said. "We do as we are told."

"Who spoke that truth into your ears?" Adison asked. "And why did you listen?"

#

Kene awoke in the early of the day, and found himself still among people he knew, and still encamped on the unsteady ground of sandscape.

The authority Moska had tried to be awake before the keepers, perhaps his purpose was to have control over the keepers by dragging them half asleep from their cloaks. He did not know keepers well if he thought to be awake before they were.

The days, even ones where they jaunted through

the sandscape, began with training. They were shown how to use the rifles, they were obligated to shoot at targets, trying to hit near the center. Not more than a handful of the keepers were able to shoot as well as the authority.

The keepers were told they would face an ancient and terrible enemy, one which threatened all of Cityscape. The authority were sure there would be no cause for surrender, for their opponent would surely not recognize it. Therefore the keepers were told not to accept surrender on the other side.

Kene nodded as the authority told him this more than once. The doubling of their words indicating they spoke half the truth, if any at all.

The day, from the last of early to the last of late was spent jaunting under the direction of the authority, who only told which way to go. The authorities did not go out in front. There was little time to rest, and according to the authority, every need for haste.

"Kene," a keeper said as he sat down with a meager late meal. The fire was small but glowing heat around the edges. "Fare you well."

"As well as anyone," Kene said. "And all of you?"

"Authority Moska yelled at Rache today," one of the younger keepers said, indicating a young woman sitting in the shadows behind other keepers. "She could not hit the target. She was upset."

"Has she been comforted?" Kene asked.

"She has," the keeper said. "But she will miss again in the early of the day."

"I will stand by her side then," Kene said. "And miss worse than she does. I have my misgivings about this labor we are on. The authority have not named the transaction, nor have they mentioned a recompense. They are not dealing properly with us."

"You are not the only one to say so," Rache said, finding her voice. "A group of young keepers has been chattering about how we are being sent to cause harm to a harmless people."

"Have they?" Kene said. "Do we know where these young keepers are?"

"I do," Rache said. "I can show you."

"Then show me," Kene said, taking his last bites as he stood up. For keepers eating was a need, but time for eating was an indulgence.

Rache took Kene across the area where they keepers had been told to rest. The keepers would have never chosen such a place, in a depression between two hills which invited the wind. Rache walked up to a small fire where a group of young keepers was talking to a mass of keepers as they ate, and not being entirely convincing. Kene was not surprised that he knew them.

"Daine," Kene said as he sat down in the core the group. "I see you have finally found Aery."

"We have sir," Daine said. "Miko you have met, and this is Adison, from Cathedral district."

Kene nodded at them as Daine introduced them.

"I understand you are chattering about the labor given to us by the authority," Kene said.

"It is most untoward," Daine said. "We are being sent to do something dreadful and we must not."

"What is the name of the place we are going to?" Kene asked.

Miko, the one who was not a keeper, stood up.

"It's called the Shanties," he said. "We will be there within the turn of three days."

"Your home," Kene said, receiving a nod from him.

"Can you help us?" Daine asked. "If there were handfuls more of us we would not have time to tell everyone, and many are not being convinced."

Kene nodded. He was not surprised. They were young and had never been given the task of convincing people as stubborn as keepers. It was good that he had found them.

"You are working without wisdom," Kene said as he stood. "First, you hide part of the truth and expect others to believe the part you tell them. You must tell the whole of the truth or none at all. And second, you need not convince the whole of the keepers of the truth, you must talk to the ones who other look to. If they are convinced, the remnant of the keepers will listen."

"We have so little time," Aery said.

"We are keepers," Kene said. "We will jump to the task."

31

Jenne awoke with the sunrise, as was her habit. The usual smell of her house did not touch her nose, and when she opened her eyes she recalled they were emplaced in a cave on the far side of the ruinscape, well away from the Shanties.

She silently found her feet and walked to the entry. The sun was moving up in the sky heralding another summer's day.

Outside had the look of the Shanties, crumbled and torn buildings, layers of rubble. However, these days she could see where it was different. Habitation did make its mark, even when everything was done to hide it. She wondered for the moment whether that meant she was truly an initiate to the Shanties, that she knew by heart the look of it.

On their arrival, Joska had been instantly drawn to the large pools, all dry now. The pools were shallow save for the centers where large vertical tunnels traversed down into the world. It was some sort of system to store water, that much was obvious, but it would take the turn of much time before such a system could be understood or utilized.

Jenne listened as others arose with the brightness returning to the sky. They had much to do. The caves had to be turned into befitted shelter should the worst happen. Food supplies had need to be established. Winter was still a length away, but it would overtake them quickly enough if they left aside planning and working.

She had sat at the entrance of the cave with Ryalt the night before; mapping what parts of the ruinscape below would be most useful for a new city. It was a bittersweet activity, exciting by itself, but within every thought came the shadow of the Shanties being brought to cold and still.

Yet something bothered Jenne, she could not quite put the words to it.

She turned and traversed to the far end of the cave. There were scores of initiates at hand, setting up areas for the cause of sheltering. Many of them greeted her as she passed.

Once Jenne had walked the depth and width of the cave she knew what was missing, and walked direct to Ryalt, who still occupied the place they had chosen in the cave.

Ryalt was sitting on a chair as she approached.

"Where is my son?" she asked.

In answer Ryalt held up a note written on a small page.

On the note Joska begged their pardon, but said he could not stay away from the Shanties.

"He returned?" Jenne said. "We must retrieve him."

"We cannot," Ryalt said.

Jenne started to stomp her foot and considered turning and jaunting back to the Shanties on her own. For some reason she stopped herself. Where she often took the first path she could see, often he was the one to ponder before the proceed.

"Why can we not?" she asked.

"We are here to keep these people safe," Ryalt said.

"Ryalt!" Jenne said. She knew he was right, but it was a bitter truth.

Ryalt had stood, and quickly took her into his arms.

"Joska will be in the best of hands," Ryalt said. "They will do everything to keep him safe, and send him back if they can."

"Is any place safe?" she asked.

"Would you think to harm someone Sharo has put under her care?"

Jenne stopped for a moment. It was the right question to ask. Once Sharo was made aware that Joska was back in the Shanties, she would do everything to assure his continued well-being.

"That should be enough," Jenne said. "Yet I will worry."

"I as well," Ryalt said. "He is young, but he has chosen his path. We are given the task to allow it."

"When I pray," Jenne said. "I will put him into God's hands."

"I already have," Ryalt said.

#

Joska awoke as the light from the distant sun first touched the world. The Shanties had become a quiet place, quiet and dark in his estimation. In the two days since his return to the Shanties, Joska had slept in his own bed during the night and scouted the lanes and ways about in the day, assuring that everything was left in order.

His mother had taken him with the rest, but Joska

would not have it. If the Shanties were to be attacked, he would stand against that evil. Every day he expected his father to have returned to find him and take him away again. Thus far he had not.

"Perhaps the city lords will see me and know there are children here," Joska had said as they jaunted away from the Shanties. "Then they would relent and return to their towers."

"It is not the way of city lords," his mother had said. "When they arrive it would be best if you were beyond their sight, and beyond their reach."

The gardens had already begun to show the lack of attention given them. There would be plenty of labor when the crises had passed. He did some small work around the edges. It would need suffice for the moment.

Joska noted how much he missed people. For the Shanties to be emptied was most ill-befitted.

As he moved into the early of the day Joska turned his feet to the demarcation. Sharo would likely be there as she had been every day, watching for the Cityscape army which would soon arrive. His mother would cry if she knew how often he frequented that place, though hidden, and watched the remnant of the Shanties prepare for what was to come.

To this day Joska had not crossed the line into the demarcation, he had only watched. But this day he saw Sharo and noted how she was alone. She was quick to the side of him when he was in need of her most, it was time for him to do the same.

"Joska," Sharo asked as he approached. "Why are you here? You should be emplaced with your mother."

In Sharo he could see the echo of the pained look on his mother's face if she found her son in the midsts of those who would fight the city lord army. The two were certainly branches from the same tree.

"I will not cower in a house when I could help," Joska said. "I have bounders for my feet and stand ready to relay words to Taylo."

On his legs Joska wore a pair of curved steel, named bounders, which were often used by the younger initiates to traverse from one part of the Shanties to another. Sharo noted his footwear and smiled.

"Once,"Sharo said. "Your father Ryalt wore bounders in his search for me at the start of fallen winter. I had already set my feet to return to Cityscape. You are very much a son of your father."

Joska had listened to the story before, more than one version, the latest of which was in the summer past when he had first obtained the bounders and put them to his legs.

"I wish to help," Joska reiterated.

"Then do not wander far from my shadow," Sharo said. "Your mother would want me to keep you safe."

Sharo returned her attention to the sandscape. In the distance Joska could see a man running. He ran at a pace, but steadily, never stopping for rest or breath. In the course of time Joska recognized Chimo. He was one who had been sent to watch for the approach of the Cityscape army.

"Chimo must have seen something," Joska said.

"Yes," Sharo said. "He must have."

After a time Chimo arrived, running unerringly

toward Sharo and the demarcation. Sharo nodded to him as he approached, and waited until he had regained enough air to speak his report.

"They are more than we can count, and they will be here not longer than the start of the morrow," he said. "Sharo, I don't know if I have the words to speak of it further. This is a bitter report."

Joska wondered what could be more bitter than what the messenger had already said. The Cityscape army was real, it was large, and it approached with intent to destroy them all. Perhaps they did not have the knowledge of which part of the ruins the Shanties would be found, but it would not take long to search it out. Many workers can make work short. For a fleeting moment Joska hoped the place where the rest of the Shanties had moved was a befitted length away.

"Tell me anyway," Sharo said.

"The militia," the messenger said. "The militia is all keepers, men and women. The house lords direct from the back. I am told those in charge are dressed like the authority."

Sharo let bow her head for a moment, then raised it, looking into the distance. She had once been a keeper. That was before she was abandoned and left for lost in what a house lord thought was a wilderness. The Shanties and her gift had reversed that fate.

"Of course they do," Sharo said. "I should have known. Go back and care for the other watchers, Chimo, and return in front of the Cityscape militia when they proceed. Joska, deliver this message to Taylo. She has need to know."

When the messenger left, Sharo allowed the tears

from her eyes to touch her face. It occurred to Joska then that no one had ever said the first word about Sharo crying. He had heard it said keepers never let their tears out; they swallowed them back for bitter days.

"This is not a god war," Sharo said softly. "It is a keeper war, for that is who will be lost and cold, for either side."

Joska looked out over sandscape. There would be no sign of the approaching army, not yet. He wondered how many of those approaching would be known to Sharo, or to the other keepers gathered in defense of the Shanties. He thought of his own friends, and how terrible it would be to be forced to fight against them.

It was indeed a bitter report.

Joska rushed over to the flat area on the edge of sandscape where Taylo was teaching the initiates what to expect. With a final leap Joska landed to the side of Taylo.

"Joska," Taylo said. "Why are you here?"

"Sharo sent me," Joska said. "Chimo has brought back a report."

"I noted as he approached Sharo," Taylo said. "I assume the militia approaches."

"Yes," Joska said. "They will arrive early tomorrow in numbers too great to count, and the worst of it…"

"The worst?" Taylo asked. She had not anticipated this part, Joska was sure. How could anyone?

"The army is made up of keepers," Joska said. "The Authority directs from behind."

Where Sharo had reacted with sorrow, Taylo set

her face and glared back at him. Joska fought to urge to run from her, and reminded himself her rage was not for his cause.

"Do they?" she said.

"I regret bringing you such dire news," Joska said.

"Don't regret," Taylo said, standing up tall and looking out over the sandscape. "You brought me the truth, and now I have a direction. Tell Sharo I intend to take a group far to the north and return in such a direction to engage the Authority directly. If I can take off the head, the rest should be less inclined to violence. Either way, I fear this conflict will not last long."

"Yes ma'am," Joska said, a turned to bound back to Sharo.

"...and Joska," she said before he could start to traverse. "You are not required to call me ma'am."

32

Over the course of their jaunt into sandscape the keepers had taken to sleeping in large groups. The sandscape was home to relentless wind and more keepers meant more layers of cloaks as cover, and they could keep for each other. Daine took to gathering with Miko, Aery and Adison, whom she named her new brothers. They had been joined by a handful of other young keepers who had once been students. They spent the nights chattering softly of what had occurred in the old ship, of things they had been taught by Gabri, and what advancement they had made during the day in convincing the keepers to resist fighting the Shanties.

Every spare moment or short opportunity was spent warning the leaders of the keepers of what was to come. Some listened with open ears and some did not, and yet, as Kene said, there would be no way to know who truly listened until they stood between the Authority and the Shanties. He reminded them they worked for the cause of their knowing, what the keepers decided would be left to them.

Miko awoke early and stepped out of his part of the cloak shelter. The day portended some important event; it was as if he could feel it wafting in the wind. Gabri had mentioned speaking with God, and Miko wondered if this was what it was like. Every detail of the world around him was clear, the wonder in it was obvious, and his heart no longer held room for the smallest doubt.

"Thank you," he said to the God he knew was listening.

"Miko," Daine said from behind him. "You are awake before your full measure of sleep. Is all well?"

"Well enough," Miko said. "We jaunt nearer to the Shanties. I see the ghosts of hills in shapes I know, there, at the horizon."

"We've not done near enough," Daine said. "We have yet to convince all the keepers, or to talk to all of them. Kene has gone to the far end of the encampment, but I have not heard what he has done."

It was something which mattered to Daine, that every keeper be given opportunity to join them in their defection. She put her face downward, thinking she had truly failed.

Because of his gift, Miko felt the tears as they welled up in her eyes and fell to her face. There was little he could say to comfort her. He would have liked to have warned every keeper as well, though from the start he knew the task could never be done, not unless every keeper they spoke to turned and spoke to a hundred more before the end of every day.

He looked about, letting his gift color what he saw. There was no blame in anything about them, and only regret at what was left undone. It could not be helped, and the failure was not in them. He could see the water embodied in each of the keepers around him, as far as the eye could see. There were more than he could say.

Miko also touched the water under the sandscape, hidden by the dryness and the sand. He was aware of the lake, over the horizon, near the place where the old colony ship was no longer hidden. He even felt the water represented in the bodies of the people in the Shanties, just over the demarkation. There were so few when compared to the overwhelming army sent by the Cityscape to eradicate them. Every drop was in his heart.

Perhaps he could turn and make to lost some of the militia, but the thought made him weary and cold. They were not his to keep or set to lost, despite the stories of monsters told among Cityscape. Miko could not make himself think his gift could have such reach. He would have to draw the water from some at a time, and he would be forced to look into their faces as they were lost and gone by his gift.

I could not be done. It would be too terrible. Miko felt tears wanting to escape from his eyes, and he looked up into the morning sky. Surely God knew where they were, and could keep for those he held in his hands, keeper and initiate alike. It had to be.

In the sky he noted the comet. It was close, as close as it would ever be. Miko had forsaken all thought about it since abandoning the old ship and the school there. He had not looked at it once, but on seeing it he hoped Trina had been watching.

The comet was still worlds away; even he should not have been able to perceive how distant it was, nor to see that it was formed of frozen water and rock. Yet he confirmed every word of his scholarship through his gift. He cocked his head, learning of the distant thing, how it glowed with light taken from the distant sun and threw off some of its water to reflect the light in a growing trail. It was further away than anything he had ever known and so much larger than it appeared.

Beyond all reasonableness he could feel it, and

within the scholarship he was receiving from the comet Miko listened as the truth spoke directly to his face.

He could call the comet and it would answer.

"Such things are not in the habit of being." He muttered to himself.

"Beg pardon Miko?" Daine asked.

Miko looked at her, becoming aware that he had spoken, and knowing there was more for him to say.

In the Shanties Sharo had often said there was ever only one right way to go. Then Miko had held disdain for every word spoke by the displaced keeper, and for her, but now he knew she had been correct. At this moment there was a way, a clear path, and beyond all reason he could see it as clear as a new summer morning.

Aery and Adison had joined Daine by his side. They held looks of despair at the news they were close to their destination. They had yet to see what Miko was seeing. Keeper Jenne had been most correct; it seemed Miko had truly been chosen for a day such as this.

"Send word to all the keepers who stand with us," Miko said, and gave them a smile. "Make haste, run to the Shanties. Your house lords will think you eager for the battle and allow you to go."

"And then we will turn and fight with them alongside the Shanties," Aery said. "It may not turn back the battle, but it is a better plan than any I could name."

Miko smiled. It made sense that what he said would be the plan, but the battle would not go according to any plan they could think of. He could not put to words what God had told him, only that he would be given to stand between two armies, and not be touched by either.

"When you reach the Shanties tell them to take shelter and keep watch," Miko said. "Tell them God fights the strong on behalf of the weak."

Daine allowed herself a cautious smile.

"God walks before you," Daine said. "It is most befitted."

"Either he has spoken to me," Miko said. "Or my continued scholarship has driven me insane. Either way, you would all be safer in the hands of the Shanties."

"And you?" she asked. She had noted he did not include himself as among those who would take shelter in the Shanties. Indeed, he could not.

"I was appointed to stand at a time such as this," Miko said. "If a life is needed, it is given without bitterness for the cause of keeping my friends. I hold no fear, no matter the outcome."

"I will stay alongside you friend Miko," Daine said.

"Daine you need go," Miko said. "With you I send my love to my mother, and my sister. You will have a place in their house for as long as there is need. And if you would, keep for them as well."

Aery put a hand to Daine's shoulder for support, and to lend a hand should she decide not to go forward with the rest. She would be needed to spread the word to the nearby keepers. There would not be a befitted amount of time as it was.

"Gladly Miko, I will walk with them as if they were my own family" Daine said. "I will await you there and hold to hope that you fare well."

"God has me in his hand," Miko said. "I will

always be where he is."

Daine turned to go, the others had already hurried off to their appointed task and there was scant time befitted for the task. However, Miko could not help but add one more comment.

"...and if by chance I meet Gabri again, I will give her your best greetings."

#

The authority chief had little love for the keepers, and had little pleasure in escorting so many of them into the desert on a fool's errand. There had never been a threat in the sandscape before. Every young scholar knew the second city had been reduced to rubble It did not take one full of scholarship to know the chatter of a new threat was more a ploy to increase the power politic held by a new regent.

"When will our traverse be ended?" he asked Moska, who was in charge of the keepers. The authority had acted with distinction, teaching the keepers how to use the guns they held, and adding discipline where it was needed.

"It is said to be a five day trip," Moska said. "We will find the enemy within the ruins of an old city. Today if all is well, on the morrow at the most."

The chief had looked at the old maps while he was still in Cityscape. Mintel had brought him into an ancient room and showed him where the second city once stood. It was a secondary subject in his early scholarship. He had never given a second thought to where that city might have been located.

"Sooner is better," the chief said. "I doubt anyone lives in the ruins in any great number. Soon to arrive and soon to finish. The better to be done and home."

A younger authority arrived at his primary position at a run, he was almost out of breath.

"Sir," the authority said. "I have ten groups of keepers who run ahead, eager for the attack. I could not put a stop to them."

"It should not matter," the chief said. "If there is anyone to oppose them they will simply fall first, or the enemy will be drawn out. Sentry, get me an image of those keepers, I would like to assure they run for the cause of eagerness, before they are too far gone to stop."

The Sentry pointed his scope and an image appeared on the reader. There were dozens of keepers, running forward for all they were worth, many of them holding their guns up in the air."

"It seems in order," the chief said. "We will call them a diversion. Prepare the rest of the troop. We will attack from the right flank as soon as they are opposed."

"It is well," several authority echoed then moved quickly to their appointed task.

"Who is that?" Moska said, pointing out into the desert.

The chief looked up. Out in the sandscape one of the running keepers had stopped. He put his gun down to the sand, and he was standing.

"Sentry," the chief said. "Image that keeper."

The picture quickly drew into focus. It was a young keeper, quite young. He was facing back toward the troop with his arms held up high toward the sky, and his face was turned upward as well.

"The expanse of sand has taken his mind away," Moska exclaimed.

The chief knew better. In the actions of the one keeper he knew the plan of the others. He stood in place to turn all attention from those who ran, allowing them to reach their goal unchallenged. It was not a good plan, for in it was the clue to allow the chief to discover the ploy.

"He stands to cover for the others," the chief said. "They move forward to escape and perhaps even join the Shanties. We must move the troop quickly to deflect them. Intercept those keepers and have them all brought to me… and someone shoot that one. Shoot him now."

Moska retrieved his gun from his shoulder and touched the scope to the image the Sentry had gathered. The image of the keeper grew larger, and yet he stayed his ground, arms and face to the sky, unaware he would soon be met by a shot and put to lost. The authority had done the same thing regularly over the last few days, every time some keeper thought he could return to Cityscape without proper leave.

The target was in the cross site, Moska drew in a breath and prepared to fire the fatal round when the keeper suddenly disappeared in a white colored mist.

Moska looked up from this scope and out into the sandscape. The young keeper was no longer there, nor were the hills beyond. The sky was turning to light grey. It was something he had seen before, but he had not placed it. It was most unexpected.

"Blizzard!" the Sentry exclaimed.

It belied all sense, there were no blizzards in the full of summer. There could not be a blizzard without the driving wind and armfuls of snow formed on the ground. There was never before a blizzard under the light of the distant sun. But the chief saw the color and had to agree. The keeper in the sand had been engulfed, hiding him from the Sentry's scope, and it moved toward them.

"What madness is this?" Moska asked when snow began to fall around them.

It was as if the world had been turned on its side. Snow never fell gently from the sky, not on Perma. It was blown to the side, or settled to the ground. This snow was different. It was not driven by wind, and it settled from high above in large glassy clusters. It was slow and lazy in its jaunt to the ground.

A mass of the snow fell on Moska's hand. He exclaimed and wiped it form him, but the damage was done. Where the snow had rested the skin was glazed over, touched by the chill. This snow was colder than most, cold enough to touch a hand to damage in the turn of a breath. The situation, though unusual, was easy to read.

"To shelter!" the chief exclaimed. He turned, but the few tents for the authority leaders were far back. There was no shelter nearby with the keepers, they kept their tents on their back. They had already huddled into clumps together, covered in layers of their cloaks.

"To the tents!" someone yelled.

A cluster of snow hit the chief's back, and burned with the chill. He yelled out in anger and pain as he took off at a sprint toward the authority tents. Moska followed close behind.

The snow continued to settle to the ground, as it hit his arms and face, then a leg.

The chief stumbled over one of the other

authority and to the sand. Moska jumped over him and kept running. The over chilled snow had set him to panic.

The tents were too far away. The last of the authority fell in front of him, moaning as the snow increased in its falling. The air was thick and chilled, and even what was nearby could not be clearly seen.

The chief curled in on himself until all he could feel was the chill of snow on his benumbed back. The snow pulled the air from his chest, and touched him to chill with every breath.

Sheltering was beyond his reach. His arms and legs no longer followed his lead. At the end of all he closed his eyes for their last, and fell so far into chilled sleep he was quickly lost and gone-- him and the rest of the authority with him.

#

Sharo listened as a second scout returned with some guess at the number brought against them. They were sorely outnumbered, and it was given the Cityscape fighters had better weapons, even if they were keepers.

Joska appeared beside her, waiting his turn.

"Yes?" Sharo asked.

"Taylo is ready," he said. "She will take a group to the north to engage the authority directly. She says the conflict will not be a long one."

"I share her fears," Sharo said. "But we must make the attempt. Joska, when you see them at the edge of the sky you are to disappear into the ruinscape. Stay hidden. As carefully as you can make haste to join the rest of the Shanties in their new hiding place."

"My place is here," Joska said.

"Your place is at the side of your mother," Sharo said. "I will hear no other answer from you."

As she spoke, snow began to fall from the sky, at first it fell in normal tiny flakes, only unusual that they were not formed on the ground. Then they arrived in larger flakes, and finally with globs of snow as large as a man's fist. It wasn't blown by any wind; it just wafted slowly downward then settled to the ground. Joska took shelter beside Sharo, looking up at the sky.

"Sharo, do you see what I see?" Joska said. "Snow is falling from the sky!"

It was odd. Sharo had heard chatter about the first world of men, that snow did not only form on the cracks and impressions of the ground, and in every shadow to touch the ground, but it also formed in the sky and fell to the earth slowly. She had never before believed snow of such large clumps would fall at anything less than a breakneck pace. She had never seen it fly above her knees save for when it was driven by a stiff wind.

"This is something new," Sharo said.

As miraculous as it was, the Cityscape militia still approached, and now it would be hid from view until they were upon the Shanties. Unless they themselves were lost in the haze. Sharo considered what to do with this new situation. She wanted to think it a good turn of events, but could not fathom why.

"Sharo," Chimo said as he approached. "I don't know where this snow is from, but it is deadly cold. Do not let it touch you even the first time. We must take shelter and do it now."

Sharo looked at Chimo's arm, it was glassy for

being touched by the chill. She reached out her hand and made warmth to surround him, especially the whole of his arm. It was not a cure, but it would turn him from further damage, at least for a time.

"Cover yourself Joska and run ahead to open the doors of the Commons," Sharo said. "Everyone, move quickly or be touched to chill and lost."

Joska pulled his cloak around his head and bounded away. Sharo noted he was still warm, but would need to be emplaced in proper sheltering soon. Meanwhile, those who had gathered around her moved at a run toward the Shanties. Sharo used her warmth to shelter them as much as she could.

"We run from snow now?" Chimo said, making jest. He was as eager as anyone to be out from under the sky.

"It is not snow," Sharo said, looking about at it.

"Then what is this?" he asked, indicating the white clumps drifting to the ground.

"The comet falls from the sky, or parts of it," Sharo said. "It will block out the Cityscape army, and will send them back to the city."

"Are you sure they will go?" Chimo asked.

"I know it,"Sharo said, glancing back at the sandscape, now hidden by the snow. "It truly is. None but a pura could stand in this snow and hope to live, and Cityscape would not tolerate the first pura in their keepers or in their militia. They have no choice but to withdraw. God has fought for us and he has won before we could even look at our opponents."

"Taylo said this would not be a long conflict," Chimo said. "May her words always be so true."

"And may she already be hid in some befitted shelter," Sharo added.

33

"The snow is thicker," Ryalt said to Jenne. "The ground is covered to my knees. I've never seen anything more beautiful."

"Nor so very chilled," she amended. "We must have a care. Kassi is not among us, and the young sozo we have are not as strong for someone who is touched too well by the chill."

Ryalt looked behind them. The Caverns were vast, allowing for the whole number of the initiates to be emplaced. Though it was packed with feet to elbows, it would be most untoward if they were required to be made to stay in the caves for more than a turn of a few days.

"How does this occur?" she asked. The caves overlooked the pools, which were now covered with the snow. He had thought they would be constructing walls by now, making shelter. A day had gone since they started the work, and they were pushed back to the caves by snow falling from the sky. It was a snow which was not being blown by any wind; snow which was deadly chilled.

"It has been two days," Ryalt said. "We brought adequate food, and Athan can make warm these caves. But what has brought this about?"

"Perhaps," Jenne said, glancing out into the snow filled world. "Perhaps this is the way God has chosen to rescue the Shanties from the hand of Cityscape."

"We left our homes for the cause of fear," Ryalt

said. "Others felt the need to stand and oppose the Cityscape army. We hid, and now the redemption of the God is hidden from us. And we don't know what has become of Joska."

"We left our homes to assure there would be a remainder to the Shanties," Jenne said, putting a hand to his shoulder. "We are happy if the Shanties are redeemed. They are family. And we can see this snow with our own eyes, I doubt anyone in all of the Shanties can see any better, and I am sure Joska is in the best of hands."

"Do you think this is a penalty for our untoward actions?" he asked. He had been feeling dread from the moment he left the Shanties. All seemed in order, but Ryalt did not enjoy being the one to hide when there was need for bravery.

"We have done nothing untoward," she said. "We have acted to save the Shanties, and many of our friends. For now, we should enjoy what is before us for we know the one who sent it."

"Elder Ryalt," one of the young men said as he approached. "The snow can be pressed together and made into blocks, if we only handle it for a short time."

"That is unexpected," Ryalt said.

"Yes," the yound man said. "We intend to make snow blocks and use them to build a wall at the cave entrance. We will leave a doorway for entry, but most of the chill will be pushed outside."

"That may be good," Ryalt said, thinking how they had taken to sleeping like keepers, huddled together, in order to keep their warmth. "But wouldn't the warmth from our fires melt the snow blocks?"

"We will keep the fires away from the blocks," Jenne said. "If they are well pressed together they will not melt quickly."

"Do you need help?" Ryalt asked before he looked to the mouth of the cave. Dozens of people were already there, taking turns packing the snow. The wall was already four blocks high and growing quickly. It would not be the most appealing wall in all of ruinscape, but it would fill its purpose.

"Take a place with the next group to labor," the young man said. "The time for the group working circles quickly to an end."

#

By the third night a fair number of the Shanties were sheltering in the Commons. The fire pits at the corners had been lit for the first time since Sharo had arrived. The snow brought with it a chill which had descended over the city, and one pura, even one as strong as Sharo, was not enough to drive it away. Their other pura, along with two young sozo, had gone with the remnant.

"How long will it snow?" Kassi asked. She was enwrapped with Pytre in a cloak, near where Sharo had established her place. Their children were nearby, each had desired to sleep separate, which would have been untoward if they were set outside. Inside the Commons it was warm and still enough. If they became chilled they could easily join their parents.

"We do not know any more than we did at the first of early," Sharo said. The question was not unexpected. Kassi oftentimes would ask the same question more than once for the cause of her worry.

"The snow has piled up past my middle," Kassi said. "The children cannot traverse outside without being in the shadow of someone larger, and even our best cloaks and jackets will hold back the chill only for the turn of a few moments. Much more and we will be consigned to whatever shelter we are in."

"Rest easy dear Kassi," Sharo said, pulling her cloak tight around her. "I do not think we are forgotten. The God who fought for us will surely not abandon us now."

"Is it so easy for you to believe?" Pytre asked.

"Today it is," Sharo said. "I cannot but wonder at what I have seen. A few nights of deep chill are a kindness compared to what would have befallen us had the Cityscape army reached the Shanties."

"It might have been less prolonged," Pytre said, at which Kassi turned to box his arm. The children were quite amused, knowing Kassi had no true animosity toward Pytre. It took the turn of several moments to settle them all again.

"Do you think the rest are warm and well?" Kassi asked. She had shown concern over the initiates who had gone further into the ruinscape to hide more than once.

"I trust in hope that they are," Sharo said. "I doubt there are many hindrances which cannot be traversed by Jenne and Ryalt together, but we cannot know for sure until after this snow ends."

"If it does end," Pytre said.

#

The snow ended during the third night, leaving the ground with a thick covering of snow sparkling in the sunlight of morningtime. The world seemed brighter than it had ever been. The Shanties organized to dig paths through the snow so they could traverse from one side of the city to the other. It was bitter cold work, and no one could be handy to it for more than the turn of a few moments. Sharo found a crew to make a path to the demarcation and kept them warm as they worked. She had an interest to what might have become of the keeper militia from Cityscape.

It was slow work, and it gave Sharo too much time to think. She had been glad at the outcome of the war. God had interposed himself in what would have ended in ill for the Shanties. But she had to wonder what had become of the keepers. She could not help but consider whether God would be found sufficient to care for them as well.

"What is that?" one of the workers said.

Sharo looked up and saw what they had seen. On the horizon, which was higher for the cause of so much snow in their path, something shimmered and glinted in the light of the distant sun.

"I don't know," Sharo said. "It is something new. Are we close to the demarcation?"

"A few steps away," a young woman said.

Sharo melted a large circle to open the demarcation and stood at the head of it, looking out upon a vast sea of snow. The sky was clear and perhaps maybe a bit deeper blue than before. The air was cold and dry, and even Sharo had to keep herself wrapped in a cloak to stay warm.

Though, with the return of light from the distant sun, the air was not as bitter chilled, and the snow was not as deadly cold as it had been. Perhaps with the turn of a few days the world would again be open to them.

The clouds were larger than Sharo had ever seen them. They hovered over sandscape, large lumbering things, and one chanced to traverse between the distant sun and the glimmering object they had seen. It was larger and further away than Sharo had thought, and with the first glance she knew what it was.

A great shimmering mountain lay crosswise upon the sandscape. It was taller than any building in Cityscape and would be more impossible to traverse. It was made, so far as Sharo could see, completely of ice.

The work crew regained their breath for the turn of a few minutes, then moved to return to the Commons and warm themselves. Sharo stayed behind, she could not take her eyes away from the mountain.

"Only God could have called a mountain of ice out of the sky," a voice said behind her.

Sharo turned to see Trina, Miko's sister, wearing both a winter jacket and a cloak. She stood to the side of Sharo and looked out at the new sight.

"It is a wonder," Sharo said.

"Miko won't be able to return now," Trina said. "We have watched the tunnel but no one approaches, and now the way overland from Cityscape is blocked."

"Hold to hope Trina," Sharo said. "Even after keeping for us in so many ways, I do not think God has yet stopped."

Trina nodded her head.

"We will talk of this for the circle of years," Authority Taylo said as she joined the two. "I'm amazed. A comet fell out of the sky and put a stop to the

Cityscape militia."

"I suspect it is only a part of the comet," Trina said. "The whole of it would have been much larger, and it should have landed much harder. I cannot fathom."

"You need not fathom to know it is," Sharo said, motioning at the mountain. "And to know it is, one need only turn your eyes and see."

As the three looked out over the snowscape, they noted a young man attempting to run in the snow. He looked odd, having to jump up and step over something soft which reached almost to his whole height.

"Chimo," Sharo said as the young man approached. "I will warm you. What has occurred?"

Chimo stopped near the demarcation and bent over, breathing hard for his exertion, and unable to utter a sound.

"Breathe deep," Taylo said. "Regain your breath. Running in this snow is worse than running in sand."

"Keepers," Chimo said. "Hundreds of them. Near to the ice mountain."

"You go lend help as you can," Trina said. "I will traverse to the Commons and return with all manner of assistance."

"How will you follow us?" Sharo asked.

She pointed at the trail in the snow left by Chimo as he hastened to them. It showed the way over the first hill toward the ice mountain.

"I suppose I will traverse in that pathway," she said.

"Students," Taylo said, shaking her head. "We send them to scholarship and they return smarter than we are."

The trail was easier to follow than it had been to make. Chimo led them through with silent determination. Taylo followed behind. Sharo stayed between them and kept them warm as they walked.

At the top of the hill they saw a sight they would not forget. Below them, at the foot of the new ice mountain scores of keepers were huddled together in groups under layers of cloaks in attempts to stay warm. They were half buried in the snow. Somehow they had landed obverse of the mountain from the rest of their cohorts. They were many, uncountable at first glance.

"We must help them," Sharo breathed. "With the distant sun shining some of the snow will melt, and all this will freeze solid overnight. They will have no chance if they stay in place."

Taylo stood up on a rock.

"Keepers from Cityscape," she yelled. "What struggle you were brought here to fight is gone. Lower what weapons you have and allow us to traverse you to sheltering before you lose your last bit of warmth."

In one of the huddled groups not far from where Taylo had made her announcement one of the cloaks rustled and a head popped out, a young man, blinking at the brightness of the snow and looking surprised.

"Authority Taylo?" he asked. "Is it truly you?"

"It truly is," Taylo said. "And the words I have spoken are well befitted. There is no longer cause to fight."

"We had no intent to fight," A keeper named Kene said as he stood up from the gathering of cloaks. "We positioned ourselves to the front to prevent any of the keepers from approaching, and stood ready to defend the Shanties if need be. Early on the day we were sent word to run in this direction."

"Why would you do such a thing?" Sharo asked.

"The house lords lied to us," another keeper said. "They sent us here to kill those who had helped provide the holy writ."

"Who told you these things?" Taylo asked.

"Students sent from Cathedral district to the old ship told us every word of it," the keeper answered. "One given the name Adison, and the other Aery."

"The other two were Daine and Miko," Kene added. "Though Miko was in no way a keeper. The authority did not see him for who he was, and we had no thought to give him over."

Taylo looked at Sharo, and with a nod confirmed her thoughts.

"I would like to converse with those students," Sharo said. "But for now, Send word to all the groups of keepers. If you would follow, I will lead you to a place of warm shelter and gentle hospitality."

"Lead on Sharo." Kene said. "We have been chilled and hungry for long enough. Even keepers can find the end of patience in such bitter cold."

#

Angla had stayed in the house of Sharo while the snow had built up outside. At one time Sundi and her daughter Trina had joined her. The jaunt to their house from the Commons was too distant in the chill caused by the snow. Angla had seen them outside and immediately waved them in. They had sat at the fire, hesitating to leave it for even the turn of a moment.

Trina had heard the story of Angla, but had never

thought to meet her. They talked through one day and into the next.

"I have heard of Miko," Angla said. "And I had hoped to meet him, but that meeting was almost the end of us all. Luckily he traversed away and was untouched by the authority."

Finally the first of early was greeted with warm light from the distant sun. The snow covered the Shanties glistened and reflected the light so well it was hard to see at all.

Trina dressed quickly in front of the fire, she had decided to go to the demarcation, to see if there was any word of Miko.

Angla accompanied Sundi to the Commons. She was hoping for word of some kind as well, but was not hearty enough for a jaunt to the demarcation. Once inside the Commons they went directly to one of the corner fires.

After a time Angla walked through the Commons to regain her warmth and found herself surrounded by friends, old and new. She had been welcomed to the Shanties with the most open of arms. Here all friends were family, the teras were invited to use their gifts, and the holy writ was discussed openly. She had found herself in the most befitted of places.

A group of workers returned form the demarcation with a wonder to report. The Cityscape militia had been made up of keepers, not an army of young house lords--they would never risk their own children for such a task. Either way, God had turned them away. In the wake of the snow a mountain of solid ice had been placed in the midst of sandscape to block the way between Cityscape and the Shanties.

Angla had hope none of the keepers suffered. City lords could be cruel if they were not handed what they had desired.

She turned back to the doors, if she would traverse to the demarcation; it had best be done soon.

Then at once there was a commotion in the Commons. Hordes of people, keepers by their dress, entered through the door, filling the room. Even more milled about outside as Sharo and Taylo moved among them. Angla could not count so high, there were hundreds within her sight, and there were more beyond, down the lanes in every direction. If they were not yet at the Commons, they were being invited into houses and workplaces to take them from the cold.

Angla was left without words as she stood to the side and watched. She was wearing Shanty colors now, and would not be immediately recognized as a house lord. In the turn of time Kassi arrived, working through the crowd, finding those with injuries and afflictions. There were surprised yelps as she touched to healing with glowing hands, and quick, gentle instruction about what the gifts truly were. It seemed some of the keepers already knew, but also knew not to breathe a word of it. Cityscape would not have it.

Angla felt a moment of envy. She had not tolerated that healing touch as well when she had first seen it. She had been frozen by fear the first time she had seen Kassi do her work.

She stood, looking to lend a hand at whatever might be needed for the group of keepers, those who must have been caught on this side of the mountain when the battle was prevented. They had been outside in nothing but cloaks for the turn of three days, and they would be cold.

She approached the first group of keepers at hand.

"Keepers," Angla said. "Fare you well? What is your need?"

"You are Angla," One of the young women said. "We are pleased to find you here. How did you escape from the hand of Councilman Iance?"

They all leaned in, eager to hear what had happened.

"Pardon my surprise," Angla said. "How did you know I was held by the Councilman?"

"Chanta told us," the young keeper said, as if everyone would have known.

"Chanta?" Angla said. "She wasn't taken from my tower."

"No ma'am," the keeper said. "Did you not know Chanta would be too smart for that?"

"Isn't she among you?" Angla asked, looking with hopeful eyes at the crowd surrounding them.

"None of us have seen her since we jaunted from Cityscape," the keeper said. "She must have avoided the hiring corner that day. But you and authority Taylo, how did you jaunt to this place before us?"

"That is a long story," Angla said.

"I trust we have time to hear it," a young keeper said. "For we are to be regaining our warmth here in this Commons."

#

Word had been sent, keepers had been found out

in the snowscape and they had been brought to the Commons. Kassi had returned to her house to set all in order, but she was sought out in particular, and would have to clean her house on another day. Some of the keepers had been touched to ill. They would need her help.

Pytre was in the midst of it, no doubt, though Kassi could wish for him close by her side on this day. To use her gift in the Shanties was no bitter task, but among keepers recently arrived from Cityscape, and in large numbers, it could turn to ill in a mere breath of time.

Kassi put her hand to her tummy, touching the young life inside.

"I must beg your pardon again child," she whispered. "This is not the most safe of occupations, but it has need to be done. I have been called, I cannot turn away. I do plan to keep from drawing on more of myself than would be prudent for your well being."

Kassi found the Commons, and the streets about it, filled with keepers who had sheltered the length of the snow sheltered only in their cloaks and each other.

An older worker sat against the wall holding his arm, he was surrounded by friends and family. It was obvious they knew he would lose the arm, it was blackened by the chill and appeared painful to move.

Kassi could touch his pain for better. She forgot her fears and walked directly to him.

"I can fix your arm if you relent," she said clearly. In some circles of keepers they would name her adverse, but this was not Cityscape. It would be best for these keepers to learn such lessons early. The monsters of Cityscape were highly regarded in the Shanties. "In the

Shanties I am named a fixer, or a sozo."

The man looked at her for a long moment, sizing her up. Kassi could feel the presence of other initiates around her. There could be trouble, and she wondered how she could put it to silence once it began.

"Do what you can, fixer," the old man said, offering up his arm. "You cannot turn it to worse."

Kassi put her hands around the base of the blackened part of his arm. Under her hands there was a faint glow. They all recognized it for what it was. They had heard the stories from the time they were children. She heard the gasps, and tensed herself, waiting for what might happen next.

"Wonders abound," the old man said before his family could think to do something about this tera who might be harming the man.

"Is that better?" Kassi asked, letting his arm loose.

"More than better," the man said, flexing his arm. "You have done a fine work. I am in your debt."

Already Kassi was moving on, she had heard a cough nearby and heard something untoward in it. Such things could not go untouched. A cough could jump from one person to another, touching them all to ill in a short time. She would put that at an end.

Kassi found a young keeper, being held close by her mother. They were both wet and cold, and the cough had touched to ill her lungs. She was scant old enough to be keeping. Being in the warmth of the Commons was a help, but the girl had already been touched by the cold. A warm room would not be enough. She braced herself again, knowing the keepers could turn against her at any moment.

"She will help you," a keeper's voice said from behind her. "God has sent a healer to greet us when we had the most need. Let her touch the girl to well and warm."

Kassi quickly touched the cough, and brought it to an end, under the eyes of dozens of keepers who whispered their awe at the glow from her hands. These were not the voices of fear she had expected. By the time she finished with the cough, a handful of keepers with various afflictions had been brought to her, and more were on their way.

"I only have so much strength by the day," Kassi announced. "Keepers, make sure those who see me today are the worst touched of all of you. Those of you who can wait until the morrow should. I will do everything to tend to every one of you within a handful of days."

Kassi was glad she had taken a large meal at the start of the day. She had already worked well beyond the strength that meal could account for. Though she would be quite weary at the end of it, it was befitted for the keepers to be greeted so. For their part the keepers quickly organized themselves, putting the worst to the front. The only difficulty was making the other keepers stay back, they all wanted to espy the wonder of her healing with their own eyes.

She moved to the midst of the Commons where a young girl was limply laying in her mother's arms. This one was among the youngest. She must have only begun to keep. She had been touched by the chill deep in her middle, and, as Kassi noted, the frost had killed some of the skin on her face. It would be easy enough to fix, but

Kassi was aware this would need be her last touch. After which she would need to recover, at least until the mid of the day on the morrow.

"I can help," Kassi whispered as she moved to put her hands on the girl's shoulders. It would be laborious, but the need was great. This one child was in the most dire of circumstances, there was little time if Kassi would see her well again.

The girl looked up, and seeing Kassi knelt over her with glowing hands, her eyes grew wide, then she tried to move away, and then she raised up her head and screamed. She screamed as if she thought her soul would be taken from her.

Pytre was instantly at her side. He must have been nearby, and was drawn by the commotion.

"Take that away!" the mother screeched. "She is contray to us! Send her out!"

"Not in the Shanties," Pytre said firmly. "Not to us. Kassi is a gift. She can help."

A handful of the keepers were saying the same thing. Trying to convince the mother that this was not like the stories of monsters they had told in Cityscape. More than a few named Kassi as a gift direct from the hand of God.

"No!" the mother said again, pulling the panicking child closer to herself. Kassi in turn pulled Pytre further from the mother and child.

"I cannot force her," Kassi said. "Her or her child."

"But..." Pytre said, looking back. They both knew the signs of bitter chill, and could easily see them in the girl. It would not end well.

"No Pytre," Kassi said again. "She is allowed the choice. Give her warm blankets and move her close to the fire. Get her whatever she requires. And send word if I am needed for any dire condition. I should rest for the turn of the day and eat well before I return."

"This is a bitter circumstance," Pytre said.

"But you must allow it," Kassi said, holding up her hand. "A gift is only a gift if it is accepted."

"Kassi," Pytre said, putting a hand to her shoulder as she turned to depart from the Commons.

"Pytre, my heart cries for the girl more than yours," she said, putting her hand to the top of his. "But this is the Shantyway, and it is right."

34

By the day and the hour the snow turned to water and flowed from the Shanties out into the sandscape. Taylo walked over snow packed paths in the early of the day wondering how many more days the covering would last. Not many, she decided, but in places which were ever in shadow the snow would not be as quick to depart.

When she arrived at the Commons the keepers, of course, were already awake and making plans for the day. Where they could not find befitted labor at recompense, they established their own work. They were glad to do whatever was helpful and needed in gratefulness to those who showed them hospitality.

Taylo wondered if the keepers were working for the cause of a need to repay what the Shanties would give to them all without thought or worry.

Sharo was in the midst of the Commons. As Taylo understood, it was her job to keep the Commons warm in the midst of fallen winter. Winter was not far off, and Taylo had heard chatter of the need for befitted shelter for so many. The full number of the keepers could not find shelter in the Commons.

That might well be a cause to address soon, but there were other matters for Taylo to set her attention to on this day.

"Good early, Sharo," Taylo said as she approached. There were a few initiates around, asking questions about the keepers. For a time there would be a need for scholarship for either group.

"Good early Taylo," Sharo said. "Is everything well?"

"So far as I know," Taylo said. "And here is elder Kene, along with the students we talked of before."

In the shadow of Kene stood Daine, Aery and Adison. Conspicuously missing from the setting was Miko, who had a part in the events they would soon hear of. Taylo had also noted Sundi, who had been spending a befitted time in the Commons. Taylo nodded as she walked up behind them. There would be information here she would want to hear.

"Authority Taylo," Kene said as he approached. "And you are named elder Sharo."

"Authority no more," Taylo said.

"And I am not truly an elder," Sharo said. "I am sometimes named as pura Sharo. I see you have found our young students."

"Some of them," Kene said. "They will tell you the events which brought them to this place, along with us."

"It is a conversation we look forward to," Taylo said. "Sharo, this is Daine and Aery, new students from the Drydocks, and you know Adison."

"We have heard much of you pura Sharo," Aery said.

"All favorable I hope," Sharo said.

"Not all, ma'am" Daine said, bowing her head for a moment. "You were not a favored person to Miko when he first arrived at the old ship. I dare say that point of view has been reformed. There were many changes when Miko's heart was put to new."

"What happened on the night you retrieved Miko from the Holding?" Taylo asked.

"On that night we were mere steps from your cart when councilman Iance had you taken," Daine said. "With his gift Miko was able to trace the location of those set to capture us, then as they gained on us we jumped into the river, which now has water in it. Miko made a bubble of air for us to stay in as they searched above."

"They would have thought you lost and gone if you were in the river," Taylo said. "The Drydocks were flooded that day. I found out on my release. How many keepers were lost?"

"Handfuls," Aery said, and looked down. "No one knows how many. My family was lost."

"My father was lost as well," Daine said. "I am alone."

"We are but dust in a cup," Sharo said. "But you will never be that among the Shanties. If you have lost your family we all take up your care. We will see you safe and sheltered. It is named the Shantyway."

"While we were in the river Miko told me of Gabri," Daine said. "They were together until her power was depleted. He told me how she was lost and gone. The last word she spoke at the point of being lost was, 'beautiful'. We talked of it at some length. She was a machine and could not have known what beauty was unless God had chosen to take her into paradise."

"You believe this to be true?" Taylo asked.

"Miko would say he does not believe," Daine said. "He knows. Belief indicates a choice, and once it was in front of his face he could not choose but to know. I choose to know along with him."

"Miko knows God is," Aery said. "It was the final lesson at the hand of Gabri."

"It is a well befitted scholarship," Sharo said. "Wonders never end."

"We went to what remained of the Drydocks and looked for Aery," Daine said. "He was not to be found, and we thought it would be beneficial to labor for a short time to replace our coinage. At the hiring platform we were taken by the authority."

"I had gone traversing about Cityscape before returning to my life as a keeper," Aery said. "In the south I saw preparations made for the water that would soon flood the Drydocks, but I did not know what those preparations portended. When I returned the river was flooded and I could not find my family. I went to the hiring platform and was taken as Daine and Miko were. We met at the training area, to be trained as a militia. It was there we were found by Adison."

"I heard them speaking of the Shanties," Adison said. "So together, along with elder Kene, we set ourselves to warning as many of the keepers as we could; preparing for what we would do when we reached the Shanties. None of us wanted to fight against our friends."

"On that morning I found Miko outside," Daine said. "He instructed us to make a hasty jaunt to the Shanties. He knew God had a plan for him to pull down the comet and put a stop to the god war, and that is what he did."

"You haven't seen him since?" Sharo asked, but she already knew the answer.

"He told me he would ever be in God's hands,"

Daine said. "And he had no fear. He also said I would be welcome in his home, and to keep for his mother and sister as there was need."

"Keeper Daine," Sundi said. She had been standing behind Sharo, but took the opportunity to stand to the front. "Miko is my son, and he has spoken correctly. You will always be welcome in our home. We will keep for you as you keep for us."

"Thank you ma'am," Daine said, bowing her head. "It will be well."

"I can think of no one more befitted than Sundi," Sharo said. "You will be in the best of hands. Aery, you can choose whether to allow us to find a family for you, or whether you want to live in the Commons alongside the keepers in attendance there."

"I think I will stay in the Commons then," Aery said. "For at least the turn of a few days. I still cannot fathom such a place."

"You are not alone," Sharo said. "There are many who can answer every question, and walk with you in every way. You are most welcome here in the Shanties."

#

Athan kept warm the cave. Ryalt would not be more grateful for the young man. He had kept their lives over the days of snow.

Looking over the far edge of ruinscape, at the place called the fountains, Ryalt would see the large pools which had once been carved to capture water. Now the pools were all half filled with the snow that they had moved into them to clear paths to walk to the broken walls below.

Finally the snow had come to its end, and finally

the ground had begun to dry.

There had been a couple of days of talking, planning where to start building if they were found safe from the Cityscape militia. Ryalt could not put the words to how much he had enjoyed planning a new city. He did not know if anyone else would fathom how little he wanted to return to the Shanties. He would regret not seeing his friends as often, but he was attached to this new place in ways he could not put to words.

Jenne walked up the hill to join him.

"Ryalt," she said. "The scout has returned and the Shanties are safe. Joska is also safe, and found in the shadow of Sharo. We should make haste to return while it is still in the early."

Ryalt looked out over the ruins below. He could picture some of what they had planned when they thought the Shanties would be lost. It was good to find the Shanties were not lost, but this place had taken hold of his heart.

"What is it?" Jenne asked.

"It is not time for me to return," Ryalt said. "I think this could is a befitted place for us. Take the rest back to the Shanties, and return with Joska if you would."

"Ryalt?"

"I see more for me here than back at the Shanties," he said. "It is beyond understanding, but I know this is the place I should live, and if you would relent, you as well. I would not prevent the rest from their return to the Shanties."

"Elder Ryalt," Athan said as he joined them. "You know this is not the Shantyway. No one here should make such decisions without a conference. If you would relent I think I would join you in this new place, and others might as well. I will call a meeting."

Jenne turned to pass the word to some others, further down the hill, but before she traversed further she turned back to Ryalt.

"...also, <u>we</u> will talk."

"Then let us gather," Ryalt said. "I neglected to give proper consideration to the rest of you."

Several moved through the cave, spreading the word. Soon, the initiates were all gathered. The discussion had already started.

35

Daine cleaned the house. It was not in need, Sundi kept her house well and Daine had been in residence for two days more than she needed to assure everything was well kept. It was more an act of habit than need.

The two, Sundi and Trina, had seen to the comfort and needs of Daine since the moment she crossed their doorway. It was more than she ever expected, but all of what Miko had told her.

And yet Miko was not in his house, only his remembrance. Though none resented her as the bringer of ill tidings, his absence wore at Daine in ways she could not put to words. Perhaps it was part of the reason she had volunteered so rapidly for something which would draw her away from the Shanties, at least for a time.

Trina arrived with additional provision for the remainder of the week. The one day in seven was in two days and Sundi was in the habit of hospitality on that day. A meal would be prepared, and friends would arrive to share.

"Is all well friend Trina?" Daine asked. She had been discouraged from using her usual form of address for house lords. It would be tolerated, but it was not the Shantyway.

"The keepers still gather around the Commons," Trina said. "Ready to work at the first hint of labor. The Shanties have been changed."

"A change for the better I hope," Daine said.

"None of us would ever think to cause such a commotion."

"Commotion or not," Trina said. "You are all a gift."

There was a silence between them burdened by the weight of words which had need to be said, but could not resolve the matter. It was a weight they all touched.

"Must you traverse?" Trina asked again. "Cityscape is dire for any of us, even for you."

"Maybe me most of all," Daine said. "I once kept the crèche in the Drydocks. My scholarship is requisite for the task. We do not have the will to leave the children of keepers in the hands of Cityscape."

"I do not disagree, but others could go and retrieve the children," Trina added. "You need not."

"Others will go," Daine said. "And others have gone. Aery and Jenk have accompanied the family of the girl who died, along with Pytre."

"The girl is a sad situation," Trina said. "My heart has tears for them. I cannot fathom."

Trina was putting words to her honesty. She did not know the first thing of the fear instilled in children with the stories of the teras, the monsters which were told in Cityscape. It was for the cause of that fear which had set the girl to lost and gone.

"I understand how perfect fear throws love to the wind," Daine said. "I am joining a handful of keepers who will follow Aery and Jenk. Together we will search out the children and return with them."

"You know mother is anxious for your every step," Trina said. "You have taken the place of a favored child."

"Much is given," Daine said as her eyes glanced downward. In this house she had jaunted as close to a mother's love as she ever had. "Taylo accompanies us. She will keep us safe."

"Is anyplace in all of Cityscape truly safe?" Trina asked.

"It never has been before," Daine asked. "We see it clearer now. I understand the need to take care, and to return safely."

#

The Commons was filled with activity, some of it the normal commerce and discussion of the day, but in the corner the door to the tunnel was open. Kimi was at the head of a group of people, keepers and initiates alike. Taylo stood to the side of Sharo as they watched the proceedings. A handful of keepers stood by, those who would be traversing with Taylo.

"What is this activity?" Daine asked as she approached the side of Taylo.

"Kimi and her cohorts will jaunt with us to the cart in the midst of the tunnel," Taylo said. "They intend to look at it, and perhaps pull it back to the landing here at the Commons."

"Kimi is sure she can learn much from the mechanics of it," Sharo added.

"Kimi is quite skillful," Daine said. "She helped when I had difficulty with the numberplay Gabri attempted to teach me."

"Daine," Sharo said. "Returning to Cityscape is a dire situation. You need not go."

Daine put closed her eyes. She was anxious for the cause of the traverse in her heart, but she also knew it was the most befitted action. There was no room for turning away. The children of keepers had need of her.

"They are not my children," Daine said. "But I have cared for many of them. I know the names they hold and I can remember what is in their eyes. I cannot rest until I see them safe."

"I understand,"Sharo said. "But I think it would be most befitted if you were to return untouched."

"And Sharo does not stand alone in that," Taylo added.

"I will endeavor to be swift," Daine said. "But I will not relent in my will to go."

"Endeavor more to have a care," Authority Taylo said. "We cannot be seen and we cannot be found, any one of us, while we are in the shadow of Cityscape."

"It would be most untoward," Daine said.

Sharo made fire in her hand and touched it to their torches as they entered the tunnel under the world. The tunnel was chilled and dark, there was not a bit of light outside the torches they carried.

"It is a long distance," Taylo said as she led the way.

"And it will not walk itself," Daine said.

#

Deep in the tunnel the group stayed at the cart after the second day. Kimi found a way to unlock the glides on the underside of it. It rolled smoothly with but a single hand put to it.

"I could move this myself the full length to the Shanties," Kimi said. "Authority Taylo, are you certain none of us can lend help to your traverse? More of us could be helpful."

"I am certain," Taylo answered. She had since given up mentioning how she was no longer an authority. It was a battle she could not win. "More mouths to feed would be untoward. We have a number sufficient to the task, and enough food and water for us."

"Than fare well all of you," Kimi said. "We hold you in our hearts until your return."

Taylo had little time to watch the students as they pushed the cart back toward the Shanties. Their path was clear, as was hers.

Conversing was difficult in the dark of the tunnel. The group moved in silence. Over the endless turn of the tunnel's night Daine moved closer into the shadow of Taylo.

"You have not yet said I should not join this traverse," Daine said. "You are the only one who has not."

"You have heard those other voices," Taylo said. "But I know what I see in your eyes, and such words will not be heard from anyone. Yet you are anxious."

"More than I can say," Daine said. "I could have been put to lost and gone when I was last in Cityscape, but I cannot leave this task to others."

Taylo considered for a moment before she spoke.

"You think it is untoward to be worried."

"More than I dare say," Daine said. "Usually I am the one who is not. I think it is a cause for concern."

Taylo smiled.

"I worry for every venture," Taylo said. "This time I do not. We traverse for the cause of retrieving children, there is no doubt but that it is what we should do. But if the worrier does not worry and the one who does not worry finds cause to worry, there might be a reason."

"Why would that be?" Daine asked.

"I dare not guess," Taylo said. "At the very least one of us will be shown to be correct."

"I have trust it will be you," Daine said.

36

Climbing downward from a mountain of ice was not an easy matter. It did not contribute to the cause of haste that Miko kept stopping to look about and wonder. Around every turn was a wall of ice which showered the world with color, or a deep chasm cut out by chilled water. It was all too magnificent to see within one glance. He could not help himself but stop too often when every step brought a different view which had more than a befitted share of beauty.

"What could have ever caused me to doubt?" he asked, talking as much to himself as to God who listened at every word. "The world could not be without you. There are wonders at every turn."

Finally, after endless walking, he could see his way clear to the sand below, but the footing was treacherous and the surface slick, made more so when it was touched by the morning sun. He worked to make the surfaces under his feet dry with his gift, and wondered at the amount of water to be found contained in the air about him.

"This will be a change," he observed, "for all of Perma."

When the clouds cleared away Miko could see the Shanties. They were a mass of sand colored rubble hid by rubble and hills. He had never seen the whole of it before, and not from such a high vantage. It had been large at one time, set between the sandscape and a low hill—where they would oftimes hunt. There was a gentle slope to it, starting at the demarcation at the edge of sandscape then edging around the hill upslope around to where the fountains were. He could almost picture what it once was; a grand white city with homes and towers and wide flat roads.

That had all been before the last God war, the one in which the city was shattered. From that time till now the Shanties had hid from the eyes of Cityscape. In the end they were not hidden well enough. They had been found.

Yet the untold power of the militia had been brought to nothing. Cityscape was defeated at the hands of gifts they fought to destroy and a God they said was not.

Miko considered that the Shanties would no longer need be hidden. Cityscape lords knew where they were, though now if they wanted to reach them they would be obligated to take a circumventious path. He could only hope they would not be so stubborn.

Miko also considered that this was now the last god war. In this case, God had been the one to fight, and he had brought it to finality.

His feet touched the sandscape in due time. Miko chose a course to the demarcation, wondering over the source of his continued strength. He should have been exhausted when he pulled the comet down to Perma. He should have been too cold to move as fluffy snow wafted from the sky. Miko had not slept since the storm began, and it had been more than three days; he should have been asleep in his feet. And yet it all ways he was fit and comfortable.

The sand was wet, small ponds formed in his

every step. It occurred to Miko that in the turn of time sandscape could become its own lake, a very large lake. It would make traversing to Cityscape more of an adventure than it had been before.

When he topped a sandy hill he noted a solitary person on the demarcation point. It took her a few moments to see him as he traversed down the hill, and a few more recognize who he was.

"Miko!" Trina yelled then took off at a run toward him. His sister splashed mud onto her clothing as she ran, but she did not seem to have a care for the state of her clothing.

"Trina," he said as he accepted her embrace. Then he broke the embrace and stepped back to gaze into her eyes. He knew he would see her again as he returned, and had been rehearsing the words he had need to speak. "I must beg your pardon for what I have done before. I have been a most contentious brother."

She smiled, almost letting a cry escape her lips as her eyes were touched with the beginnings of tears.

"That you have," Trina said. "But I have often been a willing opponent. I will grant pardon and ask the same for myself."

"Are the Shanties well?"

"More well than ever," Trina said, pulling him under her arm as she spoke. "Hundreds of keepers were found on this side of the mountain. I understand you had part in the cause of that. We have been working to initiate them into the Shanties."

"Will they accept us?" Miko asked. "People like me and Sharo and Kassi and Athan?"

"They have adjusted to us quite well," Trina said.

"Any who cannot accept the Shantyway can go back to Cityscape in the tunnel. But we must get you warm and well fed. I will take you home so mother can care for you."

She took the first steps toward the Shanties as Miko followed in her shadow.

"Is Daine in the Shanties?" Miko asked.

Trina hesitated in her answer. For a moment Miko wondered if something untoward had occurred. He could not think it, Daine would always be well.

"No," Trina said. "She joined Taylo and some other to traverse back to Cityscape and retrieve the children of the keepers."

Miko put his eyes closed. He remembered when he had spoken to Daine last. She had cause to be anxious for him. Now on his return to the Shanties, he had cause to be anxious for her.

"How could she?" Miko asked. "It is a dire task."

"You care for her so much..?" Trina started to ask.

"Not that she is untoward in any way," he said. "But I do not think that is our direction. Still, she is the best and dearest of friends."

"To both of us," Trina said. "She has a place in our house as you request. Mother will never grow tired of the stories she speaks of you."

Miko stopped in his tracks.

"I had not considered that," he said. "What has she said?"

"Shall we traverse?" Trina said. "It is too late for you to turn and hide in the ice mountain."

#

Aysa had thought she knew what to expect when

she jaunted to the Shanties. In her turn of scholarship Jenk had told her chatter of the many ways and practices of the Shanties, and yet still she had been surprised at every turn. The Shanties acted as keepers for each other, Sharo had been very clear about it. The new keepers who had moved to the Shanties had a need to learn how to accept it when someone they would name a house lord played the keeper for them.

It was easily spoken, but not so easily done.

"Pura Sharo," Aysa said, not at all sure whether she was obligated to use the title. "We have keepers staying in every corner of the Commons, out in the street under shelter, and even into the tunnel. Might there be some befitted place to put at least some of the keepers here? There is little room to breathe and less room to move."

"You name the difficulty easily," Sharo said. "Do you have a ready solution?"

"I do not," Aysa said.

"Then I trust you will do a befitted search for one," Sharo said.

Sharo was often abrupt. She did not take to being given work when she was already hard at labor. Aysa should have realized this would be her reaction, but had not known who else to approach.

On the other side of it, she had been given labor and it would be done. She was a keeper, and she had learned from the first to always be ready for keeping.

Aysa walked from the Commons and into the Street, which only a day before had been covered with the last layer of snow. On the first of the day it had been a mass of mud and broken rubble. Now the broken rubble had been fit together over the mud to form a well befitted walkway, flat and solid enough to rival any in the whole of Cityscape.

The Shanties had been surprised at such a turn of structure, but Sharo had only said, "They are keepers and they will find work. It is the way we have always lived."

Aysa walked upon the lane, pondering her task when she noted young Joska, child of parents who were gone from the Shanties, gone to a place to hide from the Cityscape militia. Joska, chatter said, had returned to the Shanties on his own. Now he was sitting near the lane. She approached him cautiously, not sure of his reaction. They had yet to converse, yet she had wanted to from her first sight of him. He was a young boy of the Shanties who had been left with but a single eye.

"I am named Joska, I fathom you are the keeper hero Aysa," the boy said. "You can look closer at my face if you want. I do not take offense."

"None is intended young sir," Aysa said. "What was the cause?"

"An accident," Joska said. "A large rock dislodged on a street we were clearing and fell on my face."

"I understood you had teras to help with such things," she said.

"Sozo Kassi was by my side in the moment," Joska said. "She eased the pain and fixed the bleeding, but there are things even a sozo of her talent cannot fix."

"My sorrow walks with you young sir," Aysa said.

Joska simply smiled. He did not look the part of a

recipient of sorrow.

"Keeper Aysa," he said. "You have walked away from the place which was once your home and now you are in a strange place among strange people. I hear there is not even the first chatter of your family who likely were part of the militia. My loss is but a small one when shadowed next to yours."

"You are most kind Joska," Aysa said. "But in this place I walk with wonder, for I know it is God who placed me here, and he will walk with me wherever I am."

"My mother was a keeper who found her way to the Shanties before I was made," Joska said. "I could just as fast been among your friends if not for the turn of certain happenstance."

"You assume we would have been friends if we had we both lived in Cityscape?" Aysa asked.

"Of course we would have been," he said. "I've heard that when one sense is cut off, the others strengthen to cover its place. My ability to see us as friends could not be more clear."

"In that case, friend Joska," Aysa said. "I need request your help."

"I am always glad to stand with a friend," Joska said. "What is your concern?"

"Do you know where we can emplace the keepers?" she asked. "The Commons are much too full, and I do not think it was purposed as living space. In all of the ruinscape there must be some place more befitted."

Joska smiled at her. Then he jumped up on a newly fabricated wall and looked around, as if he could see much more of the Shanties from this vantage point.

"There is the open bowl," Joska said, pointing to the north and some to the east. "It is said it was once a warehouse of some sort. It has not been used since the beginnings of the Shanties and is not in good repair. It will also need a good cleaning."

"How many could be sheltered there?" Aysa asked.

"A hundred, maybe more," Joska said. "But the work crews are still finishing the lane. How do we convince them to forsake that labor for this?"

"There will be no need for that," Aysa said. "All we need is to find keepers in need of keeping to do."

#

"There is no keeping for us," one of the young men said.

Kene sat among other men. Most he had known since their birth, but none he had known in this new place named the Shanties. They were before a large building called the Commons, a place where commerce was done and for the moment, the place where the keepers were sheltered.

"We were not expected," Kene said. "Yet because of us the need is great. Much needs be done before the winter."

"And yet we sit," the young man complained. The young often complained. They had not learned the art of watching and learning. In the turn of a few days, Kene would know the needs of the Shanties, and how best to utilize the keepers. Once he was conversant in what labor had need to be done, it would be simple matter to see it done.

He had never thought to leave Cityscape, he had

never thought there was anything more than emptyscape beyond, yet he was in the midst of a city filled with a kind and gentle people. In all the wonder Kene's heart was touched with worry; if they were to traverse the next winter without loss, there would need be more sheltering, and more food.

The young keeper, Aysa, walked toward the Commons. She had been one of the students of the old colony ship. She was in the company of a younger boy, one with only one eye. Kene had seen him before and had noted how he was a well-beloved child of the Shanties.

Aysa stood atop one of the blocks outside the Commons. "Keepers," she said. "We have a place which may be a well befitted sheltering for us, but it is in need of repair and cleaning. I need a work crew—as many as can work."

Kene stood from among the group. He had suspected the opportunity for befitted labor would arise, but was still surprised to find Aysa as the one to bring it.

"Elder Kene," Aysa said as she recognized him. From the moment he set foot in the Shanties they had named him an elder. He thought to complain of being given such a position, but the keepers supported him and the Shanty elders had conferenced with him and several other keepers almost daily. Perhaps, Kene decided, he was meant to be an elder.

"Lead on Aysa," Kene said as other keepers spread the news of possible work. "We have the hands for labor and the knowledge to repair any building and turn it to proper sheltering, and nothing more befitted to fill our time."

"Joska," Aysa said to the boy beside her. "Is there a place we can obtain some befitted tools?"

"The tool maker," Joska said. "Follow me."

As they jaunted down the lane Joska looked behind them more than once, his eyes growing wide for the number of keepers walking behind them.

Not far down the lane Joska motioned for the keepers to hold their place as he went inside a shop. There were tools along the outside wall and also within. Kene wondered what the price would be for the number of tools they might need, but also recognized that those of the Shanties were as adept at barter as they were at providing proper recompense.

Kene moved to the forefront to hear what manner of deal was to be made.

"We need what you have which would be useful for changing the open bowl into a befitted shelter," Joska said.

The toolmaker looked over his tools and put his hand to his chin, then glanced outside at the keepers waiting in the lane.

"I dare say who you have here is most of what you need," he said. "However, I have a number of befitted tools. There is no need to worry over payment, I will give what I have in exchange."

"In exchange for what?" Aysa asked.

The toolmaker just smiled and gathered a handful of tools before he stepped outside.

"Keepers," he said loudly enough to be heard. "I will give what tools I have on hand for your labor. In exchange I ask four young people to echo me for the cause of learning the trade of tool making. I am no longer young, and the Shanties has the need for more than I can do."

"It is the Shantyway," Joska added. "You will work with the toolmaker in the day, and return to your families at night. You will continue by the day and the winter until you know all you need to have your own shop and do your own work. You will echo for the turn of a handful of winters, sometimes more."

Kene nodded, giving his approval to the deal and four likely apprentices stepped forward at once, three young men and a young woman. The tool maker started to warn her off but Kene saw the look on his face and read what it could mean.

"She will work as hard as they do, sir," Kene said. "Perhaps she will even make her own mark on the craft. They will treat her as a beloved sister. It is the way of keepers."

The toolmaker looked at Kene, and then several of the other keepers who nodded in agreement. Then he looked over the four young keepers.

"I believe you would say, it is well then," the toolmaker said. "Echoes, follow me. We have a number of tools to bring out to these keepers, and then you have much to learn."

Joska led them down a few broken lanes and through an open set of double doors into the largest place Kene had seen for as long as he had lived. The building was not much taller than those around it, but inside it sloped down into the ground and was at its center three times as tall as the Commons. It was also dark and scattered with rubble. The center of the ceiling was open where the pinnacle of the covering had broken away, about a third the size of the floor; it was why they had named it the open bowl.

Kene organized the keepers nearest him, sending a group of keepers and laborers inside to assure the structure was sound. As the keepers waited out on the street they cleared the rubble from underfoot. Using the rubble as building material they made a flat walkway for them to stand on then used the remainder to construct short walls around every building in sight.

Kene played the supervisor; walking about to assure the connection of quality, then listening to the report from inside the building. He sent two handfuls of young men to obtain materials needed to strengthen the structure of the building inside. In the Shanties, building materials were never far away. After a time he returned to Aysa and Joska, who were watching the keepers repair the roads.

"I suppose it is okay to clear the streets now," Joska said. "We are no longer hidden from Cityscape."

"Not hidden," Aysa said, "just blocked from them. I understand Miko is the cause of that mountain. It belies all sense."

"He was chosen for a time such as this," Kene said. "And guided on every step, despite himself as I understand."

"Speak him into whatever hero you want," Aysa said. "I was a student with him and at that time his heart was ever against us, those of us from Cityscape."

"That is another thing for which I must beg pardon," A voice said from behind them.

Kene turned and saw the young man Miko in the company of Trina, his sister. The keepers had talked among themselves, deciding in their chatter that Miko was lost and gone. He was glad they had been wrong.

"Miko," Aysa said. "I am pleased to find you warm and well. Trina, I regret not searching you out. Our stay in the Shanties has been most hectic."

"I am not affronted Aysa," Trina said. "However, I have found you now."

Miko stepped forward.

"Aysa," Miko said. "I was most untoward in my actions toward you and my words about you, you and all your friends. I must beg your pardon."

"Pardon is freely given Miko," Aysa said. "Daine was insistent that your heart had been turned to change."

Miko nodded at Aysa. If he had any amount of sense he would know her pardon was not given without hesitation. He would be obligated to prove himself to her. Kene was not overly worried on that matter. Then the young man turned to face Kene.

"Elder Kene, I understand we have been hectic for the sake of proper harborage," Miko said. "Is there anything I can do to help."

"The keepers do not mind sleeping in the streets," Kene said. "But the Shanties would rather we have hard sheltering. In front of us we have a place which could be made befitted for sheltering, but the work will take the turn of a few days.

"Elder Kene," Trina said. "You have been told how in the Shanties the teras are not the monsters in stories, and they are accepted here. Miko is one of them, he was from the Shanties and he is a pino. He can call to water. It is a very rare gift, one almost unknown even in the Shanties."

"Miko," Kene said. "We have known of what you name the gifts, but have never had leave to speak of them. We are accustomed to walking the old roads and will sometimes stay to them even when there is no need."

"I will try to help gently," Miko said.

"There is a stone pond over here," Kene said taking them to the side of the building. Three keepers had just finished cleaning the rubble and the dust from the enclosure. It was round and not overly deep and would be handy to hold water. "Can you find water to fill it so we can use it to drink and to clean?"

"Easily," Miko said. "There is water all around us in the air."

Miko held his hands almost together and water started trickling from between them. Then, after the circle of a few moments, water began to pour.

"It all seems to be some kind of trick," Kene observed. "Chatter is this was brought about by technology at the first of the colony days?"

"That would be correct," Trina said. "It was done for their survival-- and for ours."

"It is helpful on this day," Kene said.

"It is well sir,' Joska said. "Hold to your mind that it is possible to find the teras even among your own children."

"It is more than possible," Kene said.

"In the Shanties we have a young initiate to the gift shadow someone who has that gift," Miko said. "You have leave to speak of it here. Those who hold the gifts are held as most befitted, and know those of us who use our gifts here stand ready to teach those who need it."

"I believe you would say," Kene said. "I will send word to the keepers to see what they say."

"You learn the Shantyway in leaps and bounds," Joska said.

Kene smiled and tossled the hair of the young initiate.

"It is no bitter task," he said.

#

It was the mid of late when Trina and Aysa walked into their house with Miko half held up between them.

"I had heard of wonderful things happening in the Shanties," she said, taking Miko into her arms. "Your return may be the best wonder of all."

"We accomplished all," Miko said. "We have kept the Shanties safe."

"For now," Sundi, his mom, said. "What do you require?"

"I grow hungry and weary," Miko said. "I suppose it would be proper for me to feed my hunger first, for once I begin to sleep I may stay in my sling for the turn of several winters."

"Then I will prepare something with haste," she said. "Then send you to rest."

She entered the kitchen followed by Trina and Aysa.

"This is my friend Aysa," Trina said. "The one I mentioned before."

"I am glad you are found warm and well," Sundi said. "Feel free to assist as you would like."

Sundi was well on her way to preparing a simple meal for Miko. Aysa helped as she could, but by the side of one who knew her own kitchen from start to finish, she found little for her hands to do.

"He calls a comet from the sky and makes a mountain of ice in the sandscape," Aysa said. "He then spends three days climbing down, but in all that he appears rested and strong. Then he fills a pond with water and he sleeps on his feet."

"He did not stand alone in the face of the comet," Trina said. "For him alone it would not be possible."

Together they prepared a simple meal and delivered it to the weary Miko. He ate but five bites before he fell to slumber with his face on the flat table.

#

They were near the exit of the tunnel, Daine was sure of it. In the tunnel there was no sense of day or dark. It was as if she had a distant memory of how far they had walked.

It would be good for them to arrive. Daine had decided her worry would be diminished by labor on hand. The tunnel had done little to help, there was little to be done except only to walk.

"We will travel in groups of two," Taylo said. Their words had been few for the last two days, but Taylo knew as well as any of them it was time to plan for what was next.

"It may be most befitted," Daine said. "We do not know what may have occurred in Cityscape."

"May every word you say be as true," a voice seemed to come out of the darkness in front of them.

Taylo had stopped from the first word. Daine sought to cower back, but knew there were those who followed. If they heard something untoward they could yet be safe.

"Pytre," Taylo said, she relaxed noticeably once she recognized the man. "You were hiding in the dark."

"We noted your progress," he said. "Since we had no way to know who you were, we chose to traverse a good walk into the tunnel and wait until you traversed near us to see who you were. If you were untoward, those at the entrance could be gone before you reached them."

"I am glad you have found us."

"I'm glad you are here," Pytre said. "You were correct, Cityscape has not fared well. While we were there I heard chatter that Mintel sent the remainder of the authority into agriscape to collect any keepers they could find, but agriscape sent the authority back, diminished in numbers and without their weapons."

"I had not considered what Cityscape would become once it was deprived of keepers," Daine said. "They purposed to hurt the Shanties but have only hurt themselves."

"So it would seem," Pytre said.

"But we are here for the children of the keepers," Taylo said. "Is there any chatter of them."

Pytre smiled. He had been waiting for this subject to arrive.

"We have them," Pytre said. "We have them all."

Daine blinked, then blinked again.

"Grant pardon Pytre, I must have misheard," she finally said. "Speak those words again."

"How did this occur?" Taylo asked.

"It is an intricate story," Pytre said. "One best told over several nights after the evening's meal. This is not my tale to tell. We can reach the entrance by the mid of the day and you will know more then. We will need much keeping for the return jaunt."

"I trust this is something I will enjoy learning," Taylo said.

"You will," Pytre said. "Of that I am sure."

37

It was the turn of two days before Miko finally emerged from his sling for more than a few moments. Stiff but rested, he was finally awake enough to complete a solid meal and to walk about the house.

Sozo Kassi visited Miko in the mid of early, carrying a newborn daughter. While Trina and Aysa cooed over the baby, Kassi looked him over completely and declared him lucky to be living.

"Now that you have touched the results of overextending your gift," Kassi said. "You will know to avoid it. Return to your bed early for another handful of days. You will soon be warm and well."

"Has Daine returned?" he finally asked.

"I have not heard any talk of it today," Kassi said. "We expect they have arrived at the lake, but their task there may be convoluted. It may be beyond fallen winter before they return."

"She thinks I'm lost and cold," Miko said.

"Then we can hold to hope that you will both hear good news on her return," Kassi said as she stood to retrieve her child. "When you are able you should visit the Commons. The Shanties may have need of you."

#

"Pino Miko," pura Sharo said as he traversed through the doorway. "Welcome back to the Commons. Are you finally rested?"

His eyes could not focus as completely as before. But Miko was on his way to being like he once had been.

And yet he still hesitated at the title. He was still simply Miko in his own mind, and his hearing thought the addition untoward.

"Rested enough," Miko said. "Has anything of import occurred as I slept?"

"The keepers have rebuilt the open bowl into something better than any sheltering we have ever had," Sharo said. "They plan to repair the roof over the next handful of days. Almost half of those who went into ruinscape to hide as the Cityscape militia was upon us have chosen not to return. And I dare say we will have every street cobbled by winterset."

"I had noticed," Miko said. "And looked at it so much I had to recourse my way here twice. The new streets are most befitted."

"There is talk of planning a wall," Sharo said. "The initiates want to build at the demarcation where the Shanties meet sandscape."

"There certainly is enough material at hand for such a venture," Miko said. "Would a wall do any good?"

"I suspect not," Sharo said. "Yet there are those who would be comforted by having it in place."

"I think that when the mountain finally melts," Miko said. "We will have a large lake in the stead of sandscape. We should suggest to the initiates to practice patience for the way to Cityscape will continue to be hindered."

"The plan will be conversed over for the course of days," Sharo said. "I do understand it is mentioned only for the cause of anxiety."

"We need not fear," Miko said.

Sharo nodded.

"Jenne has returned to the Shanties and plans to traverse with Joska back to those who plan to start another city," she said. "They are bringing their belongings with them. I will accompany them."

"Could I go as well?" Miko asked.

"I had hoped you would," Sharo said. "We do not know whether they might have need for your gift. We will start at mid-early on the morrow, and we may stay for a handful of days. We hope to return before winterfall."

"Well enough," Miko said, he looked about, making sure no one prone to chatter was within hearing space. "Sharo, in the battle, when they were approaching, would you have used your gift to fight?"

Sharo gave a circle of a moment for thought.

"I did not want to," she said. "It would have been a most untoward use of a gift. But in the end, I would have done anything to protect the Shanties and my friends."

"I had the same thoughts," Miko said. "When I turned my eyes to the sky to complain of it, that is when I noted the comet. It was then I was shown there was a more excellent way."

"I hope we never have cause to contemplate such a thing again," she said.

"I have the same hope," he said. "But if we do, I know to look for a better direction."

#

They departed in the mid of early with Jenne in the lead, walking through newly cobbled streets. After a time they stepped from the keeper streets into the ruinscape proper. They picked their way through the rubble and could not help but notice how quickly they had become accustomed to level walkways.

"We take such a rounded path," Miko said. "Is not our goal the place called the fountains?"

"It is," Sharo said. "There is no easy way on the direct path."

"You were not a child in the Shanties," Miko said. "My friends and I discovered a way, and named it the rounded cave. Though on reconsideration, we were probably not the first to step into it."

"I used it to return to the Shanties," Joska said. I thought it a secret."

"Where is this cave?" Sharo asked.

"Not far," Joska said. "Follow me."

Joska led them on a path threading through piles of rubble until he found an opening. It was quite small, but what it led to inside was quite large.

"This may be the counterpart to the tunnel which leads to the lake," Jenne said as she climbed down into what may have once been a long tunnel. The sides were smooth, but the topmost edges had been torn open in many places.

"Does this tunnel open in the Shanties?" Sharo asked.

"In more than one place," Miko said. "There is a way into it not far from the open bowl."

"Unless the keepers have repaired it already," Jenne said as she stepped forward. "This does make the walk much easier."

They followed the tunnel through the first of the day, and emerged at the last of mid. The hill where the fountains had been made was within sight, and the three walked in that direction.

"We are being watched," Sharo said. "There are people on the hill on our right hand, and more near the broken columns."

"I would have expected as much," Jenne said. "They knew we would be here over the turn of a few days, and Ryalt knew you would accompany me. There are more hills in this place. We have talked of using some of them to house towers with which to see the whole of the area."

"Towers in the Shanties?" Sharo asked. "There are wonders all around, and they will never cease."

#

"We have been planning new homes there in the valley below," Jenne said, pointing from the mouth of the cave. "It may be well, for the time when that mountain of ice is overcome by the distant sun, to have two cities ready to face Cityscape in the place of one."

"We hope it will not be needed by that time," Sharo said.

"Hope as you will," Jenne said. "But it would be prudent to be prepared nonetheless. You know this is a befitted choice."

"I know," Sharo said. "But I will miss our conversation."

"I will visit often," Jenne said. "I would not have Joska think you a stranger."

"There is not enough of a growing season remaining," Sharo said.

"We gather what we find," Ryalt said. "The winter will be a lean one, but we hold to hope there will be enough to share among us."

"We have new keepers in the Shanties," Miko said. "The remainder of the Cityscape militia which was on our side of the mountain when it appeared. "Should I ask whether some of them might relent to help build a new city?"

"Perhaps they can bring a share of what the Shanties had grown," Sharo said. "It would be better if no one eats too well this year so long as no one is lost and gone."

"They would be most welcome," Ryalt said. "We will keep for them as they keep for us."

"It is the Shantyway," Jenne said.

"Athan," Sharo said, stepping toward the pura.

"Pura Sharo," Athan said.

"You are emplaced for these people," she said. "I know you are ready, so I will not ask."

"I cannot do as well as you," Athan said.

"You need not," Sharo said. "You need only do as you can. And, Athan…?"

"Yes," Athan answered.

"Keep for these people," Sharo said. "And allow them to keep for you. They are friends and family."

"I will always do so," Athan said. "Perhaps this is the cause for both of us to learn of our gifts so close together. I was needed in this new endeavor."

"Perhaps so," Sharo said.

37

Hera would chase the distant sun around the sky for only so long before she reached her goal and dreaded winter once again settled on the world of Perma and the Shanties. The sky of the day was dimly lit with indirect light, tinted deep blue and the world turned to cold. In every corner of the Shanties feasts were held, and the holy writ, once only glanced at on the first and last days of summer by the keepers in Cityscape, was read continually in the Shanties.

There was something new this winter. On the first fallen day of winter, thick clouds covered the sky, clouds which almost touched the ground from hills to sandscape, and in the early of the second day, snow fell gently from the sky.

This was soft snow and not as cold as what had fallen on the day of the last God war. The mass of snow seemed to blunt the chill of dreaded winter. Packing the snow to the outside walls of the houses caused more warmth to stay within.

The people of the Shanties retreated to their homes for the cause of winter, and stayed within most of the time. Fires were lit and stories were told, and Sharo kept warm the Commons.

Sharo wore a cloak, fashioned in keeper form but with Shanty colors, and not a pattern this time, but pictures woven into the threads; pictures to remind her of the unfathomable events which had occurred from the day Sharo had arrived in the Shanties, and one image from before. Every so often she would glance at the face of Rafe, and touch the remembrance of what might have been.

Sharo finished putting the room to warm and sat on a short wall which had once been sheltering for numbers of keepers. They had all moved to the open bowl, or to houses of their own and Sharo now slept in her house which she shared with Angla. As she sat she glanced at the image of Jenne woven into her sleeve, her best and truest friend.

"I trust sir," Sharo said just loud enough for God to hear. "That my friends both near and far are held in your arms."

There was also a sense of anticipation in the day. Winter had fallen, this much was true, but so many other good things had occurred, there could be hope for one more.

In the Commons trading was done and deals were made, even in the cold of winter. The activity was not at the volume of a summer's day, but the concentration was all the more. What is done in winter is only the most important. There was also a new need to shovel away the snow which so readily fell from the sky. The keepers were quick to the task, but no one could tolerate the chill of winter for more than a part of a day. It was a task invented to be shared.

It was unclear who heard it first, but there was a knock from inside the wall of the Commons.

Before Sharo could traverse to the wall of the Commons the door was already set to open, and Taylo emerged. She looked tired, blinking from the light of the Commons. Sharo could not tell, but hoped there was not a hint of sadness in her eyes.

"Taylo," Sharo said as she approached and gave her friend a warm embrace. Taylo was not always amiable to such interaction, but she tolerated it. "I am glad to see you return."

"Winter has fallen," Taylo said. "We were unsure. The tunnel did not grow cold as we thought it would."

A few of the keepers who had traversed with Taylo started to emerge from the tunnel entrance.

"Did you fare well?" Sharo asked. "The whole of the Shanties will be desperate to know."

At first they had talked of the Shanties and the keepers, as if they were separate in some way, but over the circle of days the separation had gone to the side. By the time winter fell they were all initiates. They were all the Shanties.

"I know," Taylo said, and then turned back to the entry to the tunnel. "Your answer approaches quickly."

Sharo looked into the darkness beyond the wall, wondering what Taylo was playing at. It was not her pattern to be coy.

Then a small face appeared. It was a child; he was dressed as any keeper would be, in drab colors and utility. He stepped into the room, stumbling for how he looked up and around, but never at his own feet. He was joined by another, then a handful more, then many more.

The flow of children increased and threatened to never end.

"Daine suspects we have obtained them all," Taylo said. "But we cannot be sure until we can match the children to the parents."

"How did you do this?" Sharo said. "We expected it might take longer than the full of fallen winter."

"It is a long story," Taylo said. "One we will tell more of once we have found the places for these young ones and had some amount of rest. But, from first to last, we had help from a most unexpected and befitted source."

Sharo questioned with her eyes, but Taylo only answered by a nod at the entry. In the midst of the children was a keeper, one Sharo had not seen for the turn of many winters.

"Chanta," Sharo said, recalling the name.

"By the time we reached the far end of the tunnel under the world," Taylo said. "Chanta had already gathered up the children of the keepers."

"How did she know you would arrive?" Sharo asked.

Taylo looked at Chanta, busy with two handfuls of young ones, and folded her arms.

"She trusted."

#

Children had arrived at the Commons. Excited words jaunted throughout the Shanties despite the winter and the snow. Angla stayed at Sharo's house, along with Sharo and Taylo. She could have had a house of her own, but did not see the cause. She was alone as it was.

Once she heard the chatter she put on her cloaks and prepared to traverse to the Commons. There would be needs which could only be settled with many hands. Some of the children would belong to parents who were at the other city. They would need sheltering until winter's end.

The path to the Commons had been cleared, and was filling with numbers of people, many of them keepers who had hope to find their children among the crowd. Angla hoped for them as well, she knew what it was to have someone near to one's heart who was out of reach. At least the children would be restored.

The Commons was filled with more people than was requisite for a winter's day. More keepers arrived to search while restored families took their leave. Across the room she noted one of the Keeper elders. Angla knew he would be in the midst of whatever need was most pressing. She weaved her way through the people intent on joining him and being a help.

"Angla," a voice called at her as she walked by. It took her a moment to hear the sound, it was so unexpected. It was a voice she thought she had left behind.

"Chanta?" Angla said, turning around to be caught in a sudden embrace.

Angla put her head to Chanta's shoulder and allowed her tears to fall. Chanta was chilled, and somewhat wet. She looked some worse for wear, but also glowed with a happiness she had thought forsaken.

"House lord," a voice said from near them. It was one of the Shanty elders. "You will not have a keeper here like you did in Cityscape. It is not the Shantyway."

Taylo had walked up behind the initiate, she did all to protect Angla. This time there was no need. The man had only misunderstood and would soon be set to right.

"This is not my keeper," Angla said, holding to Chanta's arm as they turned. "Chanta is my mother."

They had played at being abandoned child and favored keeper for so long-- long enough so that the words and actions were by nature, but that was at an end. In the Shanties they would be family and everyone would know.

"Did you recover all these children?" Angla asked.

"She did," Taylo commented. "Chanta is a miracle."

"There is such a fuss over it," Chanta said. "I only set myself to the task as any keeper would do, and I saw it done."

"Either way," Angla said. "I am pleased you are now emplaced in the Shanties."

"I am pleased as well, ma'am," Chanta said.

"...And you are not required to call me ma'am."

A Few Words After

Worlds are big, and I tend to have a lot of characters in mine. I honestly did try to keep the number of named characters lower, and when compared to other stories I've written, I can boast some success. However, there are a "well-befitted" number of names to keep track of here. So I offer these lists.

This time, instead of dictionary-like pages of names followed by a brief description, I chose to simply generate lists of people under the headings of where they are from.

While this may not work for everyone, perhaps if one is unsure of a character, being able to see them in sequence with their peers will be helpful. Let me know what you think.

Also, there are people who properly fit on more than one list, which will either be helpful or more confusing.

The Shanties

Sharo
Athan
Paige
Chimo
Kassi
Jenne
Ryalt
Joska
Pytre
Miko

Cityscape

(House Lords)Iance
Backe
Forst
Raisa
Mintel
Rugre
Elder Hector
Mosca
Taylo
Angla

Sundi

Trina
Jenk
Kimi
Rayma
Dathe
Yendi

(Keepers)
Daine
Nyel
Kene
Aery
Chanta
Sele
Reny
Aysa
Adison
Masey
Emne
Jerin

The Colony Ship/Scholarship

Gabri
Geo
Adison
Trina
(Students)
Miko
Daine
Jenk
Kimi
Rayma
Dathe
Yendi
Masey
Emne
Jerin

If you've gotten this far, thank you for reading.

I urge you to review this book on your favorite social media. Reviews are the life blood of independent publishing.

This is the second book in the series. The first book: A Gift of Fire is available on line through Create Space/Amazon. The ebook version is also available on Smashwords.

The Third book in the series is, as ofJune '16, still a work in progress.

-Stephen Jones